I0831771

Will's Way

Will's Way

Searching for Light on the Dark Side of Paradise

Rob Benton

Esotericom
Honolulu

ISBN# Hardcover: 0-9710702-1-0

This book was printed in the United States of America

Esotericom
P.O. Box 25692
Honolulu, Hawaii 96825-0692
U.S.A.
www.esotericom.com

Contents

FOR DEBBIE MORIKAWA

Prologue

Michelle's wedding had been the signal to Will that it was time to move on with his life. He had never had hope of marrying her himself, and his own notions of a romantic relationship with her had settled into the comfort of friendship ten years earlier. But, there she had been last month in Raleigh—hardly a southern belle and not at all "the marrying kind," despite her outward femininity and gentle ways—marrying for the first time in her mid-thirties.

If she could make such a change, then Will, at thirty-seven, might be able to stuff the remaining vestiges of his once-fruitful life into a suitcase and move to someplace where he could at least regain some of the enthusiasm for life that he no longer had.

He looked out the one window of his tiny 57th street studio, sixteen floors above Ninth Avenue. The cruise ships which so often slipped in and out of their Hudson River berths during the summer were less frequent now since Labor Day had passed, and would soon subside almost entirely.

Will would not be here to see them when they returned

next spring. Like Michelle, he was making the last possible move that anyone would have expected of him. Nothing remained in his apartment but seven years of dust and the shelving that he had installed so securely that he now had neither the energy nor the desire to remove it.

He almost savored turning the key in each of the two locks on the steel door to the apartment for the last time, partly satisfied that he would never do it again, partly wistful over leaving what had been his secure inner sanctum for so long.

The elevator quickly took him up to the twenty-first floor, to a furnished room where he would spend his last night as a New Yorker. All but the things he would need tonight and tomorrow morning were already packed, ready for travel. He checked the locks on his guitar case. They were fastened. Now he could relax.

He reached for the pewter cup on the desk. It contained, as it had nearly an infinite number times, the first of many doses of the potion that would make the world seem progressively kinder, quieter, and more peaceful. He was glad he had plenty of gin, because it would take a lot to buy him a good night's sleep tonight.

* * *

The next morning, the first day of autumn, Will's only trouble was in managing the three pieces of luggage through the lobby of the building. Once he was in a taxi, he would be okay. No. Once he was on the plane, where he could have a couple of drinks and augment them with the contents of his flask, *then* he'd be okay.

He had hardly gotten his hand above his shoulder when he saw a taxi, halfway down the block, swerving toward the curb in his direction. After making sure the driver knew the established Taxi and Limousine Commission rules for making a trip to Newark Airport, Will loaded his luggage and, within minutes, was at the nearly deserted westbound entrance to the Lincoln Tunnel.

As many times as he had traversed the tunnel, he had never gotten accustomed to the realization that he was not only going *under* the river, he was also going under the river *bed.* This had always given him a claustrophobic fidgetiness, and this morning was no exception.

At first, he found some comfort and satisfaction in thinking that he probably would not have to go through the tunnel again for a very long time. As he neared the exit on the New Jersey side, that feeling began to change into an uneasy fear that he might *never* have the *opportunity* to return and go back through it again.

Chapter 1

The Shifting Spectrum

The fragrance of the orchids was missing this time. In Will's three previous vacation trips to Hawaii, there had always been an almost overwhelmingly pleasant aroma of flowers greeting his nostrils the instant he stepped off the plane. It was missing this time.

Maybe the ocean of gin he had downed over the past few weeks had permanently damaged his olfactory system, he reasoned. Or maybe the wind was just blowing in a different direction on this day. He knew not to expect any sort of welcome this time. Contrived and artificial as the tour groups' greetings had always been, it had been nice in the past to arrive and be "met" by someone at the airport.

Not only was Will alone and on his own at the airport this time, he was acutely aware that he was alone in the *world*, without even the backing of his late last bastion of material security, his credit cards. Not having worked for seven months, he had been forced to expend their usefulness for the purpose of survival. He stood at this moment with only the cash he had in his pocket, enough to pay for a hotel room and provisions for a few weeks—provisions including, of course, a sufficient supply of gin.

As he made his way to the baggage claim area, his pores responded to the warm temperature, and he began to sweat, having been accustomed to freezer-like air conditioning during all of the past summer. The combination of the time of day and the alcohol made his gait slow and labored. It was only five o'clock Hawaii time, but it was eleven on the east coast—and he had been up since five a.m., already eighteen hours. And he had yet another difficult part of the day ahead of him.

Thankfully, the luggage carousel was not crowded, and the first of his things to come up was his guitar case—intact, he quickly noted. Before anything else, he quickly unlocked the case and checked the guitar. Amazingly, the strings, loosened three musical steps down for the trip, were still tuned almost exactly as he had left them. That was a major relief. Nothing else was really fragile enough to be as subject to damage as the guitar, even, he mused, if it *was* being mauled by airline baggage handlers.

As each piece came up, he balanced it on the cart he had rented a few minutes earlier. Once he had everything, he proceeded toward the ground transportation area to look for a van, the cheapest method of transportation from the airport to Waikiki, where his hotel was. One came quickly, and the driver loaded his bags with good nature and deftness, the *sight* of which would have given a New York taxi driver a heart attack. Will, with the driver's permission, hoisted himself into the passenger-side bucket seat at the front of the van, thinking to himself that this was one of the very few advantages of traveling alone.

The driver made several more stops to pick up more passengers, seeming intent on having a packed van before he left the airport. Whatever enthusiasm Will might have had left after deplaning was diminishing rapidly with each stop. He was tired, mentally and physically and, worse, he was getting "thirsty." Finally, the driver swung the van out toward the highway, muttering something about the heavy rush-hour traffic, which seemed to Will to be fairly light. Will noted a few changes in the skyline that had been made since his last visit two years earlier. The air conditioning felt good now that the van was moving. Then there was a barely perceptible tilt in the right side of the van. The driver pulled the van into the first entrance of a large park. The right rear tire was flat. The driver unloaded ten passengers' worth of luggage only to discover that he had no spare.

Will rolled his eyes up as he looked in the direction of the ocean, hoping bemusedly to himself that this was not some sort of portent. The driver had a two-way radio on his vehicle, and within half an hour there was another van at the park to take the place of the disabled one. The driver delivered the other riders, couple by couple, to their hotels, until Will was the only passenger left.

"Look there," the driver, a young, self-described Hawaiian, said, pointing to a group of Japanese tourists. "They couldn't win this place in the war, so now they try to buy it." Will nodded, partly too tired to think of an appropriate response and partly wondering what the driver said about mainland *American* tourists when he was transporting *Japanese* passengers.

Finally, the van pulled up in front of the hotel, the Regal Arbor, which Will had chosen because a travel guidebook had recommended it as being livable and cheap for the area. It didn't look anything like the places Will had stayed before on previous vacations, but at this moment he would have settled for a pup tent and a cot. He tipped the driver, and, in three laborious trips, got his things from the curbside into the lobby. The desk clerk, a thin Asian man, dispatched his paperwork in a quiet manner, seeming unusually trusting to Will, but not showing even a hint of hospitality.

Will once again balanced his luggage on the rickety hand cart toward which the desk clerk had pointed him. Once it was loaded, he carefully guided it inside the elevator and pressed the button for the fourth floor, where he hoped to be able to rest at last.

Exiting the elevator, Will discovered that the upstairs "hallway" was outdoors, covered with what appeared to be astroturf. At the end of the hallway, finally, was Will's room. It was even hotter than outside, and Will had known when he made the reservation that it was not air conditioned. He turned on the fan and reached for the phone. He had to find out where the ice machine was and fix a drink before he could do anything else. He also knew that he was dangerously close to being out of gin, so he decided to make a quick trip outside to "procure," as he referred to it.

There were numerous convenience stores within easy staggering distance, he noted. His energy was slightly bolstered by the thought of being able to unwind for the rest of the day, and he quickly found a liter of the cheapest gin. "Procurement" accomplished, he turned to make his way back to the hotel, noticing the first signs of twilight in this overlong day. There was no ice bucket in his room, so he filled as many cups with ice as he could manage with one hand and returned to his room.

Drink in hand, he turned the television on, sat down on the bed, and, for the first time, surveyed his new temporary home. It wasn't so bad after all. The room and bathroom were clean, fairly recently painted, and everything seemed to be in good repair. Maybe it just seemed that way, since the tension he had felt all day was just beginning to subside.

It was Wednesday—what was left of it anyway. Will wanted to stay up until midnight in order compensate for the jet lag, but he knew he wouldn't last that long tonight. At about ten o'clock, he almost instinctively curled up on the bed, full glass on the bedside stand, lights and television still on.

The piercing and constant "beep-beep-beep-beep" of the garbage trucks and other service vehicles in reverse gear disrupted his sublime somnambulence at daybreak, about 6:30. The fourth floor room overlooked one of Waikiki's two main thoroughfares—almost precariously, since the building itself was separated from the street by only a very narrow side-walk—and rush hour traffic was off and running.

It had seemed to Will throughout the night that when the traffic light that hung just yards away from his window flashed red, it signaled a mandate to the Harley-Davidson riders outside that they *must* rev their engines. Closing the louvers on the windows did little to stifle the noise. Besides, it was just too warm to keep the windows closed. Even having a sizeable floor fan on a high-speed setting had not kept Will from sweating as he slept.

As he shuffled toward the bathroom, he tried to begin to plan how he would spend this day, a day of rest. After showering he replenished his ice supply, which had turned to cold water in the bottom section of the small refrigerator. It was still *very* early by his standards, barely nine o'clock. Will was accustomed to sleeping until at least ten-thirty or eleven every day. More drinking time, he reasoned about the extra hours, and fixed the first of what he called his morning "pops." As soon as he began to feel his "window of lucidity" coming on, he determined that he would walk the two very short blocks to the beach, and then decide where to go from there.

The air outside seemed not as warm as it had been the day before. The groups of people walking along seemed to be so different from the New York pedestrians to which Will was accustomed. They seemed, in general, intent on looking as slovenly as they could, and they seemed to be ill-mannered and crude, especially toward each other. These people are on vacation, he thought—they should look happier. Instead, they appeared to be going no place in particular, in a lost, half-giddy, half-morose manner.

The larger-than-life statue of Duke Kahanamoku that Will remembered from previous visits now had a plaque identifying the famous surfer. Pleased with himself that he had remembered the correct spelling of "Kahanamoku," Will turned toward Diamond Head and strolled down the sidewalk. For some reason, there weren't as many pretty women as he thought he remembered seeing here before. Maybe it was still too early in the day. Maybe this would be a good time to go to the mall and restock his dwindling supply of gin, he thought. After all, it would be much cheaper there than in Waikiki, and he could probably even find an off-brand in one of those plastic half-gallon bottles. Walking back toward Kuhio Avenue, which the buses traversed, he happened to remember that he would probably do well to buy a monthly bus pass, since he wasn't a tourist this time.

The bus seemed to stop forever at each stop. For some reason, the people who weren't sure of where they were going and were clueless as to how to get there were always the people who managed to squeeze themselves on the bus first at each stop. They would then invariably try to assert what little misinformation they had while speaking in a condescending manner to the bus driver, until they sensed that the driver and other passengers were exasperated and quickly becoming impatient. They would then either take their seats and one would tell the other that the driver didn't know what he was talking about; or, if no seats were available, they would proceed to complain loudly about *that.* All of this took place while other passengers were still waiting to get on the bus. Will instinctively thought how fortunate he was that he didn't live here. Then he realized that now he *did.*

At least the mall had a better-looking clientele, Will observed. He remembered having been to a drugstore here before that had a liquor department of substantial proportions. He walked in the direction which he thought it to be, and there it was. Infallible memory, even through the cobwebs, he told himself.

By the time he paid for the half-gallon, he was beginning to get the urge to proceed just beyond the "window of lucidity." The heat, to which he was unaccustomed even sober, was really hitting him hard. Even though years of practice permitted him to walk and talk normally—by his own estimation—after drinking large amounts, the heat was something with which he had no practice. Time to get to the bus stop.

On the way back, he stopped at a fast-food restaurant and got a large soda. This would give him something to mix the gin with, and, when it was finished, he would have a sizeable container for transporting ice so that he wouldn't have to make so many trips to the ice machine. The little refrigerator only had two small cube trays, and constantly having to go and get ice would defeat the purpose of drinking, Will reasoned.

Back in his room, he sat down to watch the news on television. He began to feel that he had finally stopped travelling. For once, it felt good to relax, knowing that he was finally where he wanted to be, geographically speaking. For several months now, he had not been able to *completely* relax, feeling but not knowing until recently that this move was impending.

A news story on the television showed an aerial camera shot of the New Jersey Turnpike. The scene looked very similar to the area in which he had stored most of his belongings, in a rented storage locker in one of those towns with an Indian name somewhere along the turnpike. Of course, all of that section of the turnpike had always looked so, so *industrial* to him.

At least he had managed to squeeze some of his "toys" into his luggage. His three cameras rested on top of the flap of a canvas bag in the corner. He had considered the possibility that he might have to sell one in order to survive once he got here. That possibility was quickly entering the planning stages in his mind.

He would sell the underwater autofocus camera, he determined. That would still leave him his SLR with its lenses and accessories, and the ultracompact autofocus. The underwater camera would sell fairly quickly here, Will guessed; and he would never miss it, since his alcohol-induced phobias had kept him, once a good swimmer, out of the water for years. The money would help to keep him "afloat." He smiled a rare smile at the irony of it.

That would then be his "project" for tomorrow. He phoned the newspaper to find out the rates and determined that it the cost of the ad would be worth it if the camera sold for anything close to his asking price.

Still not adjusted to the time change, five thirty saw Will yawning as he switched the channel on the television for the umpteenth time. The local news had just finished, and it seemed like a good time to walk over to the beach. It wouldn't be so hot, and he could see a Hawaiian sunset for the first time in a couple of years.

The sun was nearing the horizon as he approached the beach. He found a bench where he could sit with his face in the shadow of a palm tree trunk and peek around as the sun descended. The colors were not as saturated as last time, he thought. A cloud, pushed by a breeze that was present only in the distance, slowly eclipsed the sun just as it seemed about to touch the ocean. That was it. Sunset was over. No romantic notions, no hula girls, no steel guitar, Will thought. Not even a goddam proper sunset. Irritated, he rose from the bench.

Still not hungry although he had only eaten a small pastry all day, he decided he should get something to eat anyway. One of the fast food chains had a poster advertising cheap tacos. That would "coat his stomach" for the "serious" drinking that would begin as soon as he got back to his room.

The concrete and asphalt had a sheen the next morning when he looked out window. The air had a funny smell. It had been raining. In Hawaii. In Honolulu. In *Waikiki*, where it was supposed to be sunny all the time. In his three previous trips here, Will had seen a total of one rain shower, which had given way after a short while to a beautiful rainbow. This morning the sky, as far as he could see, was cloudy—solid gray.

He readied his ad copy while he sipped a morning "pop." He had to get really relaxed, because it would be, judging by his map, about a forty-five minute walk to the newspaper office. He was glad he had absent-mindedly thrown his umbrella in with his things as he had been packing. He knew that if he had been thinking straight, he probably wouldn't have brought it with him.

Outside the sidewalks, with their dampness, seemed so clean. His route memorized and his leather satchel secured by its strap around his shoulder, Will set off on his mission for the day. It was eleven-thirty, so he should be able to get this chore out of the way and be back by two-thirty, he figured. Taking the bus would shorten the required time, but he wanted to walk so that he could begin to get a feel for his surroundings. Besides, the overcast sky had the sun completely blocked out, so it wouldn't be so hot. The rain had abated to a light sprinkle for the moment.

Before he got half a block, *whoosh*! His right foot slipped, and he flailed both arms toward a utility pole in the same instant that he managed to regain his balance on his left foot. The metal manhole cover had been given the footing properties of a sheet of ice by the light rain. That must have looked really careless, he mused. He told himself to be more careful.

The further he walked, the more he sensed the area changing from a tourist area to a normal city business district. Not like New York, he thought, where tourists and residents intermingled almost indistinguishably. There were, he noticed, grassy lots, buildings with small lawns, and lots of shrubbery, both free-standing and in planters. And how clean—*whoosh*! This time both feet slipped and he was barely able to grip with both hands a chain link fence that separated the sidewalk from an empty lot. He vowed silently that he would never make that mistake again.

The walk took much longer than he had thought, and it was about one o'clock when he finally arrived in front of the building which housed the newspaper offices. The classified advertising section was behind a large semi-circular counter just inside and to the right of the double doors. He took an ad request form and began to print his copy onto the blank spaces. He had been careful to make sure that it had the proper number of spaces so as not to exceed the amount he could afford to spend.

Pleased with himself that his copy fit exactly into the correct number of blocks on the form, he waited at the counter for the clerk, an almost attractive, thin, thirtyish woman with long, straight, dark brown hair.

"Do you have a number?" she asked, turning to face him.

"A number?" Will asked, befuddled. Almost immediately, he noticed a red number dispenser that he had seen before only in places where long lines were common. "There's no one else here," he protested. "Do I really need a number?"

"Yes. You have to take a number."

He reached for the dispenser and tore off a number. Number 47. He looked at the lighted display. It read: NOW SERVING 32. The woman reached for a small metal box and began pressing the one button on it. The numbers on the display advanced one by one until number 47 was showing.

"Forty-seven," she called.

"That's me," came Will's compliant response. Without a word, she took the form he had filled out, and turned to face a computer terminal on the counter.

"I think I have the exact amount of letters to get the

lower rate," Will offered, trying to make conversation more than anything else.

"We'll see. The computer doesn't always go by the number of letters," she replied, without taking her eyes off the computer screen. "See, this is one word too long. You'll have to pay the higher rate if you want it to run this way."

"Can't I just mark out a word?" he asked.

"If you want to change it from the way it is here, you have to get another form and fill it out."

"I can't just scratch the word off this form?" he asked, beginning to lose his sense of whimsy.

"You have to get another form and fill it out," came the stone-faced answer. "But you don't have to take a number again. You can come right back to this window when you have it finished, and I'll help you.

Gee thanks, Will thought, but said nothing, noting that the whole classified advertising sales area had *nothing* that could pass for a window. Almost irritated an instant earlier, he was now becoming slightly amused by the transaction. He completed another form, deleting *two* words to be sure the ad fit this time. Back at the "window," he waited for several moments while the clerk, who had seen him approach, turned her back to him and seemed to be reading something.

She finally turned and, without a word, took the form and began typing on the computer keypad.

"Hope it fits this time," Will offered, still trying to establish a shred of a rapport. No answer. A moment later she looked up.

"We have a special rate if you run it Monday through Wednesday in addition to Sunday," she said. "Would you like to do that?"

"Just Sunday," Will answered.

"We also have a special rate if you want it to run in the afternoon edition in addition to the morning edition. Would you like to do that?" she queried.

"Just the morning."

"That will be $15.99," she announced, with all the aplomb and self-satisfaction of someone who had just completed a grueling and profitable ten-hour workday.

Will took a twenty out of his pocket and handed it to her. Her eyebrows became knitted as she looked at it. For an instant, Will wondered if she was about to tell him that United States currency was not accepted here.

"I'll have to go upstairs to get change for this. I'll be right back," she said, her routine appearing to have been upset. While she was gone, Will wondered how people generally paid for their classified ads if it wasn't by cash. Then he noticed a sign which advised advertisers to be sure to put their account numbers on their forms before submitting them to the clerks. Surely there must be people like me without accounts, he thought. Before he had time to wonder any more, the clerk came back.

"Four dollars and one cent, and there's your receipt," she said, placing the change and receipt a full two feet away from where Will was resting his folded arms on the countertop. Before he could say thank you, she turned back to her reading material, picked it up, and sat down. Will picked his money up, folded it once, and put it in his right pocket. He secured the strap of his satchel and walked toward the door.

"A-lo-ha," he said aloud as he stepped outside. It was almost now the time by which he had planned to be back to his room, which he was now beginning to think of as his home. Even though he had his bus pass with him he decided to walk back because of the clouds, taking a different route than the one by which he had come.

It was almost five when he put the chain on the inside of his door after placing the just-filled large cup of ice on top of the refrigerator. He was not used to walking so much, but the tired feeling, for once, was a good one. He turned on the television, quickly downed a large glass of ice water, and then fixed himself a strong mix of gin and Diet Coke.

Will had barely leaned his back against the pillow propped up against the headboard of the bed when he realized that he had one more small chore left to do. He went to his large suitcase which was still almost full, and he grunted as he lifted it up onto the bed. He opened it and reached under the packed mass of clothing. There it was—his answering machine.

He hadn't figured on it coming in handy so early. He had planned to hook it up only after he had started his job search. But now, with the ad for the camera coming out in the Sunday paper, it might have a sooner occasion to justify the space it had taken up inside his luggage. It took him only a few minutes to connect it to the hotel phone and plug it in to make sure it still worked after the jostling it must have gotten during the trip. There was just one more thing he had to do. He flipped up the plastic cover that protected the tapes from dust and pressed the record button.

"This is Will Tyne," he began. "I'm unable to take your call at the moment . . ."

This had been a productive day, he told himself. He deserved to relax tomorrow. But there was still plenty of drinking time left in today. He poured himself another gin and Diet Coke, this one with more gin and less Diet Coke. He didn't really care what was on television. And even if he had cared about the Waikiki nightlife just beginning four floors below, he was much too tired from all the walking to go outside again. Besides, this was not a vacation. He knew he had to budget his money wisely. Gin, to him, was not an unwise choice.

The traffic below the window was steady, and not so noisy. Will put the wooden chair so that its back was to the window, and he straddled it as he sat, watching the pedestrians and cars below. Will didn't remember seeing so many police vehicles when he had been here before, especially the little police golf carts, which frequently went tearing down the center lane of the street.

Will looked at the clock. It was just before noon. Why, he wondered, hadn't the "beep-beep-beep-beep" of the trucks awakened him this morning? Then he remembered that it was Saturday. At least, he reasoned, he was over the jet lag. He swung his feet off the bed and onto the floor, letting out a groan as he stood. The bottoms of his feet were sore, and his knee joints felt stiff.

No heavy walking today, he told himself. He would just find a shady spot at the beach and sip his "pop." That thought gave him inspiration if not energy, and he limped off toward the bathroom and the momentary comfort of the shower.

Although the streets still had puddles and there were some clouds in the sky, the sun was steaming down as Will walked down the outside "hallway." There was an older couple already inside the elevator as he stepped on it. They turned away from his glance. Maybe it's the gin breath, he figured, although, from what he had noticed so far, this was not a likely locale for a temperance union.

Out in front of the hotel, the air almost felt comfortable, although the sun irritated his face. He had a small canvas bag, used especially for this sort of outing, strapped to his shoulder. It contained his local map, paper to write on, his CD player, and, most importantly, his flask and an additional small plastic Evian bottle filled with gin. Trendy *and* health-conscious, he smirked to himself, as he tightened the cap of the Evian bottle.

He quickly wound his way through the clumps of people, grumbling to himself about how slow they were. People always walked in little mobs, it seemed to him—never alone as he did. He slid past four people—a family, he guessed—who were gathered in the main aisle of the fast-food restaurant. Why can't they ever stand to one side, he wondered silently. It appeared to him that people always stood in the very place where they could obstruct the greatest possible amount of traffic.

Jumbo Diet Pepsi in hand, he exited the side door of the restaurant, jaywalked across a side street, and trotted across the main thoroughfare just before the light turned green and released the four lanes of revving engines. He was completely out of breath. The sidewalk on this side, the beach side, had fewer pedestrians, and he could relax his pace a bit. It was only a short walk to the grassy area he had planned to make his resting place for the next little while.

He found a shady spot in the thick, close-cropped grass. Most of the people were closer to the beach, the sandy part of which was about twenty-five yards away from Will. There was no one within fifty feet of him. Heaven, he mused. He put his towel on the grass, anchoring it with his shoulder bag. Both knees made loud pops as he curled his legs, sore at the joints, under him.

The plastic top easily slipped off the top of his soda, and he quickly almost inhaled about one-fourth of the contents of the cup. His real thirst slaked, he removed the Evian bottle from his bag. Dumping well over half its contents into the cup, he stirred the mixture until it was no longer clear at the top. He took a sip, and then let out a long satisfied sigh.

"Perfect," he said aloud. "Just perfect."

He took his discman out of the bag, adjusted the earphones in his ears so that they blocked out as much outside noise as was possible, and pressed the "play" button. The familiar tones of Vollenweider's harp took the tenseness from his knitted eyebrows, and he began to relax, taking in another mouthful of his gargantuan drink.

Out of the corner of his eye, he noticed a young couple coming toward him. They stopped just a few feet away, and dropped their bags. Not here, he groaned to himself. They spread their blanket not five feet away, and directly in front of where he was sitting. Why here, of all places, he wondered.

There was plenty of shade all around, and there were plenty of other areas where they could have had some space to themselves. That ended Will's hope for solitude. He tried to ignore them.

That would not be allowed. As soon as they were settled, the man took a small portable radio/cassette player out of one of the bags. Soon, Vollenweider's harp had the unwanted accompaniment of Neil Young's three-chord whine. Will grimaced. The couple seemed to be completely oblivious to his presence. Will knew that there was a park rule prohibiting loud radios in this area, but this one really wasn't that *loud*, it was just so *close*. He decided he would move.

Gathering up bag, towel, walkman, and drink with as much disgust as he could exhibit, he cast a dirty look at the couple, who seemed oblivious of him, and trudged away in search of another resting place. He soon found an area better than the first, but with almost no view of the beach. Solitude was more important, so, grunting quietly with each leg position change, he parked himself in hopes that he would have more peace here.

The irritation and the move had opened his pores and he was now sweating freely. This time it almost felt good, though. He swilled his drink as he began to feel the relaxed sensation that it brought coming over him. Now, he thought, this is why I came here.

As soon as he was comfortable, his drink appeared as though raindrops were landing in it. Almost immediately, Will felt the rain on his skin. He looked up, but couldn't see any clouds except those in the distance. He turned and looked up and to the rear, and saw that the whole sky behind him was cloudy. None of the clouds was dark or ominous-looking, but the now-steady rain told him that they could get him very wet.

Not as bothered by the rain as by the couple earlier, he carefully returned his towel and earphones to his bag, which he lifted with his left hand, and he started back toward the hotel.

It rained steadily the whole way, but Will didn't feel like hurrying. He knew he was going to get thoroughly wet anyway, and why, thought he, should he spoil a good buzz? At least the sidewalks had fewer people, he noticed. As the rain increased its intensity, Will saw that some of the people were even beginning to leave the beach. It didn't look as though it was going to let up anytime soon.

Within a few minutes, Will approached the side entrance of the hotel. The sun shone through a break in the clouds. As he, quite waterlogged, reached for the door, it occurred to him that the rain had completely stopped. He looked in the direction of the beach. Arcing over the two block stretch of street that led in that direction was a rainbow. Exasperated, he went inside.

Because he had gotten up so late, the day so far had seemed to go by quickly. It was almost time for the news. And time to replenish the ice supply. He had discovered that he could take the elevator to the second floor, then descend to the first by way of a back stairway that led directly to the ice machine.

By taking this route, he could completely avoid the lobby and, he reasoned, the watchful eyes of the hotel employees who would surely notice his numerous trips to the ice machine. He had already been careful to bag his empty gin bottles in the closet, away from the trash can in his room, so that he could take them outside to a dumpster across the street. No need to have the maid report to the manager that there was a boozer in the house.

As his eyes followed the news pictures that flashed on the television screen, Will decided that, even though he had plenty of gin for tonight and to get tomorrow started, he might as well bus over to the mall and augment his supply. He could pick up something to eat there, as well. It wasn't as enjoyable going to the mall now as it had been when he had been here on vacation, though. Before, he had had plenty of money to buy gifts to take back to friends and family on the mainland, and he hadn't had to worry about the cost of his booze or food.

Now, knowing that he would probably come close to exhausting his money supply before he could find a job and cash a paycheck, he had to weigh each prospective purchase carefully, no matter how small it might be. But enough gin would wash out the bridge for that train of thought, and he would enjoy the trip to the mall anyway. Just looking at the pretty women would, he imagined, make the trip worth it.

Not that there would be *any* chance of making any time with them, he thought to himself. While Will might have still overestimated his potential and value in the work place, he knew that, in his present, juniper-berried state, he had not even a snowball's chance in hell with a decent woman. And he couldn't blame anyone but himself. Maybe even Michelle had seen that coming years ago.

As he tilted the pewter cup, which had been his drinking vessel of choice for a few years now and had made the trip safely tucked away in his luggage, upward, he took in the last sip along with the one remaining bit of ice. He fixed another drink of the usual proportions, except using only half the ice. This he placed inside the refrigerator. Knowing he would be tired from the course of the day *and* his consumption, he wanted to make sure that he would not have to expend any further energy fixing a drink when he returned. He would just add some ice, and sit down.

Preparation complete, he was able to slip out into the cooler, breezy twilight satisfied. The bus came quickly, the mall was uncrowded, and he dispatched his self-assigned duty with unusual ease. As he sat on the full bus making the return trip, he looked through the several postcards he had bought to send to people who might be interested in knowing his new address. He would write and address these tomorrow morning, he figured. By the time he got home tonight, his handwriting would be noticeably askew, and tomorrow morning's pops would provide him with a perfect "window of lucidity."

As he approached the hotel, he noticed that the nocturnal traffic was of greater volume than the night before. And it was barely nine o'clock. With little that interested him on the television schedule for tonight, he looked forward to occupying his front row seat on the world—from his window.

With the first drink of the night waiting for him in the refrigerator, he had but to place his chair by the window, turn on the radio, and watch. That was the way he liked people best—at a distance, where they could not bother him. That was, in fact, the *only* way he liked people.

He noticed the unusual number of pickup trucks in the traffic, most carrying riders in their cargo beds. Must be a local custom, he guessed. Occasionally, he would see someone whose lap was covered with, he assumed, a blanket or a tarpaulin. And if the traffic slowed to a crawl for long enough, which it often did, he could see the person reach under the tarp to his lap and quickly lift a beer can or a bottle of some unidentified libation to his lips, and just as quickly return the container to the cover of the tarp—all the while, surveying the surroundings.

"What's the thrill of making it so difficult?," he autoverbalized, and took a long, slow sip as he felt himself slipping into a hazier demeanor. The traffic was steady until three and a half hours after midnight. Will lasted three of those hours before "putting his head down for a minute," as he mentally referred to it.

As Sunday morning was another quiet one, Will did not wake until ten o'clock. He lay in intermittent dozes, daydreams, and reveries for another hour before dragging himself out of bed, not as sore as the day before. He was sluggish, nonetheless.

He had looked forward to this day, his fourth full day here, because it would be his first chance to read the Sunday newspaper as a resident here. Several times over the past year he had sent a money order for a copy of the Honolulu Sunday paper to be sent to him in New York. He had noted what appeared to be ample job openings here, and had lamented the fact that he had not been here to pursue them. Today was the beginning of his long-awaited opportunity.

And—today would be the day his ad for the camera would appear in the classified advertising section. His pace quicker than it had been for the past few days, or weeks, for that matter, he showered and decided to have only two pops before going out for a paper. He had counted the six quarters out of a small packet of change that he had brought with him, and had laid them on top of the dresser the night before.

Papers were sold in all the convenience stores and there were newspaper vending machines on every corner, Will had noticed. Best of all, there was one just outside the doors to the hotel lobby. He carefully deposited the change in the slot, heard the last coin drop, and pulled on the handle. The vending machine door would not open. He pushed the coin return button and repeated the same procedure, with no luck. Gathering his coins a second time, he proceeded a block and a half toward the beach to the next machine. It was empty. Finally, after walking two more blocks, Will found a machine that had newspapers and was in working order.

His pleasure at achieving his quest far outstripping the minor inconvenience that he might have otherwise regarded as a major annoyance had it gone further, he returned to his room and the welcome company of solitude and gin.

The first order of business was to make sure that his ad had been printed correctly. He found the classified ads and, after a few nervous minutes, found the ad he had placed. It was correct.

"At least she got it right," he said aloud, remembering the laconic, inflexible clerk who had waited on him at the newspaper office. Now, all he had to do was wait for the phone to ring. That would give him an excuse to stay in his room most of the day, he first thought. Then he realized that if he stayed in the room the rest of the day, he would do nothing but drink. And if he did nothing but drink, then he would be far too "out of it" to negotiate the sale of the camera.

He decided he would prepare his canvas bag "to go," and give the beach park another try. After all, he reasoned, anyone who was really interested could leave a message on his answering machine. Within a few minutes, he was outside walking toward the beach.

This afternoon was quieter than the previous one. And there were few clouds, none threatening. Will found a shady spot in the grass, as isolated a place as he could get. The trade winds felt good to him, but they were so strong that he had to keep the paper in his bag, removing it one section at a time to read it.

He quickly scanned the "help wanted" section, several pages long, and none of the offerings immediately caught his half-attentive eye. What *did* catch his eye, however, was an ad under a section marked "airlines/tickets." Not only was there an offer to sell one-way tickets to mainland destinations at rates far below the airlines' advertised rates—there was also an offer to *buy* one-way tickets to mainland destinations.

A possibility slowly crept into Will's mind: he could sell his return ticket! He had bought a round-trip ticket to come here because it had been substantially cheaper than the one-way fare. He had even reserved the "return trip" as though he had been planning to stay just over a week. He had briefly considered the return ticket as a sort of "safety valve."

What he had never thought of, though, was of having chance to *sell* the ticket. Obviously someone had, though, and had found a market for this sort of thing. Will took his red marker and circled the ad. He would call it first thing in the morning—well, almost the first thing.

Buoyed by the thought of an uncontemplated source of money, he decided to put off reading the "help wanted" section until the evening. As he tucked the paper inside his bag, he noticed two attractive, olive-skinned, bikini-clad women several yards away. This was the first time since he had been here that his mind had had enough free space to register a brief appreciation for the aesthetics of the opposite sex. He passed the afternoon less troubled than he had been in quite some time.

When he returned in time for the evening news at six o'clock, he looked at the answering machine. Its light was not blinking, which indicated that no messages had been left. Will now used three large cups to retrieve ice, and with one trip he had what he hoped would be enough to last him the remainder of the evening.

He had just turned on the television when the phone rang. Quickly turning down the volume, he grabbed the phone.

"Hello?" said Will, trying to sound as alert as he could.

"Hello. I calling about de camera. Dis de right numbah?

"Yes. This is the one," Will answered, ecstatic, but trying not to let it sound obvious.

"It goes under water? No leak?," the voice queried.

"Yes, it's waterproof to ten meters, according to the manual," Will offered.

"I like come see," the voice said, in a strange version of slightly butchered English with which Will was totally unfamiliar.

The caller's understanding of Will's instructions on how to get to the hotel seemed to Will to surpass the clarity of Will's directions. Maybe he already knew where the hotel was and was just being polite, Will guessed. He was to come look at the camera at eleven o'clock tomorrow morning.

Happy that something seemed to be going his way at the moment, Will determined that he would read the "help wanted" ads tomorrow. Tonight, he would relax and daydream about the future. He looked out the window. The traffic was light, and he saw no pickup trucks with the riders and their tarps and concealed drinks. Tomorrow was a workday, he remembered.

He had hardly been out of work a day in the first fifteen years since he had graduated from college. He had never had to look for work—it had always found *him*. It had taken less than a year for him to very nearly forget what it was like to have to get up early on a Monday. His weeks now had no end, and thus no beginning.

The room seemed a bit tilted to Will as he sat up on the side of the bed the next morning. He had sweated through his sheets again the night before, and, since he only had weekly maid service, the sheets were beginning to have a musty odor. He felt a bit lightheaded as he started toward the bathroom and wondered what was wrong. Then he remembered that he had not eaten any dinner last night. Nor any lunch yesterday. At least he knew the reason for his uneasiness. It was of no consequence, however. He knew a couple of pops would make him feel "normal."

He propped one hand against the shower wall as he rinsed the shampoo from his head—quickly, for he could not keep his eyes closed and maintain his balance, he feared. Opening his eyes, he exhaled a shallow breath, and quickly set about finishing this tedium. He *had* to get to those pops soon.

First drink of the day in hand, he sipped slowly. He felt it sting his stomach. He knew he *had* to eat something as soon as he was able. He looked at his watch. It was 9:20, and he knew that he would start to "ease off," as he put it, by 9:40. Comforted by that thought, he turned his attention to the cable news broadcast.

Nine-forty brought only an abatement of the uneasiness, along with the emptiness of the pewter cup. Will poured just a bit more gin in the second one, but he was feeling progressively better by the minute. He was certain that he would be well into the window of lucidity by the time eleven o'clock came.

At 10:52, the phone rang. Will let it ring a second time before he picked up the receiver.

"Hello, dis Weel?" came the voice from the other end.

"Rocky? Yeah, it's me," Will answered, recognizing the voice and the accent he had heard yesterday for the first time.

"I downstairs in da lobby already," came the voice, almost apologetic.

Will explained how to find his room at the end of the outside "hallway," and within ten minutes was alone again, recounting the money from the sale of the camera. Much to Will's surprise, Rocky had not tried at all to negotiate the price downward. He had paid Will the advertised price. Reassured by the thought of having a bit more money as a hedge between subsistence and desperation, Will now turned his attention to the airline ticket.

Phoning the number listed in the paper, he got a recorded message which explained the process of how he might be able to sell his return ticket. At the end of the recorded message, the narrator gave a number that could be dialed in the event that the caller decided to follow through with the process.

It was simple: Will had but to take his ticket to the office of the broker. It would then be listed on a recording for those people calling to inquire about *buying* a ticket. They would then call the broker and either pay the asking price or negotiate another rate, depending how quickly the ticket had to be used. If the ticket sold, Will would receive half the money, the broker the other half. Simple, like hell, Will thought, having a distaste for any business matter in which he was required to participate. He dialed the number for the "live" broker.

A deep-voice with an "official" manner answered and briefly reiterated the preliminary information. He asked Will where and when the ticket was for.

"Thursday, 10:05 in the morning," Will answered.

"That's kind of short notice," the voice answered, sounding more human and less businesslike.

"Can you use it or not?" Will asked, trying not to sound anxious, but uncomfortable at feeling financially coerced into the interaction.

"You can bring it over, and I'll list it. That's the best I can do. Honolulu-L.A.-New York tickets almost always sell if they're listed soon enough. This one probably will, but it won't get as much money, being that it's kinda short notice."

"Okay, I'll give it a try," Will decided.

"Okay, but you got to get it to me. I can't list it until I have it here," the broker, who had identified himself as "Bob," responded. Will sensed that he had taken up his allotted amount of time. He got the directions on where he was to meet the broker, a street corner bus stop in Hawaii Kai. Will had never been there, but, bolstered by the thought of extra money, he reached for his street map of the area. He had arranged to meet his impromptu business partner in two hours. He prepared his canvas bag "to go."

The bus ride into a neighborhood where he had never been would have been enjoyable, he told himself, if it had not been for the business aspect of it. At every juncture, he seemed to be reminded that he was *not* on vacation this time. He got off the bus at what he was certain was the right stop. Bob had given him very clear directions. He was ten minutes early. In less than five, he saw a mid-1980's Corvette approaching slowly. It pulled up to the bus stop and the driver, a heavy-set, balding, forty-something man with a dark, bushy mustache, got out.

"You must be Will," he grinned, and Will nodded. "Not many people use this bus stop this time of day. Most people in this area have cars, anyway."

His manner put Will at ease. While he had questioned

the plausibility of leaving a useable airline ticket with a total stranger at a street corner earlier, Will now thought it could be possible that it *was* above board. At any rate, he had nothing to lose. He read and signed what looked like a tenth generation photocopy marked "Agreement" that Bob handed him.

"You going back to Waikiki?" Bob asked as he was about to get into his car. Will indicated that he was. "C'mon, I'll give you a ride as far as Kapahulu. You can get a bus quicker there. Plus, it's a lot shorter ride. Only a few minutes from there to the middle of where you're going."

Will wasn't sure where he would get dropped off, but anything was better than standing out in this hot sun, which was starting to take a rapid toll on his alcohol-soaked brain. He folded himself into the passenger seat, and inhaled the cool air blowing steadily from the air conditioning vent.

Back in the solitude of his hotel room, cooled by the fan and thinking more clearly, Will wondered if he would ever hear from Bob. It was just too easy, he thought. But, all it had cost him to give it a try was the time it had taken. The ticket was worthless otherwise. He turned his attention to the "Knight Rider" rerun on the television.

About seven o'clock that evening, as Will was tucking into his satchel the four postcards he had just addressed so that he could mail them the next day, the phone rang. It was Bob.

"Your ticket sold," Will heard Bob say without even a "hello" first. "I got $150 for it. Not bad, considering how late it is. I can meet you tomorrow morning if you want to pick up your money. Cash."

"Uhh. Yeah, umm, what's a good time?" Will sputtered, partly from gin deceleration, partly from happy disbelief at what he had just heard.

"How's eleven? Bus usually goes by about then, if you catch it at the right time."

Will understood. "I'll be there no later than eleven," he answered.

"See you then."

"Okay. Thanks," Will responded, his mind starting to catch up with the moment. His pensive, doubtful mood was rapidly becoming one of satisfaction, restrained only by his contemplative nature. Sure, he would have had no place to go had he returned to New York. But it was a different feeling now that he had no *means* of returning. The concern quickly wore off.

No more tunnels, he thought.

Chapter 2

Plunging Into Darkness

Found money. That's how Will regarded the $75 he had gotten from the sale of the airline ticket. And that's how he felt that it should be spent. After all, he had already sacrificed one of his "toys," a camera, for the sake of survival. He deserved to be able to use *this* money to have some fun, something he felt he had not been permitted in a long time.

First and foremost, he would fortify his stock of gin. A couple of half gallons would take about $30, he calculated; and he would save another $15 for gin, just in case. Just in case *what*, he didn't know. That would leave $30. October was just a few days away, and he would need another bus pass. That would be $20. That left him $10. He reassured himself that the day was not that far away when he would once again not have to worry about such trivial expenses.

He picked up the "help wanted" section of the classified ads, laid aside since Sunday. It was now Tuesday afternoon, and far too late to respond, he decided, to the two job possibilities he had just read about. By the time he could get copies of his resume made, it would be too late to send them out in today's mail. And if he mailed them out tomorrow, they probably wouldn't reach the right person until Friday. That person, he told himself, would be thinking about the weekend and would forget by Monday about any resumes that might have caught his eye on the previous Friday. Thus, Will decided, he had no choice but to wait until next Sunday's paper came out to start his job search. That left him with a few days to relax without any pressure, he determined.

What a good time to get really blasted! he thought to himself. After all, it had been nothing but go, go, go since he had been here—or so it had seemed to Will, for whom a walk up a flight of stairs was a "workout." Although he had already seen the bottom of his cup several times today, those drinks didn't count. The first few had been for the purpose of making him feel "normal." The next few had been to "relax" him for the bus ride to go pick up his money from Bob; and now, at three-thirty, his drink was only to "tide him over" until he got back from his liquor run at the mall.

Remembering that he *must* eat something in order to keep from being so woozy in the morning, he decided he would pack his bag "to go," and have dinner and an altered soda at one of the fast food restaurants in the mall. It would be, for him, vaguely reminiscent of happier times he had spent there before.

The bus was slow in getting to the mall. Day-shift hotel workers and people from the military post in Waikiki were getting off work for the day, and traffic was thick. Will had found a window seat, and the air conditioner on the bus was strong, so he didn't mind. He, too, was "off" until Sunday, he told himself.

Arriving at the mall, Will went directly to the food court, an expansive area in the bottom floor of the mall, supplied with a few hundred tables and chairs, and surrounded on three sides by a few dozen fast food eateries. Choosing—not surprisingly— pizza, Will found a table which stood alone in a corner, on a side section that was raised about a foot above the center section of the cavernous dining area. He sat with his back to the other tables in the section, and braced the front legs of the chair opposite him with his own legs. He did not want any unwelcome company joining him, unfounded though his concern may have been.

The pizza was good, and he was hungry. Not like Ray Bari's pizzerias at 76th and 3rd, or 56th and 3rd, or 69th and Amsterdam in Manhattan, he told himself, but still good. Over the past few months, he had only seemed to be able to enjoy food when he was in a good mood. Other times eating was like a necessary chore, although the rounded belly on his otherwise normal frame belied his finicky appetite.

Finished with his pizza, he turned his attention to his soda, already modified by a few generous splashes of the contents of his Evian bottle. The color of the soda was still too dark, he told himself, so he added more. The loudness of the throng of people slowly turned from an annoying din into a low-pitched hum as Will's restless hunger vanished and was being replaced by a sated stupor. He sat at the table for another hour, feeling comfortably unnoticed as he watched the neon signs begin to grow fuzzy edges.

He slowly realized that he had better get his errand done and find his way back to the bus stop. He knew this feeling; he was "tiring" quickly, and wanted to get home before it became obvious to others. Will was so accustomed to heavy drinking that it took a lot to make him less than steady on his feet, but it seemed to be hitting him harder tonight. He plodded toward the bus stop, his "procurement" swinging in the plastic bag that hung from his hand almost to the pavement.

The bus filled up quickly, which didn't bother Will, since he had a seat. It glided past the first few stops, since it was too full to hold any more people, and Will smiled at the thought that there was, after all, a tiny advantage to being inside the packed bus in this instance. As the bus pulled onto a main Waikiki thoroughfare, though, Will's tolerance of the complaining chatterboxes on the bus diminished almost instantly, and he pulled himself up out of his seat so that he could exit at the next stop.

As he stepped off the bus, he reached for a signpost near the door so that he could make sure that he would be steady in case his knees started to give way. They held him up, and he started toward the hotel, now pausing to let people walk around his path, rather than assuming his usual deliberate, undeterred, straight-line gait.

Will looked toward a night club that he had noticed a few times before, in the daytime. The door was open, and there were two women entering. He stopped to get a longer look at the entrance and facade of the establishment. It looked as though it might be the sort of place he would feel comfortable in. But, he told himself, even if he *did* manage to meet someone and have a conversation that lasted longer than thirty seconds, he was just too exhausted to be in a "sociable" frame of mind. He knew that he had about another half hour of functional thinking left in him, and that after that, he would just be drinking himself toward a sound sleep.

The best thing for him to do, he conceded, would be to get home, stock up on ice, and watch television. He hadn't been in a bar in the last six months that he had been in New York, anyway. By the time of night that they usually got busy, he had almost always been already "relaxed." He smiled at his own indolence, indulgence, and the notion that he was always too drunk to go out drinking.

Without the pressure, Will had hoped that he would be able to enjoy the remainder of the week. The stark reality was, however, that he would soon have to pay rent in order to extend his stay at the hotel. In order to do so, he would have to find a job that he could begin by no later than a week from the next Monday. The only alternative he had to this would merely be a stop-gap stall: selling his other camera equipment, something he hoped to avoid.

Sunday came, and Will examined the "help-wanted" section of the classified ads more seriously this time. He had made photocopies of his resume during the week, and had bought a box of the cheapest envelopes he could find. About midway through the section he was scanning, he found a listing that he thought he might have a chance at. An advertiser was looking for a insurance billing clerk. Will had done that for almost seven years in New York. He knew that the specifics of the job varied from state to state, but that his general experience would probably generate interest with a prospective employer. At least he hoped it would.

It was still mid-afternoon when he dropped the envelope containing his resume into the mailbox outside the Waikiki Post Office. He had made certain that he had gotten the task accomplished before too many drinks had knocked the corners off of his handwriting. Along with the response to the first ad he had seen were two others, possibilities that presented less hope, but ones which he deemed worth trying.

Once the envelopes fell into the box, so fell the weight of the matter from his conscience. He had done all he could do for now, he reasoned, and it was time to relax. The impending gravity of his plight would not allow him to completely forget his concerns, however, and he speculated that he would be awake well into the night.

As Will entered his room, he noticed for the first time that it had a strong, sour, musty odor throughout. He remembered that he had been asleep the previous day when the maid had knocked on his door for the once-weekly room cleaning. All he had managed to say was "not now," instead of asking her to come back later. She had not returned. She had probably remembered that he had given her a smaller tip last week than he had the previous week. Oh well, he thought. Can't blame her.

That night no amount of gin, it seemed, could flood his worries about the job situation. Prospects had seemed so good whenever he had read the papers that had been sent to him in New York. Now, the pickings had gotten slim. It was just his luck, he told himself. What he could not consider was what would happen if he simply could *not* find a job. That had never happened to him before. What Will *knew*, however, was that he had never consumed gin in such huge quantities before, either. Maybe he would quit in a few days . . .

Will was in the middle of his third pop on Tuesday morning when the phone rang. He had awakened still weaker than usual, since he had been too worried to eat anything more than a cheeseburger the day before. Even though he had calmed the early morning nausea that had dogged him recently, and was entering his window of lucidity for the day, the phone still startled him.

Trying to sound as alert and pleasant as possible, he answered.

"May I speak to Mr. Tyne, please?" inquired the slightly Asian-sounding female voice at the other end.

"Speaking," he answered.

"This is Pauline with Epa Hauna Personnel," came the soft voice. "I'm calling regarding the resume you sent us. Can you tell me how long you've been in Hawaii and what brought you here?"

Will had glib, well-rehearsed answers for at least a hundred questions. This was not one of them. He sputtered for a moment, but recovered quickly and managed a plausible-sounding response about making the move because of the area's seeming promise of "economic opportunity." He knew he was talking to an above-average interviewer.

"Can you come by for an interview this Thursday?" she asked, apparently satisfied for the moment that he was worth more time.

"Yes. Anytime on Thursday afternoon would be good," he was careful to respond, knowing that anytime on Thursday *morning* would find him looking so beaten from the previous night that the interview would undoubtedly be a short one.

"How about two o'clock?" she offered.

"That's *perfect*," came his answer, followed by an almost syrupy, "Two o'clock. I look forward to meeting you."

"Okay."

"Thank you for calling," he oozed, trying to sound as enthusiastic and positive as he could sound, and as he was now beginning to feel. The combination of the phone call, the relief from the early nausea, and the initial impact from the alcohol all hit him at once, and he felt good for an instant. Then, almost immediately, he began to worry. If he had been feeling horrible in the morning lately, how could he make himself feel any better on Thursday? Sure, he could make certain he ate something Wednesday night, but what about going out without his morning pops, something he had not done in months? He knew he could not show up for the interview with liquor on his breath, but he had no idea how he could get through it sober, especially if he was nauseous in the morning. He would not be able to eat anything, he knew, and how would he mask his bad breath? What if it was a hot day,as he *knew* it would be, and he broke out in a sweat? He knew that the odor of the alcohol would quickly seep through his pores. And he knew without a doubt that it would be noticeable. Worst of all: what if she wanted him to take a typing test? His hands would be shaking, and that would be a dead giveaway.

He would white-knuckle it, he supposed. He had managed to cover himself many times over the years, even as his consumption had increased; and even though he was in a different situation now, Will was cautiously optimistic that he would be capable of yet another display of bravado that would make him appear normal.

It was becoming apparent to Will that if he managed to

accomplish the near-impossible and get the job, it would take longer than he had imagined. It was time, he determined, to take measures to make sure that he would have enough money to pay rent for another month. His rent had been on a weekly basis when he had arrived, but the hotel manager, whose family owned the business, had allowed him to change to a monthly rate when it became necessary for him to extend his stay. That had made his rate lower, but it also meant that he would have to pay the full month in advance, rather than paying a week at a time.

The other cameras would have to be pawned. He wouldn't worry this time, he told himself. He would have an income and be able to get them out of hock before the forfeiture date, two months from the date of the pawn transaction. It would be okay, he reasoned. Besides, he hadn't taken any pictures since he had been here. And even if he had, there was no extra money to get the film developed.

Will's other concern was his hope that he could transact enough money not only to supplement his dwindling remaining cash and cover the rent, but that he would have enough left over for food and other necessities, especially those in liquid form. He had been consuming gin so quickly lately that his trips to the dumpster across the street to dispose of his bottles had become more frequent.

He tucked his two remaining cameras and their saleable accessories into his canvas bag. He wanted to make the transaction so that he would have an idea of where he stood financially *before* his interview on Thursday. He knew that having a roof secure over his head would bolster his confidence, which had been sinking until he had gotten the phone call on Tuesday.

As he entered the pawn shop, the owner eyed him and paused before nodding and forcing a tight-lipped smile. Will knew that pawning all of his equipment would mean that he might not fare as well as if he just pawned one camera. While pawning one item might make him appear to be someone who just needed some quick cash between paychecks, carting all of his photography equipment into the pawn shop would surely identify him as a more desperate person.

If the owner thought this, he didn't show it, however; and Will left the shop without any of the equipment, but with very nearly the amount he had calculated he would need from the transaction. As he crossed the four lanes of the street, he stopped for a brief moment and let out an audible sigh as he looked upward.

"YES!" he whispered loudly. Maybe this was the turn of luck he had been looking for. Maybe the odds which he thought seemed always to be so stacked against him were about to concede him a tiny bit of relief. There was still another day between now and Thursday. That meant he could drink tonight to celebrate his temporary reprieve from uncertainty. But first he would return to the Regal Arbor, fortify himself, and make an appointment to see Mr. Sing, who had expressed some concern about the rent situation.

Tom Sing was about Will's age, but very energetic and fit in appearance. He appeared to Will to be of Asian descent, but Will hadn't been around Asian people enough to be able to distinguish his country of origin. Sing's hair had a sort of Brylcreem sheen that made it look like shiny black plastic. Will had noticed that the hotel's transient guests regarded him almost as a celebrity. They practically bowed to him in person, and whispered about him in almost reverential tones as they were riding the elevator. Mr. Sing, in turn, was friendly, but it was evident that he was first and foremost a businessman.

Bolstered by his pawn transaction and by his liquid edification, Will stepped off the elevator and walked toward lobby desk, behind which Mr. Sing was standing, looking at a chart full of numbers.

"Mr. Tyne," he acknowledged, smiling, "What can I do for you?" His speech had only a slight trace of an accent.

"Well, I have some rent money for you," Will began,

"and maybe some good news. I've got a possible job prospect lined up."

"That is good news," Sing said flatly, his smile turning to a serious look. Will handed him the money, which he quickly passed to the desk clerk, who began writing a receipt for Will. His eyes returned to his reading material. "Some people come here and they go *months* without finding work. If you come from the mainland without a job already, it's usually hard to find a good one here. So when do you start?" He rolled his eyes upward toward Will while his face still pointed down at the chart.

"Well, it's not for certain yet. I have an interview Thursday, but I think I have a good shot at it," Will fidgeted, expressing far more confidence than he really felt.

"Oh, you know?," Sing began in a friendlier tone, "November begins our busy season here. Everything is reserved already starting in mid-November."

"Wow! That's incredible, considering how the newspaper is always talking about tourism being down these days," Will enthused, not realizing what Mr. Sing was politely trying to tell him. Backing away toward the elevator, he continued, "My Fodor's guide says this is a good place. Must be a lot of people who have found that out."

Sing nodded, smiling slightly as Will stepped on the elevator.

Rent paid, money supply in better shape, job possibility on the horizon, thought Will, counting his accomplishments as he turned the key in the lock on the door to his malodorous abode. Time to relax tonight and use tomorrow to get in the right frame of mind for the interview the next day, he thought. Of course, alcohol was integral to *any* sort of adjustment that he deemed necessary. He slipped out the door and down the stairs to the ice machine, walking in a confident manner for the first time in several days.

Wednesday passed with Will becoming increasingly

nervous about his upcoming interview. By mid-afternoon, he had sedated himself to the degree that he couldn't see the television straight. A period of semi-consciousness, or "nap" as Will thought of it, rendered him able to venture out later for two cheeseburgers, his meal for the evening.

As the evening wore on, the television screen became more distorted, and the dialogues of the programs made less sense to Will. But his uncooperative, impaired eyes stayed open. The gin would not do its assigned job for the night. At three in the morning, his mind finally let go of its concerns, and he fell into a fitful, sweaty sleep.

The alarm was first a part of his half-reverie, half-sleep at ten-thirty Thursday morning, then a dreaded interruption of it. Will's first thought on awakening: it'll be over by three, and I can really let loose then. He hadn't even begun to get ready for his interview, and he was already anxious for it to be over.

The voluminous amount of booze he had consumed in his attempt to get to sleep Wednesday night made him slow, and made him wonder if he might have cold molasses in his veins instead of blood. His dread slowed him further. Unable to eat because of his usual nausea, he smiled a sardonic smile, thankful that he was a man, especially if this was a feeling similar to that which gestating women had during their pregnancies.

Finally clad in an *aloha* shirt, khaki trousers, and loafers which he had dusted off the night before, he started slowly for the door. The closing door eclipsed the sight of the almost-empty gin bottle and the full, unopened one next to it. If only . . . he thought, and knew he couldn't. But it would be there when he got back. Just two and a half hours, and he could relax.

Having allotted himself an hour to get downtown to his appointment, he stepped off the bus well ahead of schedule and still not having broken a sweat. Pleased with himself, he sat on the edge of a planter out of the sun, and removed his map of the downtown area from his satchel. Certain of his bearings, his next move was to find the lobby of the building where his appointment was, and to hope that it had strong air conditioning.

At exactly one-fifty, Will turned the knob of the door to suite 1311 and entered the Epa Hauna Personnel office. That the building actually had a floor numbered thirteen had not escaped him, but the thought was quickly crowded out of his mind.

Seated behind a desk was a partly-Asian looking woman of about forty, who smiled immediately when he entered. "May I help you?" she asked in a whispery voice, which matched her flawless appearance and pretty face.

"Um, I'm Will Tyne. I have a two o'clock appointment to see Pauline," he managed to get out without stammering.

"I'm Pauline." She offered her hand, but did not grip his in return when he grasped it. "It's nice to meet you. Why don't you have a seat right here?"

Will thanked her, took the seat and glanced around, placing his satchel on the floor beside the chair. There was no one else in the small office, and it had only one other door that appeared as though it might lead to another room or a large closet. The floor-to-ceiling window he had faced when he first walked in offered a panoramic view of western Honolulu, but the chair in which he was seated had its back toward the window.

"You know, employers here are sometimes wary about people from New York and L.A.," Pauline began.

What an odd thing to start off with, Will thought, but bit: "Oh, really? I wonder why that is." He caught himself about to look at his watch, and didn't.

"Because some people think they're too aggressive and headstrong."

"I was brought up in North Carolina. I just *lived* in

New York for the last ten years," will countered quickly, helping to illustrate Pauline's point. "I only lived the last ten years in New York. People from North Carolina are easier-going folks." He tried to smile, but was already too rattled.

"You came here because you thought Hawaii was full of opportunity?" Her eyebrows raised, but she smiled. "Where did you hear that? We're in a recession right now."

Will quoted his source—accurately, he hoped. He managed to sound credible, and was beginning to forget his withdrawal misery, distracted by the novel experience of the interview. He hadn't had many conversations *period* in the last few months.

Pauline continued, "Employers also shy away from people who pick up and move here in the middle of their lives. A lot of people come here to get away from their problems, you know. A bad marriage, child support, or just a mid-life crisis. Employers train them, and then they decide to go back to the mainland. A lot of companies here have been burned like that"

Will tried to assure her at length that he did not fit into any of those categories. He acknowledged to himself that what he was trying to escape was very similar, but Pauline did not have to know that. Seeming to be satisfied with his intentions, which he had managed to deliver without seeming too eager, Pauline proceeded with questions about his experience. This put Will less on the defensive, and he responded with the rehearsed answers that his training had told him she would want to hear.

After another round of disclaimers about the trepidations of local employers, Pauline paused. "I have to check your references," she told him. "Sometimes that can take as much as a week. If they can't take my phone call, or don't return it, then I have to mail a reference form for them to fill out, and that takes even longer. If they even bother to fill it out." Seeing the furrow between Will's eyebrows, she continued, "I'll give you a call Monday to let you know what I find out. If I can just get one reference, I'll go ahead and set up an interview with my client. But I'll give you a call either way. Okay?"

How pretty she is for her age, Will thought. And such perfect diction . . . "Okay," he blurted, realizing what she was saying. "Thank you. It was nice meeting you. I look forward to hearing from you," he effused, almost giddy that he had survived the grueling marathon without making a major faux pas. Will stepped into the hallway and realized that now his forehead had started sweating freely. He looked at the business card she had handed him as he had been leaving. After her name was her title: owner. Not even a typing test, he thought, smiling as he approached the elevator. God, I must have been in there two hours, he thought as he looked at his watch for the first time. It was two forty-five.

His ordeal over, Will didn't mind the perspiration that seemed to be flowing from every pore in his body. He was so relieved, not only that he was done with the interview, but that he had apparently passed the first phase of the employment process. Then he realized that he had not yet had a drink. The twitches that would plague him whenever he failed to wash away the previous day's after-effects slowly began to make his hands jump intermittently, seemingly without any stimulus. He reached to scratch his forearm, even though it didn't itch.

He had been comfortable the first moment after he had stepped on the bus that would take him back to Waikiki, but now he felt an urge to rise out of his seat so that he could get off at the next stop. Each time he started to move the urge would go away, only to return the instant he tried to relax in his seat again. The inside of the bus seemed tiny and constricting to him.

"I *need* my pops," he whispered to himself, louder than he intended, for the woman seated next to him glance at him with a half-bewildered, half-annoyed look on her face. He tapped the floorboard with his right toe as if he had an accelerator underneath his foot, but the bus would go no faster. It seemed to Will that it paused for an interminable length of time at every stop, and that it was caught by the traffic light at every intersection. Will felt his heart racing. He tried to check his pulse by feeling the underside of his right wrist with his left index and middle fingers. He couldn't feel it long enough to time it.

Just as he felt ready to scream, but knew that he wouldn't, the bus pulled up to the stop just before the one where he usually got off. He stood, pushed the rear doors open, and stepped onto the pavement. That part of his trauma was over. In a pace that was as fast as his spindly legs would take him, he threaded a path through the groups of people who were not in quite the desperate hurry he was.

Finally, he reached the lobby of the Regal Arbor. The elevator was on the top floor, the sixth, and Will knew that it was slow. He didn't have the energy left, however, to take the stairs up to his room. The elevator came and Will, impatient with the leisurely manner of its passengers, brushed past the last couple onto the elevator before they could get off. He pressed the button for the fourth floor, and repeatedly poked the "door close" button with the knuckle of his forefinger. The one quilted wall of the small elevator reminded Will of a coffin; he shook his head and his body shuddered involuntarily. The door opened, and Will was almost free.

Will could not steady his hands as he struggled to get his key in the door.

"Goddammit!" he grunted loudly, hoping his neighbors were not in. "Get in, goddammit," he urged the inanimate key. The door opened. Then he remembered he had no ice in the refrigerator. He grabbed his two cups and, propping the door ajar with a shoe, he started downstairs. He returned a few minutes later, very nearly out of breath, panting audibly, and feeling as if he was about to pass out.

He managed to get the gin into the glass without spilling any. As he took the first sip and frowned, his malaise lessened slightly. "Twenty minutes," he said to no one, "Twenty minutes and I'll start to feel normal." Or at least more like his usual self.

Exulting in his apparent first-round victory, and sipping on his third drink an hour later, Will's eyes passed over the answering machine. It was blinking. Who'd be calling me, he wondered. Rising, he walked toward the refrigerator and stiffened his drink. He pressed the playback button on the machine.

It was another employment agency! One of the other resumes had gotten someone's attention. His hands now sure, Will jotted the name and number down. He was still too rattled from today's earlier demands, but he would, he reasoned, call tomorrow morning. It would be Friday, he knew, and there would be no way they would schedule an interview until next week. If he called today, he feared, they might want to see him tomorrow, and he didn't want to go through another episode of the same ordeal from which he was just now recovering—especially after experiencing what had been caused by too long a period without alcohol. He inhaled as deeply as he could and took a long sip of his drink.

By ten o'clock the next morning, Will was up, showered, dressed, and sipping on his first drink of the day. He was allowing no chance that the after-effects of the previous day's alcohol would begin to overtake him before he was prepared. By eleven, he felt ready to return the phone call of the second employment agency. Within minutes, he had an appointment for noon the following Tuesday.

Now it's really rolling, he told himself, knowing that he would hear from Pauline on Monday. He had two good chances for jobs that would rescue him from the risk of facing a bleak and uncertain future. It was time to celebrate, but he was going through money and gin more quickly than he had estimated.

That meant that it was time to pawn something else, this time his portable CD player. A couple of half-gallons and some food, he guessed, could be extracted from the proceeds of the transaction. By this time, he had no worry about dealing with the pawn shop owner. He knew he was a good customer.

Confidence outstripping his physical condition, Will set out for a walk on the beach Sunday afternoon, not having eaten anything all day, but having many drinks under his bulbous waistline. The sun was no hotter than usual, and Will seemed to tolerate it better than usual at first. He normally tried to follow a path that led through the shaded areas, but today he stayed closer to the beach watching the women, his eyes lingering on the more attractive ones. Not so long from now, he nodded to himself, one of them will be mine. He imagined himself sitting in a lawn chair, his "bar" on one side and a slender, olive-skinned woman on the other.

Will coasted on his reverie all the way down to the end of the park, about a half-mile away, and much of the way back, before he began to feel tired. It was getting late in the day, but the sun seemed to be getting hotter. Will's forehead began to ache and throb. Time to head home, he groaned silently. He was sure that a couple of strong ones would wash away his headache.

As he entered his room, he grabbed one of his ice cups from the refrigerator. It was over half-full of water, since some of the ice had melted. Will guzzled it down. Without stopping to pour a drink, Will switched the fan on to its maximum speed and lay down on the bed. His stomach felt as if it had a fold in it. Maybe it was time to lay off the booze, he told himself, hoping that his admission and his ailing state would generate some sympathy for him from somewhere in the universe.

He had known that the sun could exacerbate the negative effects of alcohol, and that it was in fact *dangerous* to drink too much and venture out into Hawaii's tropical sun for too long. In his happier-than-usual state of mind, though, he had felt that he might have been granted some sort of immunity from this consequence. He knew he had been wrong.

He would just drink tonight, he determined. Tomorrow, no more. He would sober up and be ready for his interview on Tuesday, and back in top-notch form by later in the week, in case Pauline scheduled another interview. Soothed partly by his decision and partly by the fan, he sat up on the bed, then stood and walked toward the refrigerator.

Anticipating Pauline's call, Will decided to stay in his room the next day, Monday, until he heard from her. Without the seemingly calming effect of his gin, though, he was in misery. Though the claustrophobia that plagued him in elevators and on buses was absent, he still endured the uncontrollable twitches, the undefined anxieties, and the unsettling sensation of being unable to catch a full breath. He had been through this before, and he knew that, without medical help, all he could do was wait. He knew that he would live through it, but his unrelenting anxiety made the time drag.

At just after two, the phone rang.

"Hello?" Will answered, his voice weak and tinny.

"Is Will there?"

"Yes, this is Will," he responded, trying to sound okay.

"This is Pauline at Epa Hauna Personnel. I just wanted to let you know that I haven't heard anything from any of your references," she began, sounding almost *too* cheerful to Will. "I'm going to mail out reference request forms to them, and maybe they'll fill them out and mail them back."

"You didn't even hear from Harriet?" will asked, grimacing at the sound of his own voice, which sounded almost like a whimper. "She told me when I left there that I could count on her for a good reference. Did you talk to her or to her secretary?"

"I left a message with her secretary last Friday morning," Pauline said firmly, sounding slightly irritated at Will's inquisitiveness. "She hasn't returned my call."

"I'm sure she'll call eventually," Will assured her, trying desperately not to sound desperate.

"I'm going to send her a form anyway. I can't set up a meeting with my client until I can give him a positive reference," Pauline continued, sounding even more impatient. "If I hear anything, I'll let you know. You can call me before then if you want to, but I won't be in my office on Thursday and Friday."

"Okay. Well, thanks for calling," Will said, feeling defeated. He heard the phone click at the other end. Desperately wanting a drink, he took a step toward the refrigerator before he remembered that he had poured the last bit of gin down the sink drain earlier. He sat back down, knowing that he still had to get through the remainder of the day, and that, with his system still purging weeks of steady drinking, he would get no sleep that night.

Night came, and the twitches worsened. Not only did his pulse continue to race, so did his mind. He visualized an endless stream of disturbing images, but nothing to which he could affix a name. Each time he almost drifted off to sleep, his head would jerk up off the pillow and he would struggle to get a full breath, seldom succeeding. The pattern repeated itself minute after minute, hour after hour. His one minuscule fragment of relief was that he had been through this several times over the course of twelve years of heavy drinking.

He had many times fancied himself to be an "alcoholist," not an alcoholic, since he thought he knew his limits and the price that would be exacted from him if he exceeded them. Knowing this didn't actually relieve the moment-to-moment malaise, but unlike his first withdrawal, when he was sure he was going to die, he knew that this feeling would pass if the minute hand would just go around the clock enough times. He also knew that the first two days would be the worst.

Daylight came and Will had not slept. He could not lie in bed any longer, although he didn't really feel like getting up.

He had already been to the bathroom at least fifteen times during the night, and his legs had become more spindly with each trip. He knew that if he showered too early, he would be coated with perspiration before he got to the interview. The perspiration, he knew, would emit a strong, unpleasant odor, and it would certainly hurt his chances of getting the job.

The twitches were beginning to subside, and Will felt a slight twinge of hunger. But he feared that his uncontrollable throat muscles would not be able to swallow the food, and that he might choke. He dared not eat for at least another day. That would make him weak, he conceded, but he would just have to bear it.

How ironic, he thought, that he was facing an interview having been sober for a full day, and he felt worse than he had before the interview with Pauline, when he had been drinking the night before. No going back this time, he told himself. If he made it through this interview, there would be no need to drink any more, because the worst would be over. By tomorrow, he would be able to start eating again, and would begin to recover his strength, and by the weekend he would feel well enough to . . . to start drinking again. No! he thought. He chuckled at his own self-absorbed, twisted manner of thinking. This time, he vowed silently, it's for good. Time to get serious about life.

Coaxing himself mentally with each step he took in the process of getting ready, Will unplugged his electric shaver from the recharger. His face was clammy, and the shaver would not move smoothly over his prickly-feeling skin. He tried to at least scrape the morning shadow away, but he knew that no amount of time spent going over and over his face would leave him looking clean shaven.

Worried that his casual attire at the last interview might have hurt his chances, he took a gray pinstriped suit out of the closet. It would serve two purposes. It would draw attention away from his beaten-looking face, and he could put the jacket on just before going inside the office so that he could cover up the sweaty smell of alcohol that would undoubtedly begin to soak through his shirt on the way there. After retying his tie three times to get it to drape the right length over his slowly expanding midsection, he was ready. Or, as he self-deprecatingly thought of his effort, he had washed off some of the ugly and covered up some of the rest of it.

His appointment today was at a large high-rise building half a block away from the mall. The agency's office was on the fourteenth floor. As Will noted, it was on the same floor as the other appointment. He just had to press a button with a different number to get there.

He entered an outer office that led to a large suite of offices, some separated by cubicle dividers. The receptionist coldly handed him a clipboard holding several forms for him to fill out.

"Where's the table of contents?" he tried to joke, only to have his nervous smile met with a stone-faced glare. Two days of not having eaten *anything* was beginning to make Will feel weak and unsteady all over. As he began to write, he noticed that on some letters, his hand would just not execute the proper motion. He struggled with the forms for the next half hour, hoping that his handwriting, which was at least legible, would not give him away.

Finally, he finished, returned the clipboard to the humorless receptionist. He had only sat for a few more minutes when he heard his name called. He mopped as much perspiration as he could from his forehead, which had not stopped seeping sweat since he had left the hotel. As he rose from the chair and then bent over to pick up his satchel, Will noticed that there was a large damp spot in the plastic seat of the chair where he had been sitting. He rolled his eyes upward as he imagined what the seat of his *trousers* must look like. He followed the woman who had called him into a cubicle and took the seat that she offered.

After the preliminary questions to which he was accustomed, the woman, who appeared to be in her late twenties, softened her expression.

"Our client is really anxious to get someone started in this job," she began. "In fact, when I told him about what was on your resume, he said he could see you this afternoon if you were available. Would you be able to do that?"

"Sure," said Will, smiling, but with his heart falling at the thought of having this ordeal extended. "Just tell me where to go and what time to be there."

"Um," she started, then paused. "I just have to check with him first. In the meantime, I need to find out your typing speed. If you'll just come over here to this terminal." She led him to a long table on which rested three computer terminals. Will's heart started to beat even faster and he tried to dry his sweaty hands on the underside of his jacket.

"The computer will show you each step on the screen," the woman explained. "You get up to two chances to practice, and you can press the F1 button when you're ready to take the test.

Will sat down in front of the terminal. A year ago he had been able to type sixty words per minute with reasonable accuracy. He knew he wouldn't do that well today. The woman had seated herself at a desk inside a cubicle next to the testing area. She was facing in the same direction as Will, but she had a clear view of him. He began the practice session. The cursor on the screen responded to the buttons he pushed differently than the way the computer at his last job had. As he got into the middle of the test, his right hand began to shake as if it were being operated by a remote control from outside his body.

Knowing that the computer wouldn't give him any extra time or lie about his speed or number of errors, Will decided that he might as well forego the second practice session, and take the real test. He pressed F1. Suddenly, he

seemed to be unable to think what to do next. Finally, he found the home keys and began typing. His right hand continued to shake. He looked back toward the woman's cubicle, but she appeared to be engrossed in her paperwork.
That didn't mean she *hadn't* seen his hands shake. The harder Will tried to make his hands work, the more they seemed to resist. Finally, he stopped forcing them, and managed to finish the test. The sound of the printer, recording his scores on paper, alerted the woman that he was done. Just as it finished its job, she arrived in front of it, quickly tearing the paper from the cylinder. She wasn't too fast for Will, who got a brief glimpse of the scores: twenty-nine words per minute, ten errors.

"You can have a seat out front," she told him. "I'll be out shortly." Will noted a wry but serious expression on her face. He picked up his satchel and moved back to the outer office. The chair in which he had left the wet spot had been removed. At that moment, he was so embarrassed that he wanted to just keep walking, out the door and to the elevator. But he knew he had to stay. After Will had waited about fifteen more minutes, the woman appeared in the reception area.

"Sorry to keep you waiting," she said sheepishly, and in a hushed voice even though there was no one else in the area. "I just spoke with our client, and you're not going to believe this. He told me that he just hired someone to fill the job an hour ago. So he doesn't need to see you now." Will had already noted that she had not invited him back into her cubicle again, and that she was standing almost as if she was ready to run.

Still trying to fathom the situation, Will responded, "So that was the only thing you had me in mind for?"

"Right now, yes. I'm really sorry. He didn't tell us about this until just a couple of minutes ago."

"Well," Will smiled weakly. "Keep me in mind in case

you get any other leads that I'm qualified for."

"Okay. I'm really sorry," she repeated, squirming as though she could not wait for the conversation to end.

"Thank you," Will mumbled, already just outside the doorway. He exhaled as he walked toward the elevator. His shaking hands had cost him a chance at the job. He was certain of it. Try to do the right thing, to quit drinking, he groused, and *this* is what happens.

The drugstore with the cheap gin was less than two hundred yards from Will as he exited the building. He didn't even need to think before he started in that direction, toward the "libation station," as he was fond of calling it.

Somewhere in the solace of his room and at the bottom of his third glass, Will began to sense that he was thinking clearly. It was becoming apparent that his optimism had been unjustified. It wasn't him, he told himself. It was these people here. They didn't want to give anyone from the mainland a fair chance, especially those who, like himself, had come from New York. Will began to sense impending defeat, but had no idea what its consequences would be.

Three and a half more weeks passed as Will methodically sent out two or three resumes each Monday, all going unanswered. He was just two short blocks from a beach that was a mecca for thousands of different people each week, and he seldom went farther than was necessary to get food or more liquor.

The first of November came, and rent was due, but Will didn't have the money to pay it. He had avoided people as much as he could lately, feeling he had been wronged somehow by the rest of the world. But he knew that he *had* to speak with Mr. Sing, or else he would have no place to stay. Picking up the phone, he dialed the hotel office.

"Mr. Tyne," he heard the distinctive voice say. "What can I do for you?"

"Mr. Sing, I know rent is due now, but I don't have it.

I've got a good job prospect lined up," Will blurted, knowing he wasn't fooling a man who knew every desperate tourist's ploy. "If you can give me a couple of weeks, I should have the money."

"Do you have anything to offer as collateral until then?" came the unexpected query. Will was caught completely off guard.

"My guitar," he said almost reflexively, knowing that it was by far the most valuable thing he could offer. "I can let you hold my guitar. It's custom-made, worth a *lot* of money."

"I'll have to see it first."

"Okay," Will sputtered, sensing he had found a way to avert disaster. "Want me to bring it down to the lobby?"

"Yes," Sing answered, sounding satisfied. "In about fifteen minutes."

Will thanked him, hung up the phone, and groaned at the realization of what he had just done. Playing guitar had been his greatest source of comfort since he had started at age eleven. Nowadays he played only infrequently, but took great comfort in just having his favorite guitar nearby. The one he had chosen to bring with him was, of everything he owned, his most prized possession. It had been made specifically *for him*, rather than being one that he had selected from a music store. It represented to him his reward to himself for his years of practice and dedication to the instrument, practice that had given him skill that had at one time almost propelled him into a career in the music business. The guitar also was Will's best reminder of his once-prosperous, happy life.

He unlocked the case, telling himself that he would find a way to redeem it soon. He carefully turned each tuning key to loosen the strings, not knowing where Mr. Sing would keep the guitar. Closing the case, he paused to finish his drink before going to the lobby.

Mr. Sing was behind the desk, chatting cheerfully with a hotel guest, one whose bill, Will supposed grimly, had been paid in advance. Conversation over, he turned to take one end of the guitar case to lift it up atop the counter.

"Ahhh. Electric," he murmured as the open lid of the case revealed the guitar's flawless finish. Will was anxious to get this painful matter concluded.

"So this will cover me until I can pay you?" he nodded, hoping Sing would nod in return.

"You may remember, Mr. Tyne, I told you that we are completely booked starting in mid-November. I can keep you here for two more weeks after this Sunday. After that, I have no place for you."

It finally dawned on Will what Sing had been trying to tell him before. Today was Friday. That meant that Will had sixteen days. He had no choice but to surrender possession of his beloved guitar in order to keep *this* roof over his head for another half-month. He would *have* to leave then, and he had no place to go, nothing to put up as collateral, and nothing left to pawn.

As he trudged, nearly in a state of shock, back to his room, he realized one more thing. There would be no need to send out any more resumes, because he would soon have no phone number for prospective employers to call. He entered his room, poured himself a drink, and took three sips as quickly as he could. For once in his life, he had no other alternative but to drink. Many times he had wanted the freedom and the means to do just that, but these were not the conditions under which he had envisioned getting his wish.

Faced with a situation which, in his present state, he had no hope of changing, Will could only endure, not enjoy, his remaining time. The mid-November Sunday came with merciless quickness, and found Will facing the lobby desk with his bags packed, looking worn and haggard, just as when he had arrived two months earlier, except that he had no guitar and his luggage, absent the camera equipment, was substantially lighter.

Already in a juniper-berried fog, braced for what was about to happen, he looked at the desk clerk. Mr. Sing was off that day, he had been told.

"I don't have any place to go yet," he began, hardly believing what he was hearing himself say. "None of the social services places are open today, so I can't find out anything until tomorrow. Can I leave a few of my bags here until tomorrow? I don't have enough hands to carry them."

"I have to ask Mr. Sing," the clerk answered, carefully avoiding looking at Will. He reached for the phone and turned away from Will completely. After a few brief whispers into the phone, he put the receiver down and turned back in Will's direction, still looking down. "He says you can put them in the corner over there. We can keep an eye on them until you can come back and get them."

Will slid the bags across the floor into the corner behind the desk. With him he kept his leather satchel and a heavy nylon bag, which he had carefully packed earlier with his most necessary things. As he walked through the double doors into the bright sun of the outdoors, he looked at his watch. It was twelve thirty-five. It occurred to him that in his self-absorbed state he had let his manners lapse. He had forgotten to say "thank you" to the desk clerk.

Chapter 3

Perpetual Twilight

The strangeness of seeing his empty apartment the night before he had left New York was nothing to compare with the feeling of disorientation Will was now feeling. The day was far from over, and his self-prescribed anesthesia was working against him. He now *literally* had no roof under which he could escape the hot sun. Couples, families, and other groups of people passed by him as he stood on the sidewalk, satchel suspended from his shoulder and his other bag hanging from its handle gripped in his right hand. Neither did he have four walls behind which he could hide from these people who, he felt, were *not* his friends or allies.

Having no idea of what else *to* do, he began walking slowly in the direction of the beach. He had known this was coming, but his mind was unprepared for dealing with a situation that had never even been approximated by anything he had ever faced in his life. He had always had a home of some sort, and most of the time it had been a good one. It was incomprehensible to him now that he had no base of operations, no sanctuary, no privacy, no refuge.

Reaching the grassy area that was near the beach, he lowered his satchel and his bag to the ground, and then sat on the grass, not even feeling it with his hand to check for dampness, nor caring whether it was wet. Being able to put down his bags and rest made him slightly less befuddled by what had just happened. He reasoned that he would probably have spent some time sitting outside today anyway. The only time he would *really* miss his sweaty, smelly room at the Regal Arbor would be when it was time to sleep, and that was hours away. Of course, there would be no television news tonight. Nor would he be able to get ice from the ice machine. And he would not be able to drink from his favorite pewter cup, or get really drunk in order to forget about his troubles. Other than that, he tried to tell himself, life would be normal much of the time.

Part of him could not be convinced of this, but *all* of him knew that he had no choice. Since it was Sunday, there were no social service organizations open; so he would have to spend at least one night outside, without a tent or even a sheet on which he could lie down. He had read something a couple of weeks ago about a shelter somewhere in which homeless people could spend the night, but he hadn't been worried enough at that time to write down the phone number. He had done little other than drink his last two weeks away hoping that either he would be magically granted some sort of last minute reprieve, or that, if he drank enough, he would be removed from this life entirely and be permitted to start a new one with a clean slate. He had silently told a god whose existence he wasn't sure of that he wanted to "concede" this "game," clear the board, and start a new one.

Nothing worked, and here he was being made to keep playing the *old* game. If there is really a god, he now told himself, he really is an asshole. He recalled the final words of

Mark Twain's The Mysterious Stranger, and reminded himself that Twain's swipe had been *mostly* right. Will, however, did not prize his life lately, and he wished that Twain's imaginary god *would* "stingily cut it short."

Consumed by his ruminations for well over an hour, Will's mind began to redirect itself to reality, and he realized that he was thirsty, but not for booze. Thankfully, his money had not run out at the same time his luck had. He picked up his bags and began trudging the hundred yards or so to the snack bar at the far end of the beach. He started to realize that getting around would now be a more difficult task with the unwieldy bags in tow, and that he had to be judicious about how much he drank and where he went.

After paying for his jumbo Diet Pepsi, he walked across the street to another section of the park, farther away from the beach. There were few people around. Within minutes he had slaked his thirst and over half of his gargantuan soda still remained. In addition to the fifth of gin Will had tucked into his satchel, he had been able to fill his flask and two of his small Evian bottles with the gin he had remaining at the Regal Arbor that morning. There was no need to be wasteful, he had told himself, and his thriftiness would come in handy now. Feeling that he "owed" himself a good drink, he poured the entire contents of one of the Evian bottles into the cup. Taking the plastic straw, he stirred the concoction thoroughly. This, he was certain, would keep him occupied until almost dark.

At least he wouldn't need a paper today. His bags were already full, and he certainly had no need for the "help wanted" section. He didn't have a phone number or an address to which anyone could respond. And he shuddered to speculate what he might look like, unshaved and dirty, in a few days.

As dusk approached, the Sunday afternoon beachgoers thinned, with some coming away from the beach and stopping in the park to cook on the stationary grills that were spread out over the area. As it began to get dark, Will noticed that there were less children's voices, and that the people who were *not* leaving were those who he wished *would.* His feelings muted by his greater-than-usual consumption, he felt only a slight twinge of envy when he imagined the groups of people going somewhere he could no longer go—home.

Soon the sky was dark except for the stars. The park had ample night lighting, almost bright enough in some places to read by; but the sight that became most commanding to Will was that of the Waikiki beachfront skyline. It appeared that at least half of the hotel rooms in the distance had lights on in them. All of those people, Will groused, have nice, cool places to sleep. They weren't any smarter than him, he determined, just luckier.

Armed with another soda, Will commandeered the use of a concrete picnic table for the first time. By this time, there was only one other picnic table in use, and it appeared to him that it was being used by a bunch of homeless people, who were drinking beer. But, wait a minute, he thought. What, exactly, was he?

Will removed the fifth from his satchel and refilled the lighter plastic Evian bottle. He would use the contents of the glass bottle first and then discard it, he decided, so that he wouldn't have to lug the extra weight. For the first time, it made sense to him why the homeless people in New York had only picked up *cans* to redeem for the deposit on them. The bottles, each redeemable for the same amount as the cans, couldn't be carried as easily as the cans could; so the cans were more lucrative.

As he drank and therefore became more aware of his vulnerability, Will began to look around again. Several more people had come into the park. Will remembered a smaller park he had visited and photographed years before when he had been here on vacation. It was farther away from the hotel district, just past a small residential neighborhood, and a little more off the beaten path. Maybe, he hoped, it would be quieter there.

It was midnight when he tossed the empty bottle into a trash can and laboriously hoisted his bags for what would either be his last walk of that day or his first walk of the next. As he made his way down the sidewalk, he noticed that there was very little traffic, for which he was grateful. His slow but steady walk belied the amount of gin he had consumed. Adrenalin, he thought to himself.

The park, as best he could tell, was deserted as he entered it. It was fronted by the road, a sidewalk, and a wrought iron fence. The fence extended down both sides of the park, separating it from the houses that were on either side. At the other end was a seawall, against which the surf of the low tide was only rushing gently. Will sat at the concrete picnic table nearest to the ocean, and closest to the one overhead light in the park. It had taken him forty-five minutes to get there.

Wrapping the straps of his bags around his wrists in case he fell asleep, he lay his head on his forearms, which were resting on the table. Sleep, though, was too much for Will to ask for on this night. He tried to rest and forget about his predicament while trying to remain alert enough so that he could not be surprised by any predator. It was an impossible combination.

Hours had passed when he heard the increasingly loud rumble of a large motorcycle. It came inside the park, which it was not supposed to do, and its headlight bore down on him, coming closer. He reached for the inside of his bag, searching for a long pair of scissors he had placed in the bottom. The light went out, and the low rumble of the engine was choked off. Will looked straight ahead, away from the motorcycle, just wishing it would go away. After about fifteen minutes, he heard the rumble begin again and saw the light flash on, this time in the direction of the gate to the park. In a moment he was alone again.

The intermittent breeze almost made the night chilly, especially since Will was too tired to walk around. As Will put his head on his arms again, he noticed that the sky didn't look as dark. He checked his watch. It was five-forty. He stood up to stretch and, in what seemed like a matter of a few minutes, the sky became light. Will had spent his first night as a homeless man.

It was still too early to make any phone calls, but Will had spent enough time in time in this park. He decided to walk to another larger but more isolated section of the beach about a quarter of a mile up the road. His skin felt rough and tacky to his touch, and the day's growth of beard made his face feel prickly. Even though it was still early, the almost chilly breeze had surrendered its influence to the warm sun in the almost-cloudless sky.

There was no shade in which Will could rest at the next beach, and after walking the length of it and back, he decided to go back toward Waikiki. He would at least be able to use a public bathroom there. His gait was still slow and labored, and even though the effect of the liquor had worn off during the night, he still was not experiencing any of the dreaded after-effects. Stopping to rest in the shade near the table that had been his "bar" the previous evening, he decided he would get a soda and wait until early afternoon to find out about the shelter.

As he let his bags slide to the ground while carefully guarding his cup with both hands, he felt the familiar spindly feeling in his legs. This let him know that it was time to put some of the contents of the Evian bottle to use. Maybe then, he reasoned, he would be able to eat something and get a little bit of strength.

It was two o'clock when Will finally found a coin-operated public phone that had a directory attached. He managed to find what he imagined to be a correct phone number for the information he wanted and dialed it. Within minutes, he had the address for the shelter and instructions on how to get to it. He had been told that it was best to get there after six o'clock if he wanted a place to sleep.

At five o'clock Will, moving very slowly, plodded to the bus stop at the edge of the park. Waiting for twenty minutes before the bus he needed came along, he took a seat and put his bags in the seat next to him. The endpoint of the route of this bus was the airport, and Will knew that the shelter was closer to that end of the route than it was to the beginning. As the bus pulled away from the stop, Will leaned his head against the window.

"Airport! Last stop!" came the loud voice. Will opened his eyes. He and the bus driver were the only two people on the bus, and he had missed his stop. The driver explained that he would have to exit the bus, walk across the thoroughfare, and wait for the next returning bus. The driver suggested that Will ask the next bus driver to let him know when the right stop for his destination was coming up.

Will waited for another twenty minutes before the bus came. As he stepped onto the bus, he asked the driver to let him know where the stop for King's Discount Store was. He had been told that it was right across from the shelter, and he didn't want to tell the driver what his destination really was, even though he knew his appearance was conspicuous. The bus soon became packed with airport passengers on their way to Waikiki. Too cheap to even pay for the *wiki wiki*, Will snorted, recalling the inexpensive van ride that had delivered him to the Regal Arbor.

Lost in his misery for what seemed like only a few minutes, Will noticed that the bus was going through the downtown area. That meant he had missed his stop again.

Guessing that any bus that went on this route would be full by the time it got downtown, Will decided to stay on until it got all the way back to Waikiki. That way, he could just wait for the driver to take his break and start back toward the airport again.

When the bus pulled up to the last stop in Waikiki, Will meekly reminded the driver, a good-natured black man whose southern accent Will had noticed earlier, that he had forgotten to alert him to his stop.

"Naw, I said it," the driver protested, tapping his microphone. No sound came out. "Aw, no, the P. A. must be out. Sorry about that. You goin' back there? Just sit up front, an' I'll let you know when it comes up. It won't be but 'bout forty minutes."

It was now ten minutes after eight, and Will was far more than exhausted. His last "dose" of gin had worn off and his ordeal had more than expended the small amount of food he had managed to get down. Retrieving his bags, he placed them beside him as he sat down near the front of the bus.

Before it had gone the length of Waikiki again, the bus was packed with people again. It slowly wound its way through downtown again and Will became increasingly vigilant, looking for the store. As the bus slowly made its way around a turn on a smaller street with two-way traffic, Will noticed a large group of rough-looking, poorly dressed men standing in a small parking lot outside a barren-looking cinder block building. It briefly reminded him of a part of the Bowery in Manhattan. But what was such a group of people doing here?

"King's Discount Store," he heard the driver's booming voice announce. Finally, Will thought, maybe I can get in, find a cot, and get some rest. He picked up his bags for what he hoped would be almost the last haul of the day, and stepped off the bus. He saw the store and, having been told that the shelter was just across the street, he looked around for anything that would identify it by the description he had been given. He saw nothing.

Walking toward the front of the building where he had seen the group of men on the other side moments earlier, he noticed that it was well-lit on the inside and that there were people moving around. Maybe, he hoped, someone in here knows where the shelter is. He trudged up the steps of the small porch, opened the door, and walked inside. There was a short hallway or foyer, at the end of which was an office enclosed in part by a large glass reception window. Will waited for someone to come to the window. Finally a husky, masculine-looking woman with short, dark hair and thick glasses came to the window.

"May I help you?" she almost demanded.

"Yes," Will croaked, taken aback by her manner. "Can you tell me where the homeless shelter in this neighborhood is?"

"This is it," she frowned, seemingly incredulous at his ignorance.

"H-h-how do I sign up?" Will could barely get out.

"Sign up for *what*?" she inquired, as if she was beginning to wonder if he was sane or not.

"To sleep h-here," he whispered, almost ready to turn and run, but without the strength.

"*Ohhhhh!*" she let out, slightly softening her expression. "I just have to get some information from you. Do you have any I.D.?"

Will produced his old driver's license, which had a picture that hardly resembled the disheveled, unshaved, weary countenance he now wore. She wrote his name on a logbook-type form, stood, and beckoned for him to follow. He walked through a doorway into a large, dimly-lit room where he could see what appeared to be endless rows of gym mats spread out on the floor, side by side and end-to-end with no space in between them, almost all occupied by people who, from what Will could see, looked even worse than *he* did. The woman pointed to a red mat on the floor near the doorway through which he had just entered.

"You can sleep here tonight," she said. "Wake-up is at five-thirty, and if you want to stay after tonight you have to fill out an intake form in the morning. Okay?" Without waiting for Will to answer, something of which he was momentarily incapable anyway, she abruptly turned and walked back toward her office. Will sat down on the mat and looked around.

"No shoes on the mat," he heard. Louder and more authoritatively the voice repeated, "Get your shoes off the mat," before he could react. He looked up. A large, dark-skinned man with some sort of picture-I.D. badge was standing over him, looking at him squarely. Will quickly removed his shoes without untying the laces, and the man turned to move on.

Looking around, Will noticed that some of the people had placed their footwear underneath the foot end of their mat, and that most of the ones who had bags had placed them under the head end, as sort of a pillow. Will did the same, and lay down on the mat. The bare parts of his arms and legs, already sweaty from the effort it had been to carry the bags, sweated even more where they touched the non-porous mat. His face, for some reason, felt a hot, burning sensation. He turned on his side, and tried to find a comfortable position for his head, the support of his bags being too high.

He was still squirming on the mat when the lights in the room went out. There was a clock on the wall above the inside window to the office—it showed that it was exactly ten o'clock. The low din of the people subsided some, except for an occasional wisecrack by a self-appointed comedian. After several of these, a deep, ominous-sounding voice came over the P. A. system strongly urging silence.

Will closed his eyes but, even as tired as he was, he could not sleep. He hadn't been troubled by the after-effects of the alcohol yet. Maybe he had sweated it out of his system, he hoped. Finally, he began to doze off in brief episodes of light sleep, gradually becoming longer and more restful. His fatigue and weakness had finally overtaken him.

He opened his eyes. Why were the lights on, he wondered, and *so bright*? Before he could wonder further, a loud, imperative voice pierced the quiet mutterings of the half-sleeping crowd.

"*Let's get up, people! This is not the Kahala Hilton!*" The clock on the wall showed five-thirty. Slowly the people around Will began to move, some taking their mats and placing them atop one of the stacks of mats that was forming in the middle of the large room. Will was careful to sit on the edge of his mat as he put on his shoes; and he took the mat, heavy to his still-weak arms, and placed it on one of the stacks. As he was doing this, he was careful to watch his bags, still on the floor, out of the corner of one eye.

He realized for the first time in over twelve hours that he desperately needed to relieve himself. The entrance to the bathroom, a slatted wooden door missing a few slats, was at the end of the room that was opposite the office. Will moved slowly toward the door, dodging other men, a few of whom almost appeared to have trouble just standing.

The bathroom was so small and so full of people that moving about in it was difficult. There were people waiting to use the two lavatories that faced the entrance. There was a line of four people waiting in the area of the two urinals, only one of which was working. Next to them, the two toilets, Will guessed by the foul smell, were in use. Three open shower stalls were on the side of the bathroom opposite the toilets and urinals. In the small amount of floor space between the showers and the toilets was a wooden bench, about six feet in length, which looked worn and beaten. It was laden with clothing, toiletries, and other belongings.

After a short, impatient wait in the urinal line, Will found a hook on the wall, where he hung his bags and removed the soap, shampoo, and towel which he had placed in the top of the larger one two days before. He stripped to his underwear and waited his turn for the shower. After several minutes, and having to remind someone that it was his, Will's, turn, he stepped into the shower stall, still keeping his eyes on his bags. Once the water was adjusted, it felt good. It almost made up for the foul smell which was accompanied by thick cigarette smoke that filled the bathroom in spite of the "No Smoking" sign that hung on the wall. The open shower stalls faced the open toilet stalls. This insured, Will presumed, that no one would want to spend any longer than he *had* to in either one.

Will had carefully put his head under the shower head to rinse off the shampoo, still with one eye squinting toward his bags, when a toilet flushed. The warm shower water turned scalding hot for a full second. Startled, his hand slammed against the tile wall of the stall. He adjusted the water so that it was as cool as he could stand it, and finished his shower.

Stepping out in his thong sandals, he looked for an area with enough space so that he could put on his shorts without stumbling and having them brush against the wet, dirty floor. He couldn't imagine where all the muddy dirt had come from, and the floor was fast becoming littered with soaked masses of toilet paper, which some of the people were using to dry themselves. Will dressed as quickly as he could, moved his bags to a hook closer to the lavatories, and waited his turn there. Facing a mirror for the first time in two days, Will quickly and shockedly understood why his face felt so hot. Normally more "colorful" than the faces of most other people anyway, it was now an angry and unhealthy shade of red. And he had no cream to put on it. Taking his turn at the lavatory, he looked at its basin as he brushed his teeth, unable to bear the frightening sight of his own face.

He exited the bathroom and went back into the main room. It was now empty of mats, which had been stacked and stored in a room secured by a chain link gate, and several men were using push brooms to sweep and gather the litter that had accumulated on the floor overnight. To Will's surprise, there were a few women in the room, and he wondered where they had come from.

All along the wall, there were people who were sitting on the bare concrete floor, going through their belongings, talking loudly with each other, or just staring into space. A few of the people who had been sweeping were beginning to set up tables and chairs in the room. Will searched for a spot to sit, and had to walk around before he could find a place on the floor that was not damp. Finding a place, he let himself slowly drop to the floor, and searched through his larger bag for his electric shaver. He had made sure he had charged it before he had left, and he began dragging the shaving head across his face. His pores were still open, and the sweat hampered the effectiveness of the shaver. He finally just gave up.

Will heard someone tell another person that breakfast was at seven. He looked at his watch. The normally simple process of waking and showering had taken him an hour and fifteen minutes. It was only fifteen minutes until breakfast. Will hoped that his hunger would overcome his mild nausea and nervousness. He knew that he needed the food for strength, especially in this crowd. In the meantime, he decided to find out about the "intake form" that the woman had mentioned the night before. This had not been by any means a great place to sleep, but it was far better than sitting at a picnic table by the beach all night.

There was a man in the office behind the reception window, a pleasant, soft-spoken, dark-skinned man with a mouthful of crooked teeth. He introduced himself as Jerry, and Will guessed that he must be in his late twenties. He gave Will two forms to fill out, along with a copy of the house rules and regulations. Will looked at the top of the form. The heading read: Center for Social Aid. So that was where he was. Will decided to take Jerry's suggestion that he get on the breakfast line and wait until after he had eaten to fill out the forms.

From the rear of the line, which ran out of the main room onto a long covered porch in the back of the building, Will could not see the front. But he could hear the crowd's noise quickly become hushed, followed by a loud voice reciting the Lord's Prayer. Shortly thereafter the line began moving, right on time. By the time Will was handed his plate, on which was a scoop of rice, a cinnamon bun, and a small chicken thigh, all of the chairs at the tables were occupied. He picked up a small cup of juice, the last stop on the line, and looked for a place to sit on the floor. At the back of the room, just to the side of the chain-link gate that guarded the room full of mats, he found a clean-looking spot on the floor.

Will slowly began to nibble at the cinnamon bun, then took larger bites. It was gone. The chicken followed, then he ate the rice hungrily. He was relieved that it had been such an easy chore. He gulped the almost-too-sweet juice down, and got up to throw the paper plate and cup and the plastic fork in one of the two aluminum trash cans next to the table where the juice dispenser rested and by which its operator sat. Trying not to bump against anyone with his bags, Will walked toward the door. But before he could get out, two people had run into them. Neither had even seemed to notice, even though each impact had left Will worried about the condition of the bags.

On the front porch, where two people were already halfway through their post-breakfast smokes, Will again dropped his bags and sat, curling his legs underneath him. He took the two forms out of his satchel and began filling in the requested information.

The unmistakable bellow of the same voice that widened his eyes two hours earlier returned, "*Let's go! I need everybody off this porch! We have to wash it down! Let's go! NOW!*" The woman's delivery was not mean-spirited, but no less demanding than if it had been. As if to show that she was just doing her job, she smiled at one of the women she had just displaced, saying, "You stay out of that bad crowd today, now."

Will, only slightly energized by the rest and the food, grabbed his things and scrambled off the porch. He went down the sidewalk, which was separated from the building by a ten-foot strip of grass that ran the nearly hundred-foot length of the front of the building from the porch to one end. Once at the far end of the building, he sat down in the grass and resumed his work on the forms.

Just as he had finished and stuffed them in his satchel, he saw a man with a rake combing the cigarette butts and small bits of trash out of the short, thick grass. He was slowly working his way in Will's direction, and beside him on the grass was a coiled garden hose with a spray nozzle. So that's what they mean by 'wash it down,' Will supposed. He didn't want to be told to move again, so he picked up his things and walked back toward the entrance, figuring he would finish his business with Jerry.

The front door was now locked, so Will went around to the side door, ascended the six steps to the doorway, and entered the building. Jerry, still pleasant in the midst of all of the confusion, asked him if he understood the rules. Will nodded, and Jerry asked him to sign the rules sheet. Jerry explained some of the other necessary information to Will, such as the storage area, or "cage," in which Will would be allowed to store two bags of his belongings. He also told Will he had to maintain contact with a case manager in order to receive the Center's services. His name would be posted with others on the bulletin board in a few days, Jerry told him, to notify him of the date and time of his first appointment with the case manager that would be assigned to him.

Will, just beginning to realize a tinge of gratitude for Jerry's patience in making sure he understood the "ropes," nodded in understanding of and agreement with everything Jerry was saying, even though he knew he would not remember all of it the first time. Jerry asked Will if he had any questions. Thinking of what would be his next concern, where to go between now and lunchtime, Will wondered aloud why he could not sit on the porch. Again, Jerry patiently explained that everything outdoors, including the grass, had to be cleaned each morning, and that he would be allowed back on the porch at eleven o'clock. The door to the building and to the large room that served as the sleeping room at night and the dining room in the daytime would be opened at eleven-thirty.

His mind having been assaulted with more information than it could possibly assimilate in such a short time, Will thanked Jerry profusely and went back out the side door. By now, the entire grassy area and sidewalk bordering the building were soaked. Will saw two people across the street seated on a foot-high wide concrete wall that separated the sidewalk and the large parking lot for King's Discount Store, which was now beginning to appear that it might be open for business.

Will sat down on the wall, but even the early morning sun was too hot for his sore, burned, ailing face. He walked back across the street to the small parking lot outside the side door of the Center for Social Aid. Just a few feet to the rear of the steps leading to the door was a recessed section of the wall. Judging by the angle of the sun, Will figured that it would soon be in the shade; and even now the sunlight would not strike his face if he kept his head down. Maybe, he hoped, the loud woman wouldn't find him out here and chase him off again.

Awake, sober, and not anxious for a drink for the first time in many days, Will's mind began to understand the magnitude of what he was in the midst of experiencing. The very worst of it, he told himself, was over. He had survived for two nights without a home, and was only slightly the worse for the wear; and he was still safe and hopeful that he would again have a place to sleep indoors tonight.

The slow trickle of people approaching the building alerted Will that it must be getting close to lunchtime. The nausea that had worried him earlier had left, and had been replaced by a strong appetite. His watch indicated that it was twenty minutes before twelve. He could go inside. The dining/sleeping room was much quieter than it had been earlier, since only a few people had made their way back inside. He looked around for Jerry, but didn't see him. In fact, none of the faces he saw were those of the Center's workers he had seen during breakfast. Will surmised that the workers had changed shifts and hoped that this crew wouldn't be as demanding as the last.

There were far fewer people in the lunch line than there had been for breakfast. And there was more food on his plate than there had been earlier. *Much* more. He quickly scanned the room to find that, even with less people, all of the chairs were still taken. He returned to the same spot by the chain-link gate where he had sat earlier and, trying to ignore everyone else, turned his attention to his food, which he ate hungrily and without hesitation.

"Got fresher bread today than yesterday," Will heard a cheerful voice project in his direction. "I think the food's been a lot better lately." Will looked up to face a wiry man who appeared to be in his early forties, and who almost radiated a sort of nervous energy. Will nodded, his mouth too full to speak, even though he was anxious to give a friendly response. "I don't remember seeing you here before," the man continued, not waiting to for Will to clear his mouth and answer. Finally, Will was able to speak.

"I just got here last night," he managed to get out. "My name's Will." Shifting the paper plate to his left hand, he extended his right.

"I'm Johnnie. I don't stay here. I just come here to eat sometimes," the man offered, seeming to Will to be anxious to make that distinction. "I mean, this is not that bad a place to stay if you got nowhere else, but I have a tent up in Manoa."

"You stay in a tent?" Will's interest had been captured for the moment.

"Up in Manoa, yeah. V. A. says they'll give me more money if I get an apartment, but if I do that then next thing they'll do is ask me to get a job. And I can't work somebody else's schedule. I tried that, and it just doesn't work." He crammed almost half of an egg salad sandwich into his mouth.

"V. A.?" Will asked, his own mouth too full to utter anything lengthier.

"Yeah," Johnnie answered, the mouthful of sandwich well on its way to his stomach. "I'm a vet. Vietnam. PTSD. Half-disability. Enough to live on."

Will nodded, skeptical of anyone who was too quick to claim Vietnam veteran status. He had known of a few people who had claimed that in order to attempt to generate sympathy or admiration for themselves, but who were unable or unwilling to give plausible answers when pressed for details about their military service. Will *despised* people who did that, especially since his own brother had been killed in Vietnam.

"You won't have any problem around here," Johnnie was continuing, unfazed by Will's lapse of attention. "They run a tight ship, and they don't usually have any trouble. Maybe a fight once in a while, but not much more than that. You want to know anything that you can't get an answer for, just ask me. I don't sleep here, but I usually come here for lunch. Sometimes for breakfast, most of the time for lunch."

It was twelve-thirty, and the Center's employees, called "duty managers," Will had learned, were beginning to herd the remaining diners toward the door. Will shook Johnnie's hand and thanked him for the information, and walked toward the "cage," a room that was to the left of the entrance hallway of the building, partly walled with two-by-fours and chicken wire. Jerry had told him that he should see a person named Sam about storing some of his belongings there. Not knowing how patient Mr. Sing would be about looking after his remaining bags, Will wanted to get them out of the Regal Arbor as soon as he could.

Sam was efficient in his explanation of how the "cage" worked. It was open at certain times during breakfast, lunch, dinner, and just before lights-out. Will would be allowed to keep two gym-bag size bags or one large suitcase there. He had to make sure the bags were tagged with his name on them, and he had to re-register at the beginning of each month so that the bags would not be considered abandoned, or else they would be kept in a holding area for a week and then discarded. With this information, Will determined that it would be safe for him to leave the larger bag he had been carrying around. Everything he would need for getting about, and more, was contained in his satchel. Will was grateful not only for the chance to have some secure-looking storage space, but also for Sam's thoroughly understandable and clear-cut rules.

With his load greatly lightened and both of his hands now free without the large bag, and feeling more relief with each step of understanding he gained about the system at the Center, Will ambled out the door. He knew that it was over five hours before dinner time and he didn't want to spend the afternoon hanging around this building. He decided to take the bus to Waikiki.

Going to the bus stop next to King's Discount Store which, with its parking lot, took up almost the whole block, Will sat on the bench and waited for the bus on which he had spent so much time the previous night. It was a long time coming, not like the buses in Waikiki, which sometimes came one right after the other. And when it got there, it was crowded.

Will climbed aboard anyway, and after almost an hour of being jostled and swung about by the motion of the packed bus, he alit from it in Waikiki. Since he knew that he could take another bag and store it in the cage, he decided to go by the Regal Arbor, which was only a few blocks from the bus stop where he was standing.

He entered the hotel and approached the desk. The clerk who had watched him leave the other day was on duty. Will saw that his bags were just as he had left them. He asked the clerk, who this time faced him with an indifferent look, if he could get some of his things. The clerk nodded, and pointed toward the bags.

Will had only planned to take the two bags with him when he left and had packed them accordingly with the things he knew he would need. Everything else he had crammed haphazardly into the remaining bags. Now he had to cull what he needed from each of the two bags and the large suitcase, and pack it into one of the small bags, then replace the remaining things into the remaining pieces of luggage. The only place he had space to do this was in the lobby. He first brought everything out into the lobby, then began the sorting process, embarrassed that he had to attend to so personal a matter in front of any stranger who happened to pass by.

Will worked as quickly as he could, hurt somewhat by the fact that the desk clerk didn't even seem interested enough to wonder where he had gone after he had been evicted. He was just closing the lid on his large suitcase when an elderly man stepped off the elevator and walked through the lobby, noticing him. "Getting ready to leave, huh?" he heard the man say as he looked up to face the broad, friendly, genuine smile.

"Yes, sir. Getting ready to leave."

"Have a good trip home," the man said, continuing on his way out the door. Will fastened the zippers on the bag he would be taking with him, and carried the suitcase and the remaining bag over to the corner behind the desk. Remembering his manners this time as he lifted his things to leave, he turned toward the desk and offered a distinct "thank you" in the direction of the clerk, who neither responded nor looked up.

It was still only mid-afternoon and Will did not want to go back to the shelter, but he had nowhere else to go. A bus was approaching the stop that was not on the airport route, but which would take him near the shelter, and he boarded it. It was almost four o'clock as he exited the bus. The stop was on a busy four-lane street that intersected with Malualua Road, the narrower street that led to the Center for Social Aid.

As Will walked approached the building he noticed that the side door was open, though there was no one in the parking lot and no one that he could see in the hallway. He could hear voices and intermittent laughter, however, and followed the sound to an eight-foot high chain link fence with an open gate at the rear of the building. He walked up to the gate, which secured the area in the rear of the building, and saw several men sitting in the shade playing cards on the long concrete porch .

Looking for a quieter place to sit, Will walked to the front of the building. The front porch was empty of people, but not a square foot of it was shaded from the afternoon sun. He turned to walk back to the side of the building toward the tiny parking lot which consisted of four parking stalls and a short passageway which led to Malualua Road and which was accessed at the other end by Hoka Street, which ran past the front of the building. He curled himself into the recessed area where he had sat earlier in the day to fill out the intake forms. As it became later, some people began to filter into the parking lot and toward the back porch.

Anxious to store the bag he had retrieved from the hotel, Will went inside the building to the cage. It was five o'clock, the time Sam had told him the cage would be open. He could see that the padlock was still on the door and decided to wait for Sam. The dining/sleeping room door burst open and out strode a well-dressed, fortyish man.

"You can't stand in the hallway," he said to Will.

"But I'm waiting for the cage to open," he explained.

"You have to wait outside. We have to keep the hallway clear." Will moved quickly toward the front exit and onto the porch which was, by now, occupied by several people. Averse to the cigarette smoke, he continued around to the corner of the building to the edge of the parking lot, where he found the shade of a small tree. He stood there until he saw Sam walking in a deliberate manner through the parking lot, then hurrying up the steps to the side door. Will followed shortly behind him.

As Will entered the hallway, he noticed immediately that there were three men waiting in the hallway outside the cage. He took his place with them and waited his turn. His bag stored within a few minutes, Will exited the cage and noticed that the door to the dining/sleeping room was open. His load was lighter again, and he walked into the room and looked around. Although the windows were small, the afternoon sun that shone through them lit the room brightly. There were a number of people in the far rear area of the room watching a news program on a large screen television.

Realizing that he had to use the bathroom, Will walked toward the other end of the room and into it, noticing how much larger it appeared now that it was empty. His relief at the urinal done, he had an inclination to use the toilet—which was stymied the moment he peered into the doorless stall. The toilet seat appeared to be smeared with dried feces, and its smell made Will quickly decide that he could wait.

As he walked back out into the main room, he noticed that the line for dinner was already long enough to stretch out the back door onto the porch, which he had heard someone refer to as the "lanai." It was nothing more than a long section of concrete a foot above ground level, covered by a roof. It overlooked a twelve-foot wide section of asphalt opposite which was the side of the four-story building next door. The building and the strip of asphalt ran the entire length of the rear of the Center's building, leaving the tall chain-link gate at the parking lot end as the only outdoor egress.

Noticing that it was five-forty, Will thought it a good idea to take a place in the line. He also noticed that quite a few of the people who came in after him paused to speak to their friends who were close to the front of the line, and somehow ended up blending into the line permanently.

A few minutes after six, the crowd got quieter. Will

guessed that it was for the recitation of the Lord's Prayer again, but he was too far out the door to hear it. Soon after the talking resumed, the line began moving. After he got his plate, Will sat down to eat and looked around, hoping to see Johnnie, but Johnnie was nowhere in sight. He finished his food quickly, tossed the plate and utensil into the trash, and made his way toward the door.

A duty manager was stationed by the door, handing out small white cards to people who held out their hands. Will took one and saw that it had a number on it.

"What's this for?" he inquired of the duty manager.

"To get a mat," came the flat reply, followed by a louder, general directive: "*Keep moving, people! As soon as you're done eating, move outside so we can clean up!*" Will decided that it would be best to go outside. Maybe he would see Johnnie out there and he could find out what the card with the number was for. Johnnie was still not to be found, and Will moved away from the crowd to find a place in the grass where he could sit, away from the cigarette smoke.

It was already dusk outside, and through the window Will could hear the duty managers barking instructions to the people who were cleaning the inside. With his stomach full with its third meal of the day, Will was able to tune out the din and close his eyes for a brief minute. After a short while the noise of the moving tables was replaced by a noise which Will could not identify. He stood on his toes and peered through the window. The workers were now arranging the mats on the floor.

Within another fifteen minutes, Will noticed that most of the people were beginning to gravitate around the corner of the building toward the parking lot. Shouldering his satchel, he followed. He had been standing for another ten minutes when a duty manager came out onto the porch.

"Women only," he announced. "Stand back, guys. Let 'em through. The sooner they get in, the sooner you get in."

About twenty women wound their way through the crowd and up the steps to the inside of the building. As soon as it appeared that there were no more coming, the duty manager went inside. The remaining group of men became more condensed as they crowded closer to the porch.

In another minute he reappeared, announcing, "Blue cards. Blue cards only. Have them out so I can see them. If you don't have one, stay back and let those who do have 'em come through." Will's card wasn't blue, but he guessed that he would at least soon find out what the it was for. The duty manager again disappeared inside, and stayed longer this time.

"One through ten," he projected, as he stepped back out onto the porch.

"What did he say?" Will asked the man standing next to him.

"One through ten," the man answered and, sensing that Will didn't understand what was going on, asked him, "Did you get a number?"

"You mean this?" Will showed him the card.

"Yeah. What number you got?" the man asked.

"Sixty-three," Will responded, turning the card face up.

"Well, then, soon as he calls sixty-one to seventy you can go in," the man explained. "For now you might as well stand back and let the people with the lower numbers get by." Will moved farther away from the porch.

"Sixty-one to seventy," Will finally heard, and he started toward the steps. No one moved to let him by but, strangely to him, no one seemed to mind that he pushed them out of the way, either. Will ascended the steps, handed his card to the duty manager, and started down the hallway.

As he entered the sleeping room, there appeared to be a near-riot in progress. People were tossing their bags at mats, talking loudly across the room, and scrambling to claim the open mats. The three duty managers were walking about, insisting on order.

"You cannot save a mat for someone. If you get caught saving a mat for someone, you can get eighty-sixed. You have to put something on a mat to save it for yourself," they instructed. Guessing that he should claim a mat quickly rather than try to pick a location, Will dropped his bag on the open mat closest to him. He sat down and, remembering the admonition from the previous night, was careful to keep his feet off the end of the mat.

Will had brought a set of sheets with him in the bag he had gotten from the hotel earlier. He wanted to go to the cage to get it, but he didn't want to leave his satchel on the mat and out of his sight while he went to the cage. Searching through the satchel, he found a cap and placed it on the mat. Standing, he let a weathered-looking older man pass before he proceeded down the two-foot wide aisle that ran the length of the room.

There was yet another line of people waiting to get into the cage, and Will had to search for his bag since it had been moved after he had left it there earlier. Will took the bag into the hallway and began rummaging through it, looking for the sheets.

"You can't open your bag in the hall," he heard a voice behind him say. "You have to take the bag to your mat or put it back in the cage. You can't open it here." Will hurriedly picked up his bag and re-entered the sleeping room. He removed his sheets from the bag and folded one of them in half, lengthwise. Kneeling on the mat, he tucked one end of the sheet under the head of the mat. Pulling the other end of the sheet toward him, he lifted up first one knee, then the other, extending the end of the sheet under him and toward the foot of the bed, where he tucked it under. He smoothed the sheet with his hand and rose to return his bag to the cage.

Returning to his mat, he removed his shoes and shoved them under the foot of the mat. Placing his satchel under the head of the mat, Will lay back and rested his head against his arms, then sat up quickly and looked around. His cap had been taken.

After the initial hubbub had settled, Will noticed that one of the duty managers had turned on the large-screen television. Will's mat was off to one side of the room, at a sharp angle away from the television and, even if it had been facing his way, there was a support column in the room between him and it. He could only hear its low rumble, unable to discern any of the sounds coming from it. Some of the people who had remained in the room were already lying down, apparently sleeping, or trying to. Others had bags that they had removed from the cage, going through their belongings. A few had books and appeared to be reading.

Will was absorbed in his thoughts. He had begun to understand the nature of his predicament, and he was feeling slightly relieved that he had been able to deal with it as well as he had so far. He had a full stomach and a place to sleep, and he felt that as long as he was inside, at least, he was safe. He hadn't had a drink in a day and a half, either, but he was already planning a way to be able to "knock the edge off" tomorrow.

The Center had an explicit rule concerning substance abuse. Alcohol and drugs were not allowed on the Center's property, and the rules stated that anyone under the influence of either who engaged in any sort of disruptive behavior would be asked to leave. Will supposed that meant the same thing as being "eighty-sixed." Will, of course, was *never* disruptive when he was drinking; he had always gotten tanked so quickly in recent years that he had never had *time* to cause any trouble.

He still had a fair amount of money left, since he had not had to use any of it to stall his eviction. He had not had the *opportunity* to use any of it for that purpose. He began to plan the next day, not thinking of how he could begin to extricate himself from his predicament, but instead how he could make it more palatable.

The food he had eaten during the day was far more than

he had been able to consume in a single day in quite some time. He was feeling stronger and thinking more clearly than he had in weeks. He was also enthused about the possibility of being able to drink again tomorrow, and not having to worry about having a place to sleep.

As the clock wound its way toward ten, the assortment of men found their way back inside the building. Will had noticed a sign on the door which indicated that anyone not in the building by ten o'clock would not be allowed in afterward. Will turned on his side and closed his eyes, but it was still too noisy for him to sleep. Soon the lights went off, but the din of the voices remained unaffected. Shortly, a deep voice came over the P. A. system.

"Gentlemen! Quiet. Please!" The talking immediately softened, but low voices could still be heard. Will again closed his eyes, now beginning to feel tired. Out of the past two nights he had slept a total of about two hours. His adrenalin had almost run out and he was soon sleeping a light sleep.

Chapter 4

Capitulation

Knowing what was encompassed by the run of a day at the Center for Social Aid made Will slightly more sure of himself on Wednesday morning. The morning procedure took the same amount of time as it had the previous day, but Will at least had a sense of what to expect and an experienced-based knowledge of some of the things he could and could not do.

Shortly after Will finished breakfast, it became clear to him that he would soon be in dire need of a toilet other than the ones at the shelter. He first thought of taking the bus to the mall, then realized that it didn't open until nine o'clock. It was only twenty minutes before eight as he walked on the side of Malualua Road on his way to the bus stop, facing a warm morning sun. He could hardly appreciate the rested feeling he felt as a result of the reasonably good night of sleep he had had, because he had to concentrate on managing his bowels.

Seeing a bus bound for Waikiki approaching the stop, Will boarded it. He knew of a place in one of the open air shopping centers where there was a bathroom, and it would most likely be clean. The bus shifted its way slowly through the downtown traffic, with Will cringing at almost every stop and start. Finally he reached the stop closest to the shopping center. He pushed his way off the bus and began walking as quickly, but as smoothly, as he could. The bathroom was open and it was clean, and Will breathed easy as, his relief complete, he flushed the toilet. None of the shops had opened, and the large bathroom had been otherwise unoccupied since Will had entered it. As he stopped in front of the mirror first to wash his hands, then comb his hair, he decided he would bring his toothbrush and toothpaste with him next time he came. Maybe he would make this bathroom a regular stop, as long as no one told him not to.

Now he could go to the mall in comfort, and it would be open and busy by the time he got there. He crossed the street and a bus bound in that direction arrived shortly. Will first went to the bookstore for a newspaper, then to one of the already-open fast food shops for a soda. He had no gin to add to it, and it tasted almost too sweet to him, even though it was sugar-free. He sat down at a table to take his time with the paper. He had two hours to kill.

Arriving at the shelter just twenty minutes before lunch, Will walked into the entrance hallway to look at the bulletin board. He half-expected one of the duty managers to tell him to move along, but no one bothered him. Guess they *have* to let people stop to read this stuff once in a while, he mused. There were notices for temporary housing, religious services, Alcoholics Anonymous meetings, Narcotics Anonymous meetings, and a whole other assortment of information which, Will chuckled, might be of interest to the shelter's denizens if they could read it.

In the middle of the bulletin board were three long strips of paper containing lists of names along with the notice that the listed people should make appointments to see the people named at the bottom each strip. On the middle strip will saw the name "William Tyne." The person he was to make the appointment with was someone named John Marin.

Will approached the office behind the window, wondering what exactly it was that Marin was supposed to do. A young, Amazon-like woman was seated in the office, but she was so tall that Will at first thought that she was standing. Her skin was very pale, much like that of some of the newly-arrived tourists Will had seen, and her short hair appeared as though it had been last trimmed with a hatchet. Thank god she's got tits, Will observed, or else no one would know she's a woman. After finishing a phone call, she turned and saw Will, then turned back to her paperwork. After another two minutes she turned and saw that he was still there.

"Yeah?" she drawled.

"Ah . . . uh," Will started, taken aback by her surly manner. "There's a list with my name on it on the bulletin board. It says I should make an appointment to see John Marin." Without a word she opened a ledger book to her left.

"Name?" she asked, staring balefully.

"Will Tyne," he croaked. She began writing in the ledger.

"Two-thirty tomorrow," she said, closing the book and pushing it away from herself. She turned away from Will.

"Excuse me," he called after her.

"Yeah?" she gritted her teeth as she whirled around in her chair, rolling her eyes upwards in apparent exasperation.

"Where will I find Mr. Marin?" Will asked meekly.

"In his office," came the hissing reply. Will's meekness was quickly being replaced by indignance.

"And where might that be?" Will queried, his knitted eyebrows showing his irritation. This time she managed a sarcastic smile.

"Upstairs." She turned away from Will again, and he knew that he would not accomplish anything by pressing her further. He hoped that she would not remember him.

Will's appetite soon distracted his mind from thoughts of the receptionist. Lunch consisted of a slice of leftover pizza, warm pasta, a small piece of sponge cake, and a large scoop of rice. For Will's hunger, it was as appreciated as a plateful of tortellini from Guido's had once been. Feeling energetic, Will left the shelter to return to Waikiki for the afternoon. His morning had been relatively smooth with the minor exception of the Amazon woman, and he felt ready to relax during the afternoon.

Knowing that he could not fit a half-gallon of liquor into his satchel, Will stopped at a convenience store and bought a fifth. He knew he would not drink the whole thing during the afternoon, and he didn't want to return to the shelter with an obvious bulge in his satchel. The anticipation of the gin fog enveloping him put him in an uncharacteristic good mood. He buckled the straps on his satchel and picked up his soda, then exited the convenience store.

He realized that he was farther away from the park than he cared to walk, but he knew he couldn't find a peaceful, shady place to drink anywhere along the main street. He decided to walk to the canal which bordered the side of Waikiki that was opposite the ocean. He had seen park benches there before, and he hoped that he might be able to find one that was in the shade. As he crossed the boulevard that ran along the canal, he looked in both directions and noticed that there were only two people jogging on the side-walk that ran beside the canal. All of the benches that he could see were vacant.

The afternoon sun had not yet dropped behind the apartment buildings across the street, but Will had his back to the sun and didn't have to worry about further damage to his still-ailing face. He glanced furtively in both directions and saw no one coming, so he removed the bottle of gin, still in a paper bag, from his satchel. He didn't know what the laws were about drinking in this area, but he knew that all of the parks had signs indicating that alcoholic beverages were prohibited.

Will had noticed people drinking in the parks in many instances since he had been in Hawaii, but he didn't want to find out firsthand how the police would react if they saw him drinking. As a jogger approached, he placed the bottle sideways on the bench, tucked between him and his satchel. As soon as she had passed, he quickly removed it, opened it, and doctored his Diet Pepsi amply. He knew that the canal would soon be bluer, the mountains greener.

After watching several joggers pass on the sidewalk and a number of kayaks glide down the canal, Will began to feel that familiar, warm feeling, and time passed more quickly. He smiled at the irony of the realization that he no longer had to worry about losing the roof over his head. *He had already lost it*, and it hadn't been so bad. Chiding himself silently for all the worry he had wasted on a situation that had been unavoidable all along, he smiled to think that it seemed to be of such little importance now.

Looking at his watch, Will noticed that it was already four-thirty. He knew that he would quickly have to walk back to Kuhio Avenue and find a bus that would take him back to the shelter so that he would not miss dinner. He tossed his empty paper cup into a trash can next to the bench and tucked the half-empty gin bottle into his satchel. As he stood and began to walk, he knew that the sluggishness that had taken over his legs was not just momentary stiffness brought on by his long sitting spell on the bench. He had walked quickly to the canal earlier; now he moved as though he had aged twenty years in two-and-a-half hours.

The wait for the bus was longer than usual, and the rush hour traffic kept it from moving quickly. Will arrived at the shelter just minutes before six o'clock. He walked through the front entrance to the dining/sleeping area and out the back door and was surprised to see that the line extended to the far end of the lanai, doubled back the entire length of the lanai, then extended onto the asphalt area. He made his way to the rear.

It was already six-twenty when he reached the front of the line and ten minutes later, before he had eaten half of his food, the duty managers were beginning to coax the crowd of diners toward the door. Will took his plate and went toward the doorway, but there was no one handing out numbers. Seeing a man with a photo I. D. name tag standing near the front door, Will approached him.

"Where's the person giving out the numbers?" he asked anxiously.

"Don't need a number tonight. House meeting," came the terse reply.

"House meeting?" Will asked, starting to back toward the doorway to show that he was following directions.

"If you come to the house meeting at seven, you don't need a number to get a mat. You just stay inside the building after the meeting."

Will continued out the door as he tried to understand what that meant. Like everything else, he guessed, I'll find out about it when I do it. At least he would be let back in the building at seven, about forty-five minutes earlier than he had gotten in the night before. As he sat down in the grass, he again heard the sound of the duty managers directing the cleaners on the inside. He wished that he could have another drink before the meeting, and there *was* a soda machine inside, but he had no cup. He decided that he had better wait.

Seven o'clock came, and Will noticed that the crowd did not move toward the front door as quickly and anxiously as it had rushed the side door the previous night. Inside, he saw that chairs had been set up in rows in the dining/sleeping area. At the end of the room near the doorway, there were two rectangular tables set up, backed by seven chairs. On the table were two microphones held up by desk stands.

The assembly of "guests," as the Center's rules sheet referred to its clients, seemed noisy and boisterous to Will as he sat in a chair at the end of one of the back rows. As seven approached, several people began seating themselves at the chairs behind the tables. The tall, thin, well-dressed man who had ordered Will out of the hallway the day before sat in the center and tapped on the microphone.

As he called for quiet among the group the noise abated, but there were still occasional audible voices engaged in conversation at the back of the room. The well-dressed man was Dick Mengel, operations manager for the shelter. The four noticeably more humbly-dressed people to his right were members of the "guest council," residents of the shelter who were chosen to represent the concerns of the other guests. To Mengel's far right was a very young-looking somewhat attractive woman. She was introduced as a graduate student who was doing some of her thesis research at the shelter.

As Mengel started to introduce the woman to his immediate left, the microphone started to crackle. She was a fairly young-looking woman, *very* pretty, Will noticed, with shoulder-length straight almost-black hair and an expression of mild concern on her face. Will could not hear Mengel's introduction, but guessed that the woman was another graduate student.

The meeting, Mengel explained, was not for the guests to air their gripes, but rather for the guest council to present its concerns to the shelter management—Mengel, Will assumed. A woman wearing army boots stood in the back of the room and began directing something unintelligible toward Mengel, and he again explained that there would be another meeting in two weeks which would be for the purpose of having the guests air their complaints. *This* meeting was *not* for that purpose, he stressed.

As the meeting wore on, Mengel's expression began to become increasingly resigned-looking. He was clearly uncomfortable in such a hostile crowd, but he continued to answer the guest council's questions with patience that did not escape Will's observation. Twice he referred questions to the dark-haired woman to his immediate left, but she was too soft-spoken for Will to be able to hear her answers. He's just giving her some practice, Will assumed.

Just after seven-thirty the meeting concluded, and the duty managers began ushering the assembly toward the door in the far rear corner of the building, urging people to stack their chairs as they left. Will followed the crowd, wondering not so much where it would go, but where it *could* go, considering the narrow strip of asphalt that separated the Center from the building next door. As soon as Will got outside, he could see that they were filing toward the lanai area and forming a thick, poorly-defined line there. He took his place amid the clicks of cigarette lighters and the smell of igniting matches, which was soon followed by a hovering cloud of smoke in the windless enclosure.

So much for getting in earlier, Will groused to himself, noting that it was now after eight o'clock. Occasionally the door opened and Will could see that the mats were being arranged on the floor inside. Will had noticed that there were no women in the crowd, and he had heard someone guess that they must have gone upstairs already, so he assumed that was where they slept. After another twenty minutes or so, the duty managers began allowing people to go inside, ten at a time. By this time, the line had become so thick in front of Will that there weren't many people *behind* him.

Finding a vacant mat near the doorway as soon as he stepped inside, Will claimed the mat and sat down to rest and inhale some of the almost smoke-free air inside before going to the cage to get his sheets. By quarter to nine he had settled on his mat, and noticed that most people had claimed mats and left the building. He wanted to go outside, but he had already lost a hat the night before, in just the time it took to go to the cage.

He didn't want to go outside badly enough to risk losing his sheets, so he decided to stay in. He knew that he wouldn't be able to drink enough to enjoy himself in the hour before the doors would be locked and the lights turned out, so he decided to wait until after his appointment with Marin tomorrow to finish the bottle.

Will was eager to meet John Marin and find out exactly what a case manager did. He was sure that he would be able to get Marin to realize that his homelessness was just a fluke, that he was far more intelligent than his fellow guests, and that he would soon rise like a phoenix out of ashes and become the shelter's biggest success story. This appointment, Will was certain, would mark the beginning of his "comeback" in the work world. Satisfied with his thoughts, Will lay back on his mat, a two-and-a-half foot by six-foot piece of vinyl-covered foam rubber that offered a two-inch cushion between him and the solid concrete floor.

As his fellow guests began to come back inside, Will began to get an idea of the sort of company with which he now shared sleeping quarters. The men came in all ages, all sizes, and all races, it seemed. There were some who were dressed well enough to disguise their homeless status, and there were those who were so dirty and ragged that Will wondered how their clothes stayed on. A few appeared to be so infirm that they either used a cane or walked feebly without assistance, and some appeared to be in such good shape that they could very nearly pass as body builders.

Almost all of them, however, had a beaten or hurt look on their faces, advertising clearly that all was not well in their lives. Some tried to cover it with false bravado, or forced smiles, or stoic expressions; but their eyes mirrored a certain melancholia that none could hide. Will had only to look around the room to know that everyone, including him, had been stitched with a common thread. Will had not been in the shelter for long, though, and he still had a glimmer of optimism, a hope, even as he closed his eyes for the night, that the next day would be the beginning of his renaissance.

Will's waking thought of being able to finish his bottle of gin the next morning was squashed when he remembered that he had an appointment with John Marin at two-thirty. He had wanted to go to the mall, get a paper, a soda, and a table in the food court there, and drink the morning away. But he also wanted to make a good impression on John Marin. No one in the shelter needed to know, thought Will, about his adventures as an "alcoholist." If they thought he was sober and merely down on his luck, he believed, they might be more willing to help him.

With that thought in mind, Will drank only soda during the morning hours, the weight of the half-full gin bottle in his satchel keeping him reminded that he could have a couple of strong ones after his appointment was over.

Lunch was over at twelve-thirty, and Will passed the time until his appointment by reading the newspaper's more uninteresting portions, which he had passed over during the morning. Finally, the time for his appointment neared.

Passing through the entranceway of the building, Will reached for the closed door to the dining/sleeping area. It was locked. He stood at the office window and waited for the Amazon woman to turn around. This time she glanced up at him, then quickly turned to face him, almost smiling.

"May I help you?" she asked. Will's mouth dropped open at this display of propriety on her part.

"Uh, yeah. I have a two-thirty appointment with Jack, ahhh, John . . . Marin," he sputtered. She opened her ledger book.

"Your name?" she asked, inexplicably pleasant compared to her manner during Will's previous encounter with her.

"Tyne. Will Tyne," he answered.

"Okay, come inside." Just as he was about to explain that he had already tried the door and found it locked, he heard a buzzing sound and he pulled the door open. He moved to his right, toward the stairway.

"Wait!" she called. "You have to get a pass first." Will walked toward the office's inside window. She handed him a small slip of paper on which was written his name, the case manager's name, the date, and the time of the appointment. Will started upstairs.

The upstairs room was similar to the dining/sleeping room downstairs, except that a row of offices lined the street side of the floor. Each office had its occupants' names posted on construction paper, written and colored in crayon. Will found the one with John Marin's name and knocked on the door.

There was no buzzer on this door, and a man about Will's own age rose from his chair to open it, since it was locked. Will nervously introduced himself and was beckoned to sit down in the metal folding chair in front of Marin's desk. Marin had a lit cigarette in the ashtray, and he had an Irish-Italian look that reminded Will of one of his old drinking buddies back in New York. He was heavy-set, with a harried, hangdog, overworked look. The stacks of papers that cluttered his desk further substantiated Will's impression.

"So tell me how you got here," he began, the hangdog look turning to a squinty smile as he inhaled from his cigarette. Will began with his departure from New York, and concluded by emphasizing his failed job search, without mentioning his prodigious consumption of liquor. Marin leaned back in his chair as he listened, nodding empathetically and occasionally chuckling in a knowing manner at Will's recounting of his job search.

Will explained that he was a college graduate, and that he had never had trouble finding work before. Marin repeated what Paulette had told him weeks ago about the leeriness of local employers where people who had recently arrived from the mainland were concerned.

"Know what you do?" Marin asked, and continued without waiting for an answer, "Go down to the state employment office and sign up. Do you know where that is?"

"Downtown?" Will guessed.

"Yes. On Punchbowl Street. If you get lost, just ask someone down there. Everybody knows where the employment office is. Anyway, go in there and register. It won't take that long. They have a computer system in there that has job listings, so you can look at that while you're there and see if they have anything listed that you might be qualified for."

"Okay," Will agreed. "I'll go there tomorrow morning. But I've never had much luck with employment offices."

"Another thing," Marin began. "Do you have any local I.D.? Will shook his head.

"That might help. If you can show employers that you've got some sort of I.D. here, that would indicate to them that you might be intending to stay."

"But I've already been here for two months," Will protested. "Doesn't that show that I'm serious?"

"Lots of people come over here for two months," Marin countered. "And if you tell someone you've been over here for two months and then show him that you still have your New York driver's license, then he's gonna figure that you probably plan to go back."

"I still have a North Carolina driver's license," Will explained. "I always kept it because it was the only place I used to drive. I never owned a car in New York."

"Doesn't matter," Marin continued, not derailed by Will's irrelevant aside. "If you can trade that license in for a Hawaii driver's license, *that* will show that you have some intention of staying here."

"Okay, okay, I'll do it," Will conceded. He was not anxious to give up a license that had a twenty-one year history of no traffic violations, but Marin had convinced him that it would be for the best.

"Now, you've got the rules sheet, right?" Marin asked.

"Yeah, they gave that to me when I did the intake."

"So you have a pretty fair idea of how things work?" Will nodded. This wasn't exactly the kind of help he had hoped for.

Marin continued, "You have to make an appointment to see me at least once every two weeks or your case will be closed and you won't get mail and laundry service." Whoa! Will thought.

"Mail and laundry service?" Will's eyes lit up.

"They didn't sign you up for that? Ohhh, I forgot. We have to do that up *here* now. Yeah, you can get your mail here as long as you keep your case open. They have mail call every day, Monday through Friday, at two and then again at eight. No mail on Saturdays though. As for the laundry, I think they do that by alphabet. Maybe A through L on Sunday and M through Z on Monday. They give you a pillowcase and you put what you want washed in it and leave it with the duty manager one night, and then you pick it up the next night. You can ask one of the duty managers about that. They'll know more about how it works than I do. And you can also get phone calls and messages here, too. They'll page you for phone calls between wake-up time and breakfast, and then again from eight till ten at night. The rest of the time they take messages. You probably already saw how they post them on the bulletin board downstairs." Will's mind was considering the possibilities.

"So I can send out resumes and put the phone number here on them?" he asked.

"Of course," Marin assured him. "The only alternative to that would be to get a pager. But not everybody can afford those. And not everybody can afford to rent a mailbox at the post office, either. That's why we offer those services. Sometimes I get job listings, too. If I have an idea of what you're looking for, I can let you know if I hear anything."

"I can bring you a copy of my resume," Will offered.

"It's in one of my bags in the cage. What would be a good time for me to bring it to you?"

"Just leave it with Bertha downstairs. She'll put it in with my messages and mail."

"You mean the tall woman?" Will asked, unsure about her and dreading the thought of having to ask her for *anything*.

"Yeah. Just leave it with her." Marin shifted in his chair as though he might be about to stand. Will knew what that meant.

"Well, thanks for your help," said Will, extending his right hand. Marin responded with a firm grip.

"Just be sure to check in at least every couple of weeks. And in between if you have any questions or problems here."

"Okay, thanks again," Will oozed, anxious to get out the door. It was already after three o'clock and he had precious little time to get somewhere to drink in time to be back at the shelter for dinner. The most practical journey, he figured, would be to the beach park across from the mall. He could get there in less than an hour, and it would take him about the same amount of time to get back. That would give him more than an hour to drink, and he would have to make do with that.

The meeting with Marin fresh in his mind, Will decided he would go to the driver's license office the next afternoon. As the bus wheeled its way through the light mid-afternoon traffic, Will had a cautious, hopeful feeling. With a phone number and a mailing address, he would be able to make up a new resume and continue his job search. And, maybe Marin was right about the driver's license switch. Maybe it *would* make a difference. The bus squealed to a halt at the bus stop in front of the mall's parking lot. Will's thoughts turned to drinking.

He first hurried into the food court at the mall for a soda, then made a hasty path back toward the park, which was across the four-lane, divided road from the mall. He could almost taste the sting of the first sip as he waited for the traffic light to hold the traffic and allow him to traverse the crosswalk into a quieter place and state of mind. Rush hour had already begun, and he had to wait a couple of minutes before he could cross.

Will felt the grass before deciding on a place to sit. It was dry, but the dirt beneath it was still damp, probably from the sprinklers that had drenched it earlier in the day. Will took a plastic grocery bag from his satchel and spread it on the ground, then carefully sat directly on top of it, so that the part of him that would press against the ground the hardest would be protected from the dampness. Looking up, he made sure that, although he was in the shade, there were no tree branches on which birds could sit directly over him. One glance at the top of a nearby picnic table had told him that the birds in the park were well-fed.

Before the alcohol had even had time to reach his system, Will was already daydreaming about landing a good job and getting a place to live. Another hour passed, but in what seemed like only a few more minutes, it was time for him to cross the street back into the real world, now seeming less somber than it had just an hour and a half before.

As he squeezed his way toward the back of the bus, Will noticed someone he had seen at the shelter the previous night. He wasn't sure at first if the person was a man or a woman, but had seen the individual in the men's sleeping area. Trying not to stare, Will decided that the person must be a man, even though he had long, thick, black hair, feminine-looking features and mannerisms, and carried a battered purse. He was wearing paint-smeared jeans and a sweater.

Unable to keep from looking, as the man was paying no attention to him, Will noticed that the edges of his fingernails were silver-colored, and that his hands looked as though they had been lightly sprayed silver. As Will looked gradually upward, he noticed that the same trace of silver surrounded the man's mouth and nose. Periodically, the man's hands and head would shake slightly, as if he was unable to stop them. Will had never seen anyone who was a paint sniffer, but he had seen something about these people on television, and this man looked the part.

Forcing himself to turn away, Will saw that others had noticed the man, too, and that even though there were people standing on the bus, no one would sit next to the paint-man. The fast drinking had put Will in a mellow mood, and for a moment he felt sympathy for the paint-man, who obviously had a serious problem.

Another man Will had seen at the shelter boarded the bus just before it turned to enter the high-rise section of the downtown business district. It was a man Will had seen Johnnie speak to during lunch earlier in the week. He was fiftyish, short, and pudgy, grizzled-looking with bad teeth. His hair was yellowish-grayish-white, thick, straight, and slick-looking, with curly ends. He was dark-skinned and wore an olivedrab field jacket.

Calculating that the bus would get him to the shelter in time for dinner, Will rested his head against the window as the bus bumped through the downtown area. He was sufficiently sedated even though he had not yet finished the fifth, and he knew he would have food to eat at the end of this ride. The bus, traveling the airport route, stopped next to King's Discount Store rather than at the beginning of Malualua Road, making the walk to the shelter a very short one.

As Will entered the main room at the shelter, he dodged two men who, seemingly oblivious to his presence, almost ran directly into him. He found his way to the end of the line, which stretched out to the far end of the lanai. The crowd was noisy, but Will's mind had returned to his daydream about finding work.

He got a plate and squeezed into a corner on the concrete floor, placing his satchel beside him so that no one could sit close enough to touch him. He had noticed that many of the shelter people had persistent coughs and other cold-related symptoms. Will wanted to avoid illness if it was possible.

The short, pudgy man was sitting only a few yards away from Will, but Johnnie was, once again, not around. Will could also see that the paint-man had managed to sit down without spilling the contents of his plate. His hands were shaking so badly that he was eating his food straight from the plate—he didn't even *try* to use a fork. Each time he tried to bring his cup to his mouth to take a sip of juice, he would end up spilling as much as he drank, until the cup was less than half full. Even at his worst, Will's own hands had never shaken so badly.

Will got another cup of juice from the dispenser after tossing his empty plate into the trash can and, taking a numbered card from the duty manager, went outside to wait the hour and a half that it would likely be before he would be allowed in to find a mat. The porch was already crowded, so Will went toward the far end of the building and searched for a clean, dry place in the grass.

Even though the grass was the only available relatively comfortable place to sit after dinner, Will was leery of it. He had already been around the shelter enough to see how often people spat in it, threw chewing gum in it, and tossed still-burning cigarette butts into it. He was careful when he sat down, and he began to wish that he had a soda so that he could finish the last of the fifth.

There were a few people carrying fountain sodas coming from the parking lot at King's Discount Store, and Will guessed that there must be some sort of restaurant there. Maybe, he speculated, he would go over there one night and find out. He was still too comfortable at the moment to drag himself up and look.

Suddenly, about twenty feet to Will's right, there was a commotion of two raised voices. A tall, pony-tailed, muscular man in his mid-twenties was taunting a skinny, puny-looking older man, who was angrily and drunkenly yelling back at him. The younger man swung at the older man, the brunt of his blow landing on the man's shoulder.

"You fucking bony piece of shit!" the younger man yelled. "Always trying to scam somebody! You think you're smart, don't you? You fucking smart ass!" He tried to grab the older man, who darted backward toward the wall of the building. "You sorry fuck!" the younger man screamed, clearly enraged and starting toward him.

The older man scrambled toward Will and jumped behind him. He put one hand on Will's shoulder, and Will quickly knocked it off, still uncertain what had provoked all of this and not wanting to become party to it. The younger man followed, his scowl showing that he was missing two teeth, and the scars on his face making him look even more fearsome. Stopping directly in front of Will, he lunged forward and swung again at the older man.

"You sorry fuck!" he repeated as he swung, his lunge carrying him directly onto Will, who reflexively shoved him away hard with both hands, but who had still not understood the conflict. The younger man backed away slightly and continued to direct his rage toward the man who was still cowering behind Will.

"You piece of shit! You think you can always hide behind your friends don't you?" he began again. "I'll get your ass." Sensing that the barrier had worked, the older man jumped up and ran across the street. The younger man, surprised by the quickness, stayed perched on his haunches, hovering uncomfortably close to Will as he momentarily sized up the situation.

"You fat fuck," he snarled at Will, looking at Will's rounded belly. "Let your sorry-ass friends hide behind you." Will sat transfixed and expressionless. His mind had still not managed to catch up with the situation. "You fat fuck!" the man exclaimed, seeming to become more enraged by Will's failure to respond.

Knowing without a shadow of a doubt that he was overmatched, Will dared not change his expression, which had been blank when the outburst had begun and remained blank. The pony-tailed man put his face closer to Will's.

"You fat fuck," he said again, "I'll get you, too. I'll get your ass, you fat fuck." With that he stood and walked away without looking back.

Will still sat unmoving and expressionless. Part of him was just beginning to become angry and part of him was already feeling relieved that the situation had passed. He was finally able to move, and he looked around. There was not a duty manager anywhere that he could see. Despite the fact that the pony-tailed man's voice had been loud and that there had been a lot of motion, no one nearby seemed to have noticed what had happened.

There had obviously been no rhyme or reason for anything the man had done, yet Will felt he had been threatened. What, he wondered, if the man tried to make good on his threat? Would he, Will, be safe while he slept? The only form of protection that Will had was a flip knife that he kept in his satchel. The only thing he had ever used it for was to open boxes that had contained his mail-order purchases in the past.

The concern and fear that Will felt at first slowly began to turn into anger, as he began to realize how absurd it was that he had been unwillingly made a part of the conflict between the two men. He was still silently swearing revenge as he picked up his satchel to walk to the side door to wait for the numbers to be called.

As soon as Will had his mat claimed and his sheets spread over it, he lay down and tried to refocus his thoughts on his job-finding daydream. He could only think of the pony-tailed man, and he continued to seethe. Looking around, he saw that there was almost no one in the shelter. Most people had claimed mats and gone back outside. A few had even left their bags on their mats. If their bags are safe, Will thought, then my sheets are. He decided he would go outside until just before the doors were to be locked for the night.

That would mean he could finish his fifth if he could find a spot to mix it, and then a spot to sit. He walked across the parking lot leading to King's, entered the store, and saw that the snack stand was just inside the entrance. Sodas were more expensive here, but Will was "thirsty." He exited the store and walked across the parking lot toward the other end of Hoka Street. There was a thrift store on the corner, and just to the left of it, next to a wall and partly behind a large bush, was a small, flat area of concrete, set about six inches above the ground. It was just about big enough for two people to sit on or, Will thought, for one person, a satchel, and a drink.

Partially out of the sight of the parking lot traffic, and totally out of view of the passing cars on Hoka Street, Will took out his bottle and carefully poured its remainder into the cup. Replacing the cap on the bottle, he tossed it further behind the bush, out of sight. Soon, he hoped, the anger he that remained from the episode that left him feeling victimized earlier in the evening would be masked by the hazy feeling he would get from the quick, heavy dose of gin.

There were few people passing by on the sidewalk, all shelter denizens, and none taking notice of him. The head-lights from the cars exiting the King's parking lot were a minor annoyance, but one which he gladly endured in exchange for having such a comfortable, otherwise-secluded place to sit and drink. Nine o'clock passed and instead of wishing time would pass so that he could sleep, as he had when he stayed at the Regal Arbor, Will now wished that the clock would move more slowly. Although he was still tense from the earlier incident, he had been able once again to let his mind drift to other things.

In the morning, he determined, he would go to the mall and get a paper and a soda, but would not drink. After lunch he would go to the driver's license office and, if he was successful in obtaining a Hawaii driver's license, he would go get another bottle of gin, this time a half-gallon. He could carry some of the contents in Evian bottles in his satchel, he figured, and leave the larger bottle in one of his bags in the cage. And he would spend the afternoon's remaining time, if there was any, at the beach park across from the mall again.

Assuaged by his plans for Friday, Will ambled back toward the shelter entrance, eight minutes before ten, ready to sleep. He paused in the hallway to read the bulletin board, and heard the voices of two black men in the hallway by the cage entrance.

"Maaannn! Somebody done conked him a good one!" said the first.

"Wouldn't pay no 'tention to what the man was tellin' him," said the other. "The man wid the night stick tell you to stop, you best do like he say." Both men passed Will and went into the main room. Will looked around the corner and saw two duty managers enter the building by the side door at the other end of the hallway. Just inside, they stopped, and immediately after them came the pony-tailed man who had threatened Will earlier. He was holding a large white washcloth partly over one eye and partly over the side of his head. Will watched as one of the duty managers gently pulled the cloth away from the man's head. There was a huge, dark bruise in the middle of which was a jagged, deep cut. That must have been what the two black men were talking about, Will guessed.

Having seen enough, he went into the main room. So fate *hadn't* singled him out, after all, he thought. The pony-tailed man had just been out *looking* for a scrape and found someone up to the challenge. Will smiled. He could sleep now, and dream. Maybe even good dreams. He had been threatened earlier, wronged without a reason. He had already spent valuable time worrying about his safety and plotting revenge. Now, with no more effort on his part than he had exerted earlier in the evening, he had just as quickly been avenged—without a reason. It was going to take some time to get used to this shelter, this life.

The next morning Will had finished showering and was sitting on the floor of the main room, shaving. His head ached slightly, a residual effect of his rapid consumption the previous night; but he felt good otherwise, and was looking forward to the day. The sweepers had already passed over the area in which he was sitting, and he knew he would be ready to take the bag containing his towel and toiletries back to the cage shortly.

"*I want everyone out of this room and on the lanai or outside!*" came an loud female voice from nowhere. Will looked up, momentarily startled. It was the same woman who made the wake-up call, but she was not using the P.A. system. "You *must* clear out so the sweepers can sweep," she continued. Coming toward Will, she pointed to him and made a sweeping motion toward the doorway with her finger, "Let's go! Now!" she yelled.

"Fat-ass bitch," Will mumbled to himself, not quite loud enough for the broad-beamed, middle-aged woman to hear. He switched his shaver off and scrambled up, moving himself and his belongings out the door as quickly as he could. It was not yet light outside, and Will had not finished shaving. He sat down in the grass, still damp with dew, and switched on his shaver.

The woman, called Mama Kamaka by some of the residents, seemed to Will to show a preference for people of local color and a dislike for white people. "Racist, fat-ass twat!" he grumbled to himself, adding her to his fast-growing mental list of those on whom he swore he would one day seek revenge.

Breakfast passed without any further disruptive occurrences, and Will left the shelter, heading down Malualua Road to the bus stop. He hoped he would have more peace in the bathroom at the small shopping center in Waikiki. Even with the air conditioner of the bus blowing cool air directly on him, the direct sunlight coupled with Will's alcoholic metabolism to make him uncomfortably warm during the forty-five minute ride.

He stepped off the bus just outside a shopping area. The sidewalk was already bustling with tourists and tour hawkers even though it was only eight-thirty, and Will dodged them as he hurried toward the shopping center. As he entered the partially open mall, he noticed that the only shopkeeper who had her kiosk open already was the woman who ran the sunglasses business. Will saw no one else in the mall, and he stepped on the already-moving escalator to ascend to the second floor where the bathroom was.

After what was becoming a ritual morning break on the porcelain altar, Will picked up his satchel and exited the stall. He paused in front of the mirror to comb his hair, then took a small leather toiletries kit out of his satchel. He removed his toothbrush and toothpaste from the kit and brushed his teeth. As he zipped the kit closed, he half-smiled and half-grimaced at the thought of such an item finally becoming useful at such an unfortunate time. He tucked the kit back into his satchel and left the bathroom, content that he had been able to use it a few mornings now without having been displaced or even hassled by any of the shopping center's employees or security people.

Will was at the mall in what seemed like a short time. It was after nine, and everything, even the food court, was open and busy. He first went to the book store to get a newspaper. The cashier was a chubby, brown-skinned young woman with long, dark hair who had smiled at Will earlier in the week, and it had made him feel good. He had no interest in her, nor did he assume that her smile was anything more than a good business practice, but kind expressions directed toward him had become rare lately. He picked up a paper from the stack on the counter beside the cash register, and handed the young woman, who appeared to be about twenty, the coins to pay for it.

"Mahalo," she said, looking up and smiling, this time registering a hint of recognition toward Will.

"Thank *you*," Will answered, trying to manage a pleasant expression, even though he knew his lingering sunburn must still make him look awful. He tucked the paper under his arm and ambled back out into the breezeway, on his way to the food court. Even with a newspaper for company, the morning passed slowly, and Will found himself waiting for the bus to return to the shelter shortly after eleven. He was thinking about the driver's license transaction and becoming edgy. Even though he knew he did not have to take a road test, the thought of taking a written test was unsettling. He knew that his increased appetite and decreased consumption of late would ensure that his hands did not shake, but he was not certain that his mind could still remember all the right answers to questions about information he had only occasionally used over the past ten years.

Just after he settled onto the concrete floor with his lunch and began eating, Will felt a tap on his right shoulder at the same instant he heard a friendly "Hey!" His head jerked to the right, and he saw Johnnie.

"Hey, man. How's it going? Haven't seen you the past couple of days," Will effused. Johnnie's face was ruddy.

"Been up in Manoa. In my tent. Rains a lot up there. I started out the other morning, slipped in the mud. Had to go back and change. By then I wasn't hungry. Besides, I go other places, like the mission by River Street." Johnnie seemed tense.

"Well, I'm still trying to figure out the ropes here," Will offered, trying to be *just* conversational.

"So, you hangin' in?," Johnnie asked, gradually easing into a more relaxed posture.

"Yeah. I saw one of the counselors—ah, caseworkers—yesterday. I'm going to get a driver's license as soon as I eat, but I'm starting to get a little nervous about that," Will responded.

"Written part's easy. Thirty questions. Multiple choice. But if you got to take a road test, that's where they get you. Especially if you're from out of state."

Will exhaled. "Having a North Carolina license, I don't have to take the road test," he told Johnnie. "Maybe it'll be pretty easy after all."

"Yeah, well, good luck," Johnnie said, backing away toward the door as he swallowed his last mouthful. "I'll probably see you tomorrow." Will nodded. He had only eaten half his food in the time that Johnnie had wolfed down a whole plate.

After he finished his lunch, Will went out the building's side door and found a tiny patch of shade next to a recessed area in the building's exterior. He removed his well-worn map of the state from his satchel, and unfolded it. The driver's license office was a substantial distance away, but Will saw that there was no practical way to get there by bus. He decided to walk.

When he finally approached the building, and the first shaded area he had encountered since he had left the shelter, Will was damp with perspiration. He hoped that the air conditioning on the inside would be cold, and as he passed through the doorway, he could tell that it was.

After filling out the forms that were handed to him, Will sat down at a desk in the testing area and began working on the thirty-question test. Common sense, he told himself; all of the questions just required common sense. Within fifteen minutes he was back at the counter, handing the examiner his test paper. He had only been sitting down to wait for the result for a few minutes when he heard his name called. He approached the desk again. He had answered twenty-eight of the questions correctly!

There had been five other people who took the test at the same time Will had taken it. Three of them had failed. Will felt a feeling of near-exhilaration as he stood waiting to have his picture taken for the license. He would finally have something to prove that he was serious about being here.

Minutes later, he paid the fee for the license and the clerk handed the paper version of the license to him with his receipt. The actual card, she told him, would be mailed to him. He was to notify them if he had not received it in a couple of weeks. He was slightly disappointed that he wasn't able to leave with the *real thing* in his pocket.

License acquired, it was now time for his reward. The walk back to where there was a bus stop took less than fifteen minutes, and in another forty minutes Will was at the mall walking into the "libation station." His money was holding out well so far, now that he didn't have to pay for rent or food; but he was aware that it wouldn't last much longer. But he had enough for today, and he bought a half-gallon plastic jug of gin. There was plenty of time left in the afternoon, and he had a small reason to celebrate.

Stopping at the food court for a jumbo soda, he asked the girl to put extra ice in it. He knew that it would melt quickly if he made the drink a half-and-half mixture of soda and gin. As he approached the intersection where the mall parking lot met the road, the crosswalk light flashed the "walk" symbol, and Will hurried across the road into the park. He was in a better mood than he had experienced in a long time.

He found the shaded area where he had sat earlier in the week, and the ground was now dry. Sitting down, he took the Hawaii driver's license out of his pocket to look at it again before he fixed his libation. It was only a piece of paper, but just having the license made him feel that he now belonged in some small way in his environment.

The drink stung Will's tongue at first. Perfect, he

thought. He stretched his legs out in front of him as straight as he could comfortably position them. For the first time in days, they didn't ache at all. The gin went to work quickly, and Will for the first time began to feel that becoming homeless had lifted more weight from him than it had added to him.

His mind was more free than it had been in over a year. He no longer had to concentrate on the day-to-day challenges of meeting bills and deadlines. He now had a roof over his head at night, food to eat, and a few people on *his* side.

He knew that he still had to concern himself with protecting his remaining possessions but, as he saw it, he was now in a very picturesque abyss from which he could only rise.

Chapter 5

Groping for Solace

Will's throat was sore. There were two industrial-size fans in the sleeping room that were turned on at night to keep it from being so hot. Two hundred living bodies packed into one room generated a lot of heat, and none of the common area at the shelter was air-conditioned.

The double doorway that led to the lanai was kept open at night and although smoking was not permitted in the building, it was allowed on the lanai. Some of the smokers, both guests and duty managers, often stood in the doorway, sometimes literally straddling the door sill, to smoke. As the fan drew in the outside air, the smoke was also blown into the sleeping area.

Accustomed to an environment that was smoke-free indoors for most of his life, Will could not adapt to the second-hand smoke that infiltrated his respiratory system while he slept. His throat had developed a dry, burning feeling at first, and now it was sore. The pain was accompanied by an occasional cough, and his voice had also become raspy.

As he walked down Malualua Road toward the bus stop on Monday morning he swallowed repeatedly, wishing that he could swallow the soreness. He was on his way to the bathroom in Waikiki, and his throat, in addition to a slight headache, were the only things that kept it from being a great morning.

He boarded the bus for the ride that had become part of his morning routine. The few minutes of privacy that the bathroom afforded him made it worth the daily trek. The bathroom at the shelter had gotten so bad that only one urinal and two showers were in working order. Some of the shelter residents used the bathroom at King's Discount Store, but Will had heard that the shelter administrators and the management at King's were trying to put a stop to that. No one at the shopping center in Waikiki had said *anything* to Will about using the bathroom there.

The wheels of the bus squealed as it slowed to a halt in front of Will's usual stop in Waikiki, and he stepped off the bus, more spring than usual in the balls of his feet. He eased into a relaxed gait as he headed down the Kuhio Avenue sidewalk. Just ahead, he saw a woman from the shelter standing on the sidewalk, a vacant look on her face.

She had shoulder-length, dirty blond hair, and was tanned almost to the point of being sunburned. Her brown t-shirt hung on her as though her frame was no more than a wire coat hanger, and Will could only wonder what held up the camouflage trousers she wore. Two small points protruding from her chest into her shirt were the only thing that identified her body as that of a female. Still, Will saw in front of him a woman in her early thirties that might have once been very pretty, and very likely could become that way again if she were to take care of herself. She leaned toward him as he moved to pass her.

"Spare a dollar?" she asked, obviously not realizing that he was a fellow shelter "guest."

"Sorry." He shook his head as he passed, partly in response to her and partly in bewilderment. Maybe she just hadn't noticed him at the shelter. After all, there were over two hundred men and only about thirty or forty women there. He continued on his way into the shopping center and up the escalator.

A short while later, his morning routine complete, Will stepped out of the shopping center breezeway back onto the sidewalk. The traffic was momentarily halted by a red light, and he walked quickly across to the other side of the street. As he approached the bus stop, he noticed that the woman from the shelter had also crossed the street and was now stationed near the bus stop. Will slowed his pace as he got close to the stop and the woman.

"Spare a dollar?" she asked again, apparently oblivious to the fact that she had already asked him. He decided to find out if she was alert.

"No," he answered softly, "Don't you recognize me?"

She stared blankly at him, and Will, unsure what she was thinking, didn't want to risk frightening her.

"I stay at the shelter, too," he began, speaking in as soft a tone as his raspy voice could muster. "I don't have any money to give you because I'm in the same boat as you. Haven't you ever seen me before at the shelter?"

"No," came the plaintive answer. She still stared at him with a blank expression, but the fear Will thought he had seen in her eyes was no longer present.

"Well, I stay there, too," he continued. "Maybe I'll see you there tonight and I can remind you who I am." She tilted her head slightly, almost as if to look around him.

"Okay," she complacently replied, then reacted more quickly as a tourist brushed by Will: "Spare a dollar?" Will shrugged and turned to look for the bus.

He returned to the shelter for lunch, having only had a small amount to drink during the morning. He knew that he had to find a place to do his laundry that afternoon, and he didn't want to risk being clumsy with his limited amount of coins.

Johnnie was at the shelter, and Will noticed that he was talking to the grizzled-looking, pudgy man Will had seen on the bus the previous week. Will moved slowly across the room to speak, and Johnnie noticed him.

"Hey, how you been?" Johnnie greeted him, much happier than last time Will had seen him.

"Okay, okay. Got the license." Will pulled his wallet from his pocket so that he could show the license to Johnnie. Johnnie squinted slightly and looked at it closely.

"Oh, just the paper one," he observed, then turned to the pudgy man. "This is Gary. He's another vet. A friend of mine."

Will shook his hand and Gary grinned, showing that *all* of his teeth were in the same bad state as the front two. Johnnie excused himself, saying that he had to go to a PTSD meeting.

"So you were in Vietnam?" Will asked, trying to make conversation.

"No, Navy," Gary answered, his face becoming serious. "Served on a destroyer off the coast of Vietnam, but I didn't go ashore there. Serve my country for eight years, and look at me now." Will cringed inside, regretful at having brought up the subject.

"Been here long?" Will asked, knowing that this subject was not *much* better than the last, but at least better.

"I come here just to eat," Gary explained. "I don't sleep here. It's too crowded, too loud. But I was born here." He paused. "On this island, I mean. My mama was native and my father Puerto Rican. That makes me a *local*." The grin returned to his face. Will breathed a sigh of relief.

"Well, I gotta run," Will lied, wanting to end the conversation with Gary smiling. "It was nice meeting you."

"Yeah, man. I see you around," Gary waved.

Will walked out the side door, laundry bag in tow, unsure of which bus he needed to take to get to the laundromat. He found his shaded cubbyhole, made sure that there was no spittle where he was about to sit, and parked himself on the pavement. As he pulled a map out of his satchel, he noticed a tall, slender woman with almond eyes and dark hair walking toward the chain-link gate that led to the lanai. He had seen her briefly the night before, but he had guessed that she was either a shelter employee or a volunteer. She was actually pretty and well-groomed, he noticed. Surely she was not a shelter resident.

Moments later he replaced the map in the satchel and stood, peering over the top of the brick wall into the lanai area. The woman was still there, talking to two shelter guests. She now had a bag suspended from her shoulder, and Will now figured that she was a shelter resident, after all. He decided that he would pay close attention to see if she went in when the other women entered the building tonight.

Certain that the addition of the laundry bag to his load left no doubt to any observer that he was homeless, Will set out for the laundromat. He had to go almost to Waikiki, then walk two blocks to get to it. He had two "loaded" Evian bottles tucked into a plastic cup in his satchel, and he was sure that he could get a soda at the laundromat or somewhere nearby.

Once he had his two loads of laundry going, Will propped his satchel up on one of the tables intended to be used for folding laundry, then removed an Evian bottle from the satchel. Although the attendant and the only other patron were at the other end, he wanted to be sure that his mixing attracted no attention.

He was glad to have the chance to get his clothes washed, even though being homeless made it take up an afternoon. As he folded the clothes and placed them back in the bag, he began to determine how he would go about getting the clothes repacked into his bags that were stored in the cage. The gin had made everything seem more like an effort, and he walked slowly as he lugged the bag back to the bus stop.

Back at the shelter, he waited outside the side door until five o'clock came and Sam opened the cage. He took out one bag at a time, completing his unpacking with three laborious trips to the cage. He could finally rest until it was time to get in line for dinner—in fifteen minutes.

After he had been through the line, eaten dinner, and gotten a number for a mat, Will walked across the street and through the King's parking lot to the snack bar. His afternoon drinking had been no fun because of the laundry chore, and he now wanted to *enjoy* a good drink. Mindful of the Center for Social Aid's rules prohibiting alcohol, Will again sat on the concrete slab behind the bush that was just a few yards away from the Center's property boundary. It was a cool, comfortable night, and it was time to relax.

Will had not even swallowed his first sip when the rain began falling, hard and without even a single warning drop. He stood, then realized that there was no place to go to get out of the rain. The shelter was closed so that the mats could be put out, and even the lanai was locked shut. At least if he continued to sit, his sitting place would stay dry. He took his small umbrella out of the satchel and opened it. There was little wind and a high wall to his back, so he decided to sit it out. He placed his cup between his legs, periodically picking it up to sip from it.

As the air got cooler, Will noticed that his nose was beginning to run. He sniffed, and it continued. At least, he noted, the alcohol had taken most of the pain out of his throat. And by the time he finished his drink, the duty managers would be calling numbers for mats.

Will took the last sip and carried the cup toward the porch until he reached the concrete trash receptacle that stood at the end of the handrail that bordered the steps. As he discarded it, he noticed that the rain had slowed to a sprinkle, and people were beginning to move to the parking lot outside the side door. He followed.

Looking around, Will did not immediately spot the slender girl with the dark eyes. As he scanned a wooden porch by a stationary trailer, though, he saw her. She was standing up in anticipation of soon being allowed into the building. She had on a black spandex outfit that left her midriff bare, and which outlined every detail of her slim but shapely body. Her hair was wavy and thick, and her skin was smooth and clear. Will could not help but wonder what had landed her in a homeless shelter.

After he had gotten a mat and readied it for later, a process made much more tedious by the effects of the gin, Will returned outside. He had reasoned that the duty managers must keep a close eye on the mats once they were claimed, since his sheets, the only thing he ever left on them, had been there when he had left them and returned later on a previous night.

The rain had completely stopped and Will wandered slowly around the small parking area. As he looked between two of the cars parked there, toward Malualua Road, he noticed that someone was sitting in the shadows at the base of a tree that stood between the parking lot and the sidewalk. He stepped closer and saw that it was the woman who had asked him for money earlier in the day. He approached her and she looked up at him.

"Remember me?" he asked, hoping to elicit at least some sign of life from her.

"No," she said softly but flatly.

"This morning. *On Kuhio*, in Waikiki, about eight-thirty?" he queried, trying to lead her into a hint of recognition.

"Oh, yeah," she said, raising her chin and smiling weakly, enough for Will to see that one of her front teeth was black.

"*Now* will you remember me next time you see me?"

he asked. She thought for a moment.

"Yeah, I'll remember you," she nodded, and continued, "I just stay out there until I get money for cigarettes and some coffee."

Will wasn't certain what she meant, but her blackened tooth had dissuaded him from persisting with further questions. He was relieved to learn that she could at least *think*, though. Her blank expression earlier in the day had left him worried.

He turned his attention back to the side door, as the duty manager had appeared and had called for the women to enter the building. Will saw the dark-eyed woman slither through the crowd, almost seeming not to touch anyone, then quickly move up the steps and disappear inside. So she *does* stay here, he thought. She *looked* good, but Will wondered if she might have some sort of mental problem that prevented her from fitting into society. His own experience with alcohol made him certain that she could not possibly have an alcohol problem. And her mannerisms seemed normal, too.

He heard his group of numbers being called, and began pushing his way toward the door. As he was among the last group to be called, having drawn number 94, most of the mats were taken by the time he got inside. He found one near the double doors that opened up to the lanai and groaned, knowing that it would put him closer to the nighttime cigarette smoke and irritate his already-ailing sinuses.

Will had fairly quickly acquired an idea of what sort of people slept in each general area; and even if he was unable to recall who had claimed each of the mats in his area, he could sometimes look at the bags or other items that they left on the mats and recall the faces of the people to whom they belonged. He did not, however, recognize the bandanna on the mat to the left of his or the paperback book on the mat to his right. Already tired and not feeling well, Will determined that he would stay inside and rest rather than going back out for another drink. He was in a position from which he could see the projection television even if he couldn't hear it.

As it became closer to ten, Will was relieved to see that the mat with the bandanna had been taken by one of the people Will thought of as a "leftover hippie," a burned-out looking, but good-natured man whose appearance gave Will no cause for concern. Will figured that the man would sleep quietly and stay on his own mat, something that some people in the shelter seemed unable to do. The mats were positioned side by side and, in most areas, head to head, with *no* space in between them. If someone's hand or foot was not on his own mat, that meant that it was on someone else's, unless the person was on a mat at the end of a row.

Will had already been awakened a few times by another person's stray hand or foot, and he had more than once had to push the entire body of a semi-conscious drunk off the edge of his mat. A good "mat neighbor" was hard to find in the shelter.

About a minute before ten, the person who had left the paperback book returned to his mat. He was a middle-aged man, unshaved, dirty, and greasy looking, and Will saw that the legs of his trousers were spattered with mud. As he almost collapsed on his mat, a an odor of feces mixed with urine burned its way up Will's nostrils, even though his sinus ailment had all but destroyed his sense of smell.

The leftover hippie sat up and frowned. Will knew that he would not be able to sleep next to such an odor. Others in the area quickly noticed, and a dissatisfied rumble soon turned into hoots and cries of "Get a shower, man!" and "Man, go wash that shit off!" Will had read on the rules sheet that dirty guests could be required to take a shower or be denied a place to sleep.

Before the commotion became much louder, a husky, dark-skinned duty manager approached the man.

"Sir!" he said directly into the man's ear. "You need to take a shower!"

"Uhhhh. Later," the man mumbled, half-opening his

eyes.

"No!" the duty manager, whose name was Robert, said firmly. "Your lack of cleanliness is disrupting the other guests. You have to take a shower or else you have to go outside." He reached down and grasped the man's arm with both hands and began trying to get him to stand up. After muttering a few more unintelligible syllables, the man got to his feet. Robert held on to his elbow and walked him toward the bathroom. The lights had been turned off during the commotion, and Will lay down on his mat.

Within ten minutes the man returned. He had showered, *but with his clothes on!* His clothes were dripping water on the floor, and the smell was just as bad. He paused at the foot of Will's mat, apparently trying to figure out how to get back on his own mat without falling on someone. Some of the drops of water fell on Will's feet, and he quickly scrambled to his knees and pushed the man away. Robert had seen this, and was there almost instantly. He took the man's elbow again, this time more gently.

"Come with me, sir," he said, his voice less firm and more compassionate than before. "There's a mat open on the lanai. You can sleep there." He led the man through the double doors out to the end of the covered concrete porch. A single row of mats lined the lanai area, but they had some space in between them, and the man's odor would dissipate more easily outdoors. Will drifted off into a light sleep, touched by the gentle manner with which Robert had treated the man. Another duty manager might have expelled such an incoherent, uncompliant drunk.

The next morning Will managed to shave indoors without Mama Kamaka demanding that everyone leave the main room. He guessed that someone must have complained after the last time she had done it, because it had been raining that morning. Breakfast, which consisted of a cinnamon roll, rice, an orange, and out-of-date yogurt, passed without any sort of incident. Will talked briefly with Johnnie, who mentioned that he sometimes spent time in the library. The idea seemed like a good one to Will, who wanted to wait until the afternoon to start drinking anyway. Will knew that he could easily pass a few hours in the library, and was happy to find out that he could get there by taking the same bus that he rode to Waikiki each morning.

Will stepped outside onto the porch, trying to decide how to pass the time until nine o'clock, when the library would be open. He didn't want to go all the way to Waikiki, then back to the library. The library was much closer to the shelter than Waikiki, and Will could use the bathroom there. He just had to kill some time before going there. He walked toward the other end of Hoka Street, planning to sit on the concrete slab he had occupied the evening before.

A grocery store cart was positioned in front of the slab. It was packed with plastic shopping bags and trash bags. Some of the bags were even bound with clothesline cord and suspended from either side. Will sat down on the slab, just a few feet away from the eyesore. As he opened his satchel to take out the crossword puzzle he had salvaged from a discarded newspaper, he felt that he was being watched.

He looked up and saw, peering around the bush, a small, skinny man with long hair and a couple of weeks' beard growth. The man was wearing a dirty baseball cap and had on what appeared to be several layers of clothes. Will couldn't tell what age he was, but guessed him to be about forty. His expression made Will wonder if the man wanted to sit down but might be afraid to.

"You want to sit down?" he called to the man, moving his satchel closer to himself in order to make ample space for the man. "It's okay. There's plenty of room here." The man shook his head meekly, but didn't speak. Will turned his attention back to the crossword puzzle, but soon noticed again that the man was staring at him. He waved as if to say "I see you" to the man. The little man broke into a toothless grin.

He inched his way toward Will and sat down on the corner of the concrete slab. Will still held the crossword puzzle in his hand, but the little man, who had removed a pack of cigarettes from his pocket, commanded his interest.

"Got a match?" the man asked him. Will didn't want to be around cigarette smoke, but he reached in his satchel and handed the man a small book of matches. The man broke off one match and handed the book back to Will.

"You can keep the pack," Will offered. "Besides, you need the emery on the cover to strike them." The man put the single match into the pocket of his outermost shirt. He said nothing, and Will put the matches back into his satchel. His attention turned back to his crossword puzzle.

"Got any old or dead batteries?" the man asked. Will looked up, incredulous. Of all the strange things he had been asked for in his life, no one had *ever* made such a request. He quietly shook his head. The man reached into one of the bags on the shopping cart and took out a small, battered cassette player and headphones. He put the headphones to his ears, switched the player on, and listened intently for a moment before switching it off. He placed the cassette player beside him and removed a large bag of Reese's Pieces from a bag on the cart.

"Want some candy?" he asked Will, holding the bag out.

"No, thanks. Just ate breakfast," Will responded.

"They had these on sale last week. I got ten bags. Here, you can have one," the man offered, reaching into the bag on the cart and pulling out another bag of Reese's Pieces. Will didn't really want the candy, but he took it to humor the man.

"Thank you," he responded as pleasantly as he could. The man seemed pleased. As Will took a longer look at the man's face, he could see that one eye was almost closed into a squint, and that a thin trail of mucous ran from its corner down the man's cheek.

"What kind of music do you listen to?" inquired Will, looking at the battered cassette player.

"John Lennon," the man answered softly.

"A great one," Will added. "Too bad he's not still around to make more music." The man's whole body seemed to perk up.

"You know who killed him?" the man asked.

"I think it was some guy named Chapman," Will answered, not sure why the man asked that question.

"No, no. Who *really* killed him," the man said with more authority. "I *know*."

"Oh? Who?" Will had completely forgotten about the crossword puzzle and the library for the moment.

"Well, it was the people from Disneyland," the man began, serious to the point of being grave. "John Lennon went to Disneyland and he met Cinderella. And he liked her and she liked him. But he didn't want her to stay there. He wanted to take her to Disney *World*, and she decided to go with him. But the people at Disneyland didn't want her to go. But she was going anyway, so they got—um, they got . . . What was his name?"

"Chapman."

"Yeah. They got Ch—they got him to stop John Lennon from taking Cinderella to Disney World. And he killed him. Cinderella stayed at Disneyland." Will could see that the man was completely earnest and serious.

"I never knew that's what happened," he quietly said to the man, knitting his eyebrows as he pondered the sheer originality of the story. He began to buckle his satchel and ready himself for his walk to the bus stop. He knew that he wouldn't find anything in the library that would quite compare with what he had just heard. But as far from reality as the little man was, Will saw in him a mild-mannered quality that he couldn't help but like. He lifted the strap of the satchel over his shoulder, wished the man a good day, and began walking toward Malualua Road.

Will reached the library, a large yellowish-white building, just after nine o'clock. He entered it and walked around, exploring each of the three floors and noting where the copying machines were located. He had been carrying the "help wanted" section from the previous Sunday's newspaper, but had not read it yet. He also knew that he needed to find some place where he could re-type his resume and include the center's address and phone number on it.

There were a few vacant tables in the front upstairs section of the library. The tables were positioned so that they overlooked the entire first-floor lobby near the entrance. As Will sat down to read the classified ads he glanced up, and noticed that two shelter residents had just walked in.

Having the time to read the newspaper and doing so with a relatively clear mind enabled Will to find several job possibilities. Once he had them circled, his attention turned to the huge selection of books that was at his disposal. The remainder of the morning he spent reading parts of books that he picked from the shelves. As he passed by the circulation desk, about to leave, he noticed a table with library card application forms on it. He took one and slid it into the folder in his satchel.

As he entered the shelter's parking lot from the Malualua Street side, Will noticed that there were two police cars parked in front of the building. Instead of sitting down in the recessed area at the side of the building, he walked around front. Two police officers exited the front door of the building, climbed into their respective cars, and drove off. Two people were sitting on the front porch explaining to a third person that someone had his bag stolen from the cage. Will could only guess that Sam must have left the cage in the care of someone else for a time, because he knew that Sam kept a close eye on the cage when he was there.

Will had just enough time before lunch to remove from the cage the bag that contained the liquor, take it outside to refill his Evian bottles, and return it to the cage. After lunch was over he bused his way to the mall, got soda and an extra cup of ice, and walked across the road to the beach park.

His throat was becoming a problem that he could no longer ignore. His constantly runny nose had caused one of his ears to become clogged, impairing his hearing. And now he was beginning to feel run down. He knew that the shelter had a medical clinic that operated a couple of mornings a week, and he decided that he would give it a try the next day.

As he sat in the shade trying to drink away some of his annoying symptoms, he noticed that there were two people from the shelter who had sat down in the grass about twenty-five yards away from him. First the library, he grumbled to himself, and now here. He wondered if there might be *any* place that he could go where there wouldn't be any shelter people.

The afternoon passed and he felt progressively worse. As he sat outside the shelter after dinner, the cigarette smoke emanating from the porch became too irritating, so he moved to a section of grass at the far end of the building. The only other within several yards of him was a paunchy, middle-aged man wearing a baseball cap. Relieved to have some near-solitude so close to the shelter, Will closed his eyes for a moment.

"That was a pretty good dinner," Will heard someone say. He looked up. It was the man in the baseball cap, speaking to him. The last thing he wanted at that moment was to be part of a conversation, but he *had* to be civil.

"Yeah, it was pretty good," he responded, yawning and turning his head, and hoping that was the end of it.

"You been around here long?" the man queried.

"Couple of weeks," Will answered, still wishing to be

left alone.

"I just got here last week," the man continued. "I flew in from Maryland. I was staying in a hotel, but it just got too expensive." Will did not respond, not knowing what to say, but the man kept talking. "I thought I might be able to find work here, but the construction business seems to be in a slump right now. By the way, my name is Bill."

"I'm Will," Will answered, offering his right hand, but not moving any closer to the man. Bill stood and walked over to where Will was to shake his hand. Will noticed that Bill had with him what looked to be a very large doctor's bag. As they continued the conversation, he found out that the bag was all that Bill had brought with him on his trip. He had planned to stay here, as Will had when he had arrived in September. And, like Will, he had a return ticket as a "safety valve." Unlike Will, he had a family home to return to if he decided not to stay.

It soon became time to wait for the numbers to be called, and Will managed to get a mat in the same area in which he had slept the night before. Even though it had been near the doorway where people often smoked, the ventilation had been such that the air was less smoky than in the center of the main room. Bill came in just after him and claimed the mat next to his. It appeared that the "leftover hippie" had again left his bandanna on the mat on the other side of Will's.

The evening continued with more conversation with Bill, to whom Will began to take a liking, and time passed quickly. The leftover hippie came in just before ten o'clock, and Will lay down hoping that he might get a good night of sleep without getting prodded awake or having to listen to any wall-rattling snoring.

Will awakened momentarily during the middle of the night, thinking that he had heard the rumbling voice of a drunken man, then quickly returned to sleep. At four-thirty, about an hour before the lights were to be turned on, Will again awoke—this time to the unmistakable smell of urine. There was enough light casting in from the outside security light so that he could see that someone had come inside during the night and had laid down on the concrete floor—without a mat. The man was now sleeping in a puddle of his own urine, a puddle that had been large enough to flow under the mat of the leftover hippie. Part of the hippie's bed sheets had slid over on the floor and were soaked with urine, and a towel had also fallen to the side of the mat into the puddle, which had stopped about a foot and a half short of Will's mat.

Before Will could decide whether to call Jerry, the duty manager who had helped him when he had arrived at the shelter and who was on duty now, the leftover hippie stirred and then awoke. As he leaned over to raise himself, he planted his left hand in the middle of the puddle of urine. He let out a yell, and one of the duty managers hurried over, turning on a blinding Mag-light flashlight.

The duty manager began to shake the half-conscious man who was still lying on the concrete. He was still incoherent and apparently not cognizant of where he was.

"Come on, man!" the duty manager called to him. "*Look what you've done!* Get up! You're going outside. *Now!*" The man barely stirred, and the duty manager, careful not to get into the urine, grabbed the man under the armpits and pulled him toward the door. Finally the man began to wake up, and he immediately put what little energy he had into trying to break free of the duty manager's grasp.

By this time another duty manager had come to assist the first, and the two of them half-carried and half-dragged the man to the chain-link gate at the far end of the lanai. They left him outside and re-locked the gate. The leftover hippie was muttering angrily, and Will was watching him to make sure he was careful enough not to shake any of his urine-soaked things in Will's direction.

Bill had now awakened, as had several other people in

the area. Will wondered how anyone in the room had slept through all the commotion, but most of the people still appeared to be sleeping. Will lay back down, wide-awake, to wait for the lights to come on. His throat hurt so much that it reminded him of when his tonsils had been removed, thirty years before. And he now had full use of only one ear, as the other one was almost completely blocked.

As soon as he had gone through the usual morning logistics and had finished breakfast, Will walked down the hallway and into the waiting room of the clinic. The tiny room had barely enough space for four chairs on each side with a just enough aisle space in the middle to allow passage for no more than one person at a time. All of the chairs were taken, and the noise coming from the other tiny rooms told Will that those rooms were occupied as well.

A fair-skinned young woman with long, silky blond hair appeared.

"Did you sign in?" she asked Will.

"No. Where do I do that?" he answered, looking around.

"On the clipboard, there." She pointed to a clipboard, which was on a table by the doorway. Will picked it up and filled out the information. By the time he was done, one of the people had been called inside, so he had a place to sit. The woman next to him put her elbows out and spread her legs, as if she were hoping to block Will from sitting. Her elbow protruded into his side as he sat, and she glowered at him with an angry expression on her face. He guessed that whatever physical problem she might have this morning *must* be secondary to her mental condition.

The other patients went quickly ahead of him. He gathered from the whispered conversation that at least some of them were there for methadone. Within twenty minutes, the blond-haired young woman, who introduced herself as Amy, called Will inside. She looked at his throat and his ears and took his temperature, then left. A few minutes later, a tall man with bushy, curly hair walked in. Without examining Will further, he gave him Tylenol, a decongestant, and cough syrup.

Will groaned silently. He knew that if he took all of this medicine, he wouldn't be able to drink. But he *had* to get rid of the stuffiness and sore throat. The bushy-haired man, a doctor Will presumed, told Will that he had a fairly high temperature and that he should rest. He offered Will a mat pass.

"What's that?" Will asked.

"You give this mat pass to Dick Mengel to sign and you'll be allowed to rest on a mat during the day," the doctor explained. The idea did not appeal at all to Will, who had seen how the duty managers roused the people on the mats just before lunchtime.

"No, thanks," he replied, "I think I'd rather tough it out on the outside." The doctor smiled. Will guessed that he knew about the noon "wake-up calls."

Will waited until he had been first to Waikiki and then back to the food court at the mall before he took any of the medicine. He hoped he would get some sort of effect out of it since he couldn't drink. Always some sacrifice, he thought.

He knew that he needed to re-type his resume, but knew of no place where he could use a typewriter. Hoping that John Marin might know of a place, Will approached the receptionist's window at the shelter as soon as he had finished lunch. He wanted to make an appointment to see Marin. Bertha was seated in her usual place, and she ignored him for several minutes. Finally he became impatient.

"Excuse me," he projected. She turned toward him, her eyes flaring with irritation.

"Excuse *me*. I'll be with you when I'm done with what I'm doing," came her icy response. After several more minutes during which she talked on the phone, smiling and laughing happily during the conversation, she turned and faced Will again, now with a cold expression.

"Yes?" she dripped.

"I'd like to make an appointment to see John Marin," he stated. She opened her ledger.

"Next Wednesday at two-thirty," she said flatly.

"That's the *earliest* you have?" asked Will, doubting her since he could see many blank lines in her ledger.

"That's the *only* time you can see him," came her angry reply. Will was incensed, but powerless. He shrugged.

"Okay," he said softly, then, "Thank you, *BERTHA*." He emphasized her name, hoping to antagonize her by the manner in which he said it. He had hoped for an earlier appointment, but with the next day being Thanksgiving, he guessed that a week from today wasn't so bad.

He had to get to the library to turn in his application, since it would also be closed for the next four days. He didn't want to carry it around in his satchel and risk having it get mangled. He knew that once he got the library card, which would be mailed to him, he would have yet another piece of tangible evidence that showed he belonged here.

Although the shelter had announced plans to have volunteers provide table service for the Thanksgiving dinner, Will quietly wished that it would just be served in the usual manner. He had tried to avoid thinking about Thanksgiving and the upcoming Christmas season. He had several prosperous years before the previous year, and the thought of having to endure a holiday season in a homeless shelter began to depress him. He made up his mind however, that he would do his best to grit his teeth and bear it. After all, right now that was all he *could* do. Thanksgiving morning came and Mama Kamaka was apparently not enthusiastic about working on a holiday. She strode around the main room while Will was shaving, yelling for everyone to clear the room for the sweepers. Will continued shaving, still feeling tired, and well under the weather from his illness.

"Jerry, get a clipboard!" Mama Kamaka ranted, calling to the other duty manager. "I want the names of everyone who isn't out of here in the next minute!" He saw Jerry come into the main room carrying a clipboard. Shaving done, Will switched the shaver off and took the top of it off so that he could blow the dust out of it. He saw that Jerry was looking around the room and writing on the clipboard. Will decided that he would not leave the room, standing instead and walking toward Jerry.

"T-Y-N-E," he spelled as Jerry looked up. "First name, Will, that's W-I-L-L. Jerry had a slightly befuddled look on his face.

"I know how to spell your name," he grinned. "Why are you telling me this?"

"I'm just tired of that *racist* woman always hounding me when I'm shaving," Will fumed. "Besides, I'm sick and I don't feel like moving around so damn much." Jerry laughed.

"Mama Kamaka?" he asked. "You mean Mama Kamaka? She's just trying to get some of these people out so that the sweepers can clean up. She's not trying to hassle anybody. I walk around with this clipboard half the time anyway, so she just wants to make people *think* that I'm taking names. You can sit in here. No problem." Will instantly regretted that he had vented his frustration on Jerry.

"I-I just don't want to get in any trouble for just trying to get myself ready for the day. It's hard enough, anyway, and I don't have any other place to stay, so I don't want to—." He stopped as he heard his voice begin to crack with emotion. Jerry's demeanor changed.

"Don't worry," he reassured Will. "We don't want to push *anybody* out of here unless we *really* don't have any other choice."

"Thanks, Jerry," Will said, exhaling. Even his throat felt better for a moment, and he returned to where he had been sitting.

After breakfast Will made his morning trek to the bathroom in Waikiki, feeling extremely tired. He wasn't sure which was worse: the illness or the effect of the medicine. He *had* slept better the previous night, though, and taking the medicine kept him from drinking, which he knew was for the best right now.

As Will wound his way down the Kuhio Avenue sidewalk, he saw the skinny woman in the brown shirt stationed just outside the breezeway that led inside the shopping center. She appeared to be asking only the male tourists for money; and as Will approached, she leaned toward him, then backed off suddenly. A glazed look accompanied by a half-smile came over her face as she took a step back.

"I remembered you today," she said to Will, seeming somewhat proud of herself.

"Hi! How are you?" he greeted her, slowing his pace as he walked past her and entered the breezeway.

"Okay," she answered, immediately turning her attention back to the business of soliciting money. Will continued on his way, but was somewhat relieved that the woman had remembered him. It indicated that at least she had *some* of her wits about her.

After the visit to the bathroom, Will spent several minutes waiting for a bus to take him to the mall, but saw none in sight. Finally one came, and as he boarded it, he realized that the buses were on a holiday schedule. It was Thanksgiving, something that had not occurred to him until just this minute. He grimaced, knowing that the mall would be closed too, and that he would have no place to sit and read the paper.

The park would be fine for the afternoon, but he knew that the sprinkler system would still be on there this early in the morning, and that there would not be so much as a dry square inch on which he could sit. He decided to get off the bus and catch another one back to the shelter, much as he hated to return there so early. Holidays, he groused to himself, were *great* for people who had homes and jobs.

The porch and the grass outside were still wet when Will got back to the shelter, and he went down the street to the concrete slab behind the bush. There was no grocery cart there today, and Will almost wished that it *had* been there. He had been intrigued by the little man's manner and his preposterous story.

As it grew closer to lunchtime, Will noticed that there was more traffic than usual around the shelter. He had read a notice on the bulletin board that indicated that there would be table service and a traditional Thanksgiving meal today, but he had given it little thought since. He guessed that the people arriving must be the volunteers who were to serve the meal.

At eleven-fifty he walked up the steps to the porch, through the front door, and into the main room. There was *no line*. There were rows of tables set up in the main room, all of them covered with either red-check or white plastic tablecloths. The plastic utensils were laid out on paper napkins at each place. One of the duty managers was standing by the door instructing people to sit wherever they wished. Still surprised by the difference in the procedure, Will took a seat at a table near the entrance.

Most of the volunteers who brought the plates to the tables appeared to be of high-school age. There were some older people too, and Will noticed that several people had brought cameras with them. It appeared to him that some of them were more interested in having their "charitable deeds" recorded on film than in actually performing the service. But the vast majority of the young people, tentative at first, became friendly once they saw the appreciation and gratitude in the faces of many of the people they were serving.

Will had to choke back tears a few times as he ate, thinking first about how good it was of the young people to spend part of their own holiday in such a way, then thinking about how his life had been humbled to the point that he found it necessary to accept such kindness from others.

With no place to go after lunch, Will first went out the side door and sat on the concrete area next to the parking lot. The sun soon edged the shade away, and he knew that for the next few hours there would be no part of the shelter's yard that would have any suitable shady area. He closed the flap on his satchel and walked around to sit down on the front porch. No one was there.

Sitting down, he squinted as he looked around—first toward the spacious, deserted parking lot in front of King's Discount Store, then to his left, down Hoka Street and toward the harbor. He heard the front door open behind him and didn't bother to turn around, since it was almost constantly in use. No one came down the steps, though, and he turned around to see that the dark-eyed woman was sitting down on the porch, a few feet away and to the rear of him. He wanted to speak to her, but was completely unsure of what her reaction would be. He had never been much of a smooth talker with women. Finally, he dared to speak.

"Th-that was a—ahh—a good lunch we had," he sputtered, using almost the same line that he had found so unoriginal when someone had said it to *him* earlier in the week. The dark-eyed woman looked up and studied him for a moment.

"Mmmm-hmmm," she grunted, quickly looking back down at her nylon bag, through which she was fumbling.

Not encouraged by her response, Will turned to face front again. Within another minute he heard the zipper closing on her bag, and she descended the porch steps, continuing on her way down Hoka Street and turning the corner, out of sight. So much for that, Will thought. He put his head down and closed his eyes.

"Will!"

Will looked up to see that Bill was walking toward him quickly, his eyes indicating that something was wrong.

"What's up?" he asked, as Bill stopped in front of the porch.

"I went inside Zippy's to use the bathroom," Bill panted, "And when I came back out, my bag was gone!"

"Just *where* did you put your bag?" Will asked drily, wondering why Bill would leave it *anywhere* unguarded to begin with.

"There was this planter across the street, and I put it between two plants, where nobody could see it. I just went inside long enough to take a piss, and when I came back it was gone." Will was thoroughly puzzled.

"But why did you leave it there in the first place? Why didn't you just take it into Zippy's with you?" he asked, trying to figure out what Bill had been thinking.

"Because I thought it would be safe there," Bill answered. "I didn't want to take it in Zippy's because I didn't want to look like one of the people from the Center for Social Aid."

"None of us can help that," Will countered. "Besides, they don't care. They must get a lot of business from us shelter people. Anyway, did you call the police?"

"No," said Bill. "It just happened. Just a few minutes ago."

"Well, then, why don't I help you take a look around?" Will offered. "Maybe someone went through it, took what they wanted, then threw the bag in a trash can somewhere." Bill agreed and Will shouldered his satchel to begin the walk toward the direction from which Bill had just come.

Will could not believe that Bill would be so careless with the only possessions that he had brought with him. He spent the next hour and a half helping Bill search through shrubbery and whatever trash cans they encountered in the area. Feeling he had done all that could be done, he suggested that they return to the shelter. Bill refused to call the police, however. Will guessed that Bill must have been just too embarrassed by his own carelessness, so Will did not press the matter further.

The little bit of excitement made the afternoon pass more quickly, and dinnertime seemed to come sooner than usual. The evening meal consisted of the same items, leftovers from the Thanksgiving lunch. Pleased to have better food than what was normally served, and with his appetite not altered by alcohol, Will ate hungrily.

The air seemed cooler than usual as dusk was coming earlier each day. Will sat down in the grass in front of the shelter after dinner, and noticed that it was much darker at six-thirty now than it had been less than two weeks earlier. He reminded himself that he should take his jacket out of the bag in which it was stored inside the cage. The last thing he wanted was for his cold to linger.

Just as he folded himself into a comfortable position, he felt raindrops on his bare arms.

"Noooo. Not now," he groaned aloud, not caring whether anyone heard. The rain came down more steadily, and it was a cold rain. Will wrapped his arms around himself and leaned over to shield his legs. Still the rain came.

"God damn you!" he cursed, looking skyward. "If you *do* exist, you're nothing but evil!" His words to a god of whose existence he was unsure seemed only to bring more rain. It was almost pouring now, and he was getting soaked, but had no place to go for shelter. The front porch was full, and the lanai was locked. He looked upward again, this time gritting his teeth in resigned defiance.

"Go ahead and rain, motherfucker," he said quietly, almost to himself. "If you haven't been able to break me so far, this shitty little rainstorm won't do it, either."

There was still at least another half hour to go before the duty managers would have the mats laid out and the main room ready. The rain continued to fall. Will's mind drifted back to the first Thanksgiving he had spent after moving to

New York, almost eleven years earlier. He had only had enough money to eat a modest Thanksgiving dinner in a coffee shop at that time, and had vowed that he would never be so "poverty-stricken" again. How he wished he was even *that* well off now!

"Happy Thanksgiving," he said to no one. "Happy fucking Thanksgiving."

Chapter 6

Spinning at the Bottom

They had given him *expectorant*! Will's abdomen and rib cage were sore from coughing so much, even though he had been taking double doses of the cough syrup he had gotten from the clinic. Now he had discovered that it was not cough *suppressant*, but instead something that was supposed to make him cough *more*.

As he sat outside the shelter reading the Sunday paper, he knew that he would have to visit the clinic again the next morning. He could tolerate the hearing impairment, which was now affecting both ears, and the runny nose. The combined effect of the Tylenol and decongestant was even *almost* an acceptable temporary substitute for drinking. But the constant coughing and the sore ribs were just too much for him. Not only had he slept poorly the night before, his coughing had provoked the ire of several of the other shelter guests, who had the misfortune of choosing a mat near the one Will had occupied. One of them had even threatened to smother him if he ever fell asleep. Even though he had taken the threat only half-seriously, he had lain awake the remainder of the night.

Monday morning came, and Will squeezed himself into the clinic's tiny waiting room. It wasn't packed with people as it had been before, but it was still busy. He had to wait, something he didn't mind because it gave him a chance to get an occasional glance at Amy. Her smile had cheered him immensely at the time of his last visit, and he was looking forward to having a moment of her attention again today.

When he was finally called, it was not by Amy. A somewhat harried-looking young man beckoned him toward one of the treatment rooms and, after hearing Will's complaint, gave him a different type of cough syrup and hurried him back out into the waiting room. Will left without having a chance to speak to Amy. As he trudged down Malualua Road toward the bus stop, he felt slightly angry and very dejected at having been denied such a simple pleasure that would have made a monotonous day more bearable.

Sipping on an unaltered Diet Pepsi at the mall later in the morning, Will had just finished reading the "help wanted" ads in the Sunday paper when an ad caught his eye. "Need $20 fast?" the ad asked. "Donate plasma—it's simple, easy, and safe." The ad listed a number to call.

Will knew that his money would run out fairly quickly once he stopped taking the cold medicine and started drinking again. Since he had donated both whole blood and platelets before, he knew that he could tolerate the procedure, even if he happened to be hung over at the time of the donation. And he could certainly use twenty dollars. He called the number and listened to the recorded message.

Since the noticeable symptoms of his cold, the coughing and sniffling, were getting better, he decided that it would be well worth the effort for him to go through the two-hour procedure later in the week. The thought of having even a tiny bit of money to supplement his dwindling wallet contents served to neutralize the disappointment he had suffered at the clinic earlier and, still slowed a bit by the cold medicine, he plodded toward the bus stop to return to the shelter for lunch.

The crowd of diners at the shelter was half its usual size and as Will sat on the floor with Johnnie and Gary, he wondered aloud why there was such a noticeable difference. Johnnie was quick to offer an explanation.

"First of the month," he began. "All the SSI people get their checks today, so they have money. You won't see them around for a few days. Some of them get rooms to stay in until their money runs out. Then they come back here."

"You mean the welfare pe—"

"No, these are SSI. Welfare people won't get their checks until Thursday or Friday," Johnnie interjected, without waiting to hear what Will's question was. "It'll be quieter than usual around here probably for another week. Some of these people blow their whole check in a couple of days. You know, crack, stuff like that. Then they come back to wait another month for another check so they can go back out and do the same thing again. Most people try to stretch it out some." Will's interest was captured.

"Welfare, SSI, what's the difference?" he asked.

"Welfare, anybody can get. You just got to be a resident here. With SSI, you have to be crazy or crippled. They have to figure that you aren't able to work before they'll give you SSI. Almost everybody here gets one or the other." He paused, then wrinkled his brow, "You mean you haven't applied yet?"

"Of course not," Will answered firmly. "I would *never* take welfare as long as I'm able to work. I just haven't been able to find a job yet. Welfare, food stamps, all that stuff—it's out of the question. Those things are for people who are *really* bad off."

"Can't be much worse off than living in a homeless shelter," Johnnie said, his voice trailing off as he brushed the crumbs off his lap in preparation for standing up. Will knew that he had exhausted Johnnie's attention span for this meal. He bade Johnnie and Gary a good afternoon and went on his way.

That night, just after Will finished dinner and went out to sit in front of the building, it began raining again. Will thought he was ready for it this time. He walked around the building to the parking lot and exited it through the Malualua Road driveway. Just a short distance down the street was a city-owned building, and it had a small, covered front porch. Will saw that it was deserted and that it was only lit by the streetlight and light from other buildings. He sat down on the top step and let out a self-satisfied sigh, glad that he was alone and out of the rain. There was not even a trace of cigarette smoke in the air.

He had been sitting for less than ten minutes when he heard the sound of the motor that powered the electric gate to the right of the porch. As the motor switched off, a mini-van eased through the gate, and Will looked straight ahead, ignoring it. He heard the hum of an electric window.

"You can't sit there," he heard a voice from the van announce. "It's off-limits to shelter people." Will was taken aback. Was it that obvious that he was a "shelter person?"

"But it's raining," he protested. "And I've got a cold."

"I don't care," the narrow-faced, bearded man said. "I'll be back here in ten minutes, and if you're not off the steps, there'll be a police officer right behind me. He'll arrest you for trespassing."

"Motherfucker," Will muttered to himself, careful that he was not loud enough to be heard by the van driver. Now he knew why no one else was sitting on the porch. He lifted his satchel and walked out into the pouring rain.

He was thoroughly wet by the time he got inside to claim a mat, and so were most of the other people. After he got his bag from the cage, he removed a towel, a shirt, and shorts from the bag. Just as he was about to change, he noticed for the first time that there were a few women "visiting" in the men's sleeping area. It occurred to him that not only was this allowed, but one of the duty managers was also a woman.

The only place he could change clothes was the bathroom. Will knew that it would be full of people. He also knew that by this time of day the bathroom would be so filthy that it would be impossible for him to change without some part of his clothing getting soiled, possibly even stained or smeared with feces or urine. Even though both fans in the room were going full speed, Will decided to dry himself the best he could and keep his wet clothes on. He prepared his mat for the night, returned his bag to the cage, and went outside to sit on the smoky, crowded front porch. The rain had stopped, and Bill was there.

"Well, tonight's the night," Bill said, grinning.

"What do you mean?" Will asked.

"My ticket back is for 11:05 tonight, and I have to decide if I want to go or not." Will could not believe his ears—it was already almost eight-thirty. Bill had mentioned the ticket before, but not the date. And he had not yet made up his mind whether he would stay—with nothing more than the clothes on his back—or return to Maryland and the unhappy, futureless life he had described to Will.

"So what're you going to do? What *will* you do?" Will asked, mimicking an old television commercial.

"I haven't decided yet," Bill said, his expression becoming more serious. "If my bag hadn't been stolen, I wouldn't even be thinking about going back. But I don't even have a razor to shave with, or a change of underwear now."

"Well, if you wanted to stay you could probably scare up some money from somewhere to replace whatever it was you had in that bag," Will offered, trying to present a balanced perspective of the matter. "But if you think it would be better to go back, you might be able to help yourself better if you're closer to your family and friends." Bill chuckled.

"I think they've helped me about all they're going to," he said, shaking his head. "What concerns me most about that bag is that my birth certificate and some other important papers were in it. I don't really want to go all they way back to Maryland. I'm already here and this is where I want to be, but I'll *have* to get those papers replaced eventually, and I've got the means to go back and do it right now. But I don't even want to get on a plane dressed like this." Will had noticed that he was wearing jeans and a white undershirt.

"Well, whatever you decide," Will said, looking at his watch, "you're getting down to the last minute if it has anything to do with the airport."

"I guess I'll go ahead and go out there," Bill said speculatively. "If I decide to go, I'll be there for the flight, and if I decide not to, then I'll just stay out there and sleep on the floor." He dangled his legs over the edge of the porch, about to stand.

"Whatever you do, good luck," Will wished him, extending his right hand. Bill reciprocated.

"Yeah, and you just keep all these pretty island women in line," he said, grinning again. "Because even if I go home tonight, I'll be back soon." He started walking toward Hoka Street.

The next morning, a dreary, drizzly one, Will took the last of his cold medicine. By afternoon he would be able to drink again. The thought of going to the libation station for another half-gallon made Will think of his dwindling money supply. He had read on the bulletin board that a local contractor sometimes hired people from the shelter to clear land at construction sites, and it had stuck in his memory. Maybe now would be a good time to investigate that possibility. Even though he still could not hear very well, his cold was better, and he hadn't yet started drinking again.

He asked Jerry about the notice on the bulletin board. Jerry looked around the main room, where the morning diners were still working on breakfast.

"See that guy over there?" Jerry said to Will, pointing to a man with a three-day stubble and a headful of reddish-blond steel wool. Will nodded. "He's the person who's in charge of getting together a crew of people from here every morning. Talk to him."

Will thanked Jerry and approached the thirtyish-looking man.

"Excuse me. Jerry tells me that you're the person to talk to about the land-clearing job posted on the bulletin board," he half-asked.

"Yeah," the man acknowledged. "I already got a full crew today, though, if it ever stops raining. Why? You know somebody looking for work?"

"Me!" Will answered, wondering why the man would ask such a question.

"You sure you can handle it?" the man asked. "It's pretty heavy-duty, out there in the sun all day." Will bristled, even though he knew he was way out of shape.

"Sure," he answered confidently. "I grew up working in tobacco fields. A little yard work'll be a piece of cake." The younger man's expression turned into a skeptical grin.

"See me tonight and I'll let you know if I need anybody for tomorrow. The pay is eight bucks an hour, cash at the end of the day. My name is Matt Denzer."

"Will. Will Tyne," he responded. "You'll be around at dinnertime?" Matt nodded. "I'll track you down then," Will assured him.

That evening at dinnertime Will looked around for Matt, but did not spot him anywhere. Will had not bought gin earlier in the day, not wanting to be unnecessarily slow if he should get the chance to work the next day. Now he was beginning to regret his temperance.

After Will had his mat ready for bed, and before he had thought whether he wanted to go outside until bedtime, a duty manager announced that the mailroom was open. A line quickly formed, the forty or so people standing in single file since the aisle space around the mats was so narrow.

Will had sent out postcards to a few of his old friends after he had been evicted from the Regal Arbor. He had not mentioned his unfortunate circumstances, but had just put a brief greeting along with his new address, that of the Center for Social Aid. Having nothing better to do and particularly glad to have an excuse for staying indoors and away from the cigarette smoke, Will decided to go through the mail line.

After at least half an hour, he got close enough to be able to see the inside of the mailroom. One of the duty managers sat behind a small table, on which were two boxes. One box contained regular mail, the other contained government checks. Each person who had mail was required to present a photo I.D. before being given his mail, and had to sign a sheet after being given the mail. Finally, it was Will's turn. He handed the duty manager the paper license he had been given at the driver's license office, fearful that it would not be accepted because it did not have his photo on it. The duty manager did not question him.

"Tyne. Hmmm. Tyne, Tyne—ahhh. The duty manager pulled an envelope out of the box. Will had mail! His hand trembled with excitement as he signed the sheet, and he turned to walk away with his treasure, wondering for an instant who had written to him. He looked at the front of the envelope for the first time and was dismayed and puzzled to recognize his own handwriting. Then it hit him. This was one of the resumes he had sent off the previous week. It was returned marked "addressee not known." He walked outside and sat down, completely deflated.

Now he *really* wished he had bought a half-gallon earlier in the day. He looked around again for Matt and still could not see him. His second order of business for tomorrow, he decided, would be a trip to the libation station.

As soon as he was finished with breakfast the next morning, his thirty-eighth birthday, he was on his way to his first—the plasma donor facility. He had to wait a long time for the bus in the morning sun, and had a long walk to the facility after the thirty-minute ride. He spent another hour sitting in the sun, waiting for the donor center to open. His face was red and he was sweating when he walked in. He filled out the forms, took them to the desk, and sat down to wait to be called, thankful that the office had a strong air conditioner.

Soon, a small woman with gray-blond hair called his name. He rose from his chair and she led him to a small room which contained only two chairs, a flimsy table, and a blood pressure gauge. The sour-faced, unhealthy-looking woman first asked him numerous questions about his past health. He mentioned nothing about his alcohol consumption, and felt very proud that he could truthfully deny ever having used any illegal drugs.

The woman encased Will's arm in the blood pressure cuff and began pumping the rubber bulb at the other end. As soon as she stopped pumping, she squinted—first at the gauge, then at Will.

"It's kind of high," she said, "but I think we can still take you. Do you have anything on you that proves your address?" Will had only the paper driver's license, and he took that out.

"175 Hoka Street?" she asked, peering up at him over her glasses. "That's the Center for Social Aid, isn't it?"

"Yes. I—uhh—I'm just staying there until my new apartment is finished being painted next week," Will lied.

"As a rule, we don't accept donors from the Center of Social Aid. We used to, but we found that a high percentage of the donations were infected with hepatitis and other things." Will was stung. He had wasted over an hour and a half, part of which was spent in the hot sun, all of which was for nothing! Now this witch had inferred that he might have tainted blood!

He was beginning to fume.

"If you don't take people from the Center for Social Aid," he began, "then *why in hell* don't you put that in your advertising? Besides, I was an eighteen-time platelet donor, and I don't want to hear your *bullshit* insults about people down on their luck having bad blood. *You witch-looking hag!*" He stormed out of the facility, and he immediately knew that it had been wrong of him to lose his temper. He felt contrite, but this was not the first time that his desperate circumstances had caused him to act somewhat out of character. It would not be the last.

Will got back to the shelter well before noon, but too late to make a trip to the libation station before lunchtime. As he walked through the parking lot he heard a voice behind him.

"Hey, man! How you doing?" It was Gary.

"A little hot," he answered. "Mostly okay, though." Will explained what he had just been through at the plasma donor center.

"Only the people from here who can give a relative's address get through at that place," Gary commiserated. The sad part is that most of them take drugs. People like you and me—drink a little bit, you know—we go in straight and they won't take us. Me, I don't even drink lately. I been going to AA. I'm keeping the straight and narrow."

"Oh, well," Will started with a laugh. "I'm not an alcoholic, anyway. I'm an alcohol-IST!"

"You find work yet?" asked Gary.

"Nahhh. I sent out a few resumes. I guess nobody out there has any idea of what they're passing up," Will said jokingly.

"Probably not," Gary responded, completely serious. "Man, of all the people in here, I thought you would have been just about ready to get out by now." Will's shoulders drooped, and he gritted his teeth. Even in the shelter, he could not escape the expectations of others.

As soon as lunch was over, Will went to the shopping mall to get gin and bottled soda. He did not want to go to the beach park across the street from the mall. Gary's observation had put him in a misanthropic mood, and he wanted to go someplace where there would be no one from the center to remind him of how he didn't seem to live up to his potential. It was his birthday, after all, and he *deserved* to be able to get drunk in peaceful surroundings. One place he hoped he would be able to do that was the small park where he had spent his first homeless night.

The bus took him far enough so that he only had to walk a few hundred yards to the park, which he did with less than triumphant feelings. He had first enjoyed the park when he had been on vacation here. He had then spent the most unsettling, frightening night of his life here. Now he would be spending part of his birthday here, drinking. Not as good as the former, not as bad as the latter, he mused.

He sat down in a breezy, shady part of the park, away from the seawall. Soon he was on his way into a state of mind which the "witch-looking hag" would have been incapable of disrupting.

Will began to think of his last days in New York when, knowing he would be moving soon, he did little more than live to drink. He thought of his miserable days at the Regal Arbor, when he had feared almost from the start that he would end up out in the street—and had been powerless to change the self-fulfilling prophecy.

He had taken some comfort in the fact that he could now relax occasionally. Not having to worry about rent or food had freed up a significant part of his mind. This afternoon's booze session, he told himself, would not have been at all enjoyable if he was still struggling to hold onto his room at the Regal Arbor. But now he could enjoy himself in a relatively peaceful state of mind.

True, he was tethered to the schedule of the shelter—if

he wanted food and a place to sleep. It was also true that his only block of time that was really *free* was from seven-thirty in the morning until about five-thirty in the afternoon. But, aside from the menagerie of people, the shuffling around, and the waiting, Will had time to do whatever he wished.

As he packed his bag to walk back to the bus stop, Will stumbled to his feet. He almost fell over, catching himself clumsily at the last second by grabbing a tree branch. His pace was more than slow and labored this afternoon—it was wobbly. In his extremely detached state of solitude, he had poured down an unusually large amount of gin.

An hour and fifteen minutes later, he got off the bus outside King's Discount Store. Instead of walking to the front of the shelter, where he knew he would be in the sun, he sat down on the foot-high concrete wall in front of King's, which was in the shade. He knew that the duty managers would make him get up if they saw him, part of the shelter's agreement with King's, but he was too looped to care.

Will ate his food clumsily at dinnertime. He spilled milk on the floor and smeared fried chicken crumbs and salad oil on his shirt. When he moved to get up after he had finished eating, he lurched forward and crashed shoulder-first into the chain-link gate that secured the area in which the mats were stored. Because he was now like many of the others in the shelter, and because of the general commotion, no one noticed his near-mishap.

Going out the door, he could not find a duty manager handing out numbered slips. Then he remembered that he had seen a notice on the bulletin board about there being a house meeting tonight. The food helped him to begin to gather his wits about him, and he went outside to sit until seven o'clock, when the meeting was scheduled to begin.

Will got inside quickly enough to get a chair this time, and as the meeting began, he noticed that the seats at the table at the front of the room were filled only by shelter employees.

The shelter's guest council members were in the audience this time. He saw Dick Mengel enter the room, then two of the women who served as duty managers during breakfast each morning. The graduate student who had been at the previous meeting was missing from this one, but the other woman—the pretty one—again took a chair to the left of Mengel.

This meeting, Mengel announced, would be for the purpose of the guests airing their gripes to the shelter management. Almost immediately, one of the guests stood and began complaining loudly about the quality of the food. Will could hardly believe his ears. Three meals a day for free, and *this* person was complaining! Sure, thought Will, it wasn't the greatest. But it *was* food!

Mengel's explanation about the food, delivered in a monotonous, sing-songy manner, caused Will's attention to drift. It didn't return to the meeting until minutes later, when he heard the pretty, dark-haired woman speaking. Her voice was surprisingly low-pitched for someone so petite. She spoke softly and her diction was perfect. For the first time Will noticed that she had a kindhearted disposition, and that she listened with the same concern with which she spoke. For the remainder of the meeting, he looked only at her, completely captivated by a woman about whom he knew nothing. He could only guess that she must be some part of the shelter management team, not a graduate student as he had assumed at the last meeting.

Just before the meeting concluded, Mengel announced that tickets for the shelter's Christmas party would be distributed on Sunday morning just after breakfast. The party would be held at a local restaurant which was donating the space, and would be sponsored by the police department. There would be no alcohol served, Mengel added, but there would be two buffet tables. The homeless crowd, having rumbled with discontent throughout the meeting so far, let out a spontaneous cheer. Will felt a sense of camaraderie with the crowd.

As the meeting concluded and the crowd began to file out the back door, Will wondered if any of the shelter employees would be at the Christmas party—especially the pretty one. His foggy mind turned to daydreaming about what the party might be like. He wished that *he* would be allowed to drink, even though he was glad that it would be an alcohol-free event.

He realized that in order to get decent clothes for the party, he would have to make another trip to the Regal Arbor to rummage through his large suitcase. But the party would be the only social occasion he would attend for a long time, he guessed. As the thick line began to form next to the lanai, and the cigarette smoke began to cloud the air in the small, windless area, Will began to forget about the party. He was scanning the group of men to see if he could find Matt. Will had gotten fairly crocked earlier in the day, but he had stopped drinking early enough that he reasoned that he would be okay if Matt wanted him to work the next day.

He did not see Matt, and it occurred to him that he had not seen Bill, either. He hadn't thought about it until this moment, because he usually didn't see Bill during the daytime, anyway. But Bill had almost always shown up at the shelter by dinnertime since he had been here. Will guessed that Bill must have decided to go back to Maryland. Even though he reasoned that he probably would have done the same thing, he felt a tinge of sadness. He had enjoyed conversing with Bill.

Will got his mat ready for the night and went outside to sit on the front porch. The night was clear for once, and the porch had just a few occupants, only one of whom was smoking. As soon as he was seated relatively comfortably, he noticed a shock of reddish hair in the middle of the group of men across the street. It was Matt Denzer.

Will kept his seat. He wanted to have the chance to work the next day, but he knew that it would not be a good idea to interrupt Matt while he was in the middle of the group. The only type of homeless person who would do that would be one who had a bone to pick with the one in the group.

Soon Matt began walking away from the group, shaking a few hands as he left. He crossed to the shelter side of Hoka Street and approached the porch.

"Hey, Matt," Will called to him. Matt spied him and a serious look crossed his face.

"Hey, how's it?" he asked.

"Okay," Will answered. "Need anybody for tomorrow? I'm ready to work." Matt eyed him and softened his expression.

"Oh, man," he began, his face changing to a pained expression. "I talked to my boss today and he said they won't be needing any more clearing done until next week. He said there was something about a contract falling through, and he doesn't want to clear the land until he knows who *owns* it." Noticing the disappointment in Will's face, he added, "Maybe next week. I should know something by Sunday." Will quickly shifted gears.

"Sunday. The day of the Christmas party. I wonder how that is?"

"I wasn't here last year this time, so I don't know," Matt responded. "I *was* here year before last, and they didn't even *have* a party, so this one's got to be better than nothing." Will noticed that Matt had just nodded at someone to his left.

"Well, I guess we'll find out," Will added, his interest starting to wane.

"Hey, how's it?" he heard Matt say. A short, neatly dressed, bespectacled man came toward them. "You guys know each other?" Matt asked. Will and the other man didn't.

"This is Frankie," he said to Will, then to Frankie, "This is—ummm, I'm sorry, I forgot your name."

"Will."

"Oh, yeah. Will. It was right on the tip of my tongue. I just couldn't get it out," he laughed.

"Nice to meet you," Frankie said. There was something

familiar-sounding about his voice. Matt and Frankie stood talking for a moment as Will looked away.

"I gotta run. See you guys a little bit later," Matt said, turning toward the shelter's parking lot. It occurred to Will what the familiar aspect in Frankie's voice was.

"Are you from somewhere in New York?" he asked, noticing that the middle-aged man was so neatly dressed and well-groomed that Will wondered if he was homeless.

"Port Jefferson," Frankie answered quickly. "Why? You know somebody from the area?"

"I lived in New York for ten years before I came here," Will explained, knowing that his southern accent would never advertise that fact.

"Really? What part?" Frankie's interest had been captured.

"Manhattan," Will declared. "Fifty-seventh Street." Will added the last part to make sure that his present circumstances didn't lead Frankie to assume that he had come from the Lower East Side.

"Yeah? I used to work at Forty-fourth and Madison. Port Jefferson's out on the island, though."

"Yeah, I went out in that direction a few times on the Long Island Railroad," Will recalled. "It's a lot different than the city.

Frankie, Will discovered, had been a well-to-do insurance executive who had invested his savings in an attempt to start his own business. It had not been successful, and he had lost his home, wife, and children.

"You mean your wife took the kids and bailed out on you just because your business failed?" he asked, thinking that there *must* be more to the story.

"Not *just* because the business failed," Frankie admitted, looking straight at Will. "When it started to go under, I used up all of my available credit."

"To keep the business afloat?" Will asked. Frankie

shook his head solemnly.

Will looked puzzled. Frankie sniffed in an exaggerated manner.

"Ohhhh!" Will understood. Every man has his own weakness, he thought to himself. "So what brought you out here?"

"I went to Vegas to get away from the bill collectors and try to make a new start and ended up doing time for possession. Six months—I got off light because it was the first time I'd been in that kind of a scrape. Then I met a woman from North Carolina—"

"North Carolina! That's where *I* grew up," Will interjected, quickly adding, "Sorry."

"No problem. Anyway, I married the woman and moved to her farm in North Carolina. I really only married her to get a free ride for a while, and it worked out great until some of her friends started prodding her to get a background check done on me. So she hired some P. I., and he dug up a lot of crap."

"And here you are."

"No, that's not it," Frankie continued. "I got a job with a cruise line and that's what eventually brought me here—to work on one of the inter-island cruise ships. By that time I was done with the coke, and I blew the whistle on some people who were involved with it on the ship. But the person I told was mixed up in it himself, and I got fired."

"And that's what landed you here? Not being able to find a job?" Will thought he had the story this time.

"No, not quite," Frankie grinned, then chuckled. "I spent six months in Japan studying religion, *then* I ended up here. I'll spare you the details of that part of it, though."

Will decided not to press him, guessing that the part about the coke, the marriage, and the cruise ship *must* be the more interesting part of the story.

As they got up to go inside the building, Will noticed

that Frankie, born Francis Cabrino, grimaced as he bent over to pick up his backpack. He also walked with a slight limp, both for which he was quick to offer an explanation.

"I got a job a couple of weeks ago and they told me beforehand that I would have to be able to lift and carry up to twenty-five pounds at a time, a few times a day. But I bent over to pick up a box the first morning I was there, and first my back went out, then I tripped and hit my knee hard on the floor. It turned out that the box weighed closer to *forty*-five pounds, so I put in for workman's comp and I can't work now."

"That's too bad," Will commiserated.

"Not really," Frankie disagreed. "The lawyer says I should get a good settlement out of it since the box was over the weight that's listed on their job description. I could even get enough out of this to get back to Vegas and start up a P. I. business."

"Private investigator?" Will queried, amazed at the diversity of Frankie's interests.

"Yeah, I'll tell you about that one another time," he said, shuffling down the narrow aisle toward his mat.

Will did not know how much of Frankie's story to believe. He reasoned that since it did him no harm to believe all of it and no good to doubt any of it, he would believe it unless Frankie gave him cause to think otherwise. At any rate, he thought, Frankie had been entertaining. Completely distracted from his concerns for a short while, Will fell asleep quickly that night.

Will spent the next morning at the mall and the afternoon at the beach park. He was drinking, but making sure that he drank slowly enough that he would not wobble or lurch the way he had the previous day. He didn't want anyone at the shelter to see him drunk. If someone did, he might be taken for an easy mark and be forced to defend himself. He didn't want to be put in that position, since the duty managers didn't care whose fault it was whenever a fight or conflict broke out. Both or all participants were regarded as being at fault and they were treated accordingly.

That evening at mail call just after eight o'clock, the line was fairly short and Will decided again to see if anyone had written to him. Robert, the most conscientious duty manager to WIll's observation, was running the mail room and the line moved quickly. He gave his name and presented his paper license and Robert thumbed through the box of envelopes, finding two for Will. Remembering what had happened last time, Will dared not get excited.

The first envelope he looked at was from the motor vehicles department. The driver's license! he thought. He tore it open, saw the photo of himself for the first time, and was mortified. His hair was messy, his face was crimson, and around his eyes, the part shielded by his sunglasses was almost white. He looked like an aberration of a human. Nobody will ever believe that this is me, he groaned to himself. But he sadly realized that was what he looked like now.

The other envelope, brightly colored, appeared to be a greeting card. He was ready to tear it open when he noticed the handwriting on the envelope. It was from his parents. Even though he had sent them his address both times it had changed since he left New York, he had not really expected to hear from them. They had been adamantly against his moving to Hawaii, lamenting that it was so far that they feared they might die before they ever saw him again. He had dismissed their histrionics as a grandstand play to get him to go back to North Carolina, and they had not spoken or written to him since. They had no way of knowing that he was living in a shelter for the homeless, since the shelter's address was a post office box number.

He took a small utility knife out of his satchel and carefully opened the envelope. Inside was a Christmas card, and inside the card was a postal money order with a note that read: "Had no idea what you might need or like. Decided to let you pick something out for yourself. Hope this helps. Love, Mom and Dad."

Damn right, it'll help, he thought. The money order would be enough for him to buy a few necessities and to stay "afloat" in gin for a while. He tucked envelope, card, and money order carefully into the folio inside his satchel. He had been dreading the Christmas season from the moment the shelter had put up a decorated tree a few days earlier, but the money he had received would certainly go a long way toward helping it become more bearable.

The rest of the week passed quickly, with Will numbing the mounting holiday atmosphere with measured quantities of gin. His determination not to overstep his tolerance hampered what little pleasure he got out of drinking, but he had learned the habits of those with whom he shared a residence well enough to know that they would be quick to capitalize on any infirmity he might exhibit, particularly if that infirmity happened to be drunkenness.

Sunday came—the day of the party. Even though it was still over a week before Christmas, the Sunday morning diners all seemed to be on their best behavior, knowing that tickets were about to be dispensed.

The clock moved closer to seven-thirty, and Will noticed several people he had never seen before mingling among the diners. Mengel had announced at the last house meeting that the number of tickets would be limited and Will was ready to pounce, determined that he would not be shut out by outsiders.

Finally, the bellow of Mama Kamaka came over the P.A. system: "If you want a ticket for the Christmas party today, line up, *single file*, by the office window—no cuts. Anyone caught cutting in line will *not* be given a ticket."

Will assumed that could be translated to mean "any Caucasian caught cutting in line," since he had heard white people other than himself complaining that she disliked the *haoles*, a word for white people which Will found even more distasteful than *cracker*. He had even heard some of the locals laughing about how they could get away with anything as long as Mama Kamaka was on duty.

He found himself in the middle of the line, and it moved with merciful quickness. He soon had a ticket, and he moved toward the exit. The notice on the bulletin board had indicated that the party was to be from one o'clock until four o'clock. That would give Will plenty of time to go to the Regal Arbor to get clothes. He would be able to change in the bathroom at the small shopping center in Waikiki.

As there was little traffic, the bus got him to Waikiki in less time than usual. He walked into the lobby of the Regal Arbor and looked in the corner behind the desk. His bags were not there. He went to the desk clerk, the same one who *always* seemed to be there whenever Will was there. The clerk explained that the bags, for security reasons, had been moved to a vacant room on the fourth floor. Will could have access to them, but he would have to wait until there was a maintenance man available to let him into the room.

Slightly peeved, but careful not to show it since the hotel was doing him a favor by allowing him to keep his bags there, Will sat down in the lobby. It was a full twenty minutes before the one maintenance man on duty had time to take Will to the room. The two remaining bags there had a thin coat of dust on them, and Will sorted through the larger one, finding a pair of trousers, a shirt, and a jacket he thought would be suitable for the party. He thanked the man, and felt only a slight tinge of regret that he could not tip him. Will *had* cashed the money order, but his money was earmarked for things he deemed more necessary than tips to employees in a place from which he had been forced to leave.

For once, the floor of the bathroom at the little shopping center was completely dry, and the bathroom was deserted. It took Will only a few seconds to climb into the first pair of long trousers he had worn in two months. His cotton shirt and trousers were wrinkled, but he guessed that the humidity caused by his proximity to the ocean would soften the wrinkles.

The three meals a day he had been eating lately had slightly increased his girth and the trousers were a tight fit. Otherwise, he felt good to be wearing something other than the sloppy-looking knit clothes he usually wore. Even his face, devastated by a sunburn just a month earlier, now looked presentable.

Will first went to the food court at the mall since he still had an hour to while away before the party started. He wished that he could have a drink beforehand, but he was afraid that if someone at the door detected alcohol on his breath, he would not be admitted. He knew that they had to be more careful than at the shelter, since the restaurant would be open for regular business later in the day.

Not wanting to be early, Will waited until a quarter to one before leaving the mall. The restaurant at which the party was to be held was about a half-hour stroll away. To his astonishment, when he arrived shortly after one, there was still a long line in front of the restaurant. He groaned, but took a place in line.

When he finally walked inside, he was immediately accosted by a shelter volunteer who told him that he *had* to check his bag. Surrendering it without receiving a claim check put him ill at ease, and he almost wished the party was over already. The lines were already long leading to each of the buffet tables, and Will took a corner stool at the bar, slightly above the other levels of the restaurant floor.

"Get you something to drink, sir?" Will jerked his head around, startled by the crisp, friendly voice. He was completely unaccustomed to being addressed with such politeness. If the bartender had any qualms about working *this* crowd, he didn't let it show.

"Uhhh—Diet Pepsi," Will managed to get out. The sound system had begun to play soft rock music at a somewhat loud but not overbearing volume level. Will watched as some of his fellow guests began to fill the dance floor.

He noticed that none of the habitually dirty people had come to the party. Those people who had seemed to have, like Will, put on their better clothing. The homeless crowd even seemed to have brought their manners along—manners which Will had never seen some of them exhibit before. The people seemed to be rising above the usual "doom and gloom" atmosphere that normally pervaded the shelter crowd.

Even Mama Kamaka was out on the dance floor, dancing—and laughing! Will noticed that there were few shelter employees at the party. Just as he was grousing that he would probably not see Amy there, he caught sight of her blond hair on the dance floor. Maybe he would get a chance to speak to her later, but he didn't want to lose his barstool perch and its good view so soon.

The more the others seemed to loosen up, the more introverted Will felt. No one had spoken to him, and none of the people he knew—Johnnie, Gary, Frankie, Matt—were there. Finally he *had* to give up his barstool—to go to the bathroom. On his way back through the crowd, he saw Amy a few yards away. He wanted to go speak to her, but he wasn't even sure she would remember him. Anyway, she was a nurse and who was he? Just a homeless bum. He saw that the barstool on which he had been sitting was still open, and he threaded his way back through the crowd to sit down.

Scanning the crowd again, he looked to see if the shelter employee who had been at the house meeting—the pretty, dark- haired woman—was there,the "administrator lady," as he had heard Matt refer to her. He did not see her.

It was only three-thirty, but Will decided it was time for a drink. He went to the bag check area where his satchel had been tossed into a corner, asked the attendant for it, and left the party. He still had time to get to the libation station and pick up a bottle of gin and a soda.

As he sat down at the beach park across from the mall, he wondered how anyone could go to such a party and then leave to return to the bleak world of the shelter. It was one thing to exit the shelter in the hope of finding something better, he thought; but it was difficult to be reminded of the type of environment that was commonplace to ordinary people, and then go back to the environment of the "hard to love."

He had wanted so much to say something to Amy, but he had been excruciatingly aware of the disparity between their life circumstances. He knew that he could not even *hope* to be treated as a peer by her. He wondered how he would *ever* find his way back up in the world as long as he retained the posture of a homeless, nearly hopeless man.

Will knew that he would miss dinner at the shelter, but it did not matter to him. He had eaten enough at the party to last him until morning. Any more food in his system would only cause the alcohol to enter his system more slowly, and he wanted it to work efficiently right now.

He decided he would take his chances about the numbers, too. He figured that he would probably get a mat *somewhere* as long as he was back at the shelter by seven-thirty, and he didn't feel like going through the usual hurry-up-and-wait process with the numbers on this night. The breeze at the beach park felt good, and he wanted to enjoy the solitude for just a little while longer.

It was raining steadily by the time Will shuffled into the parking lot of the shelter just after seven-thirty. He wondered why there was no crowd by the side door, waiting to get in. He saw that there was a group of people standing next to the lanai, inside the chain-link gate. As he got closer to the building, he heard the sounds of "It Came Upon a Midnight Clear," accompanied by guitars.

There was a musical group, complete with amplifiers

and microphones, singing carols on the lanai. What a nice idea, Will groused sarcastically. *They* were on the lanai, under a roof, out of the rain. Here he was, along with most of the other shelter residents, standing out in the rain, not allowed to go inside to claim a mat at the usual time *because of the presence of the musical group.*

Will and the others were finally allowed inside just before nine o'clock, well over an hour later than usual. He sat waterlogged on his mat and wondered just how much more irony he could take.

The next Saturday was Christmas Day. Will welcomed it with a sense of relief, knowing that it was the last day of a season he had not only dreaded, but also had endured with a great amount of humiliation. There had been many years when he had been able to buy Christmas presents without worrying about the expense, a memory which he had tried to drink away. But the contrast had still been almost unbearable.

After he finished showering that morning, he stepped out of the stall to finish drying off, trying to squirm his way into a corner of the crowded bathroom where no one could touch him. He propped his foot on the small wooden bench and was looking through his bag for his underwear when someone bumped his shoulder.

"You fucking Americans think you own this place!" a tiny Hispanic man began shouting at him. "Especially you white ones! You are nothing but stupid scum! Get out of my way!" Will could not see how he was in the man's way.

"What's *your* problem?" he asked the young man, who was barely five feet tall.

"Shut up! *Shut up!*" the little man screamed. "I keek your ass!" The man glowered at Will and drew back his fist, poised to strike. Will realized that the man must have been drinking heavily during the night, and his shock turned quickly to amusement. He projected his left cheek in the direction of the man and pointed to it with his right hand.

"Right here," Will said, laughing. "Here it is if you want to take a swing at it."

The man turned red and the veins on either side of his neck stood out. "You worthless American! I keel you. You come outside, I *keel* you!" He picked up his bag and stormed out of the bathroom. Will looked around. It appeared that no one had even noticed the commotion.

Will was glad that the stores in Waikiki were open. The perpetual traffic of the tourists, along with the warm, sunny weather at the beach made the day seem more like any other day—certainly not Christmas. By eleven that morning Will, who had abandoned measuring his gin, was thoroughly "buzzed." He decided not to go back to the shelter for lunch, and left the shady area where he was sitting in the grass only twice more to buy sodas, until it was time to go back to the shelter for dinner.

Before it was time for him to leave, he had managed to forget about Christmas, about being unable to buy presents, about not feeling worthy enough to speak to Amy the previous Sunday. But the moment he stood up to leave, the thought of going back to the shelter made all of the buried thoughts rush to the surface. Will felt his eyes begin to well up with tears. But he would not let it happen. He bit his lip, picked up his satchel, and stumbled over to the trash can to throw away the cups that had accumulated beside him. After one last trip to the bathroom, he was ready for the bus ride back to the shelter, the excruciating, repetitious admission of defeat that occurred about this time *every single day*.

By the time Will laid down on his mat that night, any uncomfortable thoughts of Christmas, any lingering images of decorations or notes of holiday music had dissipated from him as quickly and completely as air from a worn-out bellows, leaving not even a void. This year Christmas was something *other* people celebrated, just as homes were where *other* people lived.

Chapter 7

A Hazy Flicker

The unmistakable squeaks and rattles of an approaching grocery cart made Will look up. It was not yet eight o'clock in the morning and he was sitting on the concrete slab behind the bush, just down the street from the shelter. A bad case of morning uncomfortableness had made him decide to have a drink before he left the shelter to go to the bathroom in Waikiki.

The little man pushed the cart up to the bush and stopped. As he peered around the bush he saw Will, and he walked around the cart to the slab and sat down on the corner of it. Will wondered if he would be lucky enough to get another story today, but the little man, whose right eye was now swollen completely shut, said nothing at first. He sat, barely moving for several minutes, then turned to Will.

"Got a match?" he asked. Will put his drink down and fumbled inside his satchel, producing a book of matches which he handed to the man. The man broke off a single match and held out the book toward Will.

"No, take the whole book," Will insisted. "You'll need

the emery for striking them, anyway." Seeing that the man did not retract the book, he added, "Take them. It's okay. I've got another book in my bag."

"You have another one?" he asked. Will nodded. The man put the matches in one of his shirt pockets. Will looked in his satchel again and fished out two batteries he had taken out of his headphone radio days before. They were still good, but he had already replaced them with new ones.

"Need a couple of batteries?" he asked the man, holding them out toward him. The man looked up.

"Yeahhh!" he exuded, taking them from Will. For a moment it almost looked as though he was about to smile. He stood and walked to his cart, placing the batteries inside one of his plastic bags. Will was hoping the little man had another story, but knew that he had to be leaving for the bus stop soon. Having become accustomed to visiting a bathroom every morning at about the same time, he now found it a *necessity*.

The man sat back down, took out a cigarette, then a stainless steel flint lighter, and lit the cigarette. As the man drew in a breath, Will decided that, intriguing as the little man might be, he *had* to leave for the bus stop. He fastened his satchel and stood.

"I've got to run," he said to the man, almost telling the truth. "You take it easy, okay?"

"Okay. And—and—and if you find any more batteries you don't need, I can use them." He had almost seemed to need to wind up his brain before he could speak. Will, his early morning uneasiness calmed, ambled toward Malualua Road. He hoped he could get a bus *soon* this morning.

After dinner that night, Will exited the doorway of the main room in search of the duty manager with the numbered cards. For some reason, the person handing out the cards no longer stood at the main room exit, but now changed locations every evening. Will guessed that they just wanted to keep the shelter dwellers on their toes.

He found the card dispenser at the side door of the building. It was Makolu, the masculine looking woman who had been at the desk the night he had first arrived at the shelter. She seemed to Will to have no noticeable dislike of white people—she just disliked *men* in general. He had gotten numbers in the eighties and nineties from her several times, and he wondered if she purposely handed out the cards so that it turned out that way. He waited his turn, then reached for the card she handed him, face down. He couldn't believe his eyes when he looked at it—it was number one.

He descended the steps into the parking lot, then walked around to the front of the building to find a place to sit. He had just positioned himself for the long wait when he saw Matt standing alone on the sidewalk, knapsack hung over one shoulder.

"Yo, Matt!" he called. Matt turned around, saw who had called him, and started toward Will.

"Hey, how's it?" he greeted Will, sitting down in the grass. Will noticed that he had a bad scrape on his lower lip. He guessed that it must be from the sun, since Matt worked outdoors most days.

"How's work?" Will asked, being conversational this time rather than trying to drum up a job for himself. The money order he had gotten would make work an unnecessary concern for at least a couple more weeks, longer if he was conservative.

"Ohhh, not so great," Tom frowned. "We got rained out again today. I'm hoping we'll be able to start up again tomorrow. I can use the money, but I won't know until tomorrow morning. We still have enough people, though."

"Well, I'm not really looking for work now, anyway," Will said. "Not for a while." He paused, then added, "Looks like you really got some sun."

"You mean this?" Matt asked, touching just below his lip with his index finger. "I got this from putting the wrong end of a pipe in my mouth. I got over-anxious and wasn't paying attention to what I was doing." Will pictured a pipe like his uncle smoked, and couldn't understand how the wrong end of *that* could burn someone.

"A *pipe?*" he asked, wrinkling his brow.

"Yeah . . . you know—a *pipe*," Matt answered, as if emphasizing the word would serve as an explanation to Will. Matt began to fidget.

"I gotta go see somebody over here," he said abruptly to Will. "Talk to you later." He quickly got to his feet and disappeared around the corner of the building. As Will looked toward the other end of Hoka Street, he saw Frankie coming up the sidewalk. Frankie spotted him, waved, and walked toward him. He sat down before he said anything.

"Whew! Almost like a day at the office!" he sighed expressively.

"Library again?" Will asked, having seen Frankie there on two occasions in the past.

"No—Hemmeter Building," he said. "Looking up deeds and addresses. I'm trying to find two people who have money coming to them and another person who owes money. If I can make a little bit of money out of doing this and it turns out to be worthwhile, I might take the court settlement when it comes and use it to start a business doing this."

"Whoa!" Will exclaimed. "You're *way* too fast for me. First of all, who's got money coming to them and doesn't know about it? Second, who's going to pay you for finding these people?"

Frankie explained to Will how the state government published a list of people to whom banks owed money—funds from abandoned accounts, inheritances, and other sources. His intent was to pick some of the larger amounts, locate the people, and charge them a percentage of their money as a finder's fee. Will at first could not believe that such a plan was feasible, but Frankie's confidence in it made him try harder to understand it.

"I had thoughts about being a private eye when I was in Vegas before," Frankie began. "But after I got a record, I knew I couldn't get a license from *any* state I wanted to live in. I couldn't make any money at it *without* a license because I wouldn't be allowed to do certain things that I would need to do to make money, things that I *would* have been able to do if I had the license." Will gave a nod of understanding.

"So when I found out about this list, I figured that it was a way that I could do some of the same kind of work. But instead of going to some lady and telling her that her husband is cheating on her, I could find her and tell her about a few thousand bucks she's got coming to her. Am I making more sense now?" He grinned almost mischievously as he held out both hands, palms up.

"Yeah. *Now* it sounds logical. But can you find enough people fast enough to make a good living out of it?" Will asked.

"That's what I'm in the process of finding out. The way I look at it, I can't work anyway. I'm stuck here until this work injury business is settled. So I might as well spend my time finding out how easy or hard this is going to be. Then when I get the settlement—if it looks promising—I can use the money to start a business doing this in Vegas. Just *imagine* how many people they'll have on the list there—and there's no telling how much money might be in it."

"Wish I had it figured out like that," Will mumbled.

"Are you looking for work?" Frankie asked.

"Well, I typed up a new resume after I came here, and I've sent out a few copies of it," he responded. "No luck so far, but if it lands on the right desk, maybe . . ." He didn't finish the sentence.

"You put the shelter's address and phone number *on your resume*?" Frankie asked, incredulous.

"How else is anybody going to get in touch with me?"

Will asked.

"I guess you're right," Frankie agreed. "But you can bet that most of the people who see '175 Hoka Street' at the top of your resume are going to toss it straight into the trash can."

"You think people would recognize that as the shelter's address?" Will wondered.

"Of *course*," Frankie answered emphatically. "*Every-body* knows it's the Center for Social Aid. It's in the news at least once a week." Will began to wonder if there was an alternative to that, but before he could consider it for too long, Frankie spoke again.

"Have you seen Matt?" he asked.

"Yeah, I just talked to him right before you got here. He had just walked over toward the parking lot. Said some-thing about needing to see someone.

"I can guess who that 'someone' is. Did you see the burn on his lip?" Frankie inquired.

"It was kind of hard to miss," Will chuckled. "He said something about putting the wrong end of a pipe in his mouth. I wondered if he was maybe just embarrassed that he got too much sun. I never saw him smoke a pipe."

"And you *won't* see him smoke, either," Frankie added. "He only smokes crack when he's hanging out with some of his burned-out friends."

"Hooollly shit," muttered Will, the picture finally dawning on him. "Now that I think about it, he *was* honest about it. I just didn't understand what he was talking about. How come they don't just use a water pipe or a bong for that stuff?" Frankie let out a cackle.

"You must have lived a sheltered life," he said to Will, still laughing. "Either that, or you're way behind the times." Recovering his composure, he added, "Matt knows he has a problem with that stuff. He does manual labor out in the sun every day for a week and gets a decent pocketful of money. Then he gets a hotel room on Saturday night, blows the rest on crack, and then shows up here on Sunday asking me for money to buy a cup of coffee with." He shook his head and continued.

"He's a smart guy. He's a stone mason. He built a house on St. Thomas—by himself, he told me. He's got pictures of it. But I can tell you from experience, once you get into that stuff, you lose control of everything. *It* controls *you*. And Matt will be the first one to tell you that he can't control it. He *knows* he's got a problem, and either he *can't* or he *won't* do anything about it. The shame of it is that he's really a decent person."

The course of the conversation put Will in a somber mood, and he said little until he saw the nightly migration toward the side door of the shelter. As the duty manager called for the women to enter, Will began to envision what his mat choices might be. There were, he figured, about ten mats taken already by the volunteers who had laid them out. About twenty-five or thirty more would be taken by the disabled people and the people holding work cards. His number one would entitle him to choose from among the rest of the mats.

"Alright, people—listen up!" he heard Robert, the duty manager, say. "We've been getting some complaints about how some of the same people seem to be getting the better numbers every night. So we're going to do this a little bit different tonight. We're going to go backwards. So if you have ninety-one to one hundred, you can go in. Step back, guys! Let 'em in!" Will stood speechless.

Just after breakfast the next morning, Will had an appointment with John Marin, who usually arrived at the shelter each morning before seven. Marin had allowed Will to use his typewriter to retype his resume in mid-December, and he listened intently as Will told him of the several ads to which he had responded by mailing a copy of the resume. Will wondered aloud whether having the Center's address on the resume made any difference.

"What other choice do you have?" Marin asked with

mock indignation in his voice, then added, "No, I think that if an employer sees on your resume the type of experience he's looking for, he's going to forget about the address—whether he recognizes it or not—and give you a call. I wouldn't worry about it." He inhaled through his cigarette, then put it back on the ashtray.

"I guess I'll be a little skeptical until I get a phone call," Will mused. Marin shifted in his chair.

"Have you been down to the state employment office yet?" he asked. "It might help if you at least got registered with them."

"No, I haven't." He hadn't planned on drinking until afternoon today, and spontaneously declared, "I'll go this morning. Right after I leave here."

"You never know," Marin said. "You might find something."

Will thanked him and left. As he was descending the first flight of stairs, the pretty, dark-haired woman he had seen at the house meeting ran up the stairs past him. It was his first glance at her in daylight. She ignored him in her hurry, but he quickly turned to follow her up the stairs with his eyes. She was beautiful! So neat, so well-dressed, so . . . so *perfect*, he thought.

Knowing that walking downtown would get him to the employment office at least as quickly as taking the bus would, Will turned right at the intersection where Malualua Road met King Street. As he walked past Elelu Park, he could see many of his fellow shelter guests mingling with the others in the park— people, he guessed, who preferred to sleep somewhere other than the shelter at night, who preferred to take their chances in a dark, roofless night rather than conform to the rules of the shelter. There were *so many* of them, it seemed to Will. He wondered if there were any who, like him, wanted to get out of the morass of homelessness but simply could not figure out a way.

The employment office was inside a fortress-like building, and faced a tiled courtyard. Will entered and the first thing he noticed was that there was a number dispenser like the one he had seen in the newspaper office. Unlike the newspaper office, however, there were other people waiting here.

He muttered under his breath as he sat down, "Take a number to place an ad, take a number to get a place to sleep, take a number to get a job . . ."

Will's impaired hearing made it harder for him to discern just how audible his own voice was, and the woman beside whom he sat quickly got up and moved several seats away from him. He waited until he was the only person remaining in the waiting area. Finally, a woman came out and looked in his direction. Her lips moved, but he heard nothing. She quickly disappeared into another office. Will approached the receptionist.

"Excuse me," he began. "Did that woman just call someone?"

"Yes."

"Was the name Tyne?"

"Yes."

"That was me. I have trouble with my ears. I'm sorry."

"Excuse me. I'll go get her," the receptionist offered, rising from her chair and going through a doorway behind her desk. Within seconds, both the receptionist and the woman reappeared. The woman, older than middle age and of apparent Japanese descent, moved her lips again.

"I'm sorry. Did you say something?" apologized Will.

"*I said I-am-Ms.-Ish-i-ka-wa-please-come-with-me,*" she repeated. Will guessed that the employees at this office must have been trained to be extremely soft-spoken. He had been able to hear Marin fine only an hour earlier.

"I can't hear very well," he explained. "If you can just talk really loud, it would help me." The woman offered Will a seat and peered at him over the top of her glasses as he sat down.

"What is your mailing address?" she asked him softly, but he could not hear what she said, and because her diction differed from his, he could not read her lips.

"*Pardon?*" he asked. She gave him an exasperated look.

One hour later, Will emerged from the employment office without any new job prospects, and thoroughly frustrated by the woman, who had refused to raise her volume by so much as a decibel.

He knew that he could not hear as well as usual. The stuffy feeling in his ears told him that they were not completely well. But he had been able to hear Frankie, Matt, and Marin reasonably well, interjecting only an occasional "huh?" or "pardon?" into the conversation. And he could certainly hear the rumble of the crowd at the shelter each night after the lights went out. It occasionally kept him awake.

As Will was walking away from the building which housed the employment office, he saw Johnnie quickly walking in his direction. He waved as Johnnie looked up and recognized him.

"Hey, man. What's up?" Johnnie greeted him.

"Not much," Will responded. "I just finished at the employment office. What a pain in the ass!"

"Huhhh. Not much help there," Johnnie agreed. "Just a waste of time when I was there. You hungry?" Will had to stop to think.

"Not really. Why?"

"V.A.'s got some sort of New Year's party for vets going on at ten-thirty. S'posed to have some refreshments, then hand out box lunches for later. Want to go?"

"But I'm not a veteran," said Will.

"Doesn't matter. Nobody will ask questions. If they do, just let me answer." Will looked at his watch. It was after ten-fifteen. He didn't really want anything to eat now, but if he had a box lunch, he could go straight to the beach park and start drinking instead of going back to the shelter for lunch.

"Lead the way," Will proclaimed, and Johnnie motioned for him to follow. The building was only a short distance down the same street, and they were there very shortly. Johnnie entered the building, then the office marked by a sign "Veteran Affairs." There was no one in the office.

"Must be in the other office," he speculated, and Will again kept up with Johnnie's quick pace. "I can smell fried chicken," Johnnie announced as he rounded a corner in the hallway. But the door in front of which he stopped was locked. Johnnie was beginning to appear confused.

"Hmmm. Maybe . . . it's *not* today," he thought aloud. "Maybe the announcement said that it was Thursday." He thought some more. "I'll check the announcement tonight, and I'll let you know if it's going to be on Thursday. You'll be at the shelter for lunch tomorrow?"

"Yeah, I'll be there," a deflated Will answered.

"Okay. I'll let you know tomorrow. See you then." Johnnie turned and quickly walked away. Will sat down on a nearby concrete bench for a few minutes. Then he got up to walk back to the shelter.

Will went to the beach park across from the mall during the afternoon. He was tired and slightly foggy when he got back to the shelter just before dinner, but he had been careful not to overdo the alcohol. The line was already at the end of the lanai when he joined it.

It was only minutes later that he heard the faint chorus of the blessing being recited, and the line soon began moving. Will had just inched inside the doorway of the main room when he heard loud voices farther up ahead of him in the line. Robert and another duty manager hurried to where the commotion had been, but the line was too thick with people for Will to see anything.

"*Out! Both of you!*" he finally heard Robert say, and he

saw the two duty managers ushering a tall, angry-looking man and—of all people—*Frankie* out the door. He could not imagine what Frankie, who looked like he was almost ready for Geritol and Grecian Formula, could have done to get himself "eighty-sixed." Will continued through the line, got a plate, and ate as quickly as he could.

He looked for Frankie as soon as he walked outside the door, but did not see him. Hurrying down the sidewalk, he still didn't see Frankie, and he stopped, then sat down in the grass at the end of the building. Seconds later, Frankie appeared from the loading area by the back door at the same end of the building. He was carrying a plate of food.

"Did you see what happened?" he asked excitedly.

"No," Will answered. "All I saw was you and that other character being escorted out by Robert. How'd you get food?"

"Robert told me to come to the back door of the kitchen. He gave me the plate. He just didn't want the other guy to think that *he* was the only one who got eighty-sixed." Frankie became calmer as he spoke.

"So what started all the shit?" Will wanted to know.

"The guy was in front of me, and then all of a sudden he backed into me and hit my kneecap. It was already sore, and I automatically shoved him away. Then he turned around and said 'Watch it, dicknose,' and I . . . *nobody* calls an Italian from Long Island 'dicknose'. . .I popped him in the nose. He turned around and started to swing at me, and that's when Robert and the other guy got there."

"So you—bad ass—*you* were the one who started it," Will laughingly chided him. "A fifty-two year old bully!"

"No, I didn't st—"

"You threw the first punch, didn't you?"

"Yeah, and the next one's gonna be at you," Frankie teased back. "Seriously, I wish it hadn't happened. It just makes other people want to—"

WHUMP! A smooth rock about the size and shape of a large bell pepper hit the wall of the shelter about a foot above and to the right of Frankie's head, bouncing off and landing on the grass between Will and Frankie. Will looked up. The man Frankie had punched earlier was running down the middle of Hoka Street away from the shelter. Within seconds Will saw that Robert had followed the man to the edge of the shelter's property and was standing only a few yards away. He came toward Will and Frankie.

"I saw that. I'm going to call the police and let them know to look out for the guy," he said. Turning to Frankie, he added, "If you want to make a complaint about him throwing the rock, I'll let you know when they get here."

"Nahhh," Frankie declined. "Unless what I say can help to back up what you say. I'd just as soon forget about it."

"Okay," said Robert. "I don't think you have to worry about seeing him around *here* for a while, though. At least not *in* the shelter."

"Thanks," Frankie said, a weak smile crossing his face. "I'll sleep better."

Turning to Will he asked, "Seen Matt today?"

"Nope. Maybe it wasn't raining wherever it is that he works," Will guessed. A short while later, he saw Matt, his clothes smudged with dirt from head to toe, coming toward him and Frankie. He wiped some imaginary sweat from his forehead as he sat down.

"You know, I was having this daydream. I'm going to build a garret over my garage," he began rambling. "Twelve feet high like a medieval castle. See, I've got the drawings." He reached inside his backpack.

"So where's your garage?" Will asked. Out of the corner of his eye he could see Frankie looking at him, signaling a 'no' with the motion of his head.

"Oh, I have a lot on the Big Island. I'm going to build a house there. I'm a master stone mason. I built a house on St.

Thomas. *Two* houses. But I don't own them anymore." Heeding Frankie, Will remained silent, but Matt continued.

"I had T-shirts printed with the Treasure Island logo on them. You know, St. Thomas is where Robert Louis Stevenson's treasure in Treasure Island is buried. Seven hundred thousand pounds of gold. Nobody has ever been able to find it, and I'm one of only two people who know where it is."

"Buried treasure? Really?" Will enthused, though he was beginning to wonder if Matt had gone off the deep end.

"Here, look at these maps," Tom continued, holding out two slightly worn photocopies. "One is St. Thomas, the other is the map that Stevenson drew for Treasure Island. See how similar they are? And look at the navigation lines!"

Will had no idea what navigation lines were, although the maps did have a slight resemblance at the part to which Matt's finger pointed. Accurate or not, he *had* seemed to come alive since Will had last seen him, and he gave Will no chance for more interjections.

"See this inlet? There's a cove in that section there. In that cove somewhere is the treasure. There's an underwater cave, and my pal Terry and I are the only ones who know about the cave. He's lived on St. Thomas all his life, and he used to be the only one who knew about it, but he told me. He made me swear that I would never tell where the cave was.

"I have pictures of the cove, and there's a book that has pictures of treasure hunters digging there in 1909, but they weren't in the right place. There have been two groups of treasure hunters that went there in search of the treasure, one in 1909 and the other one sometime around the 1950s. But both times, someone on their team got killed and they decided it wasn't worth it to keep looking.

"Six years ago, the newspaper there did an article on Terry. I have the paper in the bag I have in the cage. I'll get it and show it to you tomorrow. They said that Terry knows where the treasure is, but he won't tell. There's supposed to be an old island curse on anybody who tells a lot of people where the underwater cave is. But the curse didn't happen when Terry showed me the cave."

Will looked at Frankie, who had taken a notebook out of his backpack and was thumbing through it. Frankie yawned. Despite Matt's near-fanatical presentation, Will did not immediately dismiss his credibility. And such stories were high entertainment to someone at a shelter for the homeless. Matt continued.

"But Terry got mad at me when I called the newspaper and told them that he knew about the treasure. There's no curse on *that*, but Terry won't speak to me now. But it doesn't matter. I already know where the cave is."

"Is the treasure in the cave?" Will wanted to know.

"Aha! I didn't *say* that!" Matt's eyes gleamed. "It's not exactly in the cave, but I'm not going to say anything else about where it *is*."

"But if you know where it is," Will began, "why don't you go dig it up or do whatever you have to do to get it out? I mean, seven hundred thousand pounds . . ." Will took a small calculator out of his satchel and tapped on the tiny keys. "That would be somewhere near four-and-a-half billion dollars!"

"Remember the curse," Tom countered, shaking his head solemnly. "Besides, I've been working on a way to make money out of this without even *touching* the treasure. Ever hear of that Treasure Island Hotel in Vegas?" Will had not.

"Well, I wrote to the owner, and I suggested a promotion involving a new edition of the book Treasure Island. Then they could promote it with a contest and I could get a piece of the action."

"What about the copyright on the book?" Will asked. "How could *you* make money on it?"

"I already checked at the library, and the book is public domain. That means that anybody can use it or publish a new edition of it."

The sound of the mats hitting the floor inside had stopped about ten minutes ago. Will guessed that the duty managers would be allowing people to come inside shortly. He put his calculator back in the satchel and began securing the buckles.

"This is all interesting," Will told Matt. "It looks like it's about time to go inside now, but I'd like to hear more about this another time."

"Okay," Matt replied. "I'll get that newspaper and show it to you tomorrow. And I have copies of other versions of the map. And the letter I got from Treasure Island Hotel."

"Great!" Will said. Just don't tell anyone at Disneyland about this, he thought to himself—we all know what they did to John Lennon.

Once Will had gotten inside and claimed a mat, he went to the cage to get his sheets. His bags, which always got shuffled around in the same general area during the course of each day, were not in their usual location. He searched through the shelves at the back of the room and, after plowing through to the bottom of a pile, found both of them. He looked around for Sam, who had been there during the morning. He knew that Sam would be able to fill him in on the story behind the shuffle, but Sam was not there. Taking his place was a dark-skinned, dour looking man with Coke-bottle glasses and a huge stomach.

"Sam's not in tonight?" Will asked the man.

"Sam don' work heah no moah," the man answered.

"Well, can you tell me why my bags were moved from this shelf to the bottom in the back?" he asked.

"Da bag too beeg," the man snarled at Will. "It go on da las' shelf cos' it gon' be trode aweah if you no take it out."

Will was becoming irritated.

"I don't think it would be a good idea—"

"Das da new rule. If da bag too beeg, you got tree days

to take it. Den it get trode aweah. You no like da rule, you see Mengel upstaihs." Will saw other bags far larger than his at the front. He knew that those bags belonged to locals, and that some of the bags on the back shelf belonged to white people. He was livid.

"*Just don't fuck with my bags!*" he growled to the man.

"Ehhh, bra. You go make tret, you get eighty-seex."

Will took his bag and stormed out of the cage. When he went to take it back a few minutes later, he saw that the new cage attendant was talking to Robert. At least, he figured, Robert would handle the matter fairly.

Will stopped to wonder why some of the locals, like the new cage attendant and Makolu, seemed to have a deep-seated dislike of people of other ethnic backgrounds, while other locals, like Robert and Sam, seemed to treat everybody in a reasonably equitable manner. People like Robert and Sam, Will whimsically reasoned, made it difficult for him to be prejudiced.

Will woke up in the midst of a coughing spell on New Year's Eve. His hearing was still impaired, and he had never fully gotten over his other cold symptoms. The coughing was back with a vengeance, and he worried that he might soon have to visit the clinic and get more medicine. That would mean that he would have to lay off the booze again.

But, he reasoned, it was the end of the old year. Why not have one more good drinking day and then make a resolution to stop drinking in the new year? Nahhh, he thought. He would drink today and worry about tomorrow when it came. He had tried the New Year's resolution method of quitting drinking in 1986 . . . and 1987, 1988, 1989, and 1990. At the beginning of 1991 he had made a "new decade" resolution. His resolve had never worked for longer than ten days into the new year.

This New Year's Eve would be different than the others, though, since he would already be in bed by the time most revelers were beginning their celebrations. The shelter had already announced that there would be no relaxation of the ten o'clock curfew. Will would have to get his celebrating done before that time.

After his customary trip to Waikiki, Will returned to the mall and went to the book shop for a newspaper before going to get a soda. The chubby, brown-skinned young woman was at the cash register, and when it came his turn, he handed her the fifty cents for the paper. She looked up at him, as she always did, and smiled broadly before thanking him. The feeling he got from her smile always cheered him, no matter what mood he was in when he walked into the store. There had been many days when that woman's smile, he felt, had been the only *positive* acknowledgment of his existence. He wondered if she knew that he was homeless.

As he later sat down with his paper and his first drink of the day, Will wondered if his appearance advertised his predicament, not just to the young woman in the book shop, but to people in general. His satchel, once used to transport necessities to and from his work, was beginning to show the wear that had been caused by being in use twenty-four hours a day, seven days a week. A metal finding to which one end of the strap had been attached was now broken, and some of the stitching had given way. He knew that it would not hold up much longer under the present conditions, especially since he even used it to prop his head on at night.

Will showered every morning, and shaved every day, but he wondered if his hair, now longer than it had ever been and perpetually messy, and his ruddy complexion alerted others to the fact that he had only the barest means of subsistence. He was thankful that his clothes seemed to fit in with the relaxed sartorial environment in which he lived. Sometimes he felt that he stood out, other times he was confident that he fit in.

Feeling comfortable and relaxed as he sat in the food court at the mall, Will decided not to go back to the shelter for lunch. As soon as the food court got crowded, he would just get another soda and go to the beach park across the road.

Will chose an isolated area at the beach park, one which was well-shaded and as far away from the road as he could get. He watched the airplanes floating overhead toward the airport as he listened to his radio through its earphones. There seemed to be no one to be cautious about in the park, as there sometimes was, and Will lay down in the grass, partly fatigued from poor sleep at night, mostly well-oiled by the gin.

It was almost five-thirty when he woke up. He quickly felt his pockets and looked around. All of his belongings were intact. He felt relieved. It frightened him to think that he had fallen asleep so easily, because he knew that was what made homeless people such easy marks so often. Knowing that he would miss dinner at the shelter, but still hoping that he could arrive in time to get a number, Will got up as quickly as he could and headed toward the bus stop.

After a forty-five minute bus ride, Will arrived back at the shelter. He saw Makolu's pickup truck parked in the shelter's parking lot, and he knew that she was probably the person handing out the numbers. She seemed to enjoy teasing the unfortunate shelter guests, choosing a different location each day, and often making derisive remarks to the guests as she passed out the cards to them. Will saw her standing at the foot of the steps near the side door, and hurried to her.

"Any numbers left?" he asked, panting.

"Ahhhh! No more! You miss dinner, too?" she asked, her face breaking into a sadistic smile. Will turned away from her, gripping his lower lip between his tongue and his upper teeth. He would now have to wait until the work card people and the people with numbers were in, then line up with the other people who had no numbers. There would undoubtedly be someone at the front of the line who would let eight or ten people go ahead of him—in plain view of the duty manager. And Will would come in with the last of the people.

It was the end of the month, which meant that the shelter would be crowded, since most of the people had spent their monthly checks. Will would be lucky to get one of the old, worn-out mats on the lanai, and he might even have to sleep on one in back of the shelter, where there was no roof. He hoped that it would not rain.

It was not Makolu who came out on the steps by the side door, but Robert. Will was glad, because it meant that there would be less cutting in the line. The process began, and by the time all the people with numbers had been permitted to enter the building, there were only about forty people left outside. Will was tenth in line when Robert called out, "Okay! Everybody else!"

He hurried down the hallway and into the main room, which was still a madhouse as people scrambled in every direction. Will saw no open mats as he looked around, and he was about to go through the double doors to the lanai when he heard his name called. He stopped and looked around, his ailing ears unable to figure out what direction the voice had come from.

He saw Frankie on a mat near the mailroom door. Frankie was repeatedly darting his eyes in the direction of his backpack, which was on the mat beside the one on which he sat. Will quickly went to the mat and dropped his satchel on it at exactly the same moment that Frankie slid his backpack off the mat.

"Thanks!" he said, louder than he realized.

"Shhh!" Frankie warned him. He said nothing as he sat down. He knew that Frankie not only risked being eighty-sixed for saving him the mat, but he might also lose his work card privilege that allowed him inside before the people with the numbers. It made Will feel good to know that there was at least one person on his side in this crowd of unpredictable people. Despite the existence of an unspoken camaraderie among many of the homeless, the prevalent attitude seemed to be: "One for all, all for one—and *every man for himself!*" Will busied himself with a crossword puzzle he had salvaged from a discarded newspaper earlier in the day until the commotion began to die down.

"Did you hear Matt's spiel the other day?" he asked, turning to Frankie.

"Yeah. He was high."

"You mean he had been smoking crack?" Will guessed.

"Yeah. I don't know where he got it . . . in the middle of the week, that is, but whenever he talks like that, I can tell he's high. I mean—he talks about this Treasure Island thing a lot, but he usually doesn't sound like a Baptist minister when he tells people about it."

"It *was* kind of unusual to have him just start reeling the whole thing off," Will agreed, "kind of out of nowhere. But it was interesting, too. It sounded pretty plausible, too, at least until he got to the part about promoting the hotel with a new edition of the book."

"Yeah," Frankie nodded. "Hang around here long enough and you'll hear more, I bet."

"I mean," Will continued, "If he *really* knows where there's four-and-a-half billion in gold buried, why doesn't he just say 'fuck the book' and go get the gold?"

"Mmm-hmmm," Frankie mumbled. Will guessed that Frankie had already heard enough about the subject. He went to the cage to get his sheets. He assumed that Robert had put an end to the bag dispute because the cage attendant merely scowled at him without saying anything. After he had his mat ready for the night, Will went out the side door into the parking lot.

It was quiet there, as most people who were still at the shelter were either inside or out front. He slowly moved toward the driveway, inhaling deep breaths and hoping the air would help his clogged ears. They seemed to be getting no better. Close to the ground in front of him, he saw the tiny red dot of glow at the end of a cigarette. It was the brown-shirt girl who had asked him for money in Waikiki.

"Hi, how are you?" Will greeted her, as congenially as he could.

"Fine. How are you?" she reciprocated. He was nearly floored by her response, but quickly recovered.

"Some New Year's Eve, huh?" he commented, seeing if she was capable of another response.

"About like all the others," she answered. "About like any other night. They're all the same." Will decided not to push his luck any further.

"Well, Happy New Year," he said, starting to move toward the front of the building.

"Happy New Year," the girl echoed. Will strolled toward the front porch. It was almost empty, and he boosted himself onto it, rear first, dangling his legs over the edge. Across the street, a music box was blasting a rap recording. The volume was turned up too loud for the speakers—so loud that most of what could be heard was distortion.

The sting of a just-struck match hit Will's nostrils, and he turned around. The dark-eyed woman had just come outside. Before he had a chance to realize that he was staring at her, she smiled at him. Flustered by such an unexpected occurrence, he quickly looked down. She glided down the steps and walked across the street toward King's.

Will was angry with himself. She had given him a tiny chance and he had blown it. He had told himself weeks ago that if she so much as smiled at him, he would seize the opportunity. Well, she had, and he had been unable to respond. She probably thought now, he reasoned, that he was some sort of emotional cripple.

It seemed unimportant to him, as the curfew time drew near this New Year's Eve, that he had blown another year. What bore down more heavily on his mind as he went inside the shelter was that he had failed to react in such a way that he had blown another chance for a *woman.*

The next morning, in no hurry to get to Waikiki and knowing that the mall was closed because of the holiday, Will determined that he would spend some time on the concrete slab in front of the wall that stood next door to the shelter. He first went to one of the soda machines across the street in front of King's. He had in his satchel a plastic cup he had saved from the previous day. It was slipped over the top of a liter bottle of gin so that the cup would neither crack nor take up a lot of space.

He had sat on the slab for about an hour, sipping on his concoction, wondering if the little man would come by and possibly have another auditory daydream, when he saw Gary turn onto Hoka street. He waved to him. Gary walked toward him.

"Hey!" he called out. "What you up to?"

"Not much," Will called back. Gary approached and sat down on the concrete slab. "Just waiting to see if my pal with the shopping cart shows up."

"Oh, him?" Gary laughed. "His mind is gone, man. I don't know what his story is. He's *one* person that nobody knows anything about. I've been coming around here for about eight years, and he was here already when *I* got here. But nobody can tell you what his story is. And *he* sure can't. But he's harmless." Gary looked in Will's cup. "What you got in that," he asked.

"Just some gin and Pepsi," Will answered. Gary looked perplexed.

"I been on the A.A. wagon lately," Gary said. "But I don't know how much longer I can stay."

"Oh, I'm sorry," Will interjected, pushing the cup behind him and out of Gary's sight.

"No, no! That's okay," Gary assured him, then reached into a pocket on his bulky olivedrab field jacket and pulled out a pint of vodka, still sealed. "I been carrying this around for three days to prove I have control over it. Looks like a good time for my reward." With that, he unscrewed the top of the bottle and tilted it toward his mouth, taking a long time with it. When he took the bottle down, a third of its contents had been drained. Will gulped in amazement. Even in his "thirstiest" moments, he had never been able to drink liquor straight.

"Seen Johnnie lately?" Will asked, trying to draw attention away from Gary's lapse in abstinence.

"Saw him yesterday. He said he was going to move in with his girlfriend."

"And give up that wonderful tent he has in the Manoa rain forest?" Will joked.

"He said he wants to go back to school, and the V.A. won't pay for it unless he lives in a house," Gary explained. "So he's going to stay at his girlfriend's house."

"And what about you? What are you up to these days?"

"Well, I guess I have more free time since I won't be going to A.A. anymore," Gary quipped. "Nahhh. I'm just going to take it easy, finish working on my G.E.D.—"

"I didn't know you were going to school," Will interrupted.

"I only started a couple of weeks ago. I should finish up next month. I made it through half of the twelfth grade, you know, before I dropped out and enlisted."

"You dropped out that close to finishing?," Will asked.

"I always said 'no more school when I turn eighteen' so on my eighteenth birthday, I went to the principal and told him I was quitting. Then I went to the Navy recruiting office that same afternoon." Gary looked at his watch.

"Sorry, I didn't mean to hold you up—" Will began.

"No, no," Gary assured him. "I'm just checking to see if it's time for the doors to open so I can go take a shower. It's still fifteen minutes before they let anybody in."

"You *never* sleep at the shelter?" Will queried.

"A long time ago, before it got crowded, I used to sleep

there once in a while. But not in the last six or seven years. But, *don't* ask me where I sleep. No homeless man who sleeps outside will *ever* tell you where he sleeps unless he's stupid. I don't tell *anybody* where I sleep. I don't want any surprises during the night. Even the police couldn't find me at night. *Nobody* knows where ol' Gary sleeps."

Will noticed that Gary had gone from being cheerful a moment ago to an almost sullen state. He was sorry he had brought up the subject of sleep. Then he remembered the huge gulp of vodka that Gary had taken. It wasn't the subject matter that had changed Gary's mood.

Will looked at his watch and quickly downed the last of his drink, telling Gary he had to meet someone. He would go to Waikiki after all, hoping to find some solitude. It was less than ten hours into the new year and he was already drinking. He hadn't lasted ten days, he told himself, but he *hadn't* begun the first minute of the year already drunk, either.

There was a house meeting at the center the next night, and Will was close by the front door when it was opened to allow the shelter denizens to file in for the meeting. He made sure he got a seat on the right side near the front, so that he would have a good view of the "administrator lady."

The members of the guest committee filtered in, one by one, followed shortly by Dick Mengel, who was looking particularly harried and fatigued. He sat down and called the meeting to order. There was only an empty chair where the administrator lady usually sat.

Before Mengel asked the guest committee members to present their concerns, he launched himself into a monologue about the shelter's mission, stating that the goal of the shelter in dealing with its "clients" was eventually to "transition" each client out of the shelter and back into society, as one of its functioning members.

Will chuckled, almost audibly. English had been his primary course of study in college, and he had *never* heard the word "transition" use as a verb. His mind, still rendered slightly out of focus by the gin he had consumed earlier that day, drifted momentarily, imagining how funny it would be to use "transition" as a verb: "I transition, you transition, he transitions . . . they transitioned, we will have been transitioning . . . "

His body was in the meeting, but his mind was now drifting beyond even the humorous aspects of language. The administrator lady walked into the room and sat down in the vacant chair, and Will's attention quickly returned to the shelter briefly as he began studying the administrator lady.

She was well-dressed, as always. Her navy dress had red piping around the sleeves and collar, and it fit her perfectly—loose enough to be business attire, snug enough to define her slender form. Her face was expressive and sometimes skeptical, her eyes perpetually analytical. Even squinting, Will noticed, didn't seem to cause any wrinkles in her face. When she spoke, her diction and grammar seemed flawless to Will's ears.

The administrator lady was, to Will's often watery, bleary eyes, as close to perfection in a woman as he had ever seen. If there was a god, Will speculated, the administrator lady was the reason for ten ugly women existing—god took *their* beauty ingredients and gave them all to *her*.

Will tried to return his attention to what Mengel was saying, but his train of thought had been derailed. Mengel was still talking about what the shelter offered in order to help its guests get back on their feet. The idea of transitioning out of the shelter, of becoming a normal person again, seemed to Will to be no more than some sort of daydream that he could only find near the bottom of a gin bottle.

Even some of Will's shelter pals had plans for improving themselves: Frankie had his ideas about starting a business, Johnnie was returning to college, and Gary was about to finish high school. Will realized that even Matt's crazy Treasure Island scheme was his own way of trying to help himself out of the shelter.

Will had no idea what he would do to get out of the shelter. He had not had a single response from the several resumes he had sent out, not even a rejection. He was, he told himself, like a fallen tree in an uninhabited forest.

Chapter 8

Alternating Currents

Woolworth's looked like a good place for Will to pass some time on this rainy, dreary February morning. He had already finished one hefty drink and didn't feel like venturing all the way to the mall, especially with the weather the way it was. The pedestrian mall in the middle of downtown was a passable place to sit very early in the morning, but its benches became filled by mid-morning, mostly by the middle-aged and older alcoholics who Will was beginning to resemble, but with whom he did not yet acknowledge his similarities. They were dirty, disheveled people who had no self-respect, he told himself, and all they cared about was where their next drink was coming from.

Will fingered some of the greeting cards in the store, glad that he knew no one who had an upcoming birthday. The expense of a card would cut into the last of his drinking money. He stepped onto the escalator to go to the basement level, already knowing what was there, but willing to look yet again at things he could not afford and things which he had no place to put.

Wandering into the shoe department, Will's eyes were captured by a sign that read: "Men's Tennis Shoes, $5.00." He laughed. Even when he had played on the tennis team in high school in the early 1970's, a pair of tennis shoes of passable quality had cost twenty bucks. The pair he was wearing, now almost completely worn out, had cost over sixty when he had bought them two years earlier, in better times.

Picking up a pair of the advertised shoes, Will noticed that the label on the underside of the tongue read "ALL MAN-MADE MATERIALS." Plastic shoes! He laughed to himself. He looked at the ones he was wearing. They were scuffed, dingy, and worn almost paper-thin on parts of their soles. The vinyl shoes were clean, white, and appeared to have ample cushion in the bottom.

He sat down on a wooden seat at the end of the aisle, pulled his right shoe off, and slipped it into one of the five-dollar shoes. It felt comfortable. And, he observed, it looked much better than the one he had removed. He tried the other one and, with both of them, he didn't look as . . . homeless. Maybe, he told himself, the shoes would be a worthwhile investment. He would at least feel better about his appearance.

Will tucked the shoes back in the box and put his old ones back on. Five dollars was a lot, but, he told himself, it was less than half the price of a half-gallon of gin. He picked up the box with the shoes and walked toward the checkout counter. He would, he decided, buy the vinyl shoes and wear them just until he could afford another pair of good ones.

Outside the store, Will walked until he was at the edge of Elelu Park, on the way back to the shelter. It was only drizzling now, something for which he was thankful. His umbrella had been stolen the previous week, taken from the wooden bench in the bathroom when he had been showering and had closed his eyes just long enough to rinse the shampoo from his hair.

The concrete bench by the bus stop was sheltered, and

Will sat down with his back to the street. He took the shoes out of their box and laced them up loosely. They felt comfortable as he put them on and took his first steps in them. And, he noted, they *looked* good. Will was pleased with his purchase, even if it *was* a humble one. He would feel a little better about his appearance when he walked into Marin's office for his afternoon appointment, even if he *did* have liquor on his breath.

Even though it was only eleven o'clock and the shelter was only a five minute walk away, Will began the short trip up Malualua Road. He did not want anyone to see him and think that he frequented Elelu Park. It was a known hangout for drug addicts.

Will managed to down another spiked soda before lunch, and after lunch he was feeling relaxed about his one-thirty appointment—until he realized that he would have to deal with Bertha again. He entered the building and saw that Bertha was not behind the reception window. One of the duty managers was seated at the desk and Will hurried to the window.

He explained that he had an appointment, and the duty manager pushed the button to unlock the door. As Will turned to make sure the door closed slowly and quietly behind him, he saw Bertha enter the hallway from the side door at the other end of the building. He breathed a sigh of relief.

Marin greeted him cheerfully, seeming not to notice that Will had been drinking. Will had been mindful not to drink before his first few appointments with Marin, but had been drinking when he had traded jokes with Marin at lunchtime the previous week. Marin had not said anything at that time, and Will had assumed that since he was homeless, his indulgence had been, and would be, overlooked.

"Any luck with the job situation?" Marin asked, lighting a cigarette and leaning back in his chair.

"Nothing so far," Will began. "I only sent out one

resume in the last two weeks. There just hasn't been anything in the paper. And the employment office—well, I told you before it's slim pickings there. It was exactly the same when I was there last Thursday. They have some of the same jobs listed that they had *weeks* ago."

"I have something here," the squinting caseworker said. "I don't know—you *might* be interested in giving it a shot.

"Do tell!" Will effused, his businesslike manner momentarily lapsing.

"It's an opening here at the shelter," Marin said quietly, as if he were about to reveal a secret. "They need someone to organize the in-house volunteers. The person also has to go out into the community and talk to groups of people about what sort of work the shelter does." Will's mind was in motion.

"And who could do that better," he wondered rhetorically, than someone who has benefitted from the shelter's services? Wow, this could be the break I've been looking for. Where do—"

"Slow down," cautioned Marin, a trace of a smile crossing his face. "It's going to be advertised in the paper this Sunday. But they just told us about it at the staff meeting this morning. If you're interested, I can get a copy of your resume over to Karen Ling this afternoon."

"Interested?" Will almost shouted. "You *bet* I'm interested! I would be the hardest working—"

"Don't get *too* excited," cautioned Marin. "It's just that I know that if I take your resume over to Karen and let her know that you're a guest here, she'll make sure that your resume gets considered fairly."

"Who's this Karen person?" Will asked.

"She's the chief administrator of the shelter. If you go to the house meetings, you might have seen her there. I know she shows up at those whenever she can. She's petite, dark brown hair—"

"Oh, I *know* who *she* is," Will interrupted dreamily.

"The administrator lady." Marin squinted again, looking slightly puzzled for a second.

"Let's see . . . I've got a copy of your resume right here," Marin said. I'll take it over to her office right after we're done."

"In that case," Will said, rising from the metal chair, "I won't hold you up. Thanks for the recommendation."

"No problem," Marin nodded. "I know you're motivated."

Motivated to have another drink, Will thought as he descended the stairs. He darted through the doorway into the entranceway and glanced at the bulletin board, more out of habit than for any other reason. Under the "B" section, he saw a note with his name on it. He removed the thumbtack that held the message to the corkboard.

The phone call recorded on the note had been in response to one of the resumes he had sent out. He fished into his pocket and found a quarter. There was a pay phone next to the front door and, for once, it was not in use. He dialed the number that had been written on the small slip of paper.

Someone picked up the phone on the second ring. Will was coldly informed that the person he was attempting to call did not live at that number, and that the answerer had never heard of the company Will was trying to reach. Stunned, Will hung up the phone. He looked at the initials on the phone message, "BS." Bertha's initials! She had given him an incorrect number on his message.

Will wished that he could walk up to her reception window and scream at her, but he knew that would insure that he would *never* get another phone message whenever Bertha had control of the phones. He also needed to use the telephone book in her office to get the correct phone number for the company that had called him. He walked outside to the front porch to calm himself.

After a few minutes, Will returned inside and approached the reception window, behind which Bertha was seated. She ignored him. After less than a minute, he decided he wouldn't be as patient as he had been in the past.

"Excuse me. May I borrow your phone book, please?" he asked, trying to be as nice as he could bear to be.

"Certainly," she answered, handing him the white page directory through the slot in the window without looking up at him. Will knew that the white pages would probably not have the business listing he needed, but he leafed through it anyway, to no avail.

"I need the yellow pages," he said, holding the white page directory out so that Bertha could take it.

"I don't have the yellow pages," she dripped. "I let someone borrow it and it was never returned." Will felt that she might be lying, but he could say nothing. He went back out to the front porch.

A short while later Bertha got up out of her chair and Will could see through a small window that she was going up the stairway. Robert had come into the reception area. Will went inside the building, hoping Robert would know where he could find a yellow page directory. Robert had his back to the window, and before Will could get Robert's attention, he saw that the directory he needed was directly under Bertha's phone. He quietly fumed. Robert turned around and saw Will.

"May I help you, sir?" he offered in his usual polite manner, one that Will thought was unusual for a person dealing with the shelter dwellers.

"May I use the yellow pages, please?" Will asked.

"Sure, here you go." Robert picked up the book and handed it to Will through the slot in the glass.

"And," Will added, "May I have an incident report form?"

"Sure. Any problem with another guest?" Robert wanted to know. It was, after all, part of his business. Incident report forms were usually used to report complaints against other guests, but they could also be used to report conflicts involving shelter employees.

"Nope," Will answered. "An employee." Robert smiled knowingly as he handed the form to Will.

"I can take it up to Dick Mengel for you when you get it filled out," he offered. "It probably wouldn't be a good idea to leave it with Bertha." Will nodded and thanked Robert, glad to know that one of her co-workers was on to her.

Will got the phone number he needed and made the phone call. The company was interested in interviewing him, but for a position offering lower pay than the one for which he had applied. Will took down the appointment time and thanked the person at the other end of the line. His disappointment at not getting a call for the better job was overshadowed by his excitement at just getting a call for an interview. He was already encouraged by John Marin's apparent confidence in him.

As he walked toward the reception desk, he noticed that Bertha was back. He approached the window and held out the yellow page book toward her.

"Thank you," she said icily, glancing her eyes up at Will's for just an instant. She turned away from him without acknowledging the lie she had been caught in, and Will did not wish to dampen his own buoyant mood by pointing it out to her.

The pleasure he took in the two job possibilities that had come before him soon began to change to concern, then worry. Where, he wondered, would he be able to change clothes before he went to the interview? How would he carry his interview outfit around before he changed? Where would he put his regular clothes while he was at the interview? The cage was only open from twelve until one, and Will didn't want to change clothes that early for fear that he would somehow get them dirty or stained.

He would, he decided, think about it over a good, long

drink.

By the time Will settled into the grass at the beach park across from the mall, some of his uneasiness had passed. His ears were bothering him more, and he didn't want to go to the clinic for more medicine because he wouldn't be able to drink.

He tried to imagine himself becoming an employee of the shelter. The pay probably wouldn't be great, he guessed, but at least it would be a job. Even the job for which he had an interview scheduled would enable him to save enough money to get out of the shelter fairly quickly. He knew that his Christmas money, which had lasted longer than he had figured, would soon be gone.

Frankie had encouraged him to apply for welfare and food stamps, but Will had been averse to the idea. His family had always scoffed at people who were "on the dole," as they put it; and Will would *never* want to run the risk of having his family find out that he was on welfare. However, in this case, he reasoned, *maybe* just food stamps would be okay.

Of *course* they would, he thought. He now *had* to be at the shelter at noon in order to eat lunch. If he had food stamps, he could miss lunch at the shelter and still be able to eat. It would, he told himself, free up an enormous amount of useful time in his schedule, time he now used for getting to and from the shelter during the middle of the day. The additional free time, he was certain, would be of benefit by making him more flexible in terms of interview scheduling. He would be able to go to an interview *anytime* during the day instead of just the middle of the morning and the middle of the afternoon.

Will knew that Frankie had food stamps, and he *never* showed up at the shelter during lunchtime. He sometimes even left before breakfast. His flexibility, no doubt, was enabling him to get more work done toward the business he wanted to start.

By the time Will boarded the bus to go to the shelter for dinner, he had convinced himself to go to the Human Services office the next morning and apply for food stamps. It was not a matter of pride any more, he felt, but one of common sense.

The next morning Will went to the intersection from which Malualua Road originated. The food stamp office was on the corner, and several signs indicated that it would open at seven-forty-five. Will waited with a large group of people outside, and when the doors to the building were opened, he crowded inside with the rest of the people.

Within an hour Will emerged from the building, amazed at how quickly he had been able to make his application. He had filled out the forms, gotten some instructions, and had been given an appointment to come back three days later with his birth certificate and social security card. The process had not been nearly as embarrassing or as cumbersome as he had feared, and now he had time to concentrate on his interview, scheduled for that afternoon.

His ears hurt and he wanted a drink, but Will instead had to plan the logistics and clothing changes for his interview. Changing at the shelter was out of the question, because Will knew that he would *never* be able to keep his clothes clean in the filthy bathroom. By this time of day, almost every square inch of it, maybe even the ceiling, he speculated, would be dirty.

Changing at the bathroom he used regularly in Waikiki would be the perfect solution, he reasoned, except for one thing: he would probably be late for his interview if he bused there and then back downtown, where the interview was to be. There was, it seemed, no feasible way to make the change. Even if there had been, Will knew that he would have to carry his usual clothes and shoes in a larger bag with him to the interview—they would not fit in his already-overburdened satchel. And that alone would probably tip the prospective employer off as to Will's homeless status—if the address on the resume had not done so already.

So this, he groused, is why homeless people have such

a hard time getting out of the rut they're in. Discouraged, Will walked the short distance to the bus stop. Within a short while he had settled into a chair at the food court in the mall, soda and newspaper in front of him.

Normally he would enjoy this time of day, but the difficulty posed by the interview situation weighed heavily on his mind. He knew that he needed a job in order to get out of the shelter, but he also knew beyond a shadow of a doubt that the obviousness of his homelessness would preclude his being offered any job he interviewed for. He was in a situation for which there was no solution, and one from which there was no apparent escape.

Opening his satchel, Will removed a sealed fifth of gin which was covered by a brown paper bag. He twisted the cap, breaking the seal, and unscrewed the cap the rest of the way off. He then tilted the bottle over the soda and poured gin into the cup, which was two-thirds full, until the cup was completely full. He grasped the straw between his thumb and index finger and stirred the contents of the cup.

After he saw that the contents of the cup were a uniform color, Will removed the straw. He picked the cup up with his right hand, brought it to his mouth, and took several sips of the contents before placing the cup back on the table.

"That," he said aloud, "takes care of that." He would not go to an interview, he decided, knowing that just the act of showing up would eliminate him from consideration for the job. He had been on the other side of the table before. He had not only seen *others* rule out applicants for no other reason than their appearance, he had done it *himself.* And in this case, he had passed judgment on himself, thus preventing a prospective employer from having the opportunity and the pleasure of saying "no."

Will took several more sips of his drink and then opened up his paper. He could read it now. His mind was at ease. The possibility of the shelter job was more real, he told himself. And he wouldn't have the same logistics problems if he got an interview for *this* one. If any prospective employer was capable of understanding his circumstances, the shelter management would be. Some of the pain began to subside in Will's ears.

In the clinic the next morning, the doctor squinted as he looked at the LCD display on the digital thermometer.

"A hundred and two point nine," he said aloud. "I'm going to give you a mat pass for today. I want you to stay inside and rest. And if your temperature hasn't dropped by tomorrow, I want you to be seen at the main clinic. And I also want you to start taking these." He handed Will a tiny yellow paper packet containing red capsules. "This is an antibiotic. One three times a day, every day until you finish them," he instructed. Will nodded. He felt tired and beaten, but he knew it was not *all* because of the illness.

As soon as he was outside, he wadded up the mat pass and threw it in the trash can. He didn't want to wait an hour to get Mengel to sign it and then not be able to rest because of the noise from the comings and goings inside the shelter. He knew that finding a place to sit down and have a strong drink would do him more good than "bedrest" on a vinyl mat and a concrete floor. He shuddered at the thought of lying on a mat and having Bertha walk by him.

Damn the medicine, too, he thought. Taking it would not give him any relief—it would only prevent him from being able to use his only proven method of relief, drinking. He carefully placed the yellow packet into a plastic sandwich bag inside his satchel. He walked toward the bus stop, his head aching, his legs sore, and his entire body feeling like it would take little more than a strong gust of wind to fell him.

By the time Will arrived at the mall, he wanted to be as far away from people as he could get. He quickly got a soda and trudged wearily across the road to the beach park. The sprinklers, for some reason, had not been turned on and the grass was dry. Will sat down, exhausted already at nine-thirty in the morning.

After spending most of the morning in a futile attempt to mask the illness that had been dogging him, Will determined that, even though he was not hungry, he should go back to the shelter and eat lunch before drinking any more. Lunch would probably include hot soup, and it would help him sustain a dwindling energy level. More importantly, it would keep him from drinking any more for the next two-and-a-half hours. He didn't want to risk falling asleep in the park again.

When Will returned to the park after lunch, ready to resume drinking, he noticed that the very patch of grass he had occupied earlier was now taken by an older man who stared at Will as he approached. Will cursed under his breath and kept walking until he found another somewhat isolated, shady place to sit. As he sat down and looked around, he noticed that the man was still looking in his direction.

As the afternoon grew later, Will's ailments, with the exception of his hearing impairment, seemed to trouble him less. He again began to picture himself as an employee of the Center for Social Aid—the homeless phoenix rising out of the ashes of misfortune, as his pickled mind imagined it. Perhaps he would become a spokesman for the homeless and downtrodden. Maybe he would run for city council one day, or state office—maybe even governor by the time he was fifty. Maybe he would . . .

He looked at his watch. He had dozed off, but only for a few minutes this time. He was still alone in the park—no one had come near him in his moments of vulnerability. Will took the last sips of his drink and tossed the cup into a trash can. The governor's office would have to wait, for it would soon be dinnertime at the shelter.

The Thursday morning sun stung Will's face as he walked down Malualua Road on his way to the food stamp office. His appointment was not for another hour, but he had decided to get there early and wait in air-conditioned comfort rather than find a place to wait outdoors.

He walked into the office, a large room bisected by a long counter. On one side of the counter was the waiting section, four rows of chairs with twelve chairs to a row. On the other side were the employees' work stations, bordered by doorways on each side of the room.

Will signed in at the reception desk and noticed that there were only four other people in the waiting area. One by one, they were called through one of the doorways, and Will had only been sitting for fifteen minutes when he heard his own name called.

A man who appeared to be of Japanese ancestry, but who spoke English with no distinguishable accent, led Will through the doorway on the left side of the room to a cubicle in the adjoining room.

"I am Mr. Ichigawa," he told Will, who extended his right hand. The man awkwardly brought his hand out from under the desk and weakly shook Will's hand. "You are William Tyne?" he asked.

"Yes. But you can call me—"

"Do you have your birth certificate and your social security card?" he asked.

"Right here." Will had placed both in his satchel so that he could get to them quickly. He handed them to Ichigawa. The balding man took them and exited the cubicle. Will heard the whine of a copy machine, and Ichigawa returned, handing the two items back to him. He then pulled a large, thick envelope out of a drawer on his desk, along with a form.

"Sign here," he directed Will, who had his own pen ready to use. Ichigawa handed the packet to Will. "This envelope contains your food stamp voucher. Take it to any bank that distributes food stamps during their food stamp distribution hours and they will give you the coupons." That's it? Will wondered. It was just *too* easy. He took the packet, reached down beside the chair for his satchel, and started to get up.

"Thanks, Mr. Ichigawa," he began. "I really appr—"

"Wait! I have to schedule a psychological evaluation for you," Ichigawa commanded.

"A *what*?"

"A psychological evaluation. For financial assistance," explained Ichigawa. Will didn't know what the government worker was talking about, but he *knew* he didn't need or want to see any sort of shrink.

"What financial assistance?" he asked. "You already gave me the food stamp thing." Ichigawa frowned as though Will was a slow student. He took the application Will had completed earlier in the week and pointed to it.

"See this box?" he asked. Will looked closely at the form. "When you filled out this form, you put a check mark in this box. That means you are applying for financial assistance. Do you wish to withdraw your application for financial assistance?" Will now *felt* like a slow student.

"Well, umm, I—I guess not," he sputtered, unsure of *what* he was doing.

"If you wish to apply for financial assistance, then you must be evaluated by a mental health provider, at the expense of this office. If we make an appointment for you and you do not keep the appointment, you must explain within ten days why you did not keep the appointment. Otherwise your application will not be considered. If you decide in the future that you wish to apply for financial assistance, you will have to complete a new application at that time." Will was now *thoroughly* confused.

"Okay, okay. I'm applying for financial assistance, so I guess I need to get evaluated. But what do they evaluate people for?"

"To determine whether you are eligible for financial

assistance," Ichigawa explained, himself now showing just a hint of exasperation. Will had settled back into the chair in which he had been sitting, and Ichigawa reached for the telephone. Will looked away, trying to understand exactly what it was that he was doing. Within a minute Ichigawa had completed the phone call, and he turned back toward Will.

"You have an appointment to see Dr. Isaac Cotlowitz tomorrow at 3 p.m. Is that a suitable time for you?" he asked. Will nodded his assent, and Ichigawa gave him the address and directions for getting there.

"So how long does it take to get this financial thing approved?" Will asked. Ichigawa handed another form to Will.

"The doctor must complete the bottom section of this form, the one highlighted, and it must be returned to us within ten days. The eligibility will be determined as soon as we get the completed form from the doctor. If you are approved for financial assistance, your benefits will be paid to you retroactively from your date of application. You will be notified by mail of any decision this office makes. Do you have any questions?" Will was overwhelmed by the onslaught of information. He knew he would have questions *later*, but he had none now.

"No. It's all perfectly clear," he lied. "Thank you for your help." He picked himself and his bag up and walked toward the door. Once he was back in the room where the waiting area was, he moved more quickly until he was outside the building. The bus stop was less than half a block up King Street, and he wanted to get to the mall. He knew there was a bank there where he hoped he could redeem his food stamp voucher, and he was anxious to get business matters completed so he could go to the beach park.

When the bus finally came it was almost empty, and Will slid into a seat by himself. He wasn't sure exactly *what* he had done, but he *thought* he had just applied for welfare. If that happened to be the case, he thought, so be it. He knew that he could use the money.

As soon as he got to the mall, Will wanted to go settle down with a drink first, then go get the food stamps. But he didn't want to have liquor breath in the bank, *especially* this early in the morning. He sat down on one of the outside benches on the mall's lower level, shaded by the upper level parking deck.

Opening the envelope, Will found a copy of the forms he had filled out, some slips of paper containing grocery-buying hints, two brochures on government services, and the voucher. No instructions, he lamented silently. He would soon have the stamps, but he had no idea what he could and could not use them to buy, or exactly which stores would accept them. One would think, he told himself, that something worth this much money would come with instructions. He would have to find out how to use them by using them.

Will entered the bank, conscious that his appearance did not equal that of the generally well-dressed employees and customers he saw. He signed the back of the voucher carefully and made certain that he had three forms of identification ready before he went to stand on the line.

There was only one line that was designated for food stamp distribution, and Will had to let three people behind him pass by while he waited for the customer who was already on the food stamp line to complete his transaction. The teller greeted him without looking up, made a face when she looked at the photo on his driver's license, and only then looked at his face. Her deft hands returned his identification, counted out the food stamp books, and recorded the transaction. In seconds, she stacked the books of stamps neatly atop the marble countertop and handed them to Will. He thanked her and she said nothing.

Perspiring freely as he walked out the door, Will exhaled. The hard part was over. As he walked toward the food court, Will wondered if he could buy soda with his food stamps. He knew that the grocery store on the back side of the mall had a soda dispenser. He could also pick something up for lunch and avoid having to go back to the shelter until dinnertime.

As he waited on the express line with a jumbo Diet Pepsi and a huge submarine sandwich, Will's pores again opened the flood gates. He was certain that grocery store clerks treated people with food stamps like second-class citizens. The cashier might even report him to the manager, he feared, if the soda was not a food stamp item.

Will's turn came and the woman at the express check-out counter quickly totaled Will's purchase, took the food stamps and handed him his change, adding a smiling "thank you." Will walked out of the store, elated by the "magic" he had just witnessed. He had actually exchanged pieces of paper—which were not money— for soda and food. It was, his grandiose mind told him, the beginning of a brand new era.

In exceptional good humor as a result of his newly acquired buying power, Will walked across the road into the beach park. His ears still hurt and he had an occasional cough, but his spirits relegated his ailments to the back of his mind.

As he approached his favorite shady spot, he noticed that the same older man who had been there earlier in the week was there again, this time with two women and another man. Will thought he saw a snide grin on the older man's face as his arrival was noticed by the foursome. Determined that he would not be displaced from *his* spot again, Will found a place to sit that was about forty feet away from the group. The grass was thinner, and he was just barely covered by shade.

Staring the members of the group down each time they looked in his direction, Will finally felt that he was no longer under constant observation. He took the gin bottle out of his satchel and mixed a drink. The relaxation that came over him as he drank and thought of his successful morning was marred only by the fact that the two couples did not give any indication of their intention to leave any time soon.

Each time Will moved, it seemed to him that one or more of them *had* to look to see what he was doing. The shelter deprived him of privacy so much of the time, and he was becoming irritated by the constant surveillance of the four people in the park.

Will ate as much of the submarine sandwich as he had room for, then ate the remaining meat and cheese out of the middle. He was looking around to see where the closest trash can was when he noticed that a two birds had landed within a few yards of him, apparently interested in the remaining bread he was about to throw away.

That gave Will an idea. He tossed small crumbs of the bread, one at a time, in the direction of the birds. Within a minute, there were twenty birds chasing after the bread crumbs. In another two minutes there were thirty more. Will sat on the grass rhythmically tossing the crumbs in different directions, trying to make sure that different birds got them each time.

Each time a bird got a crumb, it flew up into the nearby tree so that it wouldn't have to fight the other birds to keep it. Will continued tossing the crumbs until the last one had been taken. Satisfied with himself, he added another splash of gin to his drink.

In about five minutes, Will heard one of the women in the foursome exclaim something in a language he didn't understand. He looked toward the group and saw that the woman was wiping the sleeve of her blouse with a napkin. Hardly another minute had passed when he heard another similar exclamation. As he looked up, he also saw the older man using his handkerchief with one hand to wipe something off a paper plate he held in his other hand.

One of the couples appeared to be gathering up their belongings to leave. Will looked up. Sure enough, several of the birds were sitting on the branch of the tree that extended directly above the two couples. He could now see that the woman had been trying to wipe bird droppings from her sleeve. He guessed that the older man had been similarly bombarded. Will laughed out loud.

The two men and two women quickly packed their things and left without a word to Will. He guessed that they did not equate what had happened to them with his earlier generosity to the birds. Nor did they have any idea that he had done it *on purpose*.

Will had to do laundry the next morning, or else wear already-worn clothes to the psychological evaluation that afternoon. As he worked as quickly as he could to sort his clothes on the floor of the shelter's main room before breakfast, he could hear the pouring rain outside. He hoped it would stop by the time breakfast was over. His laundry bag was bulky, and he knew that having to carry it along with his satchel would make him slow.

As soon as he had the clothes in the black nylon bag he placed it atop a chair, and quickly took his luggage bags back to the cage. He left it there, keeping one eye on it, while he went through the line to get a plate of food. None of his cohorts were at the shelter that morning, and he quickly finished his breakfast.

The rain was no longer pouring as Will went out the door, but it was still falling steadily. He hurried down Malualua Road to the bus stop as fast as he could walk, the bulky laundry bag swinging back and forth and banging into his knee the whole way. The sheltered area of the bus stop was crowded, and Will had no other place to stand that afforded him protection from the rain. It always seemed to him that the buses came less frequently when it rained. He looked at his watch, then down King Street. At least, he told himself, he already had enough quarters to do two loads of laundry. That meant he wouldn't have to wait for the laundromat attendant, an old but lively man who usually showed up at the laundromat at least half an hour after Will got there.

The bus came, but it was full. Will had to stand in the aisle, anchoring his laundry bag between his legs and covering the flap of his satchel with his one free hand. At each stop, he had to move or twist himself so that other passengers could get by him. After a bumpy forty-five minute ride, fifteen minutes longer than usual, Will pushed his way toward the rear door of the bus and got off.

It was another two blocks to the laundromat, and it was still raining. Will was wet but relieved when he got there. There were only two other people doing laundry, and he would be able to fix himself a good, stiff drink as soon as he got his clothes into the washers. He took his bag and satchel to a table in the back corner of the laundromat, a vantage point from which he could see everything—and where there would be no one behind him.

Since there were rarely more than three or four other people there, Will could leave his things on the table and walk around unencumbered. He started the washing machines and went to the front of the open-air facility. Casting a quick glance at his satchel in the back corner, he trotted a hundred or so feet down the block to a newspaper box, fed it two quarters, grabbed a paper, and hurried back. The soda machine had no Diet Pepsi button, so he treated himself to a Hawaiian Punch, gleefully mindful of the irony that would occur when he added gin to it.

Will retreated to the back corner where he removed the cup he had stored in his satchel, and poured himself his first drink of the day. He would be wet, he chuckled to himself, long before his clothes would be dry.

By the time Will had finished his laundry, the rain had stopped. He walked the six blocks to a different bus stop to take a slower, less crowded bus back to the shelter. He was glad that it was still overcast, or else the sun would have felt doubly hot on his gin-soaked head.

Will went straight to the bathroom as soon as he entered

the main room of the shelter, just before eleven-thirty. There was no one but him in it, and he decided that it would be safe, for once, to change into clean clothes while he stood on the rickety wooden bench, a foot-and-a-half above the floor. He slid the bench toward the wall so that he could brace himself as he changed. Having had a snootful of gin, he couldn't trust his already-spindly legs to keep him steady on the old bench.

Out of the bathroom before anyone else entered it, Will left his laundry bag in the main room and hurried into the cage, which had just opened. Retrieving both of his large bags, he moved as quickly as he could back into the main room. Re-packing each of his bags as he worked, he unloaded the clean clothes into them, packing everything in as tight a manner as he could. He stuffed the clothes he had just changed from into the laundry bag and crammed it into one end of one of the other bags.

By ten minutes to twelve, Will had both of his large bags repacked and back in the cage, and he stood at the end of the lunch line, just inside the double-doorway to the main room. Will saw that Nahesa, the shelter guest who usually led the group in the recitation of the Lord's Prayer before meals, had taken his place beside the head of the line.

Will didn't like Nahesa, a dark-skinned local who bullied some of the shelter's more docile denizens, and who feigned piety and goodwill whenever there was a shelter employee nearby. But Will didn't *care* who led the prayer, as long as it was recited quickly whenever he was hungry.

Remembering that he had an appointment at three o'clock, Will checked to make sure the floor was clean before he sat down to eat. He took extra care not to spill food in his lap, something that was easy to do when he sat in such an awkward position to eat.

The psychologist Will had to see was only two blocks away from the mountain, or *mauka*, side of the mall. The clouds had given way to sunshine, and Will knew that he would have time to down another drink at the beach park before his appointment.

Will particularly liked being able to use food stamps to buy sodas. The $1.09 price meant that he could give the cashier two dollars in food stamps and get back ninety-one cents in real money. That change would come in handy for buying newspapers and doing laundry. And, if he ever *really* needed to, he could easily accumulate enough change to buy a small bottle of gin.

The idea of financial assistance—welfare—still did not appeal to Will. He knew that food stamps were, in a way, financial assistance. But they were just for *food*, for subsistence, he reasoned. Welfare, to him and his family, had always been something that was handed out to people who were just too *lazy* to work. And Will was certain that he was *not* lazy.

Full of misgivings, he boarded the bus that would take him down the road that passed between the mall and the beach park. As it was no longer raining, the trip took less than twenty minutes, and soon Will was in the grocery store, helping himself to a Diet Pepsi from the fountain.

Lunch had lifted some of Will's morning fog, and he made his way quickly to the park, placing a plastic bag on the ground to sit on, and making sure he was not sitting directly under the tree. He chuckled when he thought of how his ploy with the birds had gotten rid of the two couples. He now had the whole area almost to himself.

Will became relaxed quickly in the warm afternoon breeze. He began to see that a few things had finally gone his way. He had a job prospect, he had the wherewithal to buy food, and he had even gotten the birds to help his cause. Maybe going for welfare, he told himself, would be pushing it. Besides, how could he *ever* explain it to his family if they somehow found out? No matter what he did after that, he would be shamed forever.

And what if he *didn't* pass the evaluation? He would be

wasting his time for something that he wasn't even sure he *wanted.* He certainly didn't want to have to be analyzed by some egghead he had never met. Why, Will speculated, the psychologist might even try to convince him that he had a *drinking* problem! After all, he *did* have alcohol on his breath already.

What would he tell the doctor to excuse *that*? That he had a rough morning at the laundromat? And even if he got through the evaluation, he didn't want to have to deal with Ichigawa again.

The more Will drank, the more he thought. And the more he thought, the more he wanted to stay at the park and drink. Two-thirty came and he decided that he would miss the appointment and talk to Frankie about welfare that night. If Frankie was getting welfare, Will decided, then so would *he*. After all, Frankie had been a millionaire on paper at one time.

As for Ichigawa, Will knew that he had ten days to make up an excuse for having missed the appointment. Will made another trip to the grocery store for a soda, and passed the afternoon sitting in the park.

Careful to measure what he drank, Will arrived at the shelter for dinner thinking that he still looked almost sober in comparison to some of his fellow guests. As soon as he finished eating Will went outside to look for Frankie. After hearing Frankie's customary excited monologue about his progress in locating yet another insurance beneficiary, Will changed the subject.

"I've been thinking about applying for welfare," he said cautiously. "I worry a little bit that it might not be the right thing to do. What do you think?" Frankie laughed.

"If you're asking me if I get it," he said, looking Will straight in the eye, "It's *none of your damned business!*" Will was taken aback for an instant before Frankie continued. "No, no! I'm just kidding! *Of course* I get welfare. *Everybody* here gets welfare, or *some* kind of handout. It's really no big deal."

Will inhaled deeply, immensely relieved.

"You mean," he began, "It doesn't bother you that you get money from the government?" Frankie shook his head.

"The way I see it," he said, "is that there are probably a lot of these people around here who just play the system. They live and eat here for free, and they have their welfare or SSI money to use on drugs or booze or whatever. I know that a couple of them get SSI *and* work full-time for money under the table.

"But the reason I don't mind taking welfare money is that I'm honestly working toward getting back on my feet. Sure, I let myself get involved in some bad things, but I paid my debt to society and I've acknowledged my mistakes. Now I'm trying to get my life going forward again, so welfare is one of the things that society provides to help people like me. I think that's why welfare was started—*not* so people could drink and use drugs." Will was quiet for a moment as he tried to absorb what Frankie had said. He had never thought about it like *that* before.

"So, for instance . . ." he began slowly. "If I were to go through the process and get welfare, you don't think it would mean that I was lazy?"

"Of course not," Frankie assured him. "That's why I *suggested* it to you *two months ago!*"

Despite Frankie's seemingly logical explanation, Will was still not sure that applying for welfare was the right thing to do. Anyway, he reasoned, he still had the possibility of the job at the shelter.

Shortly after the duty managers allowed the crowd inside the building to claim mats, Will heard the P. A. system click on. Makolu announced that the mailroom was open, and Will was close enough to the mailroom door that he was able to get near the front of the line.

A good haul, he thought, as he took the three pieces of mail he received back to his mat to open them. The first was a photocopied rejection form letter, informing him that one of the jobs he had applied for had been filled by "a candidate who best suited the company's needs." That's just fine, Will thought. He had, after all, only been applying for a job, not running for office. He chuckled at his own far-fetched humor.

The second piece of mail was from his last employer in New York. It was the W-2 form for the last six weeks he had worked. He smiled, because he knew that it would guarantee him a good tax refund. Realizing that there was nothing other than the form in the envelope, Will scowled.

"Not even a 'hello, how are you,' or a 'kiss my ass,'" he muttered to himself, mildly upset that an employer he thought he had served well hadn't even included a polite word of greeting.

The instant Will flipped over the third envelope, he recognized the handwriting. It was Michelle's! Will quickly and carefully tore open the envelope and began reading the two-page letter. She was fine, he read. Her design business was booming, her old MGB convertible was still running well, and she hadn't heard any good music lately but often listened to the older music to which Will had first introduced her. She wondered how life was for him in his tropical paradise. She imagined that he must be doing very well. Will laughed as he read.

One thing was missing from her letter. She had been married barely nine months, and made *no* mention of her husband or of married life. That wasn't like her. Even though she knew that Will had a tender spot for her, she had always talked about her other relationships over the thirteen years they had known each other. Will wondered if her marriage was making her have second thoughts about passing *him* over so long ago. He smiled wryly to think of how she would react if she knew what he had let happen to himself. He took his satchel out from under the mat and carefully tucked the letter toward the back of the folio that was inside the satchel.

As Will was about to leave the building the following Tuesday morning, he passed by the bulletin board and saw a message with his name on it. It was a note from John Marin, stating that Will should see him that morning. Will glanced at the reception desk and made certain that Bertha had not come in early. Jerry was still on duty, and he paged the building for Marin. Will was soon on his way up the stairs, hoping for good news about the shelter job.

Will could see through the small, square window in the door that Marin wore a blank expression as he knocked. Poker face, Will guessed. Marin beckoned for him to come in.

"Anything new?" Marin asked as Will sat down.

"Nope. Same crap," answered Will.

"You got my note, I take it?" he queried.

"Yeah, I figured it might be something about that job working for the Center that you told me about. I've been hoping for a little *good* luck for a change."

"Well, shit, Will. I hate to burst your bubble on that one," Marin grimaced. "But they filled that job. I heard about it late yesterday. That's why I left the note—so you could hear it from me first. I was sort of pissed about it."

"Not even an *interview?*" Will asked, the pitch of his voice rising. "They have people like Mengel making such a case about how important it is for all of us to 'transition' back into society, but they won't even grant *me* the courtesy of an interview!" Will could not hide his irritation. "Who got the job?" he wondered aloud.

"That's the part that pissed *me*," Marin declared. "You know the nighttime duty manager, Makolu? The one that looks almost like a man?" Will nodded. "Her girlfriend got the job. She has no experience in the field, and she didn't even finish her second year at community college. Someone told me that under the section on the application where it asked for relevant experience, she listed the two years that she spent as a prison guard."

"I'll be drinking early today," Will declared, only half-joking. He continued, "Seriously, you *know* I'm disappointed. Especially that I didn't even get called for an interview. But thanks for putting in a good word for me. Having *one* person on my side is some consolation."

"So do you have any other prospects that you're working on?" asked Marin, seeming relieved.

"As a matter of fact," Will responded, rising from his chair, "I sure do. I have to make a phone call this morning to someone named Ichigawa."

Chapter 9

Darkness Pierced

The priority mail label on the envelope from the storage company in New Jersey made Will wonder what the urgency was. As he sat down on his mat to open the envelope, the din of the shelter's main room seemed like one loud blur of noise to him. It was loud, but easy to tune out.

The storage company wanted him to know that the rent was one month past due for the locker in which he had his possessions stored. Big deal, he thought. He had paid for four months' rent in advance just before he had left New York, and he was sure that the company could wait a few more weeks until, he hoped, he got his first welfare check.

He wondered when he would finally be able to afford to go back and have the rest of his things shipped to Hawaii. He would, of course, have to find a job and a place to live first. Then he would have to save enough money to go back to New York, buy proper shipping containers, and pay for the expense of having his things transported halfway across the Pacific Ocean. But he could do without them until then.

Momentarily lost in his thoughts, Will was still sitting on his mat staring at the narrow strip of concrete that served as an aisle when he noticed in front of him the presence of a pair of feet shod in new work boots, a rare sight in the worn-out world of the shelter. He looked up and saw that it was Matt.

"Where'd you get those?" he asked.

"A place called Jobs Oahu paid for them," Matt responded, grinning. "I got into a work program at the city arboretum and this place got me the boots and some work clothes." He *had* to find out more about this, and knowing it would be easier to have a conversation outside, Will slipped his shoes on and stood. Matt followed him through the narrow aisle between the mats and out the front door. As soon as they were away from the porch, Will sat down in the grass.

"You mean all you had to do was get a job, and this place bought you work shoes and clothes?" He was agog with interest.

"Yeah. I just had to get a note from my boss saying what kind of clothes I would need. They even gave me a bus pass, too."

"Where *is* this place?" Will asked with exaggerated enthusiasm. "Where do *I* sign up?" Matt finally sat down, taking the boots off his feet and replacing them with an almost worn out pair of sneakers that he pulled from his backpack.

"Just a minute," he said. "Let me get these boots packed in here and I'll find the phone number for you." In another moment he handed will a dirty scrap of paper with the number on it.

"I don't know if they help college people, though," Matt added. "I think they mostly work with people who want to learn a skill or a trade."

"So?" Will countered. "I'm desperate. Learning a skill might be the only way I ever get a job here. So far, my degree hasn't done anything for me." He laughed as he pantomimed the motions of a person sweeping. "I'll even train to be a janitor! Some of them probably make as much money as the people whose offices they clean!"

"I don't know," Matt mused, starting to look tired. "I'm just glad that I don't have to work for that damned land-clearing slavedriver any more. This arboretum job will be a lot easier. They even have a program where I can save part of my paycheck toward a deposit and first month's rent on a place to live."

Will was interested but decided against pressing Matt for more information. He knew that it would be better to wait for Matt to *offer* more information than it would be to ask for it. He looked at the number again, and copied it into his address notebook.

The next morning Will took extra care not to let his clothes touch the floor or the walls of the bathroom while he was dressing. He had called Mr. Ichigawa earlier in the week and had gotten another appointment to see Dr. Cotlowitz, the psychologist. He had specifically asked for a morning appointment this time, worried that he might again drink himself out of the proper frame of mind for keeping the appointment.

As soon as he was done with breakfast, Will strolled outside and down Hoka Street in the direction of the harbor. He passed by the concrete slab where he occasionally sat, and it reminded him that he had not seen the little man with the grocery cart recently.

The pay phone in the entranceway of the shelter had not been in use when Will had passed it, but he knew that if he tried to use it, there would be someone who would almost immediately conjure up some sort of disturbance in the hallway. He preferred to use a phone booth at a service station three blocks away. It was quieter.

His phone call this morning was to Jobs Oahu. The woman who answered took his name and asked him several questions, then put him on hold. Will watched the traffic go by for a few minutes before the woman came back on the phone.

She offered him an appointment for March 8. He took it and thanked her even though he was disappointed. It was more than three weeks away.

Will still had plenty of time before his nine-thirty appointment with the psychologist, and he decided to go to the post office to get tax return forms. His refund wouldn't be fast in coming, he knew, but it would eventually get there. If his application for welfare didn't go through, he knew that it would come in *very* handy.

As he left the post office, a light rain was beginning to fall outside. He lumbered the hundred yards to the bus stop and boarded the first bus that arrived at the stop. He had only a short distance to go, and all of the buses went to within easy walking distance of the building where his appointment was.

It was nine o'clock when he arrived at the office of Dr. Cotlowitz, and when he examined the forms the receptionist had given him to fill out, he was glad he had arrived early. He busied himself with the task of completing the forms and the survey of questions included with them.

Dr. Cotlowitz appeared to be in his early forties, younger than Will had imagined. He was a thin, hollow-eyed man, and he was almost completely bald. Will noticed that Cotlowitz had a strong handshake, and he was glad that the doctor was starting the appointment a few minutes early. It meant that he would be able to get it over with and have a drink.

The psychologist seemed to be skeptical of everything that Will said, and he began to feel slightly defensive. The preliminary questions had been covered quickly, and the questions about alcohol were making Will uncomfortable.

"So you started drinking recreationally when you were how

old?" he asked.

"Nineteen," Will replied.

"And how much would you say you drink now—per

week?" he queried.

"Oh, maybe about a liter of gin a week," he lied. His consumption was four times that, and *that* was only because he couldn't *afford* more. "Maybe a little more," he added.

"When did you last have a drink?" the psychologist asked.

"Oh, I guess it was night before last," he lied again. He had polished off his last drink just before the ten o'clock curfew the previous night. "But that was the first drink I had in a week. What does drinking have to do with all of this?" he asked.

"To get welfare under the terms by which you applied, you have to have a disability," Cotlowitz explained. "If you have a drinking problem, it might be considered a disability. Do you lie or have you ever lied to anyone about your drinking habits?"

"*Never,*" Will asserted emphatically. "I drink occasionally, and I admit it. Why would I lie? If I thought I had a problem with it, I might lie to cover it up, but I know I don't have a drinking problem, so I don't try to hide the amount that I drink." Will thought he saw a trace of a smile on the doctor's face.

"Have you ever been warned or disciplined at work because of your drinking? Or have you ever been dismissed or asked to leave a job because of your drinking habits?"

"First of all," Will almost exploded, "it's not a *habit!*" He quickly calmed down. "No, I've never been disciplined for drinking on the job," he responded, twisting the doctor's question to fit his answer. "And I have *never* been dismissed from a job because of drinking." At least, he thought, his last employer hadn't had the nerve to *tell* him that was what he had been fired for.

"Have you ever been told that you had any kind of physical problems that could have been caused by drinking?" the psychologist continued. His quiet, smug manner was beginning to rankle Will.

"No. No physical problems," he responded. Except for a pot belly and high blood pressure, he thought to himself. Will felt a drop of water hit his lap. He realized that it had fallen from his forehead, which was beaded heavily with perspiration.

Cotlowitz paused to write on the form Will had brought for him to fill out. Will was glad for the respite, and couldn't wait to get outside.

"I'm giving you six months," Cotlowitz said to Will, who looked puzzled. His inquisitor explained, "What it means is that I'm stating that you have a disability that is expected to last for at least six months." He finished his writing on the paper and excused himself from the room. Within a minute he returned. "Do you want me to mail this to the Human Services office, or are they expecting you to take it to them?"

"I can take it to them," Will answered, relieved that his ordeal was almost over. "I'm going in that direction anyway."

"It'll probably speed up their process anyway," Cotlowitz said, smiling for the first time. Will thanked him, shoved the form into his satchel, and headed out into the hallway.

It wasn't until after he had gotten outside sat down at the bus stop that it occurred to him that Cotlowitz had said that he had a disability. He was mystified. He had detailed his sleep problems, his constant problems with his ears, his coughing, his unhappiness about being homeless . . . But none of that was really a disability. What was it, he wondered, that made him disabled?

As the bus traversed the morning traffic, Will began to plan his course of action for the afternoon. He would first drop off the form at Mr. Ichigawa's office, then go back to the mall. There he would get lunch and a soda and spend some time recovering from the strain of the morning.

The wheels of the bus squealed to a halt on King Street,

a short distance away from the Human Services office. Will stepped off and began to unbuckle the flap on his satchel as he walked toward the building. Just before he got to the doorway, he fished the completed form out of the satchel and paused to look at it.

He could barely make out the script of the psychologist. There were several check marks by certain words Will assumed must be Human Services jargon, and there was something about sleep habits. It was the handwritten word that was scrawled in the space for the diagnosis that stopped Will in his tracks: "ALCOHOLISM."

Will thought for a minute. If he had been declared disabled for six months, it meant that he had something wrong with him. If he had something wrong with him, he would have to see someone about having it corrected. Who would he see about having such a circumstance corrected? Why, of course, he told himself—a psychologist!

He was sure that he had merely been "rubber-stamped" with a disability. That way the psychologists could refer the patients they had declared disabled to other psychologists for treatment—since the Human Services rules prevented them from *treating* the people they had *evaluated.* And after six months, Will figured, the whole process would be started up again.

In the meantime, all the "disabled" people could collect their welfare checks. What a great system! No wonder they called this place paradise, he thought. The "alcoholism" notation was, Will decided, just a contrivance for allowing him to get welfare and for allowing the shrinks to perpetuate their own business.

Will rushed up the stairs to Ichigawa's office, elated that he had nothing *really* wrong with him, and anxious to get to the beach park so that he could celebrate with a good belt of gin. He had endured enough for *this* day.

Will sat in the beach park later that afternoon, contentedly optimistic about what he had accomplished during the morning. He was beginning to feel relaxed following a hearty lunch at the shelter, and the gin was slowly starting to take effect. He rummaged through his satchel, noticing that he was beginning to accumulate a collection of paperwork from the food stamp and welfare application procedures.

Taking his writing folio out of the satchel, he determined that he would discard any outdated paperwork in order to make room for the more recent additions. The folio slid out of his lap as he reached to close the flap on the satchel. As it did, several small, neatly-folded squares of pink paper fell out of one of the pockets. Will quickly grabbed them so that the steady breeze would not take them away and, unfolding one, he saw that it was a pawn ticket for one of his cameras. He sighed and his shoulders sagged when he saw that the forfeiture date had already passed. One by one, he looked at the others, each of which had passed its forfeiture date, and realized that all of his camera equipment was gone forever.

Reaching back inside his satchel, he removed an Evian bottle and added a generous splash of its contents to his drink. For once, he felt only a slight tinge of wistfulness about the loss of something. He had become so accustomed to losses and concessions, he supposed, that they no longer affected him the way they once had. He took a gulp of his drink, and looked up at the sky. A large commercial airliner was passing over the park, making an almost-silent descent toward the airport.

"Probably at least one *more* fool on that one," Will muttered to himself.

As Will gripped the railing to ascend the steps to the front porch of the shelter that evening, he remembered that there was to be a house meeting that night. That would mean that he could take his time eating dinner, since he would not have to rush to find a duty manager to get a number for a mat. He shuffled through the main room and out onto the lanai.

Coming back to the shelter at the same time each night seemed to Will to be a repetitious, endless admission of defeat.

But at the same time, it was a relief to have such a place to come to. Lately the shelter had come to seem like home, rather than reminding Will that he had no home.

As soon as he finished dinner, Will began to make his way toward the outside of the building. He saw that Dick Mengel had just come in through the side entrance and was hurrying through the hallway. Will guessed that he was there to prepare for the house meeting. Mengel slowed as he neared the congested entranceway. He looked toward Will and smiled as if in apparent recognition.

"How's it going, Bill?" he said, patting Will on the shoulder.

"Uh—fine," Will managed to say, flabbergasted not only at the fact that Mengel had spoken to him, but that he had also *almost* gotten his name right. He could only guess that John Marin might have pointed him out to Mengel.

Will threaded his way outside and walked to the far end of the shelter, exhaustedly dropping himself into the grass. He brought his knees toward his chest, folded his arms across them, and buried his head in his arms. His upper body began to shake, and tears welled up in his eyes. Will didn't understand why he was doing this, and tried to contain himself. But he could not stop, and he began to sob quietly as tears fell freely from his eyes and into his lap.

Only the realization that he might soon be noticed and be considered easy prey for someone enabled Will to begin to calm himself. He looked around as he wiped his eyes, and he saw that no one was near him or looking in his direction. He was now quiet and still, but the tears still flowed. It had felt so *good* to be patted on the shoulder. Will had not felt any kind of encouragement from anyone since long before he had left New York, and just the fact that Mengel had spoken to him had caught Will completely off guard. He just wasn't used to anything *good* happening, particularly not any sort positive initiative taken by someone with whom he had never spoken.

Finally regaining his composure, Will cleared his throat and dried his eyes. He had only sat for a few more minutes when he noticed that Frankie was coming toward him. They exchanged greetings as Frankie sat down.

"So, anything new?" Frankie inquired.

"Nah, just the shrink appointment," Will answered. "I guess I'll be 'on the dole' soon, if they approve me."

"As long as they gave you a diagnosis that says you're disabled, you'll get it," Frankie assured him. "Did you see what the doctor put?"

"Nahh," Will lied. "I just folded it up and took it to that Ichigawa person at the welfare office. He said they would contact me by mail."

"You probably got it. Put it this way—I don't know of *anybody* that went through the application process and *didn't* get it, unless they hadn't been in the state long enough or some other reason like that." Frankie reached into his backpack and pulled out a manila folder and a slightly worn wirebound composition book. Will knew that Frankie's questions had just been perfunctory pleasantries that served as a lead-in to a lengthy monologue about his latest investigative exploits.

"Looks like you've been doing some work," Will commented, nodding toward the comfortably full manila folder.

"Yeah. I found where this lady is," Frankie responded, pulling a sheet of paper from the folder. "She's got three grand coming to her, as soon as I let her know about it. I wrote this letter to send to her, but I don't know if it covers my ass legally. I want *my* cut out of that money, too." Will took the letter and read it. He knew that Frankie knew that he was good at writing. Will took his folio out of his satchel.

"Want me to make some suggestions?" he asked Frankie.

"Yeah, yeah! Why do you think I handed it to you?" Frankie exclaimed, laughing. Frankie's wording made the letter sound more like something that should have been spoken. Will began rewriting the letter in a more "official" tone, and Frankie sat quietly as Will worked. Several minutes later Will was done, and he handed his completed version to Frankie. Frankie studied it carefully.

"Well?" Will queried.

"Sounds more—ahhh—more—professional, more businesslike," Frankie nodded. "I don't know if it'll guarantee that I'll get my cut, but it's better than what *I* had."

Will looked at his watch. It was almost seven. The rewriting had spared him from hearing Frankie's detailed monologue about the day. Will slid his folio back into the satchel and began to buckle it.

"You going to the meeting?" he asked Frankie. "I want to be by the door when they open it so I can get a seat near the front. If I don't, I won't be able to hear what's going on," he explained. Or have a good view of Karen Ling, he thought.

"I'll be in later," Frankie responded. "I'm not in any big hurry to sit through another one of *those*."

Will picked himself up and walked toward the front porch of the building. Just as he started up the steps, the front door swung open and he followed the first group of people inside. Walking into the main room, he parked himself at the right end of the second row, where he would be just a few yards away from where Karen Ling usually sat, but would still have someone in front of him so that his gaze would not be as likely to be noticed.

At a few minutes after seven, Dick Mengel called the meeting to order but, to Will's disappointment, Karen Ling was not present. Mengel announced that this meeting might be longer than usual, and then opened the floor to questions from the shelter residents. Will immediately tuned out the discussion and his thoughts began to wander, first to the matter of the outdated pawn tickets, then to the realization that he only had enough money for one more half-gallon of gin.

After the meeting had gone on for about twenty minutes, the door to the main room slowly opened and Karen Ling quietly walked in, followed by two police officers. She sat down in the vacant chair that had been left for her, and the two officers seated themselves to her left. Will looked at her face carefully, and he could see no flaws. He wasn't even sure whether she was wearing makeup. Her eyes looked as dark as onyx, but with diamonds set in the corners.

After Mengel had fielded one more question from the assembly, he introduced the two police officers. They were, according to his introduction, officers who were assigned to the shelter's neighborhood. Karen Ling began to speak, and she explained that the shelter wanted to begin a neighborhood patrol on a regular basis.

The purpose of the patrol, which was to be made up primarily of shelter guests and employees, she explained, was to make sure that people who came from outside the neighborhood to buy and use drugs, or to commit other crimes, were identified and thus had their continued presence discouraged. This, she hoped, would ensure that the shelter and its residents wouldn't continue to take the blame and the heat for *all* of the neighborhood's ills.

She further explained that the first patrol would be on the coming Friday evening, and that there would be several police officers to accompany the shelter employees and guests. She also stated that, after this meeting, she would be taking the names of any shelter residents who wished to participate in the patrol.

Will had cupped his hand behind one ear in order to listen intently to her from the moment she had begun speaking. As soon as she finished her presentation and introduced one of the police officers, who began to speak, Will's mind shifted into overdrive. He would certainly sign up for this patrol, he determined, just to get the chance to speak to Karen Ling. Maybe he could remind her that John Marin had given her a copy of his resume. Maybe she would be impressed that he was willing to volunteer for the patrol, apparently a pet project of hers. Maybe she already knew who he was. Maybe he would be able to think of something witty to say to her. Maybe she would take a liking to him. Maybe this whole patrol thing would start him on a roll that would take him out of the shelter. Maybe—the meeting was over. The sliding chairs and immediate rumble of voices brought the curtain down on Will's reverie.

As he stood to leave, he had second thoughts about volunteering for the patrol. There would probably be dozens of people who would sign up for it. Will would only be another unrecognized, unappreciated face in a crowd of motley, hopeless people. Dejected, Will started to walk toward the doorway. He noticed that, amid all of the continuing conversations and motion in the room, Karen Ling was standing alone by the door. Had *no one* offered to volunteer?

Without thinking, Will walked over to her.

"I want to sign up for this patrol thing," he blurted to her. She glanced up at him, then looked away as if distracted by something on the other side of the room, and then looked back at Will.

"Your name?" she asked, pleasant but otherwise expressionless.

"Tyne. Will Tyne," he responded. Her brow furrowed.

"Dine?" she asked without looking up. Will was sweating already. So much for saying something witty, he thought.

"Tyne. T-Y-N-E," he spelled. She quickly scribbled the name on her notebook.

"We'll meet in the parking lot at seven on Friday," she explained in a matter-of-fact manner. "You won't need to get a number for a mat. The duty managers will have a list of the people participating in the patrol, and a mat will be saved for you."

"That's it?" Will asked, unable to think of anything to say that might extend the moment.

"Yes," she answered pleasantly, but cocking her head slightly to one side as if she didn't know what else Will was expecting. Will turned and walked slowly toward the door, feeling his face flush with embarrassment, even though he wasn't sure what he was embarrassed about.

As Will took his place at the end of the line outside, he could see that Karen was still there—now taking the names of other people, who would make his just another face in the crowd. The next morning Will made his usual rounds followed by a trip to the libation station. He had enough money left for one more half-gallon, with a few dollars left over. He had just enough food stamps to eat lunch on until the next ones were due to arrive in the mail. And, he hoped, his first welfare check would soon be on the way. He determined that he would enjoy this half-gallon over the next two days, then use the medicine he had gotten from the clinic until he had money to buy more liquor.

That would accomplish two things: give the medicine a chance to bring his ears and throat back to health, and make sure that he didn't show up with a hangover at the community patrol. In the meantime, he would enjoy this bottle without having the perpetual worry of wondering what would happen when he ran out.

He wanted to be sure that he was relatively clear-minded at the community patrol, since he might have another chance to speak to Karen Ling or one of the other shelter administrators. They would see, he felt, that they had passed over a qualified, sincere applicant when they had not hired him for the shelter job. And maybe, he speculated, they might just give him a chance next time they had a job opening. Since it was now only Tuesday, he would have at least most of Thursday to get over the after-effects of drinking; and that would leave him in good form on Friday.

Will spent the remainder of the day at the beach park, making two more trips back across the road to the mall for soda and food. The only other punctuations in his solitude were occasional trips to the bathroom, a slight ordeal since he had to repack his satchel and carry that and his drink with him each time he went.

His third trip across the road, just after five o'clock, was to the bus stop. By this time Will, who had been carelessly augmenting his drinks all day, was moving in a noticeably sluggish manner. He trudged across the road, barely getting to the opposite curb before the traffic began moving past him. Even with effort, he could make himself move no faster.

When the bus came, he had to grasp the handrails on either side of the doorway in order to hoist himself onto the bus. He threaded his way toward the one open seat near the middle of the bus, holding on to the rail the whole way. Just as he released his grip on the rail to sit down, the bus lurched to one side and he clumsily plowed into the man sitting in the seat next to the vacant one. He excused himself, and barely noticed the disgust in the man's face as the man waved his hand in front of his nostrils.

Having quickly downed the last third of his final drink of the day, Will's system was still absorbing the liquor as he swayed to and fro with the motion of the moving bus. When it finally arrived at the stop on Malualua Road, Will's tight grip on the door rail was the only thing that saved him from toppling to the pavement as he exited the bus. He waited for a break in the traffic on the moderately busy road, and crossed it as quickly as he was able.

Just a few yards away was the wall in front of King's Discount Store, and Will made his way to it, half-sitting and half-falling on it. He breathed a sigh of relief as he brushed the sweat from his face. At least the hard part of the trip was over. Even if he didn't make it inside to eat dinner, he could still get a number for a mat.

The late afternoon sun was still hot, but it was to Will's back. He sat on the wall, unmoving, afraid that someone arriving for the evening meal would take notice of his infirmity and then try to take advantage of him. He *knew* beyond a shadow of a doubt that, at this moment, he was completely incapable of defending himself.

As he watched the people arriving at the shelter, Will glanced in the direction of the harbor toward the far end of Hoka Street. Frankie had turned the corner and was walking toward the shelter. He knew that Frankie sometimes sat on the wall for a few minutes before going inside for dinner, and he did not want Frankie to see him in this condition. But he had no place to go, and Frankie, steadily approaching, had already seen him.

"Yo, Will!" Frankie called from the other side of the street. Will feebly raised his hand and managed a dispirited wave. He tried to answer Frankie's greeting, but an unintelligible, barely-audible grunt was all he could manage to get out. Frankie, still on the other side of the street, pointed to the doorway of the shelter, and started toward the front porch. Will exhaled in relief.

Fearing that he might not be spared embarrassment if he sat any longer in such a visible location, Will slowly rose to his feet to cross the street to the shelter. It was close enough to six o'clock that one of the duty managers was already handing out mat numbers. He shuffled unnoticed through the line and exited the side door of the building. He would forego dinner, he decided, and sit in the recessed area of the wall at the end of the building, out of the way of pedestrian traffic and partially out of sight.

As he sat down on the brown pavement, he sensed that some of his faculties were returning to him. Maybe in another couple of hours, he thought, he would be alert enough to have another belt of gin to get to sleep on. Right now, he was content just to sit and watch the cars pass by on Malualua Road.

The figure of a petite woman across the road caught Will's eye. She was crossing the street, coming toward the shelter. He quickly realized that it was Karen Ling. Surely, he fretted, she would see him and remember that he had signed up for the community patrol the previous night. And he was in *no* condition to conduct any sort of conversation. Neither did he have any means of escape from the situation he feared was about to happen.

Will held his head down as she approached, but kept his sunglass-covered eyes rolled upward so he could watch her. Her pace was deliberate and she looked straight ahead as she walked, seemingly preoccupied. Her heels clicked past him, little more than a yard away, and she quickly darted up the steps into the building.

The relief that Will initially felt as she passed was quickly replaced by disappointment. She hadn't even noticed him! Then, just as quickly, Will's disjointed mind returned him to his earlier thoughts of drinking.

Exercising more care in drinking the following day, Will even had some gin left on Thursday morning. That he used to calm the cumulative after-effects of the previous two days of drinking. By Thursday night he was able to resume taking the medicine that he had been given at the clinic.

By the time Friday evening arrived, Will was completely over the immediate residual effects of drinking. The medicine he was taking slowed him somewhat and he was still hard of hearing, but his mind was clearer than it had been in weeks. He was looking forward to the community patrol.

Just before seven, a clear-eyed Will walked from the front of the shelter to the parking lot. He noticed a few of the same people he had seen talking to Karen Ling after the house meeting earlier in the week. Then he noticed that *she* was already there, standing in the corner of the parking lot, her back to the hedgerow that separated the lot from the sidewalk.

"A violet by a mossy stone, half-hidden from the eye . . ." Will thought, recalling—for the first time in years—a line from a favorite Wordsworth poem he had studied in college. She was wearing a sleeveless denim dress, and her hair was dark and shiny in the dusk. ". . . fair as a star when only one is shining in the sky," Will's mind continued. Then he remembered who *he* was and who *she* was. He walked toward her, and stopped just in front of her. She was writing something on a piece of paper attached to a clipboard.

"Hi," Will began tentatively. "Is this where we meet for the community patrol?" She looked up.

"Yes," she said, smiling slightly. "Thank you for coming. I'm Karen Ling." She extended her right hand. Will swallowed hard as he guessed that she must not remember having spoken to him at the house meeting.

"Wuhhhhh-Will . . . Tyne," he whispered hoarsely, loosely grasping her hand for a second. As she started to write again, he added nervously, "I already signed up last, um—I left my—ahhh, I mean, ahhhmmm—"

"This is just a list for the duty managers," she explained. "This is so that they can reserve mats for the guests who participate in the patrol." She turned her attention toward three uniformed police officers who had just arrived in the parking lot.

At least, Will thought, she had recognized him as being a shelter resident. But how good a sign, he wondered, could *that* be?

The group that had gathered in the parking lot continued to grow in number until there were about twenty-five or thirty people. Even some of the shelter residents who Will knew to be involved in drug pushing and using were among the group. Karen Ling spoke briefly to the group about its purpose and objectives, to identify potentially troublesome situations or persons in the neighborhood, and the march began.

By this time it was almost seven-thirty and two local television news teams had arrived. As Will walked along with the others, it seemed to him that the bright lights that accompanied the cameras defeated the purpose of the patrol.

In all the time Will had been staying at the shelter, he had never ventured down any of the streets he was now exploring. Each morning he had gone straight to the bus stop from the shelter, and each evening he had arrived back at the shelter and had ventured no further than King's Discount Store until the following morning. The neighborhood, little more than home to an ageing pineapple cannery, seemed to Will to be a dumping ground for rusty industrial equipment surrounded by ten-foot-high chain link fences topped with razor-wire. The patrol was doing little to change his impression.

Will tried to stay within sight of Karen Ling, partly in the hope that he might get a chance to say something that would make him recognizable to her in the future, partly just so that he could *look* at her. She seemed occupied by the police officers and the attention that the television people gave her; but, Will noticed, she did not seem to revel in having the spotlight. Rather, it seemed that she merely accepted it as part of her job.

The group finally made its way through the last of the side streets and started up the short stretch of road that led to the far end of Hoka Street. Will knew that the patrol was almost over. As the group stopped, Will could hear Karen explaining some of the neighborhood's concerns to a newspaper reporter and one of the police officers. He stepped to within a few feet of her and cupped his ear, hoping to hear exactly what she was saying, but she had finished.

As she turned to look toward the rear of the group, she glanced at Will and her expression softened, almost into a smile. She noticed his satchel.

"That looks heavy," she commented. "You should have left that back at the shelter."

"I'm used to it," Will replied, almost instinctively. He first wondered if she realized that the only place he could have left it would have been the cage, which was closed just after dinner. Surely, he speculated, she knew that if he left it *anywhere* else at the shelter, it would be gone long before he returned. He offered no further explanation for why he was carrying it.

The community patrol was soon over and the group disbanded. The break in the monotony of shelter life had been short-lived and Will was soon back in his usual element, now without the anesthetizing effect of gin.

But his mood had been lifted by the mere fact that Karen Ling had spoken to him. It was not just *that*, he thought. There he had been: broke, disheveled-looking, and a shadow of the person he had once been. But she had spoken to him as if he had been a normal, credible human being. It hadn't been so much *what* she said to him. The difference was in *how* she had said it. Maybe, Will guessed, she had seen something in him that was worth salvaging—something that even *he* couldn't see in *himself*.

And maybe if there *was* something worthwhile about his miserable life, Will told himself, he could figure it out if he could stay sober long enough. Being out of money, as he now was, would certainly make *that* easier.

Will had learned that the community patrols would be done on a regular basis, that the next one was to be in a few weeks. Staying sober for this one, Will felt, had given him a good feeling. Maybe, he thought, he could stay sober for the next one, too.

Chapt er 10

From a Glimmer to a Ray

The mat didn't feel nearly as hard and unforgiv ing as usual to Will's tired body when he lay down that night. Ten o'clock came and the lights went out, but the large screen television still projected its noise and cast a dim light throughout the room. The late news had just come on, and Will, who often lay awake well into the night, had to prod himself just to keep his eyes open in hopes of seeing a report about the community watch. Within a few minutes after the newscast had started Will noticed a familiar image, a still shot of the shelter, on the television screen. Though he could not discern the words of the reporter, he knew that the story was about the community patrol. The next image on the screen was that of Karen Ling being interviewed by the reporter. Will noticed how relaxed she seemed, even though she was, to his mind, on the spot in an unenviable circumstance.

The last part of the report showed part of the videotape that had been shot during the patrol. Will sat up on his mat to make sure that he didn't miss any of it. He saw several faces that he remembered from barely two hours earlier, then Karen Ling again and—*right behind her*—himself, bulbous midsection and all. He cringed at the sight of his worn, wrinkled clothes, his dirty sneakers, and his frazzled-looking hair. Then the report was over.

What still stood out in his mind as he let himself drift into a restful sleep was the quiet, simple concern that Karen Ling had shown for him earlier in the evening. She had been in the middle of a group of reporters, television cameras, and police officers, yet she had noticed *him* and the heavy load he had been carrying.

Will's appointment at Jobs Oahu was the following Wednesday morning. Having had no liquor in his system since the previous Thursday, he tended to his morning routine with greater-than-usual ease. Even the medicine he had been taking for his impaired ears and persistent cough hadn't slowed him down nearly as much recently as it had in the past. Nor did it seem to be doing very much to relieve his symptoms.

As Will stepped off the bus in the middle of an area of downtown that contained mostly low-rise buildings, he took a long look at the five-story cube-shaped one that was his destination. Its facade of reflective, smoked-glass windows was framed symmetrically by white tile blocks, making it look somewhat like a huge television. Will entered the building, even though he was twenty minutes early, to get out of the uncomfortably warm morning sunshine.

Pausing by a full length mirror near the elevators to check his appearance, Will first raked his comb through the almost-blond straw atop his head, then through the gray temples. Shrugging at the uselessness of his effort, he punched the button to summon the elevator. He swallowed hard as the doors opened and he stepped onto it.

The receptionist blandly greeted him as he entered the Jobs Oahu office, then supplied him with six pages of blank forms to fill out. Will was glad he had come early. He completed the forms in less than half an hour and had waited for only a short while when a young, thin, Asian-looking man came from behind a cubicle wall, approached Will, and introduced himself.

Will followed him back to the cubicle and answered a number of questions about himself. He learned that one of the purposes of Jobs Oahu was to help people who were in situations similar to his own. They would do what they could to help him find employment, then assist him in buying whatever clothing and equipment he might need in order to do the job. The more Will listened to the pleasant young man, who seemed genuinely desirous of helping, the more his mood was buoyed.

As the meeting began to wind down, the man mentioned a job opening in which he speculated that Will might be interested. Will was, and he copied the address and phone number of the company into his folio.

"Should I go here and fill out an application, or should I just send them a resume first?" he asked.

"Send them a resume and a cover letter," the man suggested. "That way, they have an idea how good your language skills are."

"But I don't have a typewriter to do a cover letter on," Will countered. "I heard that the library had ones that people could use, but I checked there a few months ago, and they don't."

"Did you try the community college?" the man asked. "When I was taking classes there, they had a room with typewriters where anyone could go to practice typing."

"*Anyone*?" Will asked. "I don't have to be a student to go there?" After ten years of living in New York it was hard for him to imagine *any* sort of facility like this being open to the public, or even being left unguarded.

"As far as I know, the typing room is open to everybody," the young man responded. "You might try giving them a call before you go all the way out there. I know it's a long ride if you have to take the bus there."

"I'll call them today. I really appreciate all your help—" Will began.

"We have a workshop that's being conducted here next week that you might be interested in coming to. If you complete it, then we can continue helping you with job referrals," the man interjected. It sounded to Will like an offer which he was being coerced into taking in order to get additional help from Jobs Oahu, but he didn't mind.

"So when is it?" he asked. His apparent interest pleased the young man.

"It's Wednesday, Thursday, and Friday, noon till four. You don't have to bring anything—we furnish all the instructional materials," the man told him. Will chuckled inside at the young man's enthusiastic spiel, but he kept a straight face as he wrote down the information. He made sure he thanked the man graciously, and stood to leave.

"See you next week," he said, almost managing a genuine smile as he left.

Making sure he arrived back at the shelter well before lunch so that he could use the telephone, Will found the elusive directory laying on the shelf beneath the coin-operated phone in the building's entranceway. He saw that Bertha was seated behind her desk, working in an uncharacteristically contented manner. Nahhhh, he thought, leave well enough alone.

Will found the number for the community college and after

having his call transferred to other offices a few times, he got sketchy instructions on how to find the building which housed the typewriters. He decided he would go that afternoon.

As soon as lunch was over, Will hurried to the bus stop, happy that he would be taking a bus that would carry him into an area into which he had previously had no cause to venture.

He had been thinking about how he would compose the cover letter, but his thoughts soon gave way to speculation about other uses he might be able to find if using the typing room proved to be feasible.

The bus ride was over an hour long and the bus was crowded much of the way, but the crowd thinned out just before Will arrived at the stop across the street from the community college. Most of the remaining riders, many young people among them, exited the bus at that stop. Will crossed the street to the campus, then stopped. The person who had given him instructions on how to find the typing room had told him that it was in a brown building. Will now saw that *all* of the buildings were brown.

He walked past a row of classrooms until he came to what appeared to be an office of some sort. Without hesitating, he walked in and asked for directions. The heavy-set, middle aged woman wasn't sure where the typing room was, but she gave him a copy of a map of the campus and sent him to another office where, she guessed, he might find someone who could help him.

After talking to three more people and paying close attention to the map, Will found himself standing in a narrow parking lot at the edge of the campus, looking at a spectacular panoramic view of the Pacific Ocean in the distance. He let himself be distracted for only a moment before ambling toward a long wooden stairway that the map indicated would lead him down the steep hill to the building which housed the typing room.

As he approached a row of older buildings, he noticed that none of them had *any* windows whatsoever. He cautiously opened what he hoped to be the right door. A blast of frigid air greeted him and he walked inside. There were two rows of partitioned desks, each desk containing electric typewriters. Will looked around the room and saw not a soul.

He stood there for a full minute before a barely postadolescent girl came from an adjoining room. She walked behind a counter at the front of the room, not even looking up at Will.

"Excuse me," he said to her. "Are these typewriters for *anybody* to use? I mean, I'm not a student here."

"Oh, yeah," she nodded. "Anybody can use them." Will found a partitioned desk in the corner and sat down. He removed from his satchel a small pack of typing paper he had bought that morning, and went to work. His fingers seemed to be more nimble than they had been in months, and he enjoyed the feeling of being productive. In less than forty-five minutes he had typed out two copies of his cover letter and an envelope to mail one of them in.

Digging into the front pocket of his folio, Will found three postage stamps. He tore one away from the others and attached it to the envelope so that it fit squarely in the corner. Checking the spelling in his letter once more, he signed it, folded it, and tucked it into the envelope along with a copy of his resume. He deftly packed his things back into his satchel and exited the typing room.

The air outside was a full twenty degrees warmer than inside, but the breeze helped Will to quickly adapt to it. He spotted a postal drop box on the way to the bus stop, deposited the letter in it, and his task was complete. Now all he had to do was to wait a few days and check the message board at the shelter. As Will waited for the bus, he felt content with himself—as though he had done something which might lead him, for once, in the right direction.

As Will sat in the grass outside the shelter that night, he noticed that his coughing was less frequent. He was looking toward the doorway hoping to see Frankie when he heard a voice from the opposite direction. It was Matt.

"William! How's it?"

"Okay, Matt. What's up?" he greeted his fellow shelter denizen. Matt sat down in the grass several yards away from

Will, taking a notebook out of his backpack and, pen in hand, appearing to pore over it as if he was trying to decipher a code. Will's attention turned back to the doorway, and he noticed the dark-eyed woman step out onto the front porch. It was the first time he had seen her in several days, and she was looking particularly attractive. He followed her movements for several more minutes until he heard Matt call him.

"Hey, Will! How do you spell 'allure?' You know, like, 'The man was trying to allure the girl into his apartment?'"

Will mustered a look of mock-confusion as he turned to respond.

"It's a-l-l-u-r-e, but that's not how you use the word. The word you want for that sentence is just 'lure.'"

"Oh." Matt again seemed to focus his concentration on his notebook. Will looked toward the porch, but the dark-eyed woman had left. He gripped the strap on his satchel and closed his eyes.

"Hey, Will!" Matt called again, this time lifting his backpack and moving within a yard of Will. "What's a more polite term for 'making a lot of money?'"

"You mean profitable?" Will asked.

"No, I mean that it's got *potential*," Matt explained, grimacing slightly. "I just can't think of the right word."

"How about 'lucrative?'" Will offered. "I can't really suggest the right word unless I know what context you're going to use it in."

"*Lucrative.* That's perfect," Matt said, the frown disappearing from his face. "Maybe you can help me with some other things here?"

"Sure," Will agreed. "Glad to." He guessed that Frankie had told Matt about Will's 'editing' job on Frankie's correspondence, but it felt good to be asked for *any* kind of advice. Matt handed Will the notebook.

"See, what I'm trying to do here is, I'm writing this

letter to the owner of this casino in Las Vegas. You remember I told you about my 'Treasure Island' idea?" Will nodded, and Matt continued.

"Well, I wrote to him once before, but I didn't have my ideas and plans all mapped out. And he wrote me back and said that when I got my ideas organized to write him again, because he was interested. So now I've got a plan together and I want to let him know. But I want the letter to sound really professional. He's already said he's interested, and he's definitely got the money to advertise and promote my ideas."

"Hmmmm," Will mused. "So you just want me to look this over and make some suggestions . . . or would you rather I read it over and then write out a completely different version?" Matt looked as though someone had just handed him a hundred-dollar-bill.

"Yeah, yeah!" he enthused. "Whatever it takes. If you think that it'd be better to rewrite it, go right ahead. I can even *pay* you." Will turned to a blank page in the notebook and began writing.

"Nahh," he said, chuckling. "I only take money for *work*." Will wrote steadily for the next fifteen minutes, then handed the notebook back to Matt.

"See what you think of this," he said. Matt read the revised version, his eyebrows periodically rising, and his lips occasionally moving. He began to nod, then looked up.

"This is *great*! Now if I can just find somebody who has a typewriter, I'll be in business."

"I can do that, too," Will offered. Will told him about the typing room he had only discovered earlier that day. Matt was enthusiastic and again offered to pay Will, an offer which Will again declined.

The following morning Will again boarded the bus that would take him to the community college. He typed two copies of Matt's letter and, just for insurance, a letter to the storage company in New Jersey to let them know that his late payment would soon be on its way. He was back at the shelter in time for lunch, but Matt was not there.

Will had not been sure whether Matt had been high the night before. Matt had seemed normal enough, without talking any over-imaginative nonsense, but he had certainly been high-strung. Will guessed that he must have just been hyped on caffeine, because he knew that Matt had worked at the city arboretum that day. Will guessed that was where he was now.

Will spent part of the afternoon at the library, a place he was beginning to enjoy in this "dry" spell. He spent the remainder of the afternoon at the beach park and was back at the shelter before five-thirty. Matt was still nowhere to be seen, but Frankie was already sitting in front of the shelter as Will approached it. He greeted Frankie and asked if he had seen Matt.

"Nope. I haven't," Frankie told him. "He gets off work at the arboretum at four, but you never know if he's gonna show up here for dinner, or if he's gonna come walking up just before they lock the doors—spouting his crack-babble. He'll probably be here, though. He's been staying clean lately. I guess he hasn't gotten paid from his new job yet, and none of the guys around here will advance him anything."

Will ate dinner quickly so that he could get a mat number, then went outside to his usual after-dinner resting place. He saw that Frankie was across the street talking to another shelter resident, when he noticed Matt coming from the harbor end of Hoka Street, a noticeable jaunt in his gait. Will guessed that Frankie's speculation about the crack had been wrong, since Matt looked perfectly normal. He saw Will and walked toward him.

"Hey, Will. What's up?" Matt greeted him.

"Not much. I got your letter typed today. Two copies," Will responded. Will opened his satchel and removed the two sheets of paper and the envelope, careful not to crib the corners or wrinkle the paper. Matt took the sheets by the edges and looked closely at them. He sat down on the grass, took a folder out of his backpack, and placed the sheets and envelope inside the folder.

"Looks good. *This* is exactly the kind of treatment my ideas needed. Maybe they'll get some attention now. I've got a few more things I'd like to do, if you've got some time to help me. In the future, I mean—not right now."

"Sure," will nodded. "You know where to find me." He laughed. Matt reached for his back pocket and pulled out a wallet. He removed a twenty dollar bill from the wallet and handed it to Will, but Will would not accept it.

"I can't take any money for that," he protested. "It was actually sort of enjoyable doing it. Besides, it gave me an excuse to practice writing and then go practice typing."

"Go ahead," Matt insisted. "Take it. I got my first paycheck from the arboretum today, so I won't miss it. Believe me, it's worth it to get help with something like that. If this casino guy buys my ideas, I'll be rich anyway. I just look at it as a small investment in the future."

"No. Really, Matt, it's nice of you to offer, but—"

"Besides," Matt continued, "I might need you to do some more typing in the future. It's sort of an advance." Sensing that this argument was not working with Will, he became serious.

"Look. I just got paid today. I'll probably end up blowing most of my money on crack. You helped me out with something that might do me some good. It's better for you to take this twenty bucks than it would be for it to end up in somebody's pocket down at Elelu Park." Will was shocked by Matt's frankness—and convinced. He abashedly took the bill and put it in his pocket.

As Will lay awake on the mat long after the lights in the shelter had been turned out, he realized that he had enough money to buy a half-gallon of gin and still have some left over. He had been sober for a week now, longer than he had managed to stay sober in as long as he could remember—at least six or seven years. He felt better physically, and even though he still could not hear well, the medicine seemed to be making his cough slowly subside.

Will woke up the next morning before the lights came on, feeling more energetic than he had felt in some time. He actually had *money* in his pocket, and it was not already ear-marked for liquor or any other purpose. He would be able to walk through some of the stores at the mall and have a tiny bit of buying power for a change.

As he sat on the concrete floor of the main room sipping on his third cup of milk, he remembered that he had not yet taken his medicine. He thought for a minute, then decided to wait to take it until he was at the mall. As the duty managers began to urge the noisy crowd to finish eating and vacate the building, Will downed the last swallow of the milk and strode toward the exit.

He paused at the bottom of the front steps, inhaled deeply, and thought about the day ahead as he looked around. To his left, near the concrete slab where he had managed to find some peace and near-solitude on occasion, he saw a grocery store shopping cart. He began walking in that direction even though the shorter way to the bus stop was in the opposite direction.

Stopping as he approached the concrete slab, Will looked at the shopping cart, and he was certain that it belonged to the little man he had spoken with a few times over the past few months. Will had seldom seen the man inside the shelter at mealtime, and he had never seen him sleep there at night. The shopping cart hadn't been around the shelter in the morning for some time, and the little man was not to be seen—until Will walked past the large bush that partially masked the concrete slab, then looked behind it on the other side. The little man was sitting on the damp clay next to the wall.

"Good morning," Will said to him. The man did not

look up.

"Hey, little buddy, you okay?" Will called, becoming more concerned. This time the man looked up, saw Will, and broke into a toothless grin—still saying nothing.

"Are you doing okay?" Will asked again. "That clay looks kind of wet." The man's grin slackened, but he continued to look at Will. After another moment, he spoke.

"I'm taking the train to Texas this afternoon," he said softly.

"The *what*?" Will was caught off guard. "Don't you mean the plane?"

"No," the man said, still smiling. "I'm going downtown and get on the train in Amarillo, and then . . . Waipahu." Will wondered if the man had gotten his thoughts confused with lyrics from the music he listened to on his walkman. Then Will realized that he had never actually heard any sound coming from the man's headphones.

"So how are you going to get from Amarillo to Waipahu by train, when you have to cross the Pacific Ocean?" Will asked, hoping the man would show *some* indication of being in touch with reality.

"It doesn't matter," the man answered contentedly. "I don't drive it—I just ride it." At least he had a point *there*, Will reasoned.

"Well, you take it easy," he said to the man as he pulled the strap of the satchel up on his shoulder. "You can tell me about your trip next time we see each other." The man raised his hand as if he was about to wave, then let it fall back to his lap. Will started down the sidewalk toward the bus stop.

As the bus pulled away from the stop and rumbled past the high-rise buildings in the city's main business district, Will found himself feeling less self-conscious about being homeless the farther away from the shelter he got. By the time he stepped off the bus in Waikiki, he felt as though he fit in perfectly with the throngs of tourists. He efficiently went about his business there, then boarded a bus to go to the mall.

Will hadn't yet decided how he wanted to spend the day, but he was enjoying taking it moment by moment, especially since his cough had almost completely subsided. The distance from the shelter to the bus stop this morning hadn't seemed nearly as far as it had in the past. And as he got off the bus in front of the mall, Will noticed that the sun felt good on his face. He wasn't pouring sweat; and as he looked at his hands he noticed that there was no dirt under his fingernails even though it was already after nine o'clock.

The aluminum gates that enclosed the food court were sliding upward as Will passed them, and he started through the central walkway on the mall's lower floor. Even though it was early and not yet crowded, Will noticed that there were a number of tourists there already. He decided to go to the grocery store where he could use one of his few remaining food stamps to buy a soda. Then he would go to the book shop for a paper.

He hoped that the chubby, brown-skinned young woman would be there. She was always nice to him and, he thought, maybe today he would stop and talk to her for a minute. If she turned out to be friendly, maybe he would invite her to have lunch with him in the food court. *That*, Will was sure, would certainly make good use of the bit of money he had.

Just as he was about to enter the grocery store, Will remembered that he had used up the last of his deodorant that morning. He could get some more at the grocery store, but the drug store would be cheaper—and it was just upstairs. He walked past the grocery store and a few other shops and stepped onto the escalator.

Will quickly found the brand of deodorant he wanted and began to make his way in the direction of the checkout counters at the front of the store, glad that for once he had the money to buy something like this at just the time when he needed it. As he went by the liquor department, Will noticed a large sign that read "White Crown Gin—$12.99." He felt almost smug as he passed it, realizing how his sense of well-being had improved in the eight days since he had last drunk.

There were only two cash registers open at the front of the store, and each had several customers waiting. Will remembered that the cashier in front of the liquor department had been idle. He turned and walked back in that direction. There was only one customer ahead of him there.

Just as the customer ahead of him stepped away, Will put the small container of deodorant on the counter. Then, without understanding why he was doing it, he reached for a half-gallon of White Crown Gin and placed it on the counter beside the deodorant. He felt his pulse rate increase.

"Fifteen-sixty," Will heard the cashier say, and he reached inside his pocket for the money. A minute later he stood on the escalator, being transported downward again. His mind still was not clear. It's done—forget about it, enjoy it, he told himself. He quickly felt better, then excited, then happy. And he had not yet poured a drink.

Walking into the grocery store for a soda, Will supplied himself with two sodas in plastic bottles. They would be used at the end of the day to hold the remainder of the gin, making it more transportable—and concealable. Their contents would be used as mixer. Will had one more errand to do before he could start to the park across the road from the mall.

The chubby, brown-skinned woman at the book shop smiled sweetly at Will as he handed her the fifty cents for the newspaper. He wanted to smile back, but he could hardly look at her. The best he could manage was a meek "thank you," unable to look at her eyes, and unable to do more than twitch the corners of his mouth upward. He left the store feeling guilty. For what, he wasn't sure.

Will walked to the other side of the road and entered the park. The sprinklers were not on and the grass was not wet, but there were two lawn-mowing tractors darting about. Their noise annoyed Will and their speed frightened him. He walked away from them to another section of the park, this one closer to the ocean. It, too, was dry—and much quieter.

He sat down and took the plastic lid off the soda cup, which he had been careful to fill to within a couple of inches of its brim. Will looked around and was about to break the seal and unscrew the top of the gin bottle when he heard the raspy whine of the lawn-mowing tractor. He looked up and saw that it was entering the section of the park in which he sat.

Efficiently and unemotionally Will picked up his things and began to walk back to the section of the park where he customarily liked to sit, farther away from the ocean. There was no one around and he was able to fix a drink undisturbed. As he took the first sips, he wondered why he had so willingly—and impulsively—picked up the bottle of gin when he had been able to pass it by so comfortably only a moment beforehand. He had been becoming stronger, happier, and more confident in the days since he had stopped, and now . . .

Soon his questions and concerns gave way to a dull sense of calm. Will began to think about his one job prospect, about the Jobs Oahu workshop he would be attending the following week, and about the second community patrol that would take place the day after the workshop was over.

Surely he would get a call from the prospective employer, and he would be long sober again when the time for the interview came. Jobs Oahu would be thoroughly impressed with the skills and expertise he would exhibit at the workshop, and they would supply him with endless referrals until he found the *perfect* job. And since the next community patrol, without all the publicity, would no doubt attract fewer shelter residents, Will would get some well-deserved recognition. Maybe Karen Ling would even ask him to walk beside her.

Will missed lunch at the shelter, and barely made it back in time for dinner.

The next day found Will at the park again, busy drinking, daydreaming, and rendering himself unable to pursue any of the possibilities about which he was daydreaming. He missed lunch again, not caring whether he ate, and returned to the shelter just in time to get a mat number.

By the time Thursday morning came, Will had only enough gin left to ward off the morning shakes. After he drank that he would do without since he was out of money. He was almost glad that he was unable to buy more gin, because it seemed to him that it had taken him down much farther and much faster this time. He had almost enjoyed the eight days of sobriety that had preceded the last two-day bender.

With the Jobs Oahu workshop coming up the following week, and not having heard from the welfare office, Will was glad in a way that he would be forced into spending some more time sober.

Four months of being homeless had drastically changed his perspective of himself and had, he was sure, changed the way other people saw him. It had not been that long ago that he had been, as the phrase went, "just a paycheck away from being homeless." As a homeless person, Will had become perpetually just a bottle of gin away from having a chance to become self-sufficient again.

Will was slowly approaching the realization that he was not an "alcohol-ist", one who drank by measure and knew his limits, as he had fancied himself to be for almost his entire adult life. Even an extended drinking binge two years earlier that had nearly cost him his life and kept him hospitalized for three weeks had not forced him to confront or even admit alcoholism.

Having been forced into some degree of lucidity lately, Will was beginning to realize the severity of his predicament and to look for a way out of it. He was beginning to realize the value of John Marin's encouragement, and even the small amount of concern that Karen Ling had shown had affected

Will profoundly.

Feeling clearheaded and strong again by Wednesday morning, Will was looking forward to the workshop, which was to begin at noon. He hoped that it would provide him with an opportunity to reacquaint himself with sober interaction among normal people.

Will arrived at the smoked-glass and white tile block building at fifteen minutes before twelve. He was met by Ben, the young man who had interviewed him at his first appointment, and was seated in a large room with a conference table and several comfortable chairs.

Within a few more minutes there were five more people in the room. Then Ben came back into the room with two women. They were the workshop leaders. A local woman, Mona, and an attractive, thirtyish blond named Fran introduced themselves. Will cringed as they insisted that each of the participants introduce himself or herself in similar detail. If this is what it's going to be like for the next three days, he thought, I don't want to be here.

Before Will's reticence could take him any further, his attention was captured by Michael, a forty-seven year old Japanese-American, who openly admitted to having had a bout with alcoholism that had cost him a career with a company for which he had worked for seventeen years. Michael had spent the last nine years trying to overcome addiction and medical problems, and was finally looking to return to work. Hearing Michael, Will didn't feel as much like an outsider in the group.

After the mid-afternoon break, Fran challenged the group with some puzzle-type exercises, and Will's interest was further sparked. By the time four o'clock came, Will was almost sorry the session was over. He was already looking forward to the next one.

As Will sat on his mat at the shelter that night reading the materials he had been given at the workshop, he noticed a paragraph under the heading "dress code." It stated that male participants in the workshop were required to wear long pants. Will burned with embarrassment. He had worn shorts to the first session, and the only pair of long trousers he had at the shelter were crammed into one of his bags in the cage—certainly too wrinkled to wear.

His first order of business the next morning was to find Ben and explain why he was wearing shorts to the workshop. Ben was understanding, and Will asked him to convey his explanation to Fran and Mona. The remainder of the afternoon went smoothly. Will was beginning to enjoy participating in the learning activities. Even though some of the employment skills being taught were ones that he had learned at an early age, he still found it a pleasure to be around people who were not from the shelter.

When Will returned to the shelter that night, he was feeling unusually cheerful. He had not heard from the company to which he had written previously, but he felt sure that the people at Jobs Oahu would find some other prospective employers to refer him to. He was certain that the worst of his homeless, jobless experience was over. More important to him was the fact that he was again enjoying another extended period without booze.

The mat that Will got that night was near the mailroom door. At just after eight o'clock Robert, the local man who served as a duty manager at night, announced over the P.A. system that the mailroom was open. Will continued sitting on his mat since he figured that it was too late to expect a response from his resume and too soon to expect a response from Mr. Ichigawa's welfare office.

But Will soon noticed that the line in front of the mailroom was short, and he clambered up from his mat and took a place on the line. When it came his turn, he held his driver's license out so that Robert could see it. Robert instead looked at his face.

"Tyne, right?" Robert asked. Will was surprised. Now

he *knew* he had been around the shelter too long.

"Yep, that's me," he responded cheerfully. Robert thumbed through the large box first, then the metal one. His hand drew out a tan-colored envelope.

"Sign here," he instructed Will, pointing to the line on a form where Will's name had already been typed. Will signed, thanked Robert, and hurried back to his mat where he would be able to open the envelope less conspicuously. As he slid his finger under the flap of the envelope, tearing it as he went, he saw a dollar sign. He looked inside and saw something that resembled a check. *His first welfare check!*

Will had imagined that he would be relieved if and when the check finally came, but now that he had it, he was *ecstatic*. He began to imagine what he would be able to do with the money. He could certainly get a post office box, so that he wouldn't have to put the shelter's address on his resume. He might even be able to get a cellular telephone if the deposit was not too high. That would keep him from having to rely on the message board and its temperamental, unreliable administrator, Bertha. Thinking of how he would be able to use his newfound windfall kept Will awake long into the night.

Will was at the mall's bank to cash his check just after it opened the next day. After spending much of the morning reading the paper and sipping soda in the food court at the mall, Will left at eleven-thirty to head toward the bus stop and his third and final workshop session at Jobs Oahu. Despite the extreme amount of pleasure he felt in having a pocketful of money, Will also had a tinge of sadness.

It was the last day of the workshop, and he had thoroughly enjoyed being around people who, like himself, had an interest in finding their way back up into the world. In a very short time he had come to admire Michael, who seemed on the verge of making a poignant comeback in the work world. And he had been able to brush up on some forgotten skills and knowledge in addition to learning some new things.

Dreading the thought of returning to the day-in, day-out world of the homeless, Will had to push himself in order to maintain his concentration for the first part of the afternoon. But the session went quickly.

The final exercise of the session was a mock-interview, with each of the workshop's participants getting a chance to be "interviewed" by one of the leaders, who would be playing the role of a prospective employer. The participant would then have his performance critiqued by the workshop leaders and the other participants.

Each of the other participants went ahead of Will. When it was finally his turn, clear of mind he fielded the questions with the ease and fluency that had come with years of being interviewed and not getting the job. Fran, who had conducted the "interview," was both impressed and puzzled.

"Will! What's *wrong*?" she asked, wondering why, with his interviewing skills and education, he was unemployed. Will at first shook his head in bewilderment then, abashed, he stared at the floor.

Fran was effusive in her praise of Will's performance, and he became even more embarrassed. Will knew *exactly* what was wrong, and at that moment he knew that within the hour he was about to further illustrate the problem.

Chapter 11

"Blacker Than a Hundred Midnights"

Will left the Jobs Oahu office knowing that Fran had meant to pay him a compliment. What she said, though, only made him think of all the mistakes and miscues that had gotten him in his current predicament. And at this particular moment, it seemed to him that what had happened to him was mostly the fault of others rather than of his own doing.

It was only a short bus ride from the office where the workshop had been held to the mall, and Will, with a pocketful of money, knew exactly what his first purchase would be. He stepped off the bus and walked at a deliberate pace toward the drug store where he had found gin on sale the previous week.

The gin had been returned to its regular price, but Will did not hesitate before buying a half-gallon. Not wanting to wait in the long supermarket line to buy a soda, Will went to an outlet in the food court, where soda cost more but where he would not have to wait.

He looked at his watch and saw that it was already

quarter to five. He decided that he would skip dinner at the shelter, arrive late, and hope that Robert would let him sleep on one of the mats reserved for first-time guests who arrived late in the evening. Right now, all he wanted to do was to anesthetize the pain he felt.

He had already been somewhat depressed about the workshop coming to an end, and the manner in which it had ended had upset him. He had hoped to walk out of the Jobs Oahu office encouraged, confident, and hopeful that he would soon find work. Instead, he had left with the realization that, even if he conducted himself in a near-perfect manner during an interview, he still would probably not get the job.

Seated in a corner in the unusually quiet food court, Will used his straw to poke at the ice in his drink between sips. He hardly looked up from the table as he sat ruminating over the events of the past several months. Even the feel of the money in his pocket, which he regularly reached his hand down to check, didn't cheer him up. Will wanted to drink to numb himself.

He arrived at the shelter just before the ten o'clock curfew. Finding Robert, he asked if there was an available mat. He guessed that Robert could tell that he had been drinking, but he knew that, unlike many of the other shelter residents, he had never caused any trouble or disruption in the shelter. Robert took his metal flashlight into the darkened main room, then returned in less than a minute.

"You can sleep over there," he told Will, pointing to one of the reserved mats. Will thanked him and shuffled down the narrow aisle to the mat. The gin bottle, covered by both paper and plastic bags was still full enough that it did not make a sloshing noise, for which Will was grateful. He knew that he was lucky that Robert had let him take one of the reserved mats. Regular guests who arrived late at the shelter were usually given one of the older mats outside on the lanai.

The cage had been closed since before Will arrived, so

he had to sleep without his bedsheets. He tucked his satchel and the bottle under the head of the mat, his shoes under the foot, lay down, and slowly fell into a restless sleep.

The lights were already on when Will woke up the next morning. He had a headache and still felt very tired. The process of showering, shaving, and removing and returning his bags from and to the cage caused him to start sweating and feel edgy.

Will decided not to go to Waikiki or the mall right after breakfast. He would first have a strong morning drink to "level off" with. As he walked down the steps of the front porch, he looked toward the harbor end of Hoka street and saw that one of his favorite places to sit, the concrete slab, was already occupied by two men. He turned to his right, walked through the shelter's parking lot and down Malualua Road.

As Will approached the middle of the downtown business district, he remembered that there was a fast-food restaurant on the pedestrian mall. There he bought a soda, then a newspaper from a paper-box, and he went toward a lesser-occupied section of the pedestrian mall. He found an isolated bench in a shady area and sat down to ease his morning-after ills.

Once he was halfway through the 'soda,' Will began to feel much better. By the time he finished it, an hour and a half after he had sat down, he had read the paper and was ready to go to the mall. The bus stop was only a short walk away.

Will knew that he should use some of his money to buy some necessities while he still had the presence of mind to do so—that is, before he started to get drunk. He knew that if he didn't buy certain things, he would fritter his money away and have nothing to show for it.

He had seen an ad for one of the mall's department stores, and he knew that the store had a sale on shoes. He was anxious to get rid of his cheap plastic shoes, and now he could afford to buy much nicer leather ones, which he did. The plastic bag in which he was carrying his gin bottle was awkward and cumbersome, so Will decided to by a backpack to put it in. He had seen many of his fellow shelter denizens carrying them, and had been mildly envious. Now he could afford one.

After venturing into the drugstore to stock up on some toiletries for which his supplies had been dwindling, Will determined that he had to stop spending money until he had a chance to budget the remainder of it. He had received a check not for the full month's welfare, but for the amount dating back to when he had applied for it, slightly more than half what the usual monthly welfare payment was.

To Will's notion, it was now time for another drink. Armed with another large soda, he crossed the street, entered the park, and found a quiet place in the shade where he could examine his treasures. He had taken up more time shopping than he had thought. He knew that he had missed lunch at the shelter, but he was surprised to look at his watch and discover that it was already four o'clock.

Will decided that he would eat dinner at the mall and return to the shelter late again, hoping that Robert would again let him sleep on a reserved mat. It had occurred to him earlier in the day that if he *couldn't* get a mat at the shelter, he *could* get a room at the YMCA across the street from the park. He had heard that it was cheap to rent, and he knew that some of the shelter residents used part of their welfare money at the first of the month to stay there just to get out of the shelter for a few days.

Having some money in his pocket was making Will begin to feel indignant at having to endure the routine of the shelter. The only time that was really *his*, he groused to himself, was between seven-thirty and five-thirty each day. The rest of the time he had to spend either waiting to eat, waiting to get into the cage, waiting to get into the shower, or waiting to get a mat.

For over four months the shelter had provided Will with

food, a place to sleep, and even some encouragement. Now his gratitude was diminishing as quickly as the level of the gin in the bottle.

He determined that he needed a couple of days to 'clear his head' which, in truth, meant that he wanted a safe place to get really drunk, something he had not been able to do since he had been homeless. He would get a room at the "Y."

After going back to the mall and eating dinner while downing another drink, Will went to the YMCA and rented a room. He needed one of his bags from the shelter's cage, and he knew that if he stopped to have another drink, he would never make it back to the shelter while the cage was still open. He left the room and hurried as best he could to the bus stop.

It was just after eight o'clock when Will arrived at the shelter, which was unusually quiet. He waited on the short line to get into the cage, found the bag he needed, and quickly walked back to the bus stop near King's Discount Store. Buses didn't come to that stop as often as they came to the one on King Street, particularly at night. But Will didn't want to walk past Elelu Park at night. He knew he had drunk a lot that day, and he didn't want to risk having a run-in with any of the unsavory crowd who frequented the park.

The bus was a long time in coming, and Will stopped at the mall on the way back to pick up another bottle of gin. He knew that he wouldn't run out that night, but he also knew that he would need a good supply to get started the next morning.

Finally arriving at his rented room at ten-thirty, half an hour past his usual bedtime, Will made one more trip outside the second-floor room to get sodas from the machine on the first floor. Ecstatic at being out of the shelter for a night, Will's adrenalin was almost overpowering the liquor. He was glad that he would be able to stay up late into the night.

For the first time, he was able to take a long look around the room. There were two bunk beds, a desk built into a wall, another desk to the side of the door, and a large closet.

The room had no television, but there was a phone on the desk by the door. The bathroom was down the hallway. To Will it was a palace.

As he began to unwind and the next rounds of gin began to override his waning flow of energy, Will began to retrace the events of the day, his busiest since he had been homeless. He wondered why the shelter had seemed so quiet when he had been there.

He felt his face flush with sweat, then turn cold as he remembered: this had been the night of the second community patrol. He had missed having another chance to see Karen Ling. Will became upset with himself for having been so forgetful and irresponsible.

When the last part of the workshop at Jobs Oahu had made him feel uncomfortable, he had let everything else slip from his mind. He had wanted to be at the community patrol, energetic and sober, hoping that Karen Ling would again notice him, even if it was only in the same small way in which she had noticed him the last time.

He had instead forgotten about the patrol, about staying sober, and—for a while—about Karen Ling. Will *knew* beyond a shadow of a doubt that his presence had not been missed, but he felt a burdening sense of guilt that he had somehow let her down.

In the distance outside the window of Will's rented room was a building topped by a blinking light. Will removed a small radio from the bag he had brought with him, turned it on quietly, and sat drinking and watching the light blink on and off until he dozed off in the chair well after midnight.

As soon as he woke the next morning, Will decided that one night away from the shelter had not been enough. He went downstairs to the front desk and paid the room rent for another night. Stopping at the soda machine, he bought two more sodas and got a bucket of ice from the ice machine.

After he had showered, Will quickly downed his first

drinks of the day as he watched the people come and go through the building's main entrance, which was just below and to the left of his window. He hadn't eaten since he had arrived the night before, and he was beginning to feel hungry following the night of good sleep.

After he had selected two sandwiches at the grocery store, Will figured that it would be a good idea to get still another half-gallon of liquor. It won't go to waste, he told himself. By the time he was almost back to the "Y," it had started to rain hard. He spent the afternoon listening to the radio and watching the traffic.

The next morning, Will's hands were shaking so badly that he clumsily fixed himself a drink shortly after he got out of bed. Again, he had no food in the room, and the liquor hit him hard. He decided to stay another day, but became so drunk so quickly that he didn't want to show his face at the front desk. He had paid the day before, and he was sure that they would know that he was good for it—eventually.

He still had plenty of gin, and he went no further from the building than was required to find a paper-box. By the time he picked the paper up to read it late that afternoon, his eyes would not focus on the print.

On the morning after Will's third night in the room, he woke to find a note on the floor. It read, "Please pay rent." He looked in the mirror at his unwashed, unshaved, face and his greasy, uncombed hair. After I shower, he thought. He had not eaten and again he had a bad case of the shakes. By the time he had drunk enough to mask the after-effects of the alcohol, he had forgotten about taking a shower. It was becoming an effort to walk down the hallway to go to the bathroom just to urinate.

Will began to have periods of time he could not account for. He passed out on the bed during the afternoon and sat up drinking late into the night—then lay half-sleeping and half-unconscious until the middle of the fourth day. There was another note under the door, this one slightly more demanding. Will knew that he now owed two more days' rent.

At six o'clock that evening, Will drank the last of the gin. He checked his wallet, which lay on the desk. He had plenty of money left. But he hadn't eaten anything in three days, and he didn't have the strength to go out and get more gin. It was as if the world was about to end.

Will knew that he was in trouble. There had only been one other time in his life when he had been too weak to make his way to the liquor store. That had been the day before he had been carted off in the back of an ambulance to a hospital for a lengthy stay.

He slept for part of the night, then lay awake worrying the next several hours until daylight came. He crept down the hallway to the bathroom, leaning against the walls of the hallway as he went. Before he could finish urinating, he dropped to his knees, hanging his head over the toilet. He heaved time after time, and all that would come was a green mucus-like substance.

As Will got back to his feet and brushed the sweat from his forehead, he caught sight of himself in the bathroom mirror. His eyes were bulging from their sockets, and their whites had turned completely blood-red. He realized that he would have to find someplace where he could convalesce. But he knew that it would not be at the YMCA.

He reached for the phone to call the front desk when he got back to the room. Using his left hand to hold his shaking right hand by the wrist, Will pressed the buttons that would connect him to the operator. He explained that he would be leaving by checkout time, and that he would be settling his bill before he left. That would at least buy him some time, he figured.

The yellow pages phone book lay on the desk in front of Will. He reached for it and slowly and shakily turned the pages until he found a heading identified by a word he had never been able to face directly: "Alcoholism."

Will had heard of something called "detox." Maybe, he thought, he could find a place where he could buy some time while he dried the booze out of his system. He knew that he could not go back to the shelter in his present state. His fellow residents showed no sympathy to anyone with a *legitimate* illness, and he knew that some of them would be quick to try to take advantage of any perceived vulnerability that he might exhibit.

Several hours and many pleading, increasingly frantic phone calls later, Will had found a detox center that would agree to take him on a provisional basis. He called for a taxi and was told that there would be one to pick him up in about an hour. The delay was blamed on increased demand due to the heavy rain.

He had showered in preparation for leaving, but had already begun sweating again. And his shaver had been no match for the four-day stubble on his face, but he had done the best he could with it. He struggled, almost out of breath, to pack his things back in his bags. Finally, he called the front desk to let them know that he was leaving in a few minutes. It was two o'clock, two hours after checkout time.

Will paid his bill, and as he walked toward the front of the lobby, he saw a police officer walking toward the front desk. He couldn't hear what the officer said to the desk clerk, but the clerk's response was clearly audible: "No, he's out. He just left. Matter of fact, that's him right over there." The clerk was pointing at Will. The officer turned and left.

The taxi pulled up to the curb, and Will, weak almost to the point of collapse, struggled with the bags which he normally would have been able to handle with ease. Although it was less than a fifty-foot walk to the curb, it was pouring rain so hard that Will was nearly soaked by the time he got into the cab.

The long ride cost Will much of the money that he had

left. He got out of the taxi at the detox facility, where it was raining harder than ever, and again wrestled with his bags. Once he was inside, he saw a sign that indicated that the detox intake office was on the second floor. He began slowly climbing the stairs, one tedious step at a time. When he got to the top, a husky, pony-tailed man quickly got up from his chair and reached out to help him with his bags. Will sat down in a chair and felt dizzy.

The man and his co-worker, a small woman, asked Will question after question. He guessed that they must have known that his hands were too shaky to write, since they filled out the forms for him, only asking him for his signature. Finally, the woman checked his blood pressure. Her eyes widened as she looked at the gauge.

She removed the cuff from Will's arm and walked over to the pony-tailed man, talking with him in a hushed manner. Will, used to having high blood pressure readings, was not alarmed. He was savoring a cold, sweet, cherry-flavored liquid the woman had given him, holding it with both hands so that he would not drop it.

They told him that he would have to be seen by a doctor before he could be admitted to the detox facility. They assured him that it was just a precaution, and that they would send him there and pick him up by taxi—which they would pay for. The woman asked him if he wanted to leave his bags at the facility.

Life at the shelter had made Will distrust everyone, but he somehow felt that he was not putting himself at any risk by trusting the woman. And anyway, he reasoned, there wasn't anything valuable in the bags. The taxi soon came, and Will was on his way to the hospital.

He gave the nurse at the emergency room entrance a slip of paper that he had been given at the detox facility. Another nurse led Will down a hallway to a small room and instructed him to lie down on a padded table. As he stretched himself out on the table, he began to realize just how tired he was, but he knew that he was a long way from being able to relax.

Will's head had barely dented the pillow when his stillness began to remind him of the miserable feeling of alcohol withdrawal. Within a merciful few minutes, however, a doctor walked into the room. He first checked Will's blood pressure and frowned. Will was dreading the possibility of having to go through the same drill of questions he had already answered at the detox facility, but the doctor's first question let him know that the doctor knew why Will was at the hospital.

"When was your last drink?" the doctor asked.

"Pardon?" Will asked, cupping his hand to his ear.

"*Your last drink. When did you have your last drink of alcohol?*" the doctor asked again, louder this time, and with a trace of impatience in his voice.

"About six o'clock yesterday," Will rasped, then added, "My ears are stopped up. I can't hear very well." The doctor asked several more questions as he checked Will's breathing, then looked inside his ears. Will was now sweating profusely.

"Hold out your hands," the doctor ordered, but grabbed Will's left wrist before Will could move. Even as the doctor held his wrist firmly, Will could still see that his fingers were trembling. The stern look on the doctor's face began to soften into a kinder, more concerned expression.

"We'll give you some librium to help you relax," the doctor told him. But I want to keep you here for a while to watch your pressure. The nurse will be back in a few minutes."

In another few minutes a nurse came into the room, secured an intravenous needle in Will's arm, and connected the needle to a drip bag which contained a clear liquid. The nurse was attractive and Will wanted to be conversational, but the words simply would not come. As soon as she was done, she left him alone again.

As Will lay on the table, his cloudy eyes translated the fluorescent lights of the room into no more than an overpowering glare of chromatic aberration. The quietness of the small room was made maddening by the lack of any stimuli, as Will's body intermittently and repeatedly reacted involuntarily to nothing. Over and over he tried to time his pulse rate, only to lose count each time. His hands spontaneously reached to scratch an itch that didn't exist.

Head to toe he was enveloped by a malaise of unspeakable magnitude, yet no part of him was in pain. Will first wanted to lie still, but he could not. Then he wanted to get up and walk around, but he knew that he was too weak. The IV needle would prevent him from doing that, anyway.

Although it had been just over twenty-four hours since he had finished the last of the gin, he was just approaching the worst of the after-effects of the prodigious amount of alcohol he had consumed in the past several days.

Will lay on the table for several more minutes, feeling progressively worse. Then, just as he fought an urge to rip the IV needle out of his arm, too weak to scream, he let out a pathetic, breathy shriek and he began to feel that the worst was over. He guessed that the librium was beginning to take effect.

An artificial sense of calm that he was not quick to trust began to neutralize the twitches and nameless miseries. A few more minutes passed and Will stopped counting his heartbeats. Finally, he was able to lie still. He closed his eyes, but he knew that it would be days before he would find the solace of a restful sleep.

"Hold out your hands."

The voice startled Will, and he opened his eyes. The clock on the wall showed that it was an hour later than the last time he had noticed it. Confused, he held his hands out, palms open, to show that they were empty.

"No. this way," the soft-spoken doctor said, with only a trace of impatience in his voice. He held his hands as if he was about to play a piano. Will feebly held his out the same way.

"They're not shaking as much now," the doctor observed. Will had noticed the shake before, but he was incapable of discerning any difference now.

The doctor placed the cuff of the sphygmomanometer on Will's upper left arm. Will clenched his teeth because he knew that his high blood pressure had been what had caused the detox facility to send him to the hospital rather than admit him. Will had no idea what would happen to him if his blood pressure was still too high for him to go back to the detox facility, but he felt he had come too far to have something exclude him now.

"It's still high, but I think we've got it down enough so that we don't have to keep you here," the doctor said as he tucked the pressure cuff into a drawer. "The nurse will be back to take the needle out of your arm and give you some medicine to take with you. I'm going to give you something for your bronchitis, too."

Will finally caught a full breath of air. Now, he was sure, he would be admitted to detox.

The nurse came back into the room and removed the needle from Will's arm, then explained the dosages of the medicines he would be given. In another few minutes, he was in the waiting area of the emergency room, looking out into the rainy night and hoping to see the lighted dome of an approaching taxi.

After another half an hour, it came. As Will's tired body shifted with the motion of the cab, he tried to imagine what his next steps would be.

He hadn't eaten in five days and he could barely walk. He had an ear infection and a raspy sound in his breathing. But he knew that he would not be sleeping at the homeless shelter that night nor, hopefully, the next. Maybe, he hoped, not ever again. Even being in limbo, Will told himself, was better than being homeless.

Will grasped the handrail as he again climbed the stairs at the detox facility. The small woman saw him as he neared the top of the landing, and Will saw a smile come through the look of concern on her face. She checked his blood pressure and smiled again.

"*Now*, I think we can take you," she said. Will let his head fall backward as he sprawled out in the chair. He felt tears running down his face. When he lifted his head again, the woman held out a box of tissues in front of him. Will felt an immense sense of relief. According to what they had told him on the telephone earlier in the day, he would now have seven days to "dry out" and get his strength back.

The woman, whose name was Angela, led Will down the hallway to a large room which contained four hospital-type beds. He could rest or sleep as much as he wanted, she told him, but if he decided to get up, he *had* to make up the bed. He saw that there was also a small room with some old but comfortable-looking furniture in it—and with a television. That, Angela explained, was where he would be required to watch at least two "recovery" videos per day.

The cafeteria was downstairs and breakfast for the people in detox was served at six-thirty each morning. Lunch was at noon and dinner was at five, and other than that, Will's only requirement would be to attend the Alcoholics Anonymous meeting at eight o'clock in the cafeteria each night.

Will listened to Angela as well as he could, nodding in agreement with whatever she said. As Will sat down on the edge of the bed to which he had been assigned, Angela told him that she would have to check his bags as a final step before he would be allowed to stay at the facility. Will knew that he had nothing objectionable in his bags and he hoisted the bags, one at a time, onto the table by the large room's doorway.

Angela began removing the clothing that was in Will's larger bag, and Will noticed that she kept looking up at him as she worked. He was beginning to feel uncomfortably self-conscious until Angela spoke.

"You don't seem to be the kind of person that usually comes in here," she said, eyeing him questioningly. Will could only shrug his shoulders meekly before she continued, "Most people don't come in here with their bags packed. And not all of them are as polite as you. Or as smart." Will guessed that she must have listened to some of the phone conversations he had with someone at the facility earlier in the day, because he certainly hadn't felt very smart—or anything else—since he had arrived.

"Maybe I've just hit the end of the line with drinking," he offered, hoping that showing some contrition would help his cause.

"So many people come here just to take a break from drinking or whatever they're doing. As soon as they feel better, they go out and start all over," Angela told him. "You seem more sensitive." Will managed a tired smile.

"Maybe *too* sensitive," Will mused. "Maybe that's why I drink so much—so I won't feel so sensitive. But the way I feel now, I don't want to drink any more." It appeared to him that Angela was impressed with his declaration, but he knew that he had yet to convince himself of that intention. Angela soon finished searching Will's bags and left him in the dimly-lit room. He lay down on the bed and closed his eyes, but a spell of coughing kept him from getting comfortable.

The more Will tried to suppress his coughing, the more it seemed that he could not stop himself. In the midst of his anxiety at the hospital, he had not thought of mentioning the cough to the doctor, who had given him medicine for high blood pressure and bronchitis and not for anything else.

The door to the room opened slowly and Angela walked in quietly. She held a small plastic cup in her hand.

"Try this," she said to Will, handing him the cup. Unsure of his dexterity, Will took it with both hands.

"Do I drink it or do I gargle with it?" he asked.

"Just sip it—slowly," she instructed. "If you need some more later, just come out to the desk." Will took his time finishing the concoction, then lay back down. His cough had subsided.

The rest of the night, Will alternated between fits of restlessness and fitful sleep, pouring sweat at times and feeling cold at other times. The pony-tailed man came into the room at midnight to check his pulse, blood pressure, and temperature, and someone else came in again at six in the morning. The second man also reminded him that, if he wanted to eat, breakfast would be at six-thirty.

Will lay in the bed until six-twenty, unsure of whether he could stomach food, but feeling ravenously hungry. Finally he got up and stood beside the bed. He was still spindly, but had a little more sense of balance than he had the previous day. He decided to try to eat.

The small cafeteria was almost empty when he went in, and Will moved slowly with his tray of food, fearful that he would drop it if he tried to move too quickly. Just as he placed it on a round table and sat down, a noisy group of people began streaming through the door of the dining room. Will moved his tray so that he could sit with his back to as much of the room as was possible.

His hands were so shaky still that he continually dropped food off the fork, but hunger overcame the nausea he had felt earlier, and he ate most of the food.

As soon as he had finished, Will made his way back to the second floor. He was sweating again and feeling slightly nauseous, and he dropped himself into a chair in the television room.

A young man came into the room and introduced himself as the person to whom Will had spoken on the phone the previous day. Just as Will was beginning to feel sure that he would keep his breakfast, the man mentioned to him that detox clients were expected to participate in some light housekeeping duties each morning. Will's chore was to mop the hallway.

The man showed him where the mop, bucket, and cleaner were, and Will felt almost ready to keel over before he had even touched the mop to the floor. He worked slowly, worried that any second he would throw up before he had a chance to get to the bathroom. After ten minutes that seemed like an hour he had finished, and he slowly inched his way back to the utility closet with the mop and bucket.

Will was drenched with sweat as he moved toward the bathroom. Just when he felt he could hold back no longer he reached the toilet, and he hung his head over it. But nothing came. He rested on his knees for another few minutes and began to feel better. The nausea passed and he went back to the television room.

By eleven o'clock, Will was feeling strong enough to take a shower. The water felt good to him as he cleaned himself thoroughly for the first time in days. A fan in the room kept his face cool and dry as he shaved, and he reappeared in the television room just before lunchtime, feeling clean and looking a little better.

Just before four that afternoon, as Will was reading a book he had taken from a shelf in the television room, he heard Angela's voice. She walked into the room just as he was closing the book. She saw Will and immediately smiled.

"How are you feeling, Will?" she asked.

"Better," he responded. "I ate breakfast *and* lunch today." Remembering that her cough remedy had worked, he asked, "What was in that magic potion you gave me last night? It sure stopped me from coughing." She laughed, and for the first time Will noticed that she was pretty—especially for someone who was probably about *his* age.

"Just honey and some spices," she answered. "I can make you some more if you start coughing again."

Will was feeling both physically tired *and* sleepy by the

time Angela came into the television room to remind him and the other four detox clients that it was time for the Alcoholics Anonymous meeting. He slowly descended the stairway and walked down the hall to the cafeteria.

The meeting was something for which Will was completely unprepared. He had never been to an A.A. meeting before and, through his exasperation and fatigue, he found it almost amusing at first.

It was difficult for Will to understand at first why someone would stand to announce that he or she had been sober for ten days or seventeen days, and be applauded for that. It would be more fitting, he thought, if they were roundly booed for having become alcoholics in the *first* place. Then he realized that he had been sober for only *two* days.

When the meeting was over Will went back to the television room feeling that the meeting had been a waste of time, but admitting to himself that his attendance was a small price to pay for being able to regain his strength at the detox facility.

That night Will's cough returned but was not as persistent as the night before. Angela again prepared another batch of her "potion" for him. His fatigue made him able to sleep for brief periods of time, but he was still not completely free of the after-effects of the alcohol.

The next morning the cleaning chore seemed a bit easier to Will. He sat alone in the television room after he was finished, and Jim, the young man who had spoken to Will on the phone came in, spoke to Will, and sat down.

"Have you thought about what you're gonna do when you get out of here?" he asked Will.

"Not yet," Will answered honestly. "I'm just trying to get my legs back under me right now."

"But you *really* don't want to go back to drinking again, do you?" the man asked. "You just don't seem like that kind of person." Will tilted his head to one side and squinted.

"You know, you're the second person who's told me that," he said to the young man. "But, yeah, you're right. I think that I've gotten away with about as much drinking as I can get away with. Sometimes I think that drinking has gotten to be so much a way of life that it would be a novelty to stay sober for a while. But I've never really tried to do it." Before the last phrase was out of his mouth, Will wondered if it was really true.

"When you *do* decide what you're going to do, let me know. I might have a few ideas. You don't see yourself going back to that homeless shelter, do you?"

"I don't really want to," Will responded, "but I don't have any other place to go."

"There are lots of 'clean and sober' houses around the island," the man told him. "If you want to stay sober and get a job, that's a good place to start out."

"Yeah, but they probably want a deposit and rent up front," Will countered. "I just started getting welfare, and I can't come up with any big amount of money." The young man smiled knowingly and nodded.

"But," he added, "if you sincerely want to do it, there are people and places who may be able to help you. Where there's a will, there's a way."

As Will sat in the television room that afternoon, he thought about what the man had said. It was one thing to *want* to stay sober, Will knew, and another thing entirely to *do* it. His own experiences of the past few weeks had taught him that. He was feeling better and stronger now and he liked being that way; but what would happen next time he passed by a liquor store and had some money in his pocket? And how many times would he be able to keep doing this sort of thing and continue getting away with it?

Just after the staff had its four o'clock shift change, Will was wondering where Angela was when something tickled his nose and he sneezed.

"Will?" he heard his name called—but it was so *loud.* He looked up and saw Angela. "How are you feeling?," she asked, again sounding louder than usual. Then he realized that one of his ears had become unclogged.

"I can *hear,*" he told Angela. "*Now* I'm doing *much* better." He tugged at the lobe of the ear that had just cleared. Angela sat down in the chair next to him.

"Now that you're feeling better," she began, "have you made any plans about what you're going to do when you leave here?" Will eyed her with mock-skepticism.

"That's the second time I've been asked that question today," he responded. "I was talking to Jim about that a little while ago. He said that there were ways of getting me into one of those 'clean and sober' houses."

"But only if you *really* want to—if you intend to *try* to make a better life for yourself," Angela told him.

"I *do,*" Will insisted. "It's just that I haven't had a fair chance in the last few years. If I could get a break—like getting into one of these houses—I *know* I could stay sober."

"We can help you, then," Angela said.

"If I can get out of the homeless shelter I can guarantee you that if you see me a year from now, I'll *still* be sober," he said to Angela.

She smiled, and Will wished that his heart could be as sure of what he had just said as his mouth had been.

Chapter 12

From a Ray to a Beam

Every time Will had to climb the two-hundred yard hill that rose in front of him, he wished that it could be just a little less steep. But every time he got almost to the top he knew that it was worth it, because it led to a destination to which he was thankful to be able to go—home.

For a month now he had been re-acquainting himself with things that he had spent much of his life taking for granted: his own bed, a bathroom with privacy, a phone, a kitchen, and a television. The three roommates with whom he shared the roof over his head were a negligible inconvenience to him when he considered how much better *this* was than the shelter, where his "roommates" had numbered almost two hundred.

Angela and Jim had helped Will to get in touch with the right people. Welfare had paid the deposit and a private philanthropic organization had paid the first month's rent for him to get into the "recovery" house where he now lived. The rent was cheap enough that he would be able to pay it out of his welfare check, with just enough left over for the bare necessities. And his food stamps would keep him adequately fed now that he had access to a kitchen.

Both Angela and Jim—and others at the detox facility—had urged him to continue going to Alcoholics Anonymous meetings. They had suggested that he attend ninety meetings in ninety days. Despite the fact that some of the meetings were tedious and took a lot of time to reach by bus, Will had been to at least one every day since he had been out of detox. And he had not had the urge to drink.

The old house in which he lived stood in an older residential neighborhood. As Will reached the top of the hill and proceeded to the end of the road where the house was, he stopped to look inside the mailbox. Thumbing through the mail, he found a piece of mail addressed to him in his own handwriting. He recognized the manila envelope as a stamped, self-addressed one that he had given John Marin when he had gone to pick up his last bag from the shelter. Realizing that he would probably still receive more mail after he left the shelter, he had asked Marin to use the envelope to send him whatever came.

Will passed under the carport and around to the door, which he unlocked and opened. He flipped the switch to turn on the ceiling fan as he entered, and flopped into an old but well-padded chair.

As he tore open the envelope and looked inside, he immediately recognized the small, brown envelope he saw. It was from the Internal Revenue Service—his income tax refund. The other envelope was from the storage company in New Jersey. Will guessed that it was another past due notice, and he slipped it into the folio inside his satchel. He would look at it later that day, he determined, by which time he would have some *money* to send them.

The tax refund check was for the exact amount Will had

claimed he was owed. He had been looking for it, because it would enable him to pay Mr. Sing the back rent he owed at the Regal Arbor and get his guitar back. He would also have a little bit left over for a few household items.

When he had gone to the Regal Arbor earlier in the month to pick up his suitcase, Mr. Sing had been off the island. As Will picked up the phone to call the hotel, he hoped Mr. Sing would be there now. The hotel operator put Will on hold, and a short time later he heard a voice at the other end.

"Hello?"

"Mr. Sing?"

"Yes . . . who is this?"

"It's Will Tyne. Remember me, the one who left the guitar-"

"AHHH, YES, YES! Mr. Tyne!" he heard his old landlord say. "What can I do for you, Mr. Tyne?"

"I have the money to pay my back rent and get my guitar. Will you be there this afternoon if I come by there?"

"What time will you be coming?" Sing asked.

"About three," Will answered. "Is that okay?"

"Ohh, I'll *be* here," the hotelier assured him.

"See you then," Will told him. "Thanks." Will was half-elated and half-relieved as he hung up the phone. It had been almost six months since he had been forced to leave the Regal Arbor, and he had not even been sure that Mr. Sing would hold on to the guitar for such a long time, particularly since Will had not contacted him during that time.

After Will had eaten the two sandwiches he had fixed for himself, he picked up his satchel and headed for the door. It was one o'clock and he figured that even if he had a long wait at the bank, the bus would still get him to Waikiki and the Regal Arbor well before three o'clock.

Less than two hours later, Will walked through the front doors and into the lobby of the hotel. The same man who had been behind the front desk the day Will left was seated there on this day. Will felt confident, but not triumphant, and he was soft-spoken as he addressed the man at the desk.

"Excuse me. I'm here to see Mr. Sing," he said to the man.

"Is he expecting you?" the man asked suspiciously, without showing any sign of recognition toward Will.

"Yes. I spoke to him on the phone earlier. My name is Will Tyne."

"I'll page him," the man said. As the man reached for the phone, Will noticed a green and white ledger card that the man had been writing on when Will approached the desk. It had Will's name on it.

"He has to go to the sixth floor first for a minute, but he's on his way down," the man said, this time with some thaw in his manner. In less than five minutes the elevator opened and out stepped Sing, carrying Will's guitar case by its handle. He placed it carefully atop a bookcase to the right of the desk.

"Good afternoon, Mr. Tyne," he said to Will, offering his right hand. Will reciprocated.

"I have the money right here," Will began, anxious to conduct the transaction and have his business with the Regal Arbor concluded.

"The clerk has your bill," Sing told him, and Will gave the money to the dour-looking young Asian man, who counted it three times. He handed Will a receipt. Will then turned to the guitar case and reached for one of the latches.

"It has not been opened since you left it here. You told me that it was very valuable, so I kept it in my own apartment upstairs," Sing declared.

Sure it hasn't, *sure* you did, Will thought to himself as he released the other latch. But the straps and extra packs of strings Will had packed in the case spilled out as he raised the lid. Will knew from the way they fell out that they had been just as he had packed them. He lightly strummed the open strings. The guitar was tuned perfectly, as it had been the day he surrendered it.

Closing the case, Will again apologized to Sing for the long delay in paying the bill, although he noticed that interest had been added to the bill. He thanked Sing for taking care of the guitar and not giving up on him. Will took the guitar and walked out of the lobby and into the afternoon sun feeling like a far different person than when he had taken almost the same steps six months earlier.

It was almost nine o'clock that night and Will's fingers were tired from playing when he realized that he had not opened the piece of mail from the storage company. He hoped that he had enough tax refund money left over to pay the past due fees and get his account current again. He knew that he couldn't let the matter slide forever.

Will unfolded the contents of the envelope and noticed that there was some sort of official-looking document among them. The words "Public Auction" caught his eye. As he read further, he saw that the storage company was threatening to break the lock on his storage area and sell the contents if he failed to resolve his account by a certain date.

The date they gave was long past, but Will knew that his things would be safe if he could send the money via overnight delivery—just so the money was there before they opened his storage area. He looked further to see what the scheduled date of the auction was, and he felt as though someone had driven a utility pole into his chest when he saw it. The auction had been three days ago. All of his possessions had been taken and sold to complete strangers.

Will felt completely helpless as he sat holding the letter in his hand. His priceless record collection, his books, his audio and recording equipment, furniture, memorabilia, ten years of diaries—all of it was gone, and even if he had the money there would never be a way for him to track it down and buy it back.

The sense of loss was a strange one to Will. He was

bitterly sad that he would never see his things again but, he told himself, it was not as bad as it would have been if the things had been taken from in front of him. It had been over eight months since he had put them in storage, time during which he had learned to do without them. As Will lay awake well after midnight, his sense of sorrow eased, but he knew that tinges of it would return to haunt him badly for a long time to come.

If recovering his guitar offset some of Will's sadness and anger about losing his other things, the feeling of freedom he began to have from no longer having any material possessions tying him to the mainland gave him not only solace, but also some cheer. Everything he owned was now in one place.

He reasoned to himself that his lost property consisted of items which belonged to his old life. Now that he was beginning to live a life without alcohol, he hoped he would eventually have the opportunity to acquire things that fit with his new lifestyle. Will was beginning to feel that there had been a lot of truth in what he had told Angela.

The next morning Will boarded the bus to go to the grocery store. As he sat down he noticed that someone had left a newspaper on the seat in front of him. He took the paper and tucked it in his satchel, glad that the find would save him the cost of buying one. He bought what he needed and returned home, forgetting about the paper until after he had sat down and turned the television on.

He thumbed through first the comics, the sports, then folded the paper so that the crossword puzzle would fit onto his clipboard. Just before he was about to discard the remainder of the paper, he remembered that the editorial section had, on occasion, supplied him with a few chuckles.

On this day, the first thing he noticed about the section was that it had caption line containing the word "homeless." His eyes focused on the "letter to the editor" beneath it and noticed that its writer had a name that he had heard before:

Karen Ling.

He guessed from the content of her letter that someone had leveled some public criticism toward the Center for Social Aid, and that her letter was a response to the criticism. Will immediately saw an opportunity to assuage some of the guilt he felt over having missed the second community patrol at the shelter. But he knew that he would have to consider his words carefully.

After all the roommates were asleep that night and all the lights were out except for the tiny lamp suspended over his bed, Will began writing, as much for his own peace of mind as he was writing to share his opinions about her editorial. "Dear Karen," he began, then paused. He pulled the sheet of paper off the clipboard and replaced it with a clean one. "Dear Ms. Ling," he began this time.

Will explained in the letter that he had been a shelter resident until just recently, and that he had just begun to confront alcoholism. He wanted her to know that the support he had gotten at the shelter had been in part responsible for his decision to try to deal with his addiction. Lastly, he reminded her that her kind words to him, words which she probably did not remember saying, had made a strong impact on him.

Unaccustomed to feeling satisfied with anything he ever did, Will had an uncanny good feeling when he dropped the letter into a mailbox the next day. He could now forget about missing the community patrol.

As he trudged up the hill three days later, for what seemed like the thousandth time in the short period he had lived there, Will thought of Karen and wondered if she had gotten his letter, and if she had actually read it. As he reached the end of the road he stopped at the mailbox and pulled a handful of what appeared to be junk mail out of the box. He was about to shove it back in when he saw a letter hand-addressed to him. The letter had no return address.

Will took a small knife out of his satchel and carefully

cut open the envelope. As he read the first words he was nearly overcome with emotion, and he understood for the first time in his life what tears of happiness were. The letter was from Karen Ling!

She had received his letter, she said, and she appreciated his supportive comments . She was glad to hear that he was trying to turn his life around, and she wished him luck. She concluded the letter with a simple "keep in touch."

Will doubted that she had any idea who he was. After all, she was the head of the Center for Social Aid. She didn't hang around the shelter the whole day like John Marin and Dick Mengel and some of the others did. Someone at the shelter had once told Will that her office wasn't even *in* the shelter—that it was across the street in a separate building.

All that mattered to Will, though, was that she had taken the time to write to him. She had been willing to take the time to turn her attention away from the hundreds of other people who depended on her long enough to respond to a nobody like *him*.

And she had signed her letter, "With Aloha, Karen." *Karen*. Just her *first name*. Will wasn't sure what "with aloha" meant, but it sounded better than "sincerely," the word he had used in signing his letter to her.

Maybe, he thought, it was time for him to put *more* effort into getting his life back on track. Sure, he had been diligent about attending the A. A. meetings, and he hadn't had a drink since his stay at the "Y." But he was living on welfare, and as long as he stayed on his present course, life would not necessarily get any better.

It was, Will was sure, time for him to start looking for a job. He could now acknowledge to himself that his drinking had cost him more than one opportunity in the workplace. Seeing himself sober for a period of time made him keenly aware of how other people had seen him when he had been drunk or hung over.

Now he didn't have that pall hanging over him. His mind, he was sure, was as sharp as it had ever been. It was time for him to find a good job and get back to work.

Besides, he told himself, Karen had urged him to write to her again. He would make sure that his next letter would herald his triumphant return into the workplace. Maybe, he thought, she might even one day see him as more than just a pen pal.

Will got up early the next morning. He needed to revise his resume and put his current address and phone number on it, and he set out for the typing room at the community college. As soon as he was done, he boarded a bus to go back to the library to make copies of the resume.

From there he went to an office supply store at the mall to buy envelopes, then to the post office for stamps. Since it was a Friday, he only had to wait less than forty-eight hours for the Sunday newspaper to come out. And he was ready.

Finding only four jobs he thought he might qualify for listed in the Sunday paper didn't discourage Will. One of the ads was for an insurance biller, a job Will had done well at when he had been in New York. Before it was dark on Sunday, Will had responses to three of the ads addressed and in the mail. The fourth, the one for the insurance biller, he had to call the following morning.

Guessing the next morning that the office which had advertised the insurance biller job would open at eight o'clock, Will decided to wait until fifteen minutes after eight to call.

As the second hand crossed the twelve, he began dialing.

"Good morning," came the pleasant response. "Lapuwale Consultants. May I help you?"

"Good morning," Will began. "This is Will Tyne. I'm calling in reference to your ad in yesterday's paper for an insurance biller."

"Hold on, please," the woman told him. In a moment another female voice came on the phone.

"Billing department. May I help you?"

"Good morning," he started the spiel again. "My name is Will Tyne. I'm responding to the ad you placed in yesterday's paper for an insurance biller."

"Oh, I'm sorry," the woman said. "They've connected you to the wrong department. Hold on and I'll transfer your call." He waited another few minutes before another voice came on the phone.

"Human resources. This is Steven. How may I help you?" At last, Will thought, I've got the right department.

"This is Will Tyne," he began for the third time. "I'm interested in applying for the insurance biller job you had advertised in yesterday's paper."

"I'll have to connect you to the administration department for that," the man told him. "We normally handle applications here, but administration wanted to handle this themselves. Hold on just one moment, please." Will was still only slightly exasperated. He waited for another three minutes before a deep-voiced man came on the line.

"Walsh here," came the self-important voice over the line.

"Good morning. My name is Will Tyne. How do I go about applying for the insurance biller position you have open there?"

"In the first place," came the booming response, "we don't have *positions*, we have *jobs*. Normally, you would have to come in and fill out an application but, in the second place, this *job* is no longer *open*. This *job* has been *filled*, so there is no need for you to come in and fill out an application. Thank you for calling." Will heard the rattle of the receiver hitting the base of the phone.

Will's first thought was that his job search was over for the week unless he heard from one of the places where he had sent resumes. Then he remembered one of John Marin's first suggestions: the state employment office. Maybe he wouldn't find anything, Will acknowledged, but he *would* be trying.

It was still early in the morning and Will knew that the computer terminals on which jobs were listed at the state employment office were not in operation in the afternoon. He dropped his folio into his satchel and was quickly out the door.

The first bus to arrive at the stop was one that took a slower, more heavily populated route downtown, but Will didn't mind. He enjoyed the feeling of riding the bus with his "neighbors," sensing himself to be just another person who fit in with the crowd rather than feeling like some sort of homeless outcast who belonged nowhere. Will inhaled a deep breath of the cool bus air, and relaxed his posture as he settled into a seat. He looked at his fingernails. They were clean.

The courtyard that fronted the employment office was still damp from a brief morning shower as Will crossed it. He noticed the pleasant but curious scent of the magnolias, something he had been unable to appreciate on his last visit to this office.

He walked into the reception area and saw that there were no other people waiting, but he took a number from the dispenser anyway. Before he had gotten comfortable in a chair, he heard the receptionist's voice.

"Forty-six," she called, peering around the room in an exaggerated manner and smiling broadly as Will looked around at her.

"Oh, um—that *must* be me," he responded, playing along with her. He approached the desk and gave his name and social security number. She entered it into her terminal, waited for a moment, then frowned.

"I don't have any record of you. You said you were here before? Do you remember when?" she asked. Will had to stop and think for a moment.

"A few months ago. I can't remember the exact date," he responded.

"I can't find you on the computer. Don't worry,

though," she assured him, "We can re-register you while you're here. It won't take long." Within a few minutes Will was led into one of the several cubicles that occupied the area behind the reception desk. He answered the same questions he had been asked during his previous visit to the employment office. This time, though, he could *hear*, and the process took half the time it had taken before.

Once Will was back in the reception area, he found a chair in front of one of the computer terminals. He had *never* had much luck in offices such as this one. Maybe, he hoped, he was due some.

As he pressed the keys to activate the system, the first message he saw read: "There may be as many as 2,000 job listings in these files. Please choose the employment category which most fits the type of job you are seeking so that you may narrow your search accordingly." Two thousand, Will thought, and all I need is one.

He first checked the medical support heading, then the clerical heading. There was a combined total of fourteen listings, none of which was suited for Will. On a whim, he tried the administrative heading and one job immediately caught his eye: research associate.

Pressing another key brought more information about the job to the screen. Will read the job description. It sounded tough, but he thought he might have a chance. He looked at the educational requirements—a bachelor's degree. He had that. Then he saw the pay: $6.50 per hour! Will exited the record and retrieved it again just to make sure that the computer didn't have a glitch in it. But the same figure came up.

Out of desperation, Will began scanning each of the other categories, even ones in which he knew he had no qualifications. He kept a count of the number of jobs listed in each category, and when he had gone through them all, he saw that the total number of listings was *nowhere near* two thousand. It was eighty-three. Disappointed and disgusted, he exited the program and left the employment office.

Will had no response from the resumes he sent out that week and on the following Monday, after he had his next mailing done,

it occurred to him that he might be able to prove his skills in the workplace *and* kill some time by volunteering to work somewhere.

He recalled that the organization that ran the detox facility where he had spent time had posted a notice on its bulletin board that they needed someone to be responsible for their newsletter. Will *knew* that he had the education for the job, and he was pretty good with computers, too. He determined that he would wait until four o'clock and try to reach Angela.

In the meantime, he began writing a letter to a local politician who had just announced her intentions to run for state office. He offered to work as a volunteer in her campaign. Surely, he thought, *this* one will get a response. After all, didn't every politician need all the help he or she could get?

The clock showed that it was almost four-thirty when Will returned from the post office. He picked up the phone and dialed the still-familiar number to the detox facility. Angela answered and he told her about the notice that he had seen on the bulletin board. She assured him that she would let the right person know about his offer. But, she cautioned him, the administrative people were cautious about allowing someone so new to recovery to do volunteer work.

Another week passed without a response from either the resumes or the volunteer offers. The following Monday Will again sent out responses to the ads he had seen in the Sunday paper. The routine was becoming increasingly like an exercise in futility, and Will was becoming discouraged and depressed.

As he sat in front of the television set that evening, Will

felt frustrated, not only that his leads for the week had led nowhere so far, but also that he had nothing more to pursue until the following week. Maybe, he speculated, spending some time at the beach would make him feel better.

Will had avoided direct sunlight as much as possible since he had been in Hawaii. He knew that it exacerbated the effects of alcohol and that too much sunlight would put him at risk for some severe medical consequences. But now he didn't drink.

And he had too much time on his hands. He knew that many mainlanders would gladly trade places with him, even in his humble circumstances, just so they could be close to the beach. Now *he* could enjoy it.

Slathered with sunscreen, Will spread his towel on the already-crowded beach the next morning. The sun felt almost too warm, and there was just not enough of a breeze for him. But, he told himself, this was the *life*. Waikiki was a place people dreamed about spending time. And he would now be able to come here any time he wanted to.

Three hours later, redolent with perspiration, coated with sand, and his eyes feeling as though they had been torched, Will packed his things into the bag he had brought with him and slowly trudged toward the bus stop. As soon as he was in the shade he found a bench and sat down. Half an hour later he found the energy to walk the rest of the way to the bus stop.

Feeling completely defeated as sat in front of the television that night, Will realized that it would be a long time before he could write to Karen Ling about any sort of triumphant return to the workplace. Or even a humble return to the workplace.

But—she had asked him to keep in touch. Maybe, he reasoned, that meant she wanted to hear from him regardless of whether his news was good or bad. Will knew that it would at least make him feel better if he could tell someone about his frustrations. None of his roommates would be interested. They had their *own* lives and, like him, their *own* problems.

Writing a letter, Will decided, might not be as good as having someone to talk to, but it was better than nothing. As soon as all the other lights were out and the house was quiet that night, Will switched on the lamp over his bed and took out his clipboard, pen, and paper. "Dear Karen," he began this time.

He reminded her that he had written to her and that he was writing because she had asked him to "keep in touch." He told her how much receiving her letter had meant to him—and of how grateful he was for the sustenance he had received during his stay at the Center for Social Aid.

Will explained his frustration at the rebuffs and lack of response he had encountered in his job search. He began to feel a sense of relief and calm as he closed his letter by promising to write to her again when he had happier news to report.

The next afternoon as Will mailed the letter, he realized that there must have been something more than just Karen's kind words to him and her response to his letter that had attracted him to her. He realized that his mind had never been really clear enough when he had seen her for him to be able to form a mental picture of her now.

As he left the downtown post office, Will remembered that he needed to make a stop at the drugstore to get some toiletries. The thought occurred to him that the prices at King's Discount Store would be cheaper, but he hadn't been in that neighborhood since he had gone there to get his last remaining bag from the shelter.

Looking at his watch, Will saw that it was not quite three o'clock. He knew that the shelter would be deserted, that he would probably not run into anyone he knew—particularly if he walked along the highway that led to the harbor side of King's rather than walking along Malualua Road.

Elelu Park was, as usual, filled with faces that looked

familiar to Will, but he was relieved to see no one who might be inclined to try to engage him in conversation. As he continued alongside the highway Will began to feel more tense, wondering how the sight of the shelter would make him feel. He knew that he would only be able to see it after he had crossed the harbor end of Hoka Street, and then only if he turned completely to his right.

As he reached the intersection where Hoka Street met the highway, he looked straight ahead as he crossed, then stepped across a foot-high concrete barrier into the parking lot that fronted King's. He walked the remaining fifty yards to the front door of the store looking neither right nor left.

Will took his time browsing through the store, feeling good that he was no longer one of the store's unwanted neighbors. After he paid for his purchases he walked slowly toward the front door, and as he stepped into the parking lot he looked up and saw the shelter on the other side of the street. He continued glancing at it as he walked toward Hoka Street, finally pausing to take a long look as he stood directly across from it.

It appeared to be impossibly small for housing the number of people who slept there each night. And the tired-looking building whose every square inch seemed to have been abused or maligned in some way seemed more deserted than Will ever remembered seeing it. Will could almost imagine that he heard the structure breathing with relief at the pleasure of having such a respite.

He had not seen Frankie or Matt the night he had left to get a room. He wondered if they were even curious about what had happened to him. Maybe *they* had found a way out of the shelter, too. Maybe Frankie had gotten his settlement check and was in Las Vegas. There could be no telling what might be happening with Matt.

The concrete slab looked as though it had been cleaned, and the bush that had shielded it from most of the passing traffic had been mercilessly pruned so that it now hid nothing. Will did not see any sign of a grocery store shopping cart around the shelter.

Will glanced at his watch and began moving, taking one last look at the shelter. Once a place he had at best looked at with grudging acceptance, he now viewed it with a sense of grateful affection. It had provided him with a cushion for the last stage of his fall, and with the first nudge of motivation back in the right direction.

The following Friday morning Will packed his canvas bag for another outing at the beach. Waikiki had not been to his liking, but he remembered the beach along which he had walked the morning after he had spent his first night without a home. It had been mostly rocky, but he remembered seeing a sandy place at one end of it. Most important, there had been few people there.

The bus got him to the far end of Waikiki in just over an hour, and he began walking alongside the road that led to the beach. Will slowed down as he began to pass the small park where he had spent the night after his eviction from the Regal Arbor. It now looked more as it had looked when he had first seen it as a tourist, six years earlier, not as it had appeared when he had sat at the concrete picnic table all night. He knew that physically nothing had changed.

Leaving the park, he continued up the hill and around the curve past houses that were of the type he knew he would never be able to afford. If he had only gone *up* in the world, he told himself, there would still be hope. But now even his dreams were more humble ones.

A small road with a large sign that read "DO NOT ENTER" led down a hill to a thick concrete barricade which prevented vehicles from going further. Will sidled around one end of the barricade and continued the last hundred yards down the hill to the beach.

He crossed another patch of rocky area and then

stepped onto the sandy stretch he remembered from before. Another twenty steps in the breezy sunshine took him past a protrusion in the embankment, well away from the main road, and out of the line of view from the smaller one.

Will flattened a large towel out on the damp sand, anchoring one end with his bag and the other end with a small, round stone at each corner. He sat down, pulled a newspaper out of his bag, then looked around. The closest person to him was at least thirty yards away. Will guessed that he might be spending some time here.

Stopping to look in the mailbox as he returned from the beach late that afternoon, Will found nothing. He went inside, dropped his bag on the floor, and was about to sit down when he noticed a single letter atop the mail tray he and his roommates kept in the living room. It was Karen's handwriting. Already relaxed from a lengthy stay in the solitude of the beach, Will almost wondered what he had done to merit *two* good things happening in the same day.

Her letter showed that she understood the frustrations he had expressed in his last letter to her. She urged him to keep trying, and indicated her certainty that he would one day succeed. It was almost as if she had lived through the same circumstances he had endured, but he knew that she hadn't. He had read that she grew up in an upper middle-class neighborhood and had gone to private schools. But her *understanding*, the way she echoed his feelings, told him that she was as sensitive as anyone he had ever known.

As Will put the letter down, he began to worry. He knew that, without even seeing Karen, he was beginning to feel an attraction to her, feelings that went beyond those of a grateful homeless alcoholic.

He also knew that he didn't have a prayer of a chance with her. She was well-known and well-respected in the community, often mentioned in the newspaper and occasionally on television. She was also a woman who was beautiful by anyone's standards. And, he guessed, she probably had an extremely busy, fulfilling life.

Will, by comparison, was unemployed and on welfare. He knew that his socio-economic status alone would preclude *any* sort of social interaction with women. He stood on a slippery rock one step above homelessness and alcoholism. While Karen Ling could offer him encouragement and understanding, he knew that she could *never* see him in the way he saw her.

One of the big differences Will had noticed in being sober was that he felt emotions with far more intensity than when he had been drinking. Even happiness sometimes made him feel overloaded with emotion. Now he was beginning to feel something in which he had no recent experience at all.

Will did not want to find himself so quickly involved in another hopeless situation, but he knew that he was already falling for Karen Ling, even if it was just for the *human* side of her he had seen.

The next morning, Will went back to the quiet beach again. Maybe, he hoped, the solitude would help his mind—since there was no hope for his heart.

Chapter 13

The Enigmatic Spectrum

For the next two months Will tried diligently to find a job, if for no other reason than so he could write to tell Karen about having made *some* achievement. Each Sunday he read the "help wanted" ads in the paper, and each Monday morning he made whatever phone calls were necessary to follow up on the ads.

Then, as he got off the bus downtown to change to another one, he dropped his written responses in the mail. His effort completed for another week, he boarded a second bus that would take him to the beach. The answering machine at the house where he lived would take whatever phone calls came in response to his efforts, but when he came in at the end of each day, the incoming message tape was invariably blank.

Will disliked the feeling of being a welfare recipient, but he knew that it kept a roof over his head and food on the table while he was trying to do better. His only consolation at times was the fact that he was sober.

His almost-daily trips to the beach had become such a

diversion for Will that he began to wonder if spending so much time sitting in the sand was equivalent to burying his head in it. The quietness of the beach allowed him to forget that he was unemployed and on welfare, that he was crowding forty and didn't even have a place of his own, and that it didn't look as though anything would be changing for him anytime soon.

At the beach, though, Will's station in life didn't seem to matter to anyone. The regulars knew him and spoke to him as though they were glad to see him. There were even a few who stopped to talk at length: Nick, the retired, cigar-smoking old man who had lived in New York; Rocky, the middle-aged local man who drove a tour bus for a living; and Jerry, the older British man who was married, but who came to the beach to meet gay men, many of whom frequented the beach.

Will enjoyed the feeling of being on a par with others. At the beach no one cared that he was on welfare—no one even *knew*. Other people shared *their* ideas and opinions on common interests, and they were also interested in *his*.

The clean air and the sun made Will feel good each day, and his part-Indian skin quickly adapted to being outdoors, developing a healthy-looking, almost-brown color. One or two hours of swimming every afternoon began to give Will a growing sense of well-being and a feeling that he might be regaining some of the energy he had lost over the years of inactivity.

When he returned each evening to the house where he lived, however, Will's mind was all too quick to change its focus back onto his lack of progress. The darkness of the old house, the smell of stale cigarette smoke, and the sour-smelling furniture reminded him that he was living below the poverty level. The messageless answering machine reminded him that it would probably be a long time before he would get a chance to rise above it.

He often took out the two letters Karen had written to him. Reading them over and over just before he went to sleep had given him something to dream about many nights, and something to wake up for the next morning.

The fact that *she*, of all people, believed in him and had faith that he would stay sober and improve his life enabled him to believe in *himself*, something he had lost the ability to do many years ago. And since Karen was the *only* person who seemed to believe in him, Will felt bound to honor the faith she had placed in him.

But instead of being able to write to Karen about his success, Will found himself wanting to write to her to tell her how unfair the world had been treating him, of how hard he had tried to get ahead only to be met by a conscienceless world that seemed to turn a blind eye and a deaf ear to his every effort.

Will also knew that he needed Karen's reassurance, not just that his life would improve if he only kept trying, but reassurance that she still had faith in him. Her letters were beginning to look worn because of Will's frequent handling of them, and a new, unwrinkled letter from her would be tangible proof to Will that her faith in him was not worn, either.

Just after eleven o'clock, with the house dark and quiet, Will sat on his bed and switched on the lamp above him. "Dear Karen," he began, knowing that he had to be careful in writing *this* letter. He didn't want her to think that he never had *anything* good to write.

He told her of his diligence in trying to find work, of the shabby manner in which he was often treated because of his welfare status. He lamented that it seemed as though, in spite of the professed desire of many people to help others who were disadvantaged, the world seemed more intent on *punishing* him for his past than it was interested in helping him outdistance it.

But, he wrote, he had no intention of giving up. He would do the best he could, he declared, and try not to worry about what he could not control. He reminded her again of how his stay at the shelter had given him the means to inventory some of his problems so that he could deal with them, and of how her insightful letters had given him encouragement that he had been unable to find anywhere else.

For the first time, Will wrote of his hopes for her well-being and, full of emotion from the writing, he signed the letter, "Love, Will." He knew that the ambiguity of such a closing would not be lost on her, and he hoped that it would make her smile.

Within a few days, Will reached into the mailbox and had material proof that he still mattered to someone. True to form, Karen had written to him almost as soon as she had gotten his letter. It was obvious that, even though he had tried to make light of some of his feelings, she had understood his exasperation.

Her response again made Will wonder if she had at some time in her life endured what he was going through, even though he could not imagine that she had. She seemed to fully understand that the world made it tougher, not easier, on people like him. Will was completely struck by her reaction to his willingness to share his feelings, good and bad, with her. Not only did it not bother her for him to do so, she wrote, she was *honored* to be the one he chose to share his sadder moments with.

Will was very nearly walking on air the next morning as he descended the small access road that led to the beach. His feeling of aloneness, at times bordering on solipsism, had been altered by the sense that he now not only had someone who understood his predicament, but who was also *on his side*.

He waved to Nick, who usually arrived at the beach by nine-thirty, as he passed on his way to the patch of sand where he customarily settled down each day. The tide was low and the top layer of sand was dry where Will dropped his bag.

Still consumed by thoughts of Karen's letter as he stretched out beneath the sun, Will realized that his emotions for her were beyond what he would feel for just *anyone* who had helped him. Although he hadn't actually seen her in months and was unable to form a clear mental picture of her, his impression of her was more than adequate to remind him that she was an attractive woman.

Maybe, Will mused, he should send a card to Karen to let her know how he felt. Knowing that greeting cards *never* said what *he* wanted to say, he quickly ruled that out. Will recalled that during his college years he had occasionally written sonnets to girls who had caught his fancy. Those, he recalled wistfully, had never been understood or appreciated.

He had always told himself back then that if he ever found a girl who appreciated that archaic form of expression, *she* would be the one he would fall in love with. And he hadn't even bothered to write one in the last fifteen years. Just as Will was about to rule out the idea, he began to think that writing one for Karen might be worth a try. Maybe she would be the woman he had begun looking for back then.

Trying to imagine exactly what he wanted to say, Will began forming thoughts that ran into couplets. He stopped. Elizabethan or Petrarchan, he wondered, knowing that he had to decide on a form. Then he realized that they were words that had not come to the forefront of his mind in years. Maybe, he hoped, he still had a little bit of creativity left.

All that he could find to write on in his canvas bag was a paper grocery bag he had placed there some time ago for a reason he could not recall. He began scrawling words, scratching them out, then scribbling more. He completely lost track of time as he thought and wrote, and when the trade winds began to feel cooler, Will realized that it was late afternoon.

As he sat on the bus heading back to his place of abode he continued to write and rewrite. The lamp over his bed stayed on well into the night, but Will was not sleepy. When the lines were completed to his satisfaction, he copied them over onto another sheet of paper so that he could read them without the distraction of the scribbles and scratched-out words.

He knew that Surrey, Spenser, Donne, and others had wrested the best out of this form of writing long ago. He knew that most people nowadays frowned upon rhyming poetry. And he knew that not a single one of the sonnets he had ever written had been well-received. But what mattered most to Will was whether he said what he meant and whether *Karen* would like it. He finished the copy and carefully read what he had written:

> The changes wrought by many months have made
> My eyes, perception, and my memory—
> Diminished by impaired acuity
> For years—more lucid and yet still betrayed,
> Done in by my own course in life's charade.
> My loss is that my mind can only see
> You with the same awestruck uncertainty
> That made the memory become so frayed.
> But when you write . . . ! Your image becomes clear,
> A surreal Nadja best left undefined
> By terms that when compared to you seem dull.
> Emotions that I feel, thoughts that I hear,
> Your caring words, tell me I could be blind
> And still I'd know that you are beautiful.

Maybe a little bit corny, he thought, maybe a little contrived. But it said what he wanted to say—what he *felt*.

He placed the clipboard with the finished poem on the floor by the bed, turned the lamp off and soon fell asleep.

Will stepped off the bus in front of the post office the next morning. He had a feeling of almost complete satisfaction as he dropped the envelope containing the poem into the mailbox. He tried to imagine how Karen would react when she read the poem. Usually apprehensive whenever he had sent a poem in the past, Will now had no apprehensions about what he was doing. Karen had always positively to whatever he had written, especially so in the instances in which he had been painfully honest. He could only imagine her being happy to receive the poem.

For the next week, Will's first glance upon walking in the door at the end of each day was toward the mail tray. Each time he checked it there was nothing except for candidates' campaign literature addressed to him, his reward for registering to vote, and the piece of bulk mail addressed to "resident" that announced that there would be a community meeting on homelessness the next month. But there was nothing from Karen. He tried to tell himself that what he had written had not been solicitous of a response, that he should not worry.

Three weeks after he mailed the poem Will opened the mailbox in front of the house and removed a piece of mail with the Center for Social Aid's return address on it. His heart went to his throat only for a second, as he realized that it was only another piece of bulk mail addressed to "resident."

Opening the envelope, Will realized that it was solicitation literature—asking for a donation. He chuckled at the irony of *him* receiving it as he scanned the brochures, hoping that there would be a photograph of Karen. His eyes gravitated to a section headed "letters from former guests."

As he scanned the excerpt from one of the letters Will noticed that the words seemed familiar. He read it more closely and realized, to his dismay, that it was part of the first letter he had written to Karen. There, for all the potential contributors to read, were words that he had written to Karen, believing that only *she* would see them.

Will's eyes burned hot as he folded the brochure back into the envelope, trying to contain his confusion. He had been certain that his trust in Karen was well-placed. And now she had made his private thoughts public—just so the shelter could rake in some donations.

But had she really betrayed him? His name had not

been used. Nor had she printed the whole letter he had written. The excerpt contained no more than his praise for her and an expression of gratitude for the help the shelter had given him. Will began to wonder if he should feel flattered rather than hurt. Maybe it was a good sign that his words had made that much of an impression on her.

At that moment Will's only sure thought was that he didn't know enough to be sure *what* to think. He began to ramble through the stack of campaign mail that cluttered one corner of his desk.

* * * * * * * * * * * * * * * * * * * *

A long, steep escalator slowly conveyed Will up toward the cavernous lobby of the Shelton Hotel convention center. As he stepped onto the carpet and began walking to the elevator on the far side of the room he wondered why some hotels had such spacious areas, yet made their rooms so constricting.

He quickly traversed the empty room and stepped onto the paradoxically small car of the lift. Four floors later he stepped into another lobby decorated with paintings—original in acrylic pigment but not ideas, he noted. There were *people* in this lobby, people who were here for the community meeting on homelessness.

There were no familiar faces for Will to see as he looked around. He guessed that most of the people in attendance were either people whose jobs involved helping the homeless or those whose jobs were made more difficult by the presence of the homeless.

Stepping up to the hospitality table, he gave his name to the receptionist, signed a registry, and was given a copy of the morning meeting's agenda. Will was slightly relieved to see that the meeting would be over by noon. He was interested in finding out what happened at this sort of meeting, but not *that* interested.

As he was about to enter the side door of the meeting room, Will saw Dick Mengel about to walk past him. Surprising himself with his own forwardness, he turned.

"Hi, Dick," he greeted the harried-looking man. "Remember me?" Mengel paused.

"Ummm, oh, *sure*," he responded, seeming to come out of a daydream. "Ahh, Bill—no, Will, right?"

"Good memory," Will grinned, genuinely surprised that Mengel remembered him.

"Nice to see you," he said to Will, moving on his way. "Good luck."

Will sat down at a table near the front of the room. Although his hearing had completely returned a couple of months before, he had almost become conditioned to the fear that he would not be able to hear what people were saying.

He looked at the agenda again, this time noticing that Karen Ling would be one of the speakers. He knew that seeing her would run him through an emotional gamut, but he told himself that Karen was not the reason he had come to the meeting. He had come to listen and learn.

The opening speaker rambled for what seemed like forever to Will, and was followed by two more long-winded self-proclaimed authorities. By the time the mid-morning break in the meeting came, Will was afraid that he would flood the floor before he got to the bathroom.

As he slowly made his way through the mob of people who had gone into the hallway to smoke, Will looked around to see if he could spot Karen. She was nowhere in sight and he walked back into the room and sat down to wait for the meeting to reconvene.

He had only been sitting for seconds when he felt a light tap on his shoulder. Sure that it was a woman's touch, he quickly stood up.

"Hello, Will," came the voice from a face he knew, followed by an outstretched hand.

"You—you are . . ." he stammered.

"Karen Ling," she said.

"I know *that*," Will blurted, struggling to keep his composure. "What I mean is . . . you are the most beautiful woman on the face of the earth." Will could not *believe* what he had just blurted out. Karen put her right hand over her heart and took a step back, modestly reacting to Will's hyperbolic declaration with a look of mock-incredulity.

"How are you doing?" she asked.

"Fine. Just fine—now," Will responded, his initial shock having passed. "How are you?"

"I'm okay," she answered. "I'm the next speaker, so I'm—" The pounding of a gavel interrupted her, and the dull roar of the crowd turned to a low rumble. "They're getting ready to start again. I have to go," she said in a breathy voice. "It's nice to see you."

Will nodded and was about to extend his hand when Karen stepped toward him, then reached out with both arms and put them around him. He barely had time to touch his hands to her back when she let go, backed away, and hurried toward the front of the room. Will sat down, completely flabbergasted by what had just happened.

He watched and tried to listen to Karen when her turn came to address the audience. But he found it difficult to do anything more than stare at her. Her speech was short, and when she finished she left the podium and walked down the side of the room where Will was seated. The moderator's voice filled the room as Karen leaned over the table as she neared Will.

"Will," she whispered, "don't leave right after this is over. I want to talk to you." He nodded, and he felt his heart rise to his throat again. He scribbled on the note paper on the table in front of him as he waited for the last speaker to finish and the closing statements to be made. Finally it was over.

The instant after the last remarks were spoken, it seemed that all two hundred fifty voices in the room began talking at once. Will's attention had turned to securing the buckles on his satchel when he saw Karen sit down in the chair across the table from him.

"So, how's life?" she asked, smiling in a way that nearly rendered Will speechless.

"It's hell," he said in feigned exasperation, smiling as he managed to muster a shred of humor. "No, I'm just kidding. Really, it seems to be getting better. Still no luck at finding a job, though." He explained to her that he had wanted to come back to the shelter to work as a volunteer, but that the experience of having been homeless made it too difficult to consider. She understood.

Will asked her about herself. She responded that she was fine, that her life had its ups and downs. Just as Will was beginning to feel relaxed enough to enjoy the conversation, she slid her chair away from the table.

"Just keep trying, Will," she urged him. "You're going to make it. I *know* you will." Will stood as she stood and they both walked to the side of the table.

"You take care of yourself," she said, smiling as she again reached toward him with outstretched arms. . This time Will wasn't taken by surprise and he put his arms around her, careful not to squeeze her too tightly, wishing he wouldn't have to let go for a long while. He could feel the strength of her arms, petite as she was, then felt her embrace loosen just before she stepped back.

She looked at him and smiled, then turned away. Will reached for his satchel's shoulder strap as Karen took two steps, then turned her head toward him again, this time with a playful smile on her face.

"Keep in touch," she said.

Will knew that he would. He knew that heaven had no love like that of a once-hopeless man who had been treated with kindness.

THE END

www.ingramcontent.com/pod-product-compliance
Lightning Source LLC
Chambersburg PA
CBHW030826310726
48980CB00006B/650/J
* 9 7 8 0 9 7 1 0 7 0 2 1 9 *